# COUNTING THE WAYS

# COUNTING THE WAYS

JUDE HAYLAND

Matador
9 Priory Business Park,
Wistow Road, Kibworth Beauchamp,
Leicestershire. LE8 0RX
Tel: 0116 279 2299
Email: books@troubador.co.uk
Web: www.troubador.co.uk/matador
Twitter: @matadorbooks

ISBN 978 1788036 306

British Library Cataloguing in Publication Data.
A catalogue record for this book is available from the British Library.

Printed by Printed and bound in the UK by TJ International, Padstow, Cornwall
Typeset in 11pt Aldine401 BT by Troubador Publishing Ltd, Leicester, UK

Matador is an imprint of Troubador Publishing Ltd

*For George*
*with unconditional love*

*"How do I love thee? Let me count the ways."*

Elizabeth Barrett Browning

# Acknowledgements

Thank you to Carol Randall and Alison Mackie – my early readers who patiently offered constructive comments, ideas and support. I am hugely indebted to my sister, Jane Gaudie, also an early reader and a source of constant encouragement and positivity.

# About Jude Hayland

Jude Hayland was born in London and now lives in Winchester. A freelance writer, teacher and tutor, *COUNTING THE WAYS* is her second novel.

www.judehayland.com

# Prologue

The place: Jacob's Bottom.

The time: the latter part of the 20th century, early spring 1987.

The man and the woman left the car, walked fifty yards or so along the ridge until he halted, propelled her forward a little. Across the mesh of wet, neat patchwork fields, endless sheep, they looked down towards a flat plain that suggested signs of habitation. A church with a spire, outbuildings possibly. Certainly cows.

"There," the man said, gripping her shoulder with one hand, pointing with the other, "you see those buildings? Not the farm, but beyond that. That's the house."

The woman, Grace, pulling her coat closer against the fine rain, could see little. Just as they had approached the village, he had swung the car sharply up an incline, headed for a narrow single-track road that weaved its way steeply upwards until they seemed to be hanging precariously above the valley. Now she found herself peering through a heavy mist that shielded clear shapes, blending them into an indefinable blur with the grey sky, the undulating land. But she tried. He was so eager, insistent. The enthusiasm of a small boy who wants to share something newly discovered.

"I think so. I think I can see the house. Is it thatched?"

"No, a slate roof. Do you mind?"

"Of course not," Grace said. "Slate is better."

"Is it? I thought you'd expect thatch in this part of the world. I'm glad you're not disappointed." Archie took her arm, protectively. She leant against his shoulder.

"I didn't know what to expect. It's all such a surprise, really, so sudden. We've not even discussed it properly. The idea of this place, I mean. The country."

He continued to look down across the valley towards the house. She was unsure whether he'd heard her, her words possibly dissolving into the damp air, snatched away on the westerly wind. It was a nursery plate for children, grazing cattle and haystacks and hares nipping and darting across the land.

"We're not too far from the coast here either," he said, "and you know how that'll suit me. The sea's no more than three or four miles away, I'd say. And we're just on the edge of the village so it won't feel too remote for you. Just what we want."

Grace felt the dampness of her feet through thin city soles, her hair limp and deflated against her neck. Archie, oblivious, pulled her further down the path so that they could see a cluster of cottages, a building that could be a hall or a village school, then a car park and beyond that a narrow track that led down to a large barn and a long, low house.

"No immediate neighbours, but there are a couple of houses within view. And the lane just leads to farmland so there's no passing traffic. You won't mind?" Archie asked then answered for her. "No, you'll love the peace after London. No more complaints about aircraft noise and people playing loud music into the small hours. It'll suit you, Grace. It's what you want. What I've had in mind for us."

"It looks perfect. You're right, of course. And once there are children…"

"Exactly. Just the place to bring up children. What we've planned."

They had been married sixteen months.

# Part One

# England

# 1

Grace could not particularly remember the planning that had taken them to Jacob's Bottom, but she supposed it had been implied between them, a tacit agreement of sorts. Archie's actions so often seemed to stem from conversations she could scarcely recall yet had a sense of something remotely familiar. As if her unformed and distinctly vague thoughts somehow translated themselves into speech without her conscious awareness. Even their engagement had felt like an arrangement removed from her as if Archie had proposed while she was running a bath or engrossed in a novel and he had assumed her reply. She remembered feeling faintly astonished when friends of his had rung up to invite them round for a celebration dinner and she had chosen to ignore the alarming possibility that they had known of his intentions before she had any idea. She knew, of course, that they had become engaged, but was unable to pinpoint the exact moment of reaching such an agreement. Still, Archie's friends were nothing to complain about or choose to shun. Close neighbours of his in south-east London, they had been boisterously warm and effusive towards her from the start, affectionate and considerate as if, having been introduced, they felt all of a sudden contracted to ensure her well-being. They enveloped her wholeheartedly. The two couples, Monica and Bernard, Celia and Cyril, and their assorted children, appeared to live comfortable, established lives in large houses and could afford to support philanthropic causes and hold liberal views. They were the sort of people Grace had always quietly envied, never known, watched only from a distance and believed herself to be too ill-equipped to join. She coveted not their affluence, but their assurance of their place in the world, an ease with their privilege. They appeared able to reconcile their somewhat extravagant lives with professed egalitarian ideals and vociferous support for charitable concerns. They expressed their opinions on local and national matters with astounding certainty so that Grace found herself sitting mute at meals in their enormous kitchens, incapable of matching their convictions. She began to feel inadequate, insubstantial, reduced to nodding her head, making inaudible grunts of agreement. They appeared not to notice. Monica and Cyril in their huge house on Belmont Hill, Celia and Bernard in theirs on Lee Terrace talked on. About street crime and city riots and the miners and Aids. About starvation in Africa and communism and corruption in Russia. They possessed endless opinions, offered endless solutions. She had never personally known such people before, only glimpsed their stereotypes in satiric fiction. Archie, catching Grace's eye across the scrubbed pine table in Monica's kitchen, squeezing her hand under cover of Celia's Provençal tablecloth, would diffuse their intense debates with a flippant remark. Always she would feel grateful for his rescue, his glance of complicit affection and love.

As soon as she and Archie became engaged, the two women, Monica and Celia, took it upon themselves to steer her through the wedding arrangements so that she found herself agreeing that, "Yes, the second Saturday in November sounds fine," watching as the date was eagerly written into handbag diaries, placed on the calendar on the wall. Archie had beamed at her amidst raised glasses, clutching at her hand as if reluctant to let it go. Grace was elated yet also mildly alarmed at the assumptions surrounding her, at the speed with which matters were galloping. They had known each other only a few months, after all. A lengthier engagement might well have seemed more appropriate. However, she was sure of her love for Archie and it would have seemed churlish for her to quibble. After all, her life outside this splendid kitchen, Celia and Bernard's kitchen, with its comforting Aga and faint smell of domestic Dalmatian waiting patiently for his night-time walk across Blackheath, was hardly offering a desirable alternative. There seemed little reason to delay what had come to feel inevitable, destined, even. Archie was certain, his friends were very sure, and so she felt it the best course to be contaminated by their conviction. Procrastination had featured too highly in her life and who was she to defy people like them, always so adamant, always so sure, to wave a hand in mild query at this swift course of events?

They had met in March. By chance.

"At the ballet of all places!" Archie always said in his telling of it.

"How romantic!" people always said, Monica and Celia had certainly said.

"My first and only visit so far," Archie would go on, "to the ballet, that is. Not for Grace, of course, she's quite a devotee. A bit of a regular at the opera house."

"In the cheap seats," Grace always clarified. "Upper slips on the whole. You'd be surprised at how good the view is."

"And I'd been stood up, would you believe it!" Archie would continue. "There I was, thinking uncharitable thoughts about my supposed date for the night – it turned out her dog had died or that was her lame excuse – wondering whether to slope off home when I saw this lovely woman in… well, frankly, she looked so upset, in a bit of a state."

Grace had lost her cheap ticket for the amphitheatre. She had stood in the foyer feeling exposed, searching her bag fruitlessly and growing too warm in her cream winter coat that had suddenly felt inappropriate for the mild March evening. (Next day, she had found the ticket hidden between the pages of her Iris Murdoch where she had evidently employed it as a bookmark when leaving the tube.) The foyer had begun to thin; men in suits, women in diaphanous dresses heading for the orchestra stalls, others nipping round the side to Floral Street to begin the climb up to the top tier. Grace had been expecting to join them. She had searched her bag again, working her fingers into the place where the lining had split, producing a wad of tissue, a single aspirin in silver foil. A broken biro.

"Excuse me," a man had said, appearing abruptly at her side. She had raised her face, flushed with irritation, and noticed the ticket he was holding out in his hand. "Here, have this one, it's spare. You seem to have lost yours. But hurry, curtain's up in a couple of minutes and I don't suppose this is the sort of place to put up with latecomers."

"Your knight in shining armour!" Monica had said.

"Sir Galahad rides again!" Celia had said.

"And was it love at first sight? Please say it was!" Monica had urged, looking from Archie to Grace, from Grace to Archie, as if beseeching the pair of them to fulfil her need for a fairy tale.

"Of course," Archie had said, "for me, at least. How could I resist such an extraordinarily pretty young woman who was replacing my intended dull dog-owning companion and could explain the plot of the ballet to me into the bargain? She looks like a dancer herself, don't you think? But I'm sure it took Grace considerably longer to make her mind up about me."

It had. Or at least longer than their initial encounter. In spite of Archie's claim, they had hardly spoken to each other during the evening beyond a few obligatory civil exchanges at the interval. At the end of the ballet, Grace, distracted entirely by the rapture of the performance, the perfect synthesis of movement, music and emotion, had hardly noticed him following her down the stairs and out into the damp night air of Bow Street. But he had caught her arm with some urgency as if anxious not to lose her in the outpouring of audience onto the street. He had asked if he might see her again. And he had introduced himself, held out his hand.

"Archie Copeland," he had said. "I should have told you before." She had looked at him fully for the first time, saw sandy-coloured hair, brown eyes, a hesitant smile.

"Grace Barnes," she'd said, taking his hand. "Thank you so much for the ticket, for rescuing me like that," and she had been about to decline automatically his suggestion that they meet again, make some excuse of a husband or partner to escape and dispel the awkwardness of the moment with this stranger to whom she felt mildly indebted when she had noticed two things: Archie's dark navy overcoat, his sensible shoes. Particularly, she had noticed his shoes and had been irrationally reassured by them. They had exchanged phone numbers. Three days later, he had rung.

"I adore it!" Monica had said. "It's like...well, it's just the perfect love story."

"Swept off her feet at the ballet," Celia had said. "What could be more romantic – or more appropriate?" They had giggled endlessly until their respective husbands, Bernard and Cyril, had told them to stop being so juvenile.

She had not, in fact, been instantly swept off her feet.

Grace had returned to her small, dark basement flat on the outer edges of Earl's Court convinced she had little desire to see or hear from Archie Copeland again. She could hardly recall his features, equable rather than striking, and had doubted whether she would even recognise him should she bump into him again. Yet she had retained the scrap of paper bearing his name, his phone number, placing it near the flotsam pile of bills and bank statements and overdue library reminders that resided in the space between the two-ring electric cooker and the single larder cupboard. She had gone to bed dreaming of Manon Lescaut, dying consumptively in the arms of her lover in the fetid swamps of Louisiana, rather than of Archie Copeland, a pleasant, thoughtful man who had kindly given her a spare ticket for the stalls circle one early evening in March.

***

Her mother, Hester, had reacted pragmatically to the news of their engagement.

"The man has a house in Greenwich," she said, "and he's a professor."

"Archie's not a professor," Grace pointed out. "He's a lecturer."

Hester had shrugged away the distinction. She had already told people that Grace was marrying a professor.

"And the house is more Lewisham than Greenwich. And he shares it with his brother and one room's let to a student nurse."

"Well, she'll have to go for a start, once you move in," Hester said.

"It's a he, a male student nurse, actually. And yes, he's going at the end of the month. And fortunately his brother's always away. Archie says he spends his time moving from one crisis relief programme to another. Every time there's a famine or a flood or earthquake somewhere, Leo enlists himself as an aid worker or something. Admirable, really."

"How odd," Hester said. "Anyway, Archie will obviously buy you something bigger, a house of your own once the children come along. You are planning on children, I hope, Grace?"

"Oh yes, children definitely. That's rather the point of it all, isn't it? Marriage, I mean. Otherwise, I can't think why people really bother."

"Security. Respectability, possibly, although of course no one seems to worry about things like that anymore. Status, then. There's something so dreadfully spinsterish and dull in being called a Miss once you're past your prime."

"Like me, I presume you mean," Grace said. "Archie's eight years older, you know, he's forty."

"Then you better be getting on with these children promptly before he becomes too old for the fathers' race on Sports Day," Hester said. "At least he's not trailing a brood from his first marriage behind him."

Archie's former wife lived in Deptford with her second husband and their two children. Grace wondered whether they'd bump into each other on the heath on a Sunday afternoon.

"We well might," Archie said blandly. "I've often seen them there flying kites. With their children, I mean. It wasn't an acrimonious divorce, you know. We… it just didn't work, that's all. She moved out after six years. We both got on with our lives. Very straightforward. And really, such a long time ago now."

"And thank goodness you hadn't started a family."

"Exactly," Archie said, "exactly. As I say, all very straightforward. Now don't you give Louise another thought. I certainly don't."

Archie was a lecturer in Romantic poetry at a small college near Aldgate. Affiliated to London University, the majority of his students were mature, people who had missed out on earlier formal education and were anxious to make up for lost time. In the early days of their relationship Grace strained to remember her Wordsworth from the sixth form. She recalled Shelley drowning, Byron catching a fatal fever. She had never forgotten her adolescent sorrow at Keats' premature consumptive death halfway up the Spanish Steps in Rome. She believed she had begun to fall in love with Archie when he had quoted Coleridge over dinner in a bistro in South Kensington. It had been their third date and she had grown tired of men who cited share prices and talked about their substantial portfolios, waiting for her to be impressed by their membership of Lloyd's. Archie talked about pathetic fallacies. He talked about cadences and sonnet forms and his PhD research into *Christabel* and *Kubla Khan* and *The Rime of the Ancient Mariner.* Here was a man who appeared to share her passion for the written word and her belief in the transcendent power of literature and was unlikely to scorn, as so many had before, her obsessive reading habit. His passion for his Romantic poets had been seductive for Grace. She had sat at their small, cramped table in the South Kensington bistro, sipped bone-dry Muscadet and listened to him talk. She had noticed his eyes, lively, alert. Kind. She had felt comforted by the spare, strong gestures of his broad, practical hands, had been drawn to the warmth and ease of his voice. Instinctively, she knew she felt safe with him and yearned for the yoke of his arms around her.

So she had gone home with him that evening to Greenwich, his brother Leo conveniently away in the Congo, the male student nurse on night duty at Charing Cross. He had been gracious, his behaviour exemplary, making them coffee, deploying half an hour or so with discussion on the novels that sat on the low table in the sitting room. They had discovered a shared indulgence of D.H. Lawrence, a difficulty with Joyce. She had admired his patience with Conrad, confessed her confusion with Woolf. He had slipped his arm around her shoulder, kissed her gently and then with more intention, and had asked, "Is this all right? Is this what you want? Are you sure?" And Grace had found herself surprised to realise that yes, this was exactly what she wanted and yes, she was very sure indeed for in such situations she was usually so ambivalent and uncertain, her convictions, one way or the other, only clarified the next day or even the next when the deed had already, irretrievably, been done. Grace had always doubted her capacity for finding contentment and ease with a comparative stranger plucked, as it were, from the madding crowd. Her consolation, her easy solace had always been in books, in satisfying plots and evolving characters that demanded little more of her than attention and patience. Even platonic friendships could be hard to navigate, she found, and she feared at times her unwillingness to surrender her quiet corner, her safe refuge in imagination. She had worried that she would never be able to settle for a man less admirable than Atticus Finch, less noble than George Knightley. But Archie Copeland appeared to be a man as willing as she was to suspend connection with the raw immediate world to spend time contemplating the fictional plane, ponder people who were merely the figments of a writer's mind. Against the odds, she seemed to have found herself a man who applauded rather than suspected her solitary reading habits, her regular library visits, her devotion to the ballet, and saw no reason to encourage her to reform her ways.

She had spent little time at her basement flat after that evening. Archie liked to find her at the Greenwich house when he came home from Aldgate at night, his dilapidated leather briefcase containing notes and student essays in one hand, some contribution towards dinner, a piece of ripe Brie, a bag of cherries, in the other. They'd prepare a meal together in the small kitchen overlooking the postage stamp of a south London city garden. Often, Joe, the student nurse, would join them and one day, Archie's brother, Leo. Grace had been startled to find a strange man in the house when she arrived late one afternoon, a rucksack spilling its contents over the narrow hallway, blocking her path to the burglar alarm in the cupboard under the stairs.

"Don't worry, I've switched it off," the man said, appearing abruptly in the doorway of the sitting room, appearing to fill it and shielding any light so that Grace at first could make out only an outline, a suggestion of long, thin limbs. A shock of long, untidy hair. "I'm Archie's brother, Leo," he said. "And you are obviously the girlfriend. Or partner, should I say. That seems to be the word people are using these days." They spent the subsequent hour before Archie came home edging awkwardly through conversation, Leo seeming ill at ease with her, answering abruptly as if he had little to share or was unwilling to make the required effort. Archie's arrival diluted the tension somewhat, but Leo still appeared strained and after rapidly eating an enormous meal accompanied by a pint of milk, disappeared upstairs to bed. Archie claimed not to have noticed anything unusual in his behaviour.

"He's a loner, that's all," he said, making coffee for the two of them. "Not very good with people."

"But he spends his entire time with people, doesn't he? Rushing off to all these places of crisis, caring about people, trying to save them and feed them. I thought it was his life's work," Grace said.

"That's different. They're strangers. He's helping them practically," Archie said and switched on the machine to grind Blue Mountain beans.

"So there's never been anyone in his life? A girlfriend, I mean, or..."

"There was," Archie said, "once. It... no, he rather gave up on all that side of things when it went wrong. Look, don't take anything personally with Leo. It's just the way he is. Anyway, he's only here a couple of days. He's off to Eritrea on Friday. We might not see him again for years."

"Don't you miss him? I mean, he's your brother after all." An only child, Grace felt Archie dispatched Leo with extraordinary nonchalance. She had always imagined a fraternal bond to be something to covet rather than discard so carelessly. Archie had looked at her blankly.

"I've never really thought about it, to tell you the truth."

***

They drove up the M40 to Oxford one Sunday in early September to visit Hester. Archie bought them lunch at a pub overlooking the river and afterwards they walked in Christ Church Meadow. He was attentive, decorous, and Hester appeared charmed, admiring at some length Grace's Victorian engagement ring, garnet and seed pearls, bought at an antiques shop in Camden Passage. Grace was relieved when they left just after five. Her mother had never been hesitant in the past to show her feelings about her friends, male or female, and subject them to something of an inquisition. Archie had been spared. They appeared to like each other.

"Your mother's had such an interesting life, hasn't she? I have to say it's the first time I've actually met an actress in the flesh." Archie drummed the steering wheel as they sat in the inevitable traffic jam approaching the Hammersmith Flyover. Grace wondered how much Hester had conveniently embroidered while she was in the bathroom. To most people, her mother's life would probably appear to have been prosaic, thwarted and disillusioned, rather than graphic. "Did you never want to follow in her footsteps?"

She stared out of the car window and into the living rooms thrown into view, third-floor flats exposed through grimed net curtains. Electric lights were switched on, the flicker of a television screen filling the void of an early Sunday evening. She was grateful for Archie next to her, his broad, artisan hands. Those sensible shoes.

"In her footsteps? Certainly not," she said, "but I'm not sure there were any clear ones to follow. None that I saw, anyway. All that theatrical part of her life was a long time ago and before I was born."

"Yes, of course," Archie said and shoved the car rapidly into first gear as they managed to gain five yards, "and a bit of a bygone era, of course. Genteel comedies and matinee tea trays, that sort of thing. All very remote now."

"Besides," Grace said rapidly, in case Archie was under some misapprehension about her, "we're entirely different, nothing at all alike in character, my mother and I. I could never be… well, extrovert and assertive like her." She always thought of herself as pale and neutral, slipping constantly into a bland background to shun attention, preferring an empty room, the company of the printed page rather than the throng of a crowd. They slipped down into Marylebone and picked up some speed past the blocks of mansion flats, past Baker Street station, the Planetarium and Madame Tussaud's.

Archie said, "Will your father come? To the wedding, I mean. Will you mind if he doesn't?"

Grace watched a boy dart across the wide road, another in pursuit and the two of them dodged cars, gesticulated at drivers, in some foolish game until reaching safety the other side.

"I think," Grace said eventually, leaning forward to fiddle with the knobs on the car radio, stumbling across static until arriving at the clarity of the six o'clock news, "that I might mind more if he does."

# 2

Hester Barnes stares out of the window across the Banbury Road. For once, the summer seems to have been endless, a series of long, sultry days in which the city has heaved with too many dusty tourists. Disgorged from stuffy coaches each morning, they have dutifully followed the trail around countless college quadrangles with blank uncomprehending stares and obsessive use of cameras. *Japan*, she thinks, *Canada and America must be awash with meaningless photographs of medieval gargoyles and stone architraves.* She's benefitted from the foreign students, though. Letting Grace's old bedroom to a constant stream of disaffected teenagers attending language courses in the city has been tiresome, but financially rewarding. She's relieved now, however, overwhelmingly relieved to reclaim the flat to herself. *I am too old*, Hester thinks, *or too selfish to enjoy making stilted conversation with adolescent French children over the breakfast table. I am too intolerant to handle the sight of my young European visitors depositing my carefully prepared packed lunches in the nearest litter bin to my front door. Good riddance to the lot of them*, she thinks, but is gratified that the income will help her buy a satisfactory wedding present for Grace. Hester turns her back on the Banbury Road, sits down at her bureau and begins to write her letter:

*North Oxford – October 17th, 1985*
*My dear Fergus,*
*I have no idea whether this will even reach you in your godforsaken spot. (Notice the lower case 'g' – I imagine things to be pretty pagan and without a decent parish church in such wild climes.) I am sending it via the local post office cum village store in the place you mentioned in your last letter which was, need I remind you, well over two years ago. Goodness me, doesn't time fly when you're enjoying yourself, Fergus? I assume your silence suggests you are. Anyway, to the point.*

*Our only child is getting married.*

*I don't suppose you will come to the wedding nor is this even a formal invitation for, quite frankly, Fergus, I think your presence would be something of an embarrassment, not least to poor Grace. After all, she's got used to you as an absence in her life and a sudden manifestation, the word made flesh, as it were, could be quite upsetting. Let me elaborate for you, anyway. Grace has got herself a nice, respectable, affable man who'll do all the right things and keep her in the style to which she ought rightly to be expecting – indeed, he seems suitably intent on indulging her with more extravagance than she's ever known (which is not difficult, of course, things being the way they have been.) At last she's being spoilt a bit with endless meals out, expensive theatre tickets, thoughtful gifts, that sort of thing. Lucky girl and no more than she deserves. I was beginning to give up hope of her ever snaring herself a match given her marginally reclusive habits for how was she supposed to find a future partner with that pretty face of hers forever buried in a book? However, finally she has and she seems utterly smitten and he's clearly devoted. You can see from the way he gazes at her which is rather sweet and touching even to a devout sceptic like me. I couldn't be more delighted. And she can hardly go on forever drifting from job to job, living on a pittance of a salary and dwelling in that dreadful cellar of a home of hers somewhere south of the Cromwell Road. It's not as if I am in a position to set her up financially, after all. Let's face it, Fergus, it's always been a bit of a struggle keeping our heads above water. Need I remind you that your last cheque belongs to the annals of history although you know I've never been the sort to go demanding money from a man. It's just a pity my acting career seemed to curtail itself about the time I married you and had Grace. No doubt I could have resurrected it if I'd been willing to prostrate myself in front of some of these slick young telly producers, but the small screen has always seemed such a travesty of the profession and, of course, my agent died in 1963. The same day as President Kennedy, as it happens, although from cirrhosis, I believe, rather than an assassin's bullet.*

*Well, Fergus, enough of this. I digress in my usual manner and I wouldn't want to distract you from your sheep farming or morning milking or whatever else it is you do up there in your Welsh idyll.*

*To the facts, then.*

*Grace is to be married at the Registry Office at Chelsea Town Hall on November 9th at twelve noon – that very Victorian place halfway along the King's Road opposite Habitat. I'm disappointed it's not here in north Oxford as I've become quite friendly with our local vicar since I joined his team raising money for repairs to the organ. But evidently the idea of a church service poses a problem, for the fiancé's got a bit of a Past where marriage is concerned. He's done Time already in that department with an ex-wife living just across the hill from him in south London. Not that we should be surprised as Grace has left it far too late to get herself anyone decent who's a first-timer. Our daughter's already thirty-two, remember – although I doubt you do, Fergus. Your head's probably too full of organic fertilisers and chicken coops and swine fever to retain such family facts with any clarity.*

*Well, I've done my duty in telling you and shall no doubt be in touch in the near future when Grace and Archie bless us with grandchildren, which is, I am gratified to say, rather part of their plan. Go and commune with the fields and trees now, Fergus, and I remain, as always,*

*Ever yours,*
*Hester*

She posts the letter later in the day on her way to the cinema. The film, an intense political drama, is dispiriting and Hester's mind lifts from the complicated plot and on-screen conflict to Fergus and her letter now sitting on top of the pile of mail in the box on the corner of the Banbury Road. She regrets her tone. She is sure she sounded petulant, irritable even, and wishes she had simply sent a wedding invitation, no personal note attached. Her very occasional correspondence to Fergus over the years always troubles her after it has been dispatched for she finds herself incapable of simply writing to him openly, honestly. There's an attitude she adopts, a voice she appears to feign as if the whole matter of their long estrangement is something of a joke, a chance for light banter. It's a defence, she thinks, my armour. Against what, though? Displays of anger, recrimination, even love? After all this time, she finds it impossible to know any more the warp and weft of her own feelings. Hester gives up on the plot of the film and thinks instead of Grace. *At last she appears to have found herself some direction in life. Archie Copeland seems to be a sensible selection*, she thinks, *although Grace has never been the sort to choose a man for hard-headed reasons. More's the pity, I've often thought in the past.*

*She could have found herself a husband of sorts and settled down years ago if she'd put her mind to it. But no. This is clearly love as the two of them see it and good luck to them. He's a little older than I would have liked to see for Grace, but goodness, what do I know about the whole business of pairings and partnerships? How unreasonably rapid life is and how entirely out of control. One moment Grace is three years of age and I am as essential to her as the air we both breathe. The next moment she's a grown woman and entirely out of my sphere of influence and I am redundant. To all intents and purposes my role and function in her life are now negligible. The age-old story, of course, yet no less poignant for that. If Fergus were still with me, things would seem different. We would be growing into a late middle-aged couple with respectable late middle-aged friends talking about retirement plans and insurance policies and sizing down to realise capital from the family home. We might even have played golf. I would have been accommodated, defined, provided with a protection and solace from the terrifying abyss of old age. Somehow growing old as a couple is more socially acceptable, gracious and convivial even. Advancing years for a single woman bear the taint of desperation as if she gives off pheromones of decay. Exile her socially. Engage with her only at your peril.*

The film has finished. The audience sits on, studying the credits on the screen as if having no better place to go. Hester stirs herself, irritated suddenly by her morose mood. Introspection is aging, she suspects, no doubt depletes the collagen or whatever it is that prevents entire facial collapse. Outside it's a fine early autumn evening and she weaves her way briskly through the bevy of cyclists and pedestrians to the bus stop. She thinks of her quiet flat awaiting her, her music, the colours of the cushions, the prints on the wall, that vase, the half bottle of Soave in the fridge. The small consolations when the miraculous moments of passion, love, conception, new life are no longer available. And she is not unhappy, not at all. She watches the very young couple in the bus queue ahead of her, clutching, groping, pawing, entwined, almost inextricably attached to each other like some strange hybrid creature and she finds herself pitying their ineptitude. Their frightening, terrifying vulnerability. All that anger and inevitable heartbreak lying in wait for them. In fact, thinking now of Grace's marriage, of all the possible outcomes and events as yet unknown, she feels positively blessed. There is a future, after all. Time is not entirely behind me, error-strewn or unlived, but lurking unpredictably ahead. There's solace in that, she thinks. The bus arrives and Hester, recharged, pushes ahead of the adolescent lovers to take the front seat.

***

Fergus Barnes left his wife and daughter when Grace was nearly three years old. His departure was not dramatic. He simply packed his old holdall with a change of clothes, his razor, the Observer books of both birds and wild flowers and kissed Hester goodbye. Initially, they both talked of his absence as a prolonged holiday. Hester told her few friends in Pinner that he'd gone on one of his solitary cycling trips to the Welsh Marches. After a month she concocted a tale about a legacy that had freed Fergus from his job as a bank clerk and enabled him to realise a lifelong ambition to write travel books about the British countryside. The thin fiction became an embarrassment when he failed to return by Grace's third birthday. At first there was a little money. Fergus sent letters, containing carefully folded crisp ten shilling notes, occasionally more, taking pains to explain that there was no blame attached to either Hester or Grace. It was not so much that he had stopped loving his wife as that he had become indifferent to the idea of love and its inevitably binding aspects. He did not want to live in Pinner and travel every day to the bank in Kenton until retirement eventually released him to the bowls club in the Memorial Park, Life Treasurer of the Allotment Society. Nor did he want to accommodate any more the needs of Hester, of young Grace, who would be clearly unsuited to the new life he had chosen for himself. Hester wrote back, pointing out, reasonably enough, that if he had made his inclinations clear before they had married she could have avoided the situation of being an abandoned wife and mother. She could have made an alternative choice of husband from the serried rows of men who, she implied, had been available to her. Fergus wrote again, agreeing that his timing was unfortunate, but that he had only recently discovered where his true destiny lay. He'd always suspected that the Kenton branch of the National Provincial Bank was not his intended milieu, but it was a copy of *The Countryman* magazine that had found its way into the waiting room of his dentist in Eastcote that proved to be his epiphany. He read an article about life on Scottish crofts, the remote existence, the hardships and rewards of solitary self-sufficiency, and by the time it came for his upper left molar to be filled he was convinced. Substituting mid-Wales for the Shetlands was his only concession. His maternal grandmother had been Welsh and he claimed to Hester that the blood tie had drawn him inevitably to the Dovey Valley. He was aware, even as he wrote the words, that they were foolishly whimsical, entirely fraudulent, in fact. But that was their point, the purpose they served. For he knew he had to say something to mitigate conduct that was inexplicable even to himself.

Hester wondered whether she was incapable of retaining husbands.

Fergus was her second attempt, a replacement for Alec Adaire, who had been shot down over Norway in 1940 just six months after their marriage. There was something faintly topical about being a war widow at only twenty-two years of age; besides, she was hardly alone. Being left by a Kenton bank clerk in her late thirties with a small child in tow was far less tolerable. Besides, Fergus had been a judicious choice. In Fergus, she felt she was attaching herself to reliability, to routine and regularity, which she saw as sensible complements to her own disposition. And with his cautious yet regular salary and the eventual prospect of a pension she would be able to return to acting, dip an occasional, carefully selected toe into the profession she had previously pursued with moderate success. Fergus Barnes, a calm, quiet, affectionate man who had conveniently walked into her life at a dispiriting party at a friend's flat in west London, had caught her heart, punctured the cynicism that she had tended to employ in her relations with men since the loss of Alec. After their marriage, she would wake in the night and look at his fair head upon the pillow next to hers, regard his even, regular features, and believe herself to be contented, settled into a blissfully ordinary and delightfully regular domestic life.

She was astounded, therefore, the day that Fergus packed his holdall, searched under the stairs for his old khaki duffel bag, and walked out of the front door, closing it carefully but very firmly behind him.

Hester, despising the idea of being the subject of cheap gossip amongst the housewives of Pinner, swiftly retreated with Grace to Oxford and a couple of cold but serviceable rooms in her elderly maiden aunt's cavernous house on the Botley Road. Over the next few years, she satisfied herself with a few flings with virgin undergraduates lodging on the upper floors, a couple of brief affairs with married professors. There was a fleeting involvement with the widower French teacher from Thame, a temporary attachment to an Abingdon vet, a summer of attention from a Bodleian archivist. On the whole, however, she adapted herself to a quiet, compromised sort of life, awaiting the increasingly irregular arrival of the folded banknotes from Fergus. She worked in bookshops, antique shops, hair salons, even an outmoded draper's shop, to supplement the rare professional acting jobs that came her way. When her aunt died and left her a share of the house in the Botley Road, she sold her portion and bought a neglected maisonette in north Oxford with the proceeds. She embraced this new home, set about removing the taint of post-war austerity that it still wore and at the same time relished shedding the unwelcome coat of dependence and genteel poverty attached to life with the maiden aunt. She befriended the man in the do-it-yourself shop in Summertown who guided her through emulsions and wallpaper pastes and strippers. She made friends with a retired electrician who taught her to change fuses and attach plugs. She instilled in Grace the necessity for domestic and financial self-sufficiency at the same time as telling her only to pursue boyfriends with secure, sensible prospects. And each Christmas she sent a card and a small gift to Fergus. A pictorial calendar of Oxford colleges. A pair of thick, sturdy socks. Woollen mittens in oatmeal beige. On Grace's birthday she sent a photograph, the cake glowing with lit candles so that he could count them if he needed to be reminded of his daughter's age. Hester had little idea whether he received such things with gratitude or contempt. But she kept sending them, clutching, perhaps, at the slender hope that he might be touched by her constancy and surprised by it herself. Like Penelope awaiting her Ulysses, she thought. Another infuriating man who really had taken an excessively long and circuitous route home.

# 3

Her mother had insisted on the hotel room.

"You cannot possibly be married from that cell of yours, Grace. For one thing, it has such a peculiar smell about it."

"It's the damp," Grace said, "in my flat. That's the smell, I think. And the mould. I expect it's probably unfit for human habitation although the insect life in the bathroom seems to find it agreeable enough."

"I can't imagine what Archie thinks of you, living in a place like that. It's a wonder he didn't dump you after a first visit to the place."

"Archie, fortunately, understands. And anyway, we hardly spend any time there these days."

Archie had clearly been taken aback by Grace's flat on his fleeting first visit there. But equally he had appreciated its merits. Or so he claimed.

"It belongs to my mother's sister, Ruth," Grace had said, edging him into the condensed space, aware, suddenly, of a need to justify the place. "She bought it in 1942 when no one was exactly thinking of London property as the best investment. I can't imagine how she got the money together, but according to my mother she was somewhat unscrupulous about borrowing from random men who then conveniently disappeared into the war. She used to own the whole house, all four floors of it, but then she gradually sold bits off to developers when she was hard up. But she's always clung on to the basement, refuses to sell which naturally drives the developers mad."

Grace had looked around the small basement living space cluttered with piles of books, rows of clothes attempting neatness; the narrow bed camouflaging as a sofa by day, the posters of Impressionist painters she'd stuck to the walls to hide alarming cracks. She had grown so used to the nature of the place, to the blocked-off stairwell that offered a view of little more than the ankles, shoes and socks of passing pedestrians, to the limited cooking facilities, a Baby Belling and a couple of rings, that she forgot even to comment on its curiosity. In spite of the pervading sense of decay, she always felt some sense of affection towards the flat, the way she might towards a needy, desperate friend. It couldn't help itself; it was what it was. Archie, evasive, had commented on the cornicing. The attractive tiling of the Victorian fireplace.

"And you say this aunt of yours lets you live here rent-free?"

"She's lived in California for thirty years, but she's always threatening to come back. I think she's entirely deluded herself about the state of this place. In her mind she probably sees it as some sort of bijou pied-à-terre tucked away in a Kensington mews. I'm her sort of live-in caretaker, I suppose, a defence against the squatters. Although no doubt it would be a little below their standards."

"And the location's ideal." Archie had clearly been uncomfortable. He'd perched on the edge of the bed, sipped cautiously from his mug of coffee as if suspicious of what it harboured. "After all, a west London address is always a premium."

"Even if it's barely Earl's Court let alone Chelsea. The idea was that I'd just be here for a year or so before I moved on to somewhere decent. But it never quite happened. The move, I mean."

Of course, in truth, there had never been enough money to move. Her string of low-paid jobs had been the main factor that had kept her in her aunt's flat in SW5, living some feet below the rest of the transitory population in a two-roomed basement that had clearly never been adequately tanked. In the first few weeks of their relationship she had been loath to admit to Archie her lack of direction where a career was concerned. She hedged and dodged. No, she had never been a student unless you counted the six-month secretarial course she'd taken straight out of school to pacify Hester. Yes, she'd thought about diplomas and certificates and degrees, but she had never considered herself sufficiently academic; she read obsessively, addictively, but had no particular wish to shape her opinions into appropriately critical language to share in seminars. Indeed, she found the whole idea most alarming. It was different for someone like Archie, of course. Someone with the intellectual curiosity and dedication for trawling through the works of dead poets the way he did. She relished, she told him, his capacity for such intellectual rigour, revered and respected it. He was clearly an academic and she could only admire the long hours he devoted to his well-annotated volumes of poetry, his files of handwritten notes, his patient two-finger typing on his electric Olivetti.

When they'd first met, Grace had been working in the china department at Liberty's. She had been taken on as seasonal Christmas staff in Scarves, retained for the winter sale in Dress Fabrics and had somehow drifted downstairs to China during February. Every day she waited for someone to notice that she was still there, but the temporary nature of her original employment seemed to have been forgotten for a while. She disliked the china department, yearned to be returned upstairs, to the second floor and Dress Fabrics and the delight of silks and cottons and crêpe de Chine and spools of thread in countless shades and orderly drawers of dress patterns. But eventually she was weeded out, brought before someone senior who suggested she might wish to apply for something more permanent, away from the shop floor. Her secretarial abilities were cited, her clutch of schoolgirl qualifications noted. She was, in fact, given the option of either clerical office work or taking the exit out through the shop's magnificent revolving doors onto Great Marlborough Street. That afternoon, she bought herself a small Susie Cooper jug at cost price and left, calling in at the employment agency on her way back to Earl's Court.

Archie seemed unconcerned by her lack of focus. Unlike Hester who sent her thick envelopes on a weekly basis full of job advertisements she'd spotted in *The Times* or *The Daily Telegraph*. Grace thumbed her way through these apparently stellar opportunities in advertising agencies, in press offices, law firms, accountancy concerns, publishing houses, and felt bleak. Even if she were equipped to fill any of these estimable positions, the prospect was uninspiring. Beneath the self-important language of these adverts with their incremental salary schemes, their contributory pensions, their health club memberships and executive office suites seemed to lie so little. As if the pretentious words masked a vacuum, a pointlessness of these endeavours. Hester rang most Monday nights.

"Well? What about that one with offices overlooking Blackfriars? Or better still the Trainee Copywriter in Covent Garden? You've always had a way with words, Grace, you know you have. And it's such a lovely area now they've done up the piazza. All those wine bars where you could go after a day's work. Or surely you could get yourself something in the City. I was only reading the other day how champagne bars are now de rigueur all hours of the day and night in the Square Mile."

She saw Grace's reluctance as worrying.

"You're beginning to make me think you are your father's daughter, when it comes to earning your living. Perhaps you're going to take yourself off to live some alternative lifestyle in a remote region, eating brown rice and reading books all day long," she said. "I have friends with successful children little older than you living in penthouses, Grace. The opportunities are out there for you to grasp, you know. You're a very pretty girl, quite lovely, in fact, which is a considerable asset, I can tell you. You are capable of doing so much better, I know you are. The 80s are proving to be such exciting, profitable times for everyone. Well, for those in the right place at the right time, at any rate. And that could be you, Grace. I know it's your life and I adore you, love you to pieces, as you well know, but… just don't throw an opportunity away, that's all I'm saying. Chances don't come the same way twice in life."

Grace found Archie, however, sympathetic.

"My mother is concerned I'll end up sheep farming or pig rearing in deepest Wales," she said, "or something equally unsociable and unprofitable. She thinks I'm just being obstructive. And perhaps I am. Obstinate, anyway."

"Nonsense, it's just that you're not suited to office environments and places obsessed with money," he said. "That's no crime. Not everyone has to fit in with this current materialistic culture of ours, you know. There are all sorts of other avenues and directions for you, after all. "

"Really?" Grace said. "I can't think of a thing for which I'm qualified. Or even anything I'd be particularly good at. No one employs you for sitting in a corner and simply reading books all day long, after all."

"You could easily get some qualifications," Archie said, "if you wanted to. You simply haven't found your niche yet. I mean, there are… well, museums, perhaps. Exhibitions, libraries, galleries, that type of thing. Yes, I can really imagine you in that sort of world. It would suit you. Bring out your artistic strengths." He beamed at her, evidently pleased to solve her career dilemma and Grace had felt infinitely relieved. And extraordinarily grateful too, for it seemed as if Archie was the first person who had clearly defined her rather than viewed her as a curious aberration. The next time Hester rang she appeased her mother by talking vaguely about a degree in art history, a diploma in museum studies, dropping words like 'curator' and 'consultant' casually into the conversation and for a while the thick envelopes posted from the box on the Banbury Road stopped arriving on her dank doormat in SW5.

Meanwhile, she had moved on from Liberty's to the tourist office at Victoria station, finding cheap hotels for visitors around Bayswater and Warwick Road and Praed Street. Her knowledge of London's A-to-Z directory became expert, but the hours were tedious, requiring her to do night shifts every few weeks when she would either fall inexcusably asleep, abandoning hapless tourists, or drink too much tea. Coming home to Greenwich one early morning in late August, a day when all signs of summer suddenly seemed to have disappeared overnight and the air smelt sharp, crisp, redolent of something new, she went upstairs to Archie's bedroom, sat on the bed and watched him dress for his day at college. The new academic year was beginning to shift into gear, the last of the students enrolling, and Archie had been sifting through endless lists and course notes and seminar numbers ready for the start of term in three weeks.

"I've had an idea," she said. "Your college is mainly for

mature students. Could I apply? I mean, is it too late for this year? There must be a space for one more on some course and I just feel suddenly that the time's right. I don't want to wait another year."

Grace watched him as he continued to fiddle with his tie, rearranging the knot, and tugging his collar down firmly. He picked up a comb, stared at it a moment as if forgetting what he had intended doing with it.

"Don't be ridiculous," he said sharply and sat down on a chair to pull on black socks. "That wouldn't do at all. That's… well that's just a stupid idea." He sounded exasperated with her as if she were a whining child who had suggested Christmas presents in July. She was as shocked as if he had slapped her around the face. She knew Archie only as mild-mannered, measured and calm and was entirely bewildered by his reaction. He stood up, shifted his jacket over his shoulders and went downstairs to the kitchen where he filled the kettle, overfilled it and splashed water across the front of his shirt. He cursed under his breath.

"It was just a random idea." Grace followed him, handed him a towel. "I thought your college was for people like me, second chance people, as it were. There's really no need for you to be quite so angry with…"

"I'm not angry, but it's just an absurd suggestion, Grace. Forget you ever thought of it, all right? My college… well, it would simply be wrong for you. I wouldn't want you… I mean it's a foolish thought and not at all what you want. Please don't mention the idea ever again." He turned towards her, stared at her for a moment then dropped the towel on the floor, gathered up his briefcase and left the house.

Two weeks later, they became engaged.

***

Grace had found them a reasonably priced hotel in South Kensington where she and Hester shared an adequate twin room that had oblique views of the Natural History Museum. Now, faintly bridal in winter white, she stares out of the window of the taxi ferrying them through congested traffic towards the town hall on the King's Road. She wonders fleetingly whether she should have pushed for a church blessing, obliged Hester with a small ceremony conducted by her earnest north Oxford vicar. Perhaps she will regret something so secular and devoid of ritual. Perhaps she will not even feel legitimately married. Still, it is too late now for such thoughts and as the taxi rounds the corner and pulls up, she catches sight of Archie on the pavement surrounded by his friends, barely a dozen in number, but looking so mutually sufficient, greeting each other warmly, laughing, joking, so that she feels positively superfluous. Will they even notice if she fails to turn up? She could tell the driver to go on, randomly drive her around London for hours so that she can take a little longer to consider whether she does indeed want to marry. It is, after all, an alarmingly momentous step and how can she possibly be sure? How can love, such an irrational, untamed emotion, possibly be sufficient foundation for it? *We know so little of each other,* she thinks of Archie. *People get married with a kind of blind faith, placing ultimate trust in a relative stranger. At least if we'd had a church ceremony of sorts there would have been prayers, some chance of a deity, if any exists, taking note and offering a hopeful blessing.*

But now here is Archie, turning away from the others, looking down the road, glancing at his watch anxiously then spying their taxi pulling into the curb and walking towards it, wrenching open the door and taking her hand. *He's looking so overjoyed to see me*, Grace thinks. *He is smiling with such relief, looking so calm and reliable in his dark suit, his white shirt. Those sensible shoes. It is enough solely to be so needed by another. It is the conviction I need. Love, perhaps, can make things very simple after all.* She stands next to Archie as he takes her arm, kisses her cheek, admires her dress although he seems nervous and distracted suddenly as if following expectation rather than really noticing it. She hopes he notices it. She wishes he would exchange with her some look of complicity, an indication that they share something above and beyond the decorum and obligation of the day. He has seemed tense and somewhat remote all week as if preoccupied with matters, unreachable almost. However, she dispels such qualms as Archie holds firmly to her arm and leads her past his friends, past Celia and Bernard and Monica and Cyril and the others, the one who runs that second-hand bookshop in Camberwell, the one who works in television, Primrose something from Penge who produces documentaries, up the steps of the town hall they go, and inside. She shivers in her thin silk jacket, wishes she'd chosen wool. It is early November and the thin sliver of sun that had slipped through the hotel bedroom window that morning has dissolved behind banks of dense white cloud. Behind them, Hester is decorous, glamorous and Grace has to admire her ability, chameleon-like, to blend and adapt to her surroundings. Hers is always a consummate performance. She is animated with Cyril and admires Celia's embroidered jacket, her rather unnecessary hat. She is mildly flirtatious with overweight Bernard and solicitous to Monica's fear of a migraine. She does not know people like them, is unfamiliar with their privileges, their cushioned lives of private banks and substantial shareholdings and gilt-edged investments yet she is supremely confident in pretending that she belongs. At times, Grace wishes she had her mother's gift for acting.

Archie had invited no one from the college in Aldgate.

"Why would I do that?" he had said to Grace as they had

sat compiling the short guest list. "Boring academics are not the sort of people you want at a wedding."

"But you've been there ten years," Grace had reasoned. "Surely there must be someone you want to ask."

"No, there's nobody, Grace. In fact, I don't think I've mentioned the wedding to anyone, not even told them I'm getting married. I can't see it's any of their business. Life is best kept compartmentalised, you know. Then everyone knows where they are. And there's no need to invite my brother, by the way. He's in sub-Saharan Africa until Easter."

Grace wondered whether Archie's colleagues had been invited to his first wedding and chose to see his reluctance to include them on this occasion as being out of embarrassment. Although Archie claimed that his divorce from Louise had been uneventful, a prosaic occurrence, she could not believe that he had been entirely unaffected by it and perhaps he wished to keep his second attempt at marriage somewhat covert. Her own invitations were hardly extensive. Two close friends from schooldays now lived too far with domestic lives too demanding to be free to come and recent acquaintances made through work were solely that, transitory connections that did not merit an inclusion. So the wedding guest list, the south London neighbours, a couple of remote cousins, her mother and an old friend from Oxford, amounted to just sixteen. It was enough. Sufficient to appear respectable on the pavement outside Chelsea Town Hall, ideal to fill the back room at the French restaurant on Fulham Road that they had taken for the reception. Archie had refused to let Grace or Hester worry about costs. To Grace, Archie appeared to treat money with an abandonment that both surprised and consoled her. She had acquired a cautious respect for money from Hester and the constrained circumstances in which the two of them had always lived. They had got by through an essential frugality that had ensured bills had been paid, food provided and some semblance of a civilised life maintained. Hester had been insistent that Grace should never feel financially embarrassed by having an absent father. But money remained for Grace a commodity to be treated warily, with regard for its treacherous habit of disappearing if subjected to undue neglect. Archie had no such inhibitions. The cheques he wrote, the cash he withdrew from his wallet, the regular production of an array of credit cards, seemed spontaneous gestures, a Monopoly currency with little essential value. There was no vulgarity or ostentation in his spending, but more a lack of interest or concern for its significance. His salary at the college was adequate, but hardly generous and certainly incapable of sustaining such spending habits. Grace assumed he must have other means of financial support and had tactfully tried to ask him. He had spoken vaguely about a family trust, a legacy of stocks and shares. He had muttered something about a great-uncle who had died leaving a complicated will with various beneficiaries, waving away her enquiries as if he found the subject of money unsavoury. His father had died prematurely of chronic heart disease. His mother, increasingly frail according to Archie, lived on in the family house in Norfolk with a succession of carers in the shape of temporarily homeless friends and relations happy to exchange nursing and domestic duties for free bed and board for months at a time. He went to visit her once a month, but Grace had never met her. Her mild senility, Archie insisted, would make such a meeting difficult, upsetting for both of them since his mother would no doubt confuse her with his first wife, Louise. Grace, whilst curious about his mother, was happy to oblige, to stay in Greenwich or go and see Hester in Oxford on the Sunday afternoons when Archie drove his way up the tedious A11.

The ceremony seemed too rapid for such a binding

agreement; in a brief space of time they declared their vows, signed a declaration of sorts in front of a stern, unsmiling woman and were out onto the King's Road again. A few passers-by, bored Saturday shoppers, stopped and stared at their small group and Grace felt suddenly relieved, overwhelmingly glad to be at Archie's side, included, rather than the onlooker she seemed to have been for so long. She slipped her arm through his, felt the fine worsted wool of his dark jacket. Monica thrust a silver horseshoe into Grace's hand, Celia threw confetti rather wildly so that it pooled on the pavement at their feet. Across the road the next wedding party was clearly arriving, a more lavish celebration, this one, with several small bridesmaids fussing with muffs and a couple of black limousines spilling out guests in formal morning dress. Archie began to marshal their dozen or so party off to their nearby cars. Cyril stood on the curb waving down cabs so that they could all move on to the Fulham Road and the Restaurant Claude for the wedding breakfast.

"Hester, if you can go with Monica and Celia and the men and then there's only need for one more taxi," Archie said, attempting to guide his new mother-in-law into Cyril's care. Hester, however, resisted him. She stood rigid, staring down the road to the bus stop where a straggle of people had just got off the 22. Archie called her again, but although she turned her head for a moment towards him in acknowledgement, she then turned back and swiftly began to take some steps along the pavement away from him and the dispersing wedding guests. Amongst the unfolding pushchairs and the laden shoppers, a group of boys sporting blue-and-white football shirts and scarves and a heavily pregnant woman constraining a toddler with reins, was a very tall man with hair the colour of dark, rain-sodden sand. Dressed in a worn, windproof coat, heavy walking shoes, a bottle-green long woollen scarf, he looked incongruous among the Saturday lunchtime shoppers of the King's Road. Grace watched as her mother walked up to the man, stopped a few feet away at first then moved closer, touched his arm. The man, however, seemed more interested in staring back at her, looking with a kind of bewildered affection, a smile of slow recognition as if waking out of a prolonged unconsciousness. Hester turned suddenly and called back to her.

"It's all right, Grace, you and Archie take the taxi. I… I have something to sort out here first. Just go, please," she said firmly, waving her hand in emphasis. Archie grabbed her hand.

"Come on, Grace, people will be waiting for us."

At Restaurant Claude, in the back dining room set aside for the wedding party, Fergus Barnes, windproof coat and woollen scarf removed to reveal an old tweed jacket and tartan shirt, sits between his abandoned wife, Hester, and Primrose Larrington, the documentary film producer from Penge. Grace looks across at this unprecedented sight of her mother in the company of her father, a man who, for her, has taken on a kind of mythic status, absent as he has been for the conscious years of her life, glimpsed merely in a few photographs of the past, his identity sketchy, unformed. Yet she feels she knows him or at least she is surprised that the reality of Fergus, his stature, his presence, his reticent, almost apologetic manner as if ill at ease in social company, mirrors her latent expectations. She is drawn to him, senses an affinity of sorts although she's aware that the feeling may be charged by the emotion of the day. Hester has talked of him over the years, of course, referred to him frequently in a dismissive although not unkind way rather like people speak of a sadly eccentric remote relation. But Grace has never been aware of forming any strong image of the man nor has she particularly mourned the lack of a father in her life. As a teenager, in fact, she rather relished the slight notoriety of being different, able to indulge in the tale of Fergus' departure from Pinner and his self-imposed exile on a smallholding in Wales. She watches Primrose Larrington, her fork prodding vigorously at a chicken leg on her plate, nodding her head in agreement with Fergus. She watches Hester sipping steadily from her glass of Sancerre, eating little of her sole as if nervous and alert to anything inappropriate he may be saying. Grace cannot decide whether his presence at the wedding is touching or presumptuous. She is pleased to be seated too far away from him to make conversation possible for, after all, where would they start? Would she unfold her development and progress over the past twenty-nine years or so of his absence? Does he need to know about her average academic achievements, her first fumbling boyfriends, her allergy to avocados? Should she suggest she and Archie visit him from time to time at his rural retreat to rekindle an acquaintance? Archie has behaved impeccably, she thinks, accommodating this prodigal father at Restaurant Claude, welcoming him as if there was nothing astounding in his arrival, nor unconventional in his appearance. *Dear Archie*, Grace thinks, *I have done the right thing in marrying you. I have married you for your kindness, for your certainty and stability. For our shared affection for Austen and Forster and Greene and your tolerance of my sentimental tendencies. For that dark suit. Those sensible shoes. For the measure of your voice, the strength and safety of your embrace. Your habit of always emptying your pockets, spilling change onto the table before sitting down on the sofa, of drinking your coffee black in the morning, with milk at night, of running your hands through your hair, losing the car keys, tapping the steering wheel rhythmically in traffic jams. It's as if the smallest, most insignificant of things, barely perceptible gestures, can draw and bind us one to another, become signifiers of our love.*

Over coffee Archie made a short gracious speech. The

brief light of the November day was disappearing fast and the low back room of the restaurant became shadowy, a warm comfortable haven smelling richly of wine, of good food. Everyone seemed reluctant to move from the table, preferring to stay on and drift through the remaining hours of the afternoon even though the main business of the day was nearly over.

Hester listens to Fergus, hears him supplying answers to the questions that the very thin, close-cropped auburn-haired woman is firing at him relentlessly. The woman, Primrose Something, appears fascinated to hear endless details of Fergus' life; his daily routine in his isolated rented stone cottage with its lack of modern conveniences, its limited heating, the deficient plumbing. Hester wonders whether Primrose Something is patronising Fergus with her apparent interest and hopes she is not. Fergus is so earnest, too ingenuous to notice such an attitude and Hester has no wish to see this sophisticated, worldly media woman use him for her sport. *He is such a hopeless case*, she thinks, *a foolish innocent for whom I should have only feelings of contempt. Yet I feel protective of him in some way. Look at him, sitting here in his old clothes among these smart London people with their preposterously self-indulgent lifestyles, their fast cars and expensive houses. Why ever does Archie Copeland associate himself with this lot? Seek out their friendship when they are really so shallow, their very of-the-moment superficial lifestyles expendable? At least Fergus knows how to survive, how to dig a field, cultivate some root vegetables and batten down his hatches against any unlikely storm. Yet the man is so ridiculous. And in his own way as pretentious as Celia and Cyril and Monica and Bernard and the like, living lives self-consciously cluttered with invitations to private viewings and opera gala nights and wine tastings. Renovating their huge Victorian town houses as Celia's been regaling me, ripping out evidently serviceable and sensible kitchens to replace them with free-standing dressers and units to resemble the servants' basement quarters of old. Fergus walked away from a civilised, cavity-walled, post-war semi-detached home in Middlesex, from pensionable, clean and respectable employment, from an attractive, loving wife and delectable small child to pursue his absurd notion of a better, purer life.* Hester drains the last of her cup of bitter coffee and despairs of her own ill-placed patience with Fergus. *Let Primrose Something or Other eat the man alive, spread him on a Bath Oliver along with the sliver of Camembert she's prising now from the Assiette de Fromage circling the table.* She looks across at Grace who's resting one hand on her cheek as if the day is beginning to feel too long. Archie clearly adores her. Hester hopes this is enough and knows that it rarely is. Such a love can be stifling and she wonders whether Grace will wake up in five years' time and realise she is bored by Archie, faintly repelled, even, by his calm, ordered manner, his inability to surprise. *Still, there are worse things*, she reminds herself, with a rueful glance at Fergus, *than a husband who constantly delivers. And with the two or three children that Grace so blatantly craves and a pleasant home, they'll probably rub along all right together, coast through the ordinary and inevitable everydayness of life until suddenly they'll turn around and realise they've stuck at it for forty or so years. A marriage no worse and possibly considerably better than most. 'For richer for poorer, in sickness and in health', or something like that. After all, does anyone know what they really want? Women, in particular. And if they do, surely that could change along with the winds of time. What can seem the perfect, ideal life to covet one day can so easily feel confining and restrictive the next. I've drunk too much wine*, Hester thinks, scrabbling for a tissue in her bag, which has fallen to the floor, lost among a flotsam of white napkins and place name cards. Fergus sees her forage, fumbles in the breast pocket of his absurd tweed jacket and hands her a large, creased handkerchief.

"Here, Hess," he says. "Have this."

Hester takes it. It smells of bonfire smoke and peppermints.

# 4

They took a twelve-month lease on the house at Jacob's Bottom. Leaving London behind and driving down the A30 in late March, the fields and hedgerows splashed confidently with signs of an English spring, Grace was optimistic. Initially, Archie's somewhat cavalier behaviour in choosing the place had alarmed her. She had felt marginalised as if her own wishes were too subordinate to be of any concern. She had, of course, often agreed that they would eventually move out of London, but it had been one of those recurring conversations that most people living in the capital had. It was what was talked about while sitting endlessly in traffic jams or while reading the Sunday papers with their country property sections displaying vast homes going for a comparative song. But in truth no one seemed to move further west than Barnes Common or shift north of Crouch End. Like Moscow to the three sisters, The Country appeared desirable to city people as an idea rather than a reality. Grace, too, had thought only in abstract terms of living there and at first the idea that Archie had not only been doing more than this, but considering counties, consulting agents without bothering to inform her, had been infuriating. But she swiftly acclimatised herself to both his clandestine actions and the move itself. She was too cautious, given to procrastination, retreat, reluctant always to effect change. She'd put up for far too long with her aunt's dreadful damp basement flat, tolerated her dead-end jobs with too much equanimity. The only impulsive act of her life had been in marrying Archie after knowing him only eight months and even that could be considered acquiescent on her part. Archie had instigated, she had merely followed.

Besides, this move was what she wanted. She realised now that living in London had been something she had tolerated rather than enjoyed. In truth, London life felt too boisterous for her. It beat, throbbed and thrived constantly, a relentless and perpetual pursuit of prosperity and advancement. The place itself she loved. The churches, theatres, parks, river, bridges, buildings. The melting pot of centuries of endeavour and belief to be found round every corner as if the whole city was one historic theme park laid out for general edification. Before she met Archie she'd often go out very early on a Sunday morning to try and catch the capital before it was really awake and drawing attention to itself. There was always the odd café open, a newsagent or two, but on the whole the streets were deserted, shops firmly closed against commerce for at least one day. It was how she liked London, a peaceful watercolour, a still life. A sentimental idealised vision utterly at odds with the competitive and energetic pulse at its heart, she knew. Grace was not competitive. She felt enervated by the prospect of a life tethered to clocks and alarms and appointments and everywhere around her in the city she saw people living lives increasingly like that. Fast, energetic lives seemingly in some strange perpetual motion in pursuit of material success, getting and spending, with scant awareness of the time of the day, the season of the year. She did not want to settle for what she saw as so little.

But of course, there was the matter of Archie's career. It was all very well for them both to indulge in pastoral dreams, but salaries were required.

"I don't see how we can live here," Grace had whispered

to Archie when the letting agent had first shown them around the house at Jacob's Bottom. She had already fallen for the appeal of the place and it hardly needed the enthusiastic agent to extol its virtues. It was a skilful conversion of two small 18$^{th}$-century farm cottages into a long, low house with sanded oak floors, a good, square kitchen and rural views from every window. The previous tenants had already moved out and the empty rooms had been repainted in readiness for the new let.

"Don't you like it?" he had said.

"That's not the point, I love it." Grace had not even bothered to lower her voice as the agent showed them the two bedrooms upstairs, each with open fireplaces, oak floorboards and wooden beams. "But it's hardly commuting distance to Aldgate."

"There's a branch link from Fletwell that hooks up to the main London line into Paddington," the agent had informed them swiftly. "Lovely ride most of the way. Very picturesque. And they're cutting minutes off the journey all the time, of course. It's quite opening up this part of the south-west."

"I've looked into it," Archie had added. "About a hundred and fifty minutes, I should say, door to door. Give or take half an hour or so. It's certainly doable, Grace. And I can use the time for reading. I don't suppose you'll mind giving up your job and looking for something down here?"

Archie knew that Grace would have no qualms about handing in her resignation. She had moved on from the tourist office at Victoria station soon after their wedding to a bookshop in the Charing Cross Road where the initial incentive of swift managerial advancement had failed to materialise. Even the lure of spending her days ensconced between endless shelves of books soon waned since she was mostly dispatched to the chaotic stockroom with indecipherable lists of orders to sort. The other members of staff were disaffected and transient and she, too, was desperate to leave. The letting agent had suggested they repair to The Carpenters' Arms in a nearby village to discuss the terms of the tenancy. They had driven back to Greenwich later that day and Grace had gone into work the next morning and, exhilarated, had handed in her notice.

Four weeks later, they collected the keys from the office in Fletwell. The Greenwich house had swiftly been let to a colleague of Archie's, a temporary measure, he said, before he sorted out a sale. Since the house had originally been bought with his brother he would need to consult Leo before instructing an agent to market it. Leo, he was sure, would have no objection since he was so rarely settled in one place for long and his nomadic lifestyle made it senseless to tie himself down to property ownership. But equally, he had no idea when he would next be in England in order to sign contracts and fulfil paperwork necessities. In the meantime, the rental income from the one house would more than cover the expenditure on the other, Archie reassured her, and they could take their time in deciding exactly where they wished to buy their permanent home.

The first night at Jacob's Bottom, Grace lay awake long after she knew Archie had fallen asleep, worn out by the long day of removal from SE10. She felt conscious of being at the start of something new and was suddenly overwhelmingly relieved. The move felt like a solution to a problem that she could not even fully define. *Archie is outwardly devoted to me*, she thinks, *proud and appreciative and I never have a moment when I doubt his faithfulness, his love, his desire to be with me. It should be enough. Yet there's something between us, a detachment on his part, a defence as if he fears me drawing too close, as if he fears complete confidence. Sometimes*, Grace thinks, *it's as if I hardly know him and that sensation seems to be growing rather than diminishing with time.*

Nevertheless, she listens now to his steady breathing in bed beside her and is comforted and reassured by it.

As always.

She lies in the extraordinary darkness of this new place, listens for new noises. At first, it's the absence of sound she welcomes: no constant background hum of road noise, of sirens and accelerating cars and screech of brakes. Instead, a silence, alarming initially for its novelty, then punctuated by occasional creaks in the fabric of the old building, the remote noise of an animal in a field, possibly the hoot of an owl in a tree. Grace feels elated to have Archie away from all they have left; his Greenwich house just off the ever-hectic A2, the affluent friends and neighbours, ex-wife Louise and possible sightings with new husband and children on the heath. Here, in this rural hamlet, they are both novices, set adrift from their respective pasts, together. *It has to help,* she thinks. *It has to bring him closer to me.*

Over the first few days and weeks at Jacob's Bottom, Grace finds herself thinking of her father. As she potters contentedly around the new house, arranging furniture, staring out of the window for long stretches of time onto ploughed fields, grazing cattle, she thinks of Fergus and his departure from suburban Pinner all those years past. However outrageous the gesture, given the existence of his wife and very young child, perhaps he had a point. She has not heard from him since their wedding. She wrote to thank him for coming at the address she managed to grab before he left the restaurant, disappearing suddenly out into the dark November afternoon mumbling something about a long journey by coach followed by a spot of hitchhiking. But she's had no reply, which her mother says is to be expected. And now, at Jacob's Bottom, he's frequently in her mind, she finds, and she thinks of him with a fondness he's never remotely earned. Mentioning it in a phone call to her mother, Hester warns her against sentimentality where her father is concerned, but Grace suspects she shares her susceptibility. There is something blatantly likeable about the man with his entire lack of vanity and pretension. He is an innocent. He has a 'rabbit caught in the headlights' sort of disposition that makes him immune from blame. Or at least that is how he seems to Grace and possibly, by now, to Hester too. Grace is sure that her mother's judgement of him has mollified over the years, the passage of time no doubt dissolving bitterness that no longer has a relevance to the here and now. Hester is not one to harbour resentment. He would like this place, Grace thinks, looking out at the hares that dart over the fields at the back of the house. She abandons her furniture-sorting jobs on a whim, grabs a coat and walks up one of the steep paths which leads out of the hamlet to the ridge above, spotting wild primroses, narcissi, hawthorn. But she knows she's fooling herself if she thinks this place to be to Fergus' taste. It is too tame, polite and well behaved to be his kind of landscape. Urban niceties are safely a short car drive away with a couple of shops that sell between them a selection of decent cheeses, bread, wine. There are too many houses owned by people living in Fulham and Putney during the week who appear in pristine Barbours on Saturday morning, sniffing the air and exchanging tales of Friday night gridlock around Swindon. And there's an uncomfortable division, Grace notes after the first few weeks of living here, between the occupants of the tied cottages, farm labourers and their families who live alongside the weekenders and the owners of the two substantial Georgian houses, the Old Vicarage and Maple Lodge. No, this is not her father's sort of rural idyll at all. Fergus' idea of countryside is very Ted Hughes, rugged, raw, an elemental place that tests rather than accommodates its inhabitants. Jacob's Bottom is the opposite. Grace thinks that she could easily sink into a comfortable sort of lethargy, slide from day to day accomplishing small tasks, noting new seasons, a recipient rather than an active participant in the frenetic round of things. It would be so appealing. *It's not that I want to be indolent like the idle rich*, she defends herself, *I am happy to be purposeful and industrious as long as it is in the shadows. I am temperamentally suited to drifting rather than seizing days. I'd rather tell the time of the day, the fall of the year from the light in the sky, the height of the sun than from insistent diaries and calendars ticking off time with disturbing relentlessness.*

But it's no good, she knows. She has to be a woman of her time and stir herself into some worthwhile occupation, forge a career of sorts even if she does soon find herself to be gratifyingly pregnant. (*Please God, let me become pregnant. Surely, after all this time of trying...*) It is 1987, after all, and women are – take or leave a few biological differences: a womb and a lifetime store of eggs – as men are. Or supposed to be. On the whole.

They had filled a removal van with most of the contents of Archie's house in Greenwich and one or two of the pieces Grace had kept from her flat. A pine Victorian washstand she'd bought when she first moved to London. A cheval mirror Hester had given her for her twenty-first birthday. And her books, of course, mostly novels, well-thumbed, raddled paperbacks, had taken up two entire packing cases. They had been surprised to find an upright piano sitting inexplicably in the corner of the living room on the day they moved in. They had noticed it on their previous viewing of the house and the agent had assured them it was awaiting collection. But the days turned into weeks and calls to the rental office in Fletwell had still not uncovered anyone wanting to take responsibility for it. It appeared to have been abandoned. Grace lifted the lid every now and again, struck a few notes randomly, unable to tell whether it was in tune.

"Can you play?" Archie asked, surprising her one day, coming into the room when she thought he was at the bottom of the garden investigating the dilapidated shed. She traced her finger through dust-encrusted keys, forming her initials on middle C then firmly closed the lid.

"No, not a note," she said, "I mean I did have lessons once, when I was about ten or so. But I was hopeless. It all seemed too bewildering, black shapes on paper supposedly meaning something. I just couldn't work it all out. Can you? Play, I mean?"

Archie laughed. He opened the lid of the piano, touched the keyboard with his sturdy fingers. His broad, capable hands looked entirely out of place on the slim, neat keys.

"Me? Of course not. It's not my sort of thing at all. But you could learn, Grace. I could imagine you playing, it would suit you. I'd like to see you sitting here, playing the piano. You'd be good with the right teacher, I'm sure of that. Wouldn't you like to learn?"

Grace moved away from the piano, inexplicably irritated by his encouragement. She felt uneasy with his apparent wish to visualise her as he wished to see her, an image created to satisfy some concept of appropriate outmoded womanhood. She knelt down on the floor in front of several packing cases marked 'books'.

"No, I told you, I tried it once and I was no good," she snapped, "worse than hopeless, in fact. Why would I want to try again just to please some fantasy of yours?" She turned away to one of the cases, ripping it open and splitting the corner of her fingernail. Archie's comment was too bland, too inconsequential to have deserved such a rebuke and she felt uncomfortable with herself for making it. She heard him move towards the large inglenook fireplace that occupied most of one wall of the room. Somewhere in the distance was the sound of a tractor. Sheep bleating. A car drove past the lane at the end of their track. There was a silence between them. Grace stared at the contents of the packing case, at the empty shelves behind her as if suddenly unwilling and inadequate to the task.

Archie said, "No doubt we'll need to get the chimney swept. Before we can light any fires with safety, I mean. We should get that done."

"Yes," Grace said. "You're probably right. I'll ask around, shall I? For a chimney sweep, I mean. Someone will know of one, surely."

Archie turned around, beamed at her, gratified.

"That's a good idea, Grace, you do that. I'll leave it to you. And logs too, of course, someone will know of a good supplier. An open fire will bring this room alive."

He sat down on one of the sofas they'd brought from Greenwich, a two-seater covered in beige William Morris fabric that was somewhat dwarfed by the contours of the long room. Grace started to shift books, carefully arranging hers on one shelf, Archie's on another. She sat back to look at them then swiftly removed them all, shelf by shelf, and began again, this time intermingling them, ordering the books alphabetically by author. Absorbed now by her task, she noted numerous duplicates, which consoled her. She flicked to familiar openings, finding comfort in the rich cadences of the perfect phrase, turning to closing lines to read again the balanced resolution of rhythm and meaning. She had grown almost oblivious of Archie in the room, entirely engrossed and about to move on from his Fielding and her Fowles when she became aware of him at her shoulder. He handed her a second copy of *Lord of the Flies.*

"'The darkness of man's heart'," he said.

"Yes," she said, looking up at him, "'The end of innocence'. Poor Piggy."

***

They had been to Florence for their honeymoon. They'd waited some months after the wedding, for the warmer weather of spring and Archie's Easter break from his Aldgate college. Flying to Pisa, they'd collected a car then driven down to the city where Archie had booked a hotel for their first week. It was a perfect choice, an enchanting place, occupying the top four floors of a Renaissance building set in a piazza close to the Duomo. Their bedroom, sparsely furnished, was large and lofty with an enormous wardrobe, a marble-topped dressing table and a bed with springs that complained each time either of them moved. They ate breakfast, dry rolls, very sweet buns and coffee, dense and strong, perched at small tables in an airy room filled with paintings by artists of dubious talent. The other guests were mostly American, a contingent of ten retired teachers on a European tour that departed each morning at nine in the company of a guide. There were two elderly sisters from Norwich who sat each evening over glasses of Cinzano, ticking off sites in their much-thumbed guidebooks rather as if they were playing a game of 'I Spy'. A retired priest from Dublin was visiting his brother, an art historian at the Uffizi. Grace enjoyed watching them all, enjoyed noting the way they looked at the two of them with fondness, a tender, sentimental regard for their relative youth. They explored the city, the galleries, the churches, chapels, shops and cafes and Grace felt, at first, overwhelmingly comforted and at ease with Archie at her side.

"I feel so lucky," she said to him one evening as they slipped down the wide stone staircase of the building and out into the fading light of a day that had been unseasonably warm for early April. "To have found you, I mean. I was beginning to think I was destined to a life of spinsterhood and celibacy with only my fictional heroes for company."

He held hard to her hand so that she felt her wedding ring dig sharply into her flesh.

"What a waste that would have been," he said, "but I shall have to make sure I live up to your high expectations and emulate these perfect protagonists of yours. I intend to take good care of you, Grace, don't you worry."

Later that evening, they had made love in their ancient double bed and Grace had lain awake long after Archie had fallen asleep, assured by his steady breathing, his biddable, even temperament. And she wondered whether, here in this cavernous, high-ceilinged room, she might have conceived a child, in this building which must have witnessed countless such couplings over the centuries.

"We'll have to call her Florence if it's a girl," Grace said lightly the next morning as they left the city and headed south towards Siena. Archie said nothing in the driver's seat next to her, concentrating on the dense traffic and flinching at the constant car horns as they extricated their way out and onto emptier roads. Eventually, he pulled sharply up at the side of the road to consult the map, causing horns to blast and drivers to gesticulate in his direction. "If I manage to get pregnant while we're away, I mean," she added. "A boy would be harder to name. Cosimo, Leonardo… I suppose there's always Michael, of course." He looked across at her, his face blank as if uncomprehending then grabbed the map from the back seat and straightened it out against the steering wheel, tracing his finger along roads and routes then checking the scale.

"I think we should go to San Gimignano on the way there," he said, "just in case we don't fit it in on the trip back. We need to look at the fourteen medieval towers. That's important for us. And then possibly Volterra if there's time. You look out for the signs, Grace, so I can concentrate on the driving. You need your wits about you, the speed some of these people go."

He pushed the road map onto her lap, checked his mirror and pulled more cautiously out into the traffic.

After five days of fine weather, rain and clouds set in. They spent their second week in Umbria, first in Spoleto then in Assisi, visiting numerous hill towns and villages and too many chapels and churches each day to remember them all. But it was cold. Suddenly unseasonably cold, according to the manager of their hotel in Assisi who apologised for the penetrating winds and sudden downpours that soaked into the stones of the ancient streets and through the inadequate clothing they'd brought with them. Grace left Archie in a café in Perugia and went and bought a pair of gloves and a thick sweater. The wool itched her sunburn, acquired on the first day sitting in the sun on the steps of the Uffizi. Archie broke his reading glasses. Suddenly, she wanted to go home. She became irritated by his constant company and alarmed by her irritation. She resented his firm grasp on her arm as they toured Gubbio, Orvieto, Todi, Terni, an apparently endless list of places that he seemed compelled to show her, more the insistent tour guide than her husband. She felt his perpetual presence as an unwelcome constraint. She blamed the weather. She blamed her lack of intellectual curiosity about sites that obviously enthralled Archie. She worried that he would find her tiresome, superficial. She fretted that she would find him dull and too intense. He seemed so remote from her, polite, courteous, yet withdrawn as if he were going through the motions of accompanying her through obligation rather than choice. In her turn, she found herself withdrawing, matching his restraint, as if warm, spontaneous behaviour had become inappropriate, an embarrassment to them both.

Then suddenly, on their last day, the sun reappeared, strong and hot as if determined to shift the season firmly into summer. Back in Tuscany, they spent the morning in Lucca and Archie talked about the Etruscans and the Roman street plan and the basilicas and Grace tried hard not to recoil from his knowledge, but to tease him a little instead; his careful, scholarly manner, her need for instruction. Waiting for their flight at Pisa, staring up at the departure board so she could not see his expression, she said abruptly, "We'll be all right together, won't we, Archie? We'll be able to make things work for the two of us if... surely we can do that?" She felt him start with surprise at her side then stand up, check his watch, move a couple of feet away.

"Of course we will. Whatever do you mean, Grace? What a very strange thing to say. Coffee? Our flight's not even up there yet. It'll be a long time before we board."

***

Most days, Archie drove three miles into Fletwell, a small market town that offered a station with hourly connections to London. His evening return was more laborious with delays and slow trains substituted for the speedy morning service and he would often not be back at Jacob's Bottom before nine. Grace felt he looked tired and worried that the country experiment would become just that and he would want to return to Greenwich when their year's lease on the house came to an end. She dreaded the prospect of going back for even though she knew few people here and those only on a polite, nodding acquaintance, the longer they stayed the more she felt attached and accommodated by the place. Her initial concerns that she might find the days tedious during Archie's absence proved groundless; she relished being alone in the house, alone as she walked up the hills, across the valley to Fox Woods and down to Acorn Coppice. At weekends or on fine evenings if he was home early, she would show Archie the tracks she'd found, the bridleways and shortcuts across to neighbouring villages or hamlets. Fortunately, Archie seemed as set on staying away from London as she was. He allayed her fears one night when his journey had been particularly tiresome with a points failure south-west of Swindon and a replacement bus service that trundled slowly through several counties before eventually depositing him at Fletwell.

"I don't mind, Grace, really. These things happen, but it's not as if it's a daily occurrence."

Although it was early May the day had been dull and wet and she'd lit the fire around five. They ate her dried-up dinner and drank most of a bottle of red wine in front of it. She glanced at the crumpled copy of the London evening paper Archie had brought in with him rather as if it were a missive from a frantic alternative planet. Bomb scares, traffic chaos, threatened tube strikes glared up from the pages as if hungry for her attention.

"Besides," Archie went on, "it's worth it to come home to you." He took her hand and kissed each finger slowly. "You're happy here, aren't you? I know it's a bit of a backwater, but..."

"Of course I am," Grace said, "I like backwaters. They suit me."

"Me too," he said and refilled his glass with the last of the wine. "In fact, if it turned out that our plans to... no, it doesn't matter."

"What?"

"No, it's nothing to worry about. Nothing worth talking about. Another time, perhaps." He leant forward to shift a log into the flame. Outside the rain continued to lash against the windows and she knew that by morning the track that ran alongside the house down to the lane would be encrusted mud and deep puddles.

"I found cornflowers today," she said, "and bluebells.

Masses of them, up near Fox Woods. I'll take you there at the weekend."

***

Melanie Babbington, late thirties, perhaps forty, sat back in her office chair, pushed a plate of flapjacks across the large desk.

"Go on, help me out. They're from the health shop down the road so they must be doing us good. That's my excuse, anyway!" She pulled the black patent belt around her waist a little tighter as if to defy any surplus flesh. "So tell me a bit about yourself – Grace, isn't it? Why you're interested in the job, all that sort of thing. We're only a small concern at the moment, of course, although we have great plans to expand. Providing we can get a bit more money out of the local council and increase our sponsors, seek out some like-minded locals with a bit of spare cash. We've been running things on a shoestring so far."

They had noticed the sign in the window of what appeared to be a disused Methodist chapel undergoing some sort of renovation when in Fletwell on Saturday morning. 'Part-time Assistant for new arts centre', it read, with a phone number that promised 'more details available'. But when Grace had rung, details had been scant.

"Best thing is for you to come in and see us. Would Tuesday suit? Tuesday morning around eleven?"

So Grace had driven in with Archie, dropped him at the station and wasted time in the small library, the local museum which specialised in rural artefacts – ploughshares, a shepherd's smock, an accounts book dated 1846 – and found herself just before eleven sitting in a small cluttered office across the desk from Melanie Babbington.

"I don't really have much experience of this kind of thing," she said tentatively, "none at all, in fact, but it sounded as if it might be interesting." She felt pale and neutral next to Melanie who was dressed in a narrow black skirt, silk blouse, precariously high heels. Around her, books, piles of paper, posters, tea-stained mugs strained for space and there was a smell of new paint and wood stain in the air.

"You'll be in good company, then," Melanie said. "I've only just taken over here and really, it's the blind leading the blind most of the time. My background's in nursing, you see, and boarding schools – running the 'san' and bandaging bloody knees, that sort of thing. And, of course, we're still a bit of a building site at the moment."

"What exactly would the job entail?" Grace said.

"Oh, a little of this and a little of that, really," Melanie said vaguely, sweeping strands of blonde hair onto the top of her head with a tortoiseshell clasp. "The exciting thing is that we're entirely new so that the job could grow around you. I suppose you'd be a bit of a general dogsbody, some typing, although speeds aren't really an issue so don't let that put you off. Then there'd be answering the phone, dealing with enquiries and the post. Drafting the odd press release for the local papers, no doubt. And ideas, of course. We've just about got our first season planned, but with another mind, another pair of eyes… well, you are keen on the arts, I presume? Otherwise, why would you be interested in us? I suppose I should be interviewing you formally, but since you're our only applicant under the age of eighty and over the age of sixteen so far there really doesn't seem much point." She laughed loudly, opening her mouth wide to display a considerable number of mercury fillings. Grace thought of endless solitary winter Sundays wandering around the Tate, the National Gallery, the Royal Academy, not with any specific notion or knowledge, but as an essential escape from the basement flat. As a change from walking in the West Brompton Oratory or drinking too many cups of coffee at cafés in the Fulham Road as she sat reading. She told Melanie about her interest in theatre, no doubt inherited from Hester. She talked about music and ballet and her passion for books and seemed on the point of impressing her when she added, "Of course, I don't have any formal academic qualifications beyond school, I'm afraid."

"Oh dear, that's a pity," Melanie said, sitting back in her chair, deflated. She fiddled again with the tortoiseshell slide, attempting to confine more strands of hair that appeared brittle as if from constant lacquering. "Then you're not really what we're looking for at all. I was hoping we could say we'd taken on a young graduate, straight out of Oxford or Cambridge, Bristol or Durham at a snatch, or something like that. It would be good publicity for the local rag, you see. Make us seem so much more authentic. We're so keen to establish a credible footprint on the artistic scene here in the south-west."

"I'm sorry," Grace said, feeling fraudulent. The phone rang and, unearthing it from under a pile of flyers advertising a children's half-term event, Melanie answered it, greeting the caller with familiarity and evident affection. Grace tidied the leaflets that had consequently cascaded around her, ordered them into neat piles on the desk while Melanie talked rapidly, balancing the receiver under her chin and scribbling names and figures on the back of her hand with a leaking biro. Eventually, just as Grace was feeling it would be sensible to leave, her inadequacy for the position all too plain, Melanie finished the call. She was flushed, a bead of sweat had appeared on her forehead.

"God, look at the state of me!" she said, inspecting her hands, tattooed all over with blotched blue ink. "So sorry, Grace, but that was Giles Meredith. My other half, actually, and the one who got me into this shindig in the first place.

Unfortunately, there's a harridan of a wife in the wings too, but the less we think about her, the better for all of us. But Giles is the brains running this show and he's a dynamic operator and when Giles needs to talk… well, he's not the most patient of men, but then the gorgeous ones never are, don't you find?"

Again, the big laugh exploded from her rather like the snap of a cracker being pulled. Grace stood up, tucked her chair as best she could into one side of the laden desk. Melanie leant over for the final piece of flapjack then pulled back her hand as if remembering something more urgent she needed to do.

"So it will just be three days at first, ten until four, will that suit you, Grace? Giles has given me carte blanche to take on who I like. Of course the hours are a bit varied, I have to say, because if there's an evening event, and of course there will be quite a few of those, we'd like you here for those as well. Time off in lieu, naturally." She had changed her manner, even her voice suddenly sounded brisk, purposeful, as if a superior had walked into the room and was observing her. She retrieved a file from the floor, opened it and drew out an application form that was headed 'The Old Chapel Arts Centre'.

"I thought you said my lack of qualifications was going to be a problem," Grace said, feeling a need to remind Melanie in case the phone call with Giles Meredith had caused her to forget.

"Oh nonsense, we could never attract the calibre of person we really want," she said. "Our pay's quite pathetic for a start and we can't pretend we offer the first rung on the ladder to a stellar career. But we might fit the bill for you, Grace. We might suit you and be just your sort of thing. Could you start this Thursday? Fill this in purely as a formality, will you?"

Archie was home early that day and they walked from the house up to Fox Woods, the first mild day of May and a relief after an interminably wet, cool spring. He seemed preoccupied at first and Grace said little, supposing he was simply detaching himself from the noise and clamour of London, from his students and the stuffiness of the rail journey. He often seemed remote when he arrived home as if the transition from one place to another was awkward for him and Grace tried not to feel isolated by it. By the time they reached the bluebell fields, she had unfolded her morning with Melanie at the Old Chapel Arts Centre.

"Obviously, I'll take the job," Grace said as they left the lane and went into Fox Woods. "It's not as if there's much else around here and I must start earning some money. And Melanie seemed welcoming, quite enthusiastic about the idea of me starting. Especially when I mentioned you, actually. She seemed to think a lecturer in Romantic poetry could be a useful connection for the arts centre."

Archie looked uncertain. He slipped a hand into hers as they went deeper into the woods, which grew damper underfoot in places where the sun rarely reached. The dank smell was almost sweet like sweat, like rotted apples in an unkempt orchard. Alone, Grace found the woods claustrophobic and she panicked at the absence of sky and at the thought that she might lose sense of direction. But here with Archie she was content to suppress any such thoughts and depend on his certainty.

"I think Melanie has the idea you might give a talk or something like that. Or lead a discussion. She was particularly keen when I mentioned your PhD on Coleridge. Although she did say she wished it was Hardy. She seemed to think Hardy would have more popular appeal in this part of the world."

Archie picked up a couple of sticks from the ground, compared them, discarded one and walked on with the other as a makeshift crook. He often did this when they went for a walk as if he saw it as the mark of the genuine countryman whereas Grace felt it looked affected as if he was trying too hard to adopt rural habits that did not sit naturally with either of them. "Well, I suppose that's possible. A talk or a general discussion on poetry, perhaps," he said cautiously. "I'm not too keen on divulging too much about my PhD research and findings before I've finished the whole thing. That… well, that wouldn't be a good idea at all."

They turned and began to make their way out of the woods and back down the hill towards Jacob's Bottom. A field of docile cows on one side mirrored sheep on the other.

As always, Grace feels infected by the tranquillity of the place and is mostly overwhelmingly content. She tells herself that she needs to ignore the growing confusion of Archie's papers and catalogue cards seemingly spread aimlessly across the bare floorboards of the spare room and the scant time he appears to be giving to serious completion of his thesis. What does it matter? *We can live here,* she thinks, *make as fulfilled and happy a life for the two of us as any flawed human beings have a right to expect.* She looks across at Archie and fleetingly gives in to a recurring unease, wondering if, at times, he finds the intimacy and companionship of marriage a burden in some way. So often she finds herself wanting to reassure him, to reach out and draw him close, but at those same moments she holds back, fearing she lacks the words to convince him, not even knowing the words to use, so she shies away, removing a little of herself too.

But now they are together.

They are at ease with the hour, the moment, and Grace chooses to dispel any shadow from her mind. There's a fleck or two of grey in Archie's thick sandy hair that she's not noticed before. It suits him, she thinks. He's a man better suited to middle age than youth. Archie wears sobriety well.

***

Archie swam. Grace had realised Archie's passion for swimming when they'd spent a weekend in Cornwall during their first summer together. On a cool June day when the few occupants of Polzeath beach were sheltering behind windbreaks, attempting to constrain sand from stinging eyes and skin, Archie had headed for the waves. He shunned the black rubber body suits they'd seen the surfers wear and plunged heedlessly through the cold Atlantic waters, soon disappearing from Grace's view. On the first occasion she'd grown anxious when he failed to reappear after half an hour. She had paced the beach, trying to decide whether the occasional bobbing head, the white limbs glimpsed from a somersault, jettisoned by the surf, belonged to Archie and if these movements suggested he was in trouble. When he eventually emerged, clearly exhilarated by his exposure to the turbulence of the waves, she realised her anxiety had been entirely misplaced.

"I can't see how you get any pleasure from swimming when the water's icy and there's such a strong current," she'd said.

"It's refreshing. Invigorating." Archie took the towel she had been clinging to, rubbed his arms and legs roughly as if encouraging the return of a blood supply. "It's a marvellous feeling, being tossed around by the waves, feeling entirely free with just an edge of danger."

"Exactly, an edge of danger. I was about to call the lifeguard."

"Relax, Grace. I know what I'm doing out there. I've swum in far worse than this, I can assure you. There's no need to worry."

When a red flag was flying at the beach the following day,

Archie chose to ignore it. Grace, anxious not to displease the lifeguard or Archie, took herself off to the comfort of a café to read until he came to find her later.

"See?" he said. "Alive and well and no damage done."

"I was just..."

"I know," he interrupted her, pulling her close and kissing the top of her head, "and thank you for that."

From their house at Jacob's Bottom, Archie could reach the sea in less than thirty minutes; on early summer mornings or around dusk he could wind down through the lanes and be in the water in nearly half that time. On his return, Grace noticed his humour had always improved and any slight indifferent mood or irritation lifted, so she encouraged him to go. That first summer at Jacob's Bottom, the weather remained indifferent, the temperature rarely rising to anything remarkable through June and July, but Archie swam several times a week. Often she would be woken early by the sound of the car pulling away from the house, over the rough ground of the track down to the road and she would roll over in bed and find Archie gone. One Saturday morning, she got up in time to make coffee, load a tray with breakfast so that she could pull him back to bed as soon as he arrived home, the smell of salt and cold air clinging to his skin. But instead he walked into the kitchen and caught sight of the pile of unopened post that had cluttered the dresser for several days. He sifted swiftly through it, deposited most in the bin, slipping a couple of unopened letters into his back pocket. Grace handed him a towel. Absently, he took it, ran it through his wet hair.

"Archie?"

"What?"

She indicated the tray of toast, pot of coffee. Her bare feet felt suddenly chilled by the flagstone floor. He tidied his towel around the back of a kitchen chair, draped wet swimming trunks on the back of another. They began to drip, small pools forming noiselessly. He looked at her for a moment then turned away.

"No breakfast for me, thanks, I'm not hungry. You go back to bed, though. It's still early. I think I'll get on with some gardening. It's all in the terms of the lease for the house, you know, to keep the exterior up to scratch. That ground ivy, it's… it's completely out of control. And there's the grass too. I need to… it's going to rain later, you see. Before midday. That's what they've just said on the radio."

Grace watched him disappear out of the back door, head towards the garden. She tipped slices of buttered toast into the bin, covering Archie's discarded mail. An hour or so later, she took him out some coffee and found the overgrown ivy untouched, the grass still long. Archie was sitting on the bench at the end of the garden staring, apparently, at the beds that bordered the lawn. She handed him a mug. He smiled, thanked her.

"It seems to be keeping fine after all," Grace said. "The forecasters got it wrong."

"Yes," he said, sipping his coffee, "I'm glad of that."

***

It was three weeks before Grace met Giles Meredith. She had settled into the job at the Old Chapel Arts Centre although the days were unpredictable, the building transforming around them, evolving from out of the disused and damp space it had been for years, shedding its skin of abandonment and decay. Builders were still adapting the main chapel into two venues and although the structural work was mainly finished, there were constant visits from contracted workmen who often arrived unsure of what they were contracted to do. The site manager had already moved on to another job in another part of the county since the project had long run out of time and budget. The place, however, was attracting a lot of interest from local people, some of whom called in to berate the expenditure of their rates on worthless artistic pursuits whilst others were gratifyingly enthusiastic about the idea of the centre. The historical architect, bearded and ponderous, arrived one morning when Grace was alone and spent two hours shifting from foot to foot, inspecting every detail of the transformation.

"A pity the gallery's gone," he said morosely when Grace came in with a mug of tea. He appeared not to have moved since he arrived, occupying a spot in the centre of what was now the main auditorium and scanning the space around him. "Such a feature of these Non-Conformist chapels. The more affluent ones, anyway, like this one was. Having an upper storey. Take that away and you're losing so much of its essence."

"I believe the idea was to create a space upstairs for exhibitions," Grace said. "It's a big building, but a lot of the space was simply being wasted by such high ceilings."

He looked at her contemptuously, but said nothing for a while, drinking his tea and staring up at the clear glass windows. Eventually, he shuffled across the limestone floor towards the door to the office.

"This would have been the vestry, you know," he said, peering into the room and appearing to show disapproval of the two desks, the filing cabinet and typewriters and telephone, the piles of brightly coloured leaflets and brochures ready for distribution.

"I know," Grace said, "I've seen photographs of the original building. It's been deserted and neglected for years, hasn't it? It's wonderful to think of it having a new life, a phoenix rising from the ashes so to speak. The original chapel's Victorian, I believe. Built of Bath stone."

He appeared not to hear and walked back to the entrance hall and up the newly created staircase that was yet to be carpeted. Grace followed, watching him peer up at the ceiling, into the roof of the original nave, muttering under his breath, into his unkempt beard. Finally, he retraced his steps, holding firmly to the stair rail as if not quite trusting the workmanship. Opening the front door, he seemed about to leave when he turned and looked directly at Grace.

"Purbeck stone. Everyone makes that mistake. Even the so-called experts."

"Right," she said.

"Purbeck with Bath. A combination. I hope you'll get that right in any literature about the place."

Five minutes later, Melanie arrived with Giles Meredith. He smiled expansively, kissed her on both cheeks and introduced himself.

"And you must be Grace Copeland. Delighted you've come to join our little venture." Jeans, a black polo-neck sweater too warm for the summer day, khaki jacket, sports bag. "Melanie's been singing your praises. I'm so sorry not to have met you before, but no doubt you'll have heard how busy I am with other enterprises of mine. I only wish I had more time to spend here at the Old Chapel with you two ladies. But I'm always chasing my tail and wishing there were more hours in the day." Again, the broad smile was offered up as if in propitiation. Melanie laughed her loud, expansive laugh, firmly took his arm and led the way into the office. Once inside, Giles slipped off the khaki jacket, handed it to Melanie and sat down at Grace's desk.

"Now, bring me up to date with plans for the grand opening next month. I hope all potential patrons are invited, local business magnates, the owner of that appalling tasteless furniture emporium on the new industrial estate? Press releases all done and catering arranged by now, I presume? What is it, canapés and undrinkable Spanish plonk? Or are you bringing some of your sophisticated London ways to our West Country backwater, Grace?"

He leant back in the chair, her chair, looking at her intently while Melanie fumbled among papers on her desk for a file that she produced and handed to him. He tossed it down, unopened, and went on looking at Grace while Melanie talked him through the plans rapidly as if concerned to make a quick impression before his interest waned. Grace found herself avoiding his eye.

"I think you'll be quite pleased, Giles," Melanie said eventually when he had failed to make any comment at all. She perched on the edge of her desk, the full skirt of her fuchsia dress sweeping a box of staples and drawing pins onto the floor. "It's a gala evening, after all, and we've had an excellent response so far to the invitations. I've got that string quartet that you mentioned on board and the jazz trio. Of course if you could spare us just a bit more of your time here in the office and away from your antiques... well, no doubt the results would be even better." Melanie leant forward and patted the back of his hand as if in mock reprimand. He looked irritated at first, but after a moment responded by catching her hand, kissing it with evident affection. Then as abruptly he let it go, stood up, yawned. He looked squarely at Grace.

"How about the new girl giving me the grand tour? I need to see if the place is yet fit for purpose, after all."

# 5

Hester addresses her letter to her sister, Ruth, places it on one side and flexes her fingers before beginning her second of the afternoon. *I am like a character in a 1930s film*, she thinks, *dividing my days between writing long, newsworthy letters to relations and arranging the church flowers*. In truth, she's only a reserve on the flower rota since she hardly knows her chicken wire from her green oasis, but it is August Bank Holiday weekend and most of the congregation are in cars heavily laden with wine from French hypermarkets, heading home on auto routes in time for the new school term. *It is that kind of church congregation*, she thinks wryly.

Hester likes writing letters. She writes to Ruth, twenty years in Bakersfield, eighteen in San Diego, unfailingly once a month and covers several pages of tissue-thin airmail paper and receives, in return, the occasional picture postcard. She suspects she has become a caricature of herself in her letters to Ruth. She talks about parochial concerns and events, no doubt sounding like a cross between a Jane Austen spinster and the heroine detective of an Agatha Christie novel. She enjoys what she sees as a subterfuge of sorts and knows it feeds into Ruth's assumption about her life. On her rare visits to England, only a handful in three decades, Ruth, in her cultivated Californian twang, is scornful of Hester, of Oxford, of anyone who has chosen to live not as she has. Three times married, three times divorced, her most recent postcard to Hester was sent from

Palm Springs where she was on honeymoon with husband number four, a retired psychiatrist from Laguna Beach. Hester responded with fervent good wishes and sent the couple a beautifully bound edition of Shakespeare's sonnets that she had found in a second-hand bookshop in the city. They would expect no less of her. *We've both become clichés in our own right, Ruth and I. Perhaps that's what actresses do when their careers flounder or fail to take off fully in the first place. We turn our own lives into performances, adopt the roles we didn't manage to play. Of course Ruth was more musical comedy than straight theatre with those curly blonde, blue-eyed good looks and that rather penetrating, strong voice. A third-rate Doris Day, if the truth be told, who soon found her type to be something of an anachronism. As for me, circumstances were hardly favourable. What with losing dear Alec and then Fergus departing into the Welsh mists, the odds were rather stacked against a successful theatrical career. Of course I had my moments. What did that critic say about my performance in* Heartbreak House *at the St Martins? Something along the lines of Shaw having found his definitive Ellie Dunn. Or words to that effect.*

She turns to her second letter. In view of the long and effusive phone call she's had that morning with a virtual stranger, she's anxious to get it written and posted before the day's final collection from the box on the Banbury Road. At least, then, she can't be accused of not warning him.

*North Oxford – August 1987*
*My dear Fergus,*
*Greetings and all that sort of thing and hoping you are keeping as well as you obviously were when we last met at Grace's wedding. I was wondering if that little surprise encounter might stir you to keep in more regular contact. We did, after all, seem to have rather a jolly time of it, all things considered. But possibly that was the wine speaking. (I was on the Sancerre and*

*you seemed very partial to the Beaujolais, I seem to remember.) Or perhaps it was the emotion of the occasion that brought us together, reminded us of the conjugal rites that had created dear Grace in the first place. I'm very well in case you're enquiring, Fergus, and keeping myself busy with a spot of house-sitting every now and again. You know, it's extraordinary what people will pay to have someone live in their house, tend their geraniums and stroke their Siamese cats while they're wintering in the Bahamas. But I'm glad of the cash, I can tell you. Life doesn't get any cheaper out here in the normal world where we weak mortals have central heating and electricity bills and such like superficialities to meet. Or had you forgotten how the rest of us live, lost in your bucolic idyll, counting the daisies rather than the debts with only a recalcitrant goat or two to test your patience? Sorry, that does sound awfully sour and you know that's never been my style, Fergus. There's something so ugly and undignified about resentment, I've always felt. And, after all, we are still technically husband and wife. No Man Having Put Us Asunder, and all that.*

*But I digress as always. Fergus, do you remember that Telly woman at Grace and Archie's wedding? All that time ago? She sat next to us in the Restaurant Claude and seemed madly enthusiastic about your self-sufficiency endeavours in wildest Wales. Well, evidently, she really was. Enthusiastic and fascinated, I mean, not just being polite because the occasion demanded it. And finally, she's been in touch. Primrose Larrington wants to come and see you. She wants to track you down, Fergus darling, and since she had no idea where to reach you she reached Grace and dear Grace passed her onto me. I had the woman on the phone for nearly an hour this morning so thank goodness she was the one making the call and consequently paying the considerable bill.*

*So here I am warning you that at any moment, Fergus,*

*you could find yourself looking up from your sheep-dipping or your cheese-making to be confronted by a woman and a camera crew. I imagine these people have their ways of tracking their victims down even though my directions were little more than 'turn right at the last signs of civilisation'. She's got it into her head that you'd make an excellent subject for a documentary. She sees you as the inevitable reaction to the acquisitive lifestyles of the hedonistic 80s – her words, not mine, Fergus, for I'm hardly swilling champagne nightly or driving through Oxford in a splendid, fast car as you can imagine and I don't suppose the ranks of the chronically unemployed are either. (All the fault of that dreadful woman with the handbag, of course – but don't get me started on politics.) Anyway, this Primrose person has something of a fixation although no doubt a day or two spent at your side, frozen to the skin in her two-ply cashmere as you explain the workings of an oil lamp will be enough to send her skittering back to the comforts of urban life and the wine bars of Islington and Notting Hill or wherever such types hang out these days.*

*I'm hoping to get down to see Grace and Archie before the summer's finished now they've decamped to the south-west. Grace sounds happy enough when we talk on the phone, got herself a job she's enjoying and she's never been one for the bright lights of the city and a mad social life, of course. I have to say I'm a little concerned about the lack of a baby by now. Or at least some signs of a pregnancy and a bit of morning sickness in evidence. I do hope there are no problems in that area. One doesn't like to ask, of course, as it's like questioning them about the effectiveness of their sex life. I do so hope it's rampant at this early stage in their marriage if only for some racy memories to reflect upon in staid post-menopausal middle age. Even so, one can't help but wonder. And worry just a little.*

*Well, Fergus, I've played the role of the messenger so don't say I didn't warn you. And do be on your guard, dear man, you really are so ingenuous and I wouldn't want to see you eaten alive and spat out by some despicable Telly crew. I'm off to Derbyshire tomorrow to ensconce myself in a small dower house for a fortnight while the owners flit off to something similar in Tuscany. Fortunately, I'm incurably nosey and shall no doubt lap up the contents of their bookshelves and make censorious judgements about their neighbours.*

*Take care of yourself, Fergus, and I remain, as always,*
*Ever Yours,*
*Hester*

Later that evening, suitcase packed in readiness for Derbyshire, Hester thinks of Primrose Larrington and her imminent intrusion into Fergus' life. No doubt he'll simply show her the door, if that's the expression, although she certainly sounded fairly formidable and hell-bent on her purpose. *How entirely unreasonable fate is!* she thinks. *I've spent most of my life with an Equity card festering away in the bureau while Fergus has done his very best to shield himself from any attention or even human contact. Yet evidently he is to be the recipient of a camera crew turning up uninvited on his doorstep.* Hester pours herself the last dregs from a litre bottle of cheap Italian red that's done her service for the past week and stares out of the kitchen window at the sunset causing startling crimson streaks across the sky. *Red sky at night, shepherd's delight, red sky in the morning, shepherd's warning. Who taught her that?* She wonders if Fergus attends to such nursery rhyme folklore or if the words even possess any veracity at all.

She would like to ask him.

# 6

Archie's brother, Leo, arrived one afternoon in mid-August without prior warning. Grace found him lying on the grass in the back garden, rucksack at his side, studying a very creased ordnance survey map when she came home from work at the arts centre. He was wearing faded green shorts and a shirt that made him blend, camouflage-style, with the long grass. For a moment she was startled to find him there; it was nearly two years since his impromptu visit to Greenwich and it took her a second or two to recognise him.

"No one in," he said, unfolding his tall frame from the ground, "I've been here all afternoon. I was hoping you weren't away on holiday."

"We're not, no," Grace said, "but we might have been. It is August, after all."

"I've noticed," Leo said and let a silence fall between them as if he'd carefully contrived it. Grace hovered, noted that the grass could do with cutting again. "It's a good spot you've found," he went on eventually. "I found you on the map quite easily. Jacob's Bottom, three miles south-west of Applewood Copse, according to the old Ordnance Survey. Do you know it, Applewood Copse? I camped there last night."

"Camped? Why didn't you come straight to us? We could have met you at the station in Fletwell."

"I didn't come by train," Leo said. "I left London three

days ago and walked. Well, that's not strictly true. I cheated a bit at the start, hitched a lift as far as Reading. Dreadful place, Reading. Do you know it?"

Grace wondered why Leo disarmed her so easily. She remembered feeling similarly awkward at their first meeting as if he found her dull, pedestrian. She knew so little about him and Archie hardly mentioned his younger brother. She led the way towards the house, wondering if it would be inappropriate to suggest he might wish to take a bath.

"Archie's out," she said unnecessarily as they went into the kitchen. "He's probably swimming at South Bay. He's there most days. Did he know you were coming to see us?"

"Certainly not," Leo said, pulling out one of the chairs at the kitchen table and settling himself into it. Although the room was large, Leo's height had the effect of dwarfing it. There seemed little space left around the table without crowding him too close so Grace hovered, leaned against the sink. "I didn't know myself until an hour or so ago. Of course you were in the background, a possibility, but I hadn't actually decided. I had thoughts about heading on towards Exmoor at one point."

"But now, here you are," Grace said and wondered how long he would stay. She wished Archie would walk through the door and relieve her. The weather had been overcast, humid, the office at the arts centre hot and stuffy and Giles Meredith had spent a rare full day there, impatient and demanding one moment, fawning and foolish the next and she wanted to do no more than go upstairs, shower and change her clothes. But she felt awkward with Leo in the house and did not want him to think her rude or inhospitable. He reached down and undid the laces of his enormous walking boots.

"Do you mind?" he asked and shuffled them off without waiting for a reply. Grace turned away toward the sink, turned on both taps.

"Tea," she said, "I'm sure you'd like some tea. Or perhaps something stronger?"

"Tea," Leo said, "right now, tea would be perfect. Strong and sweet. And do you have any bread? I could do with a sandwich. Haven't really eaten today. And come to think of it, I didn't have that much yesterday considering the miles I've covered. Then we'll start on some more serious drinking once Archie's back."

"Of course," Grace said, relieved to turn her back on him and occupy herself with cheese and bread and pickle. "Tea. Sandwiches. Good idea."

An hour later, Archie was back from South Bay. Grace left the brothers at the kitchen table, catching up on news: their mother, her increasing frailty, her dependence on carers who were becoming less reliable, family friends unknown to Grace. She was pleased when she heard them begin to talk about the house in Greenwich still let to the college colleagues of Archie.

"Actually, I went there first when I got back," Leo said. "That's how I got your address here."

"I did write," Archie said, "and we spoke on the phone. Don't you remember? It was just before we moved down here when you were back in Norfolk for a couple of weeks. You had all the details."

"Possibly. I don't really keep hold of things like that, though. Either in my head or on scraps of paper. So we're selling it, are we? The Greenwich house?" Leo spoke with disinterest.

"Eventually, I suppose," Archie said, refilling mugs with strong tea. "That would be sensible, don't you think? I can't see me and Grace ever moving back any time and there's no point in holding onto the place forever. And we'd like to buy somewhere around here in the country, put down some roots."

"Ah, equity for the big family house," Leo said.

"Yes," Archie said. "Or something like that."

Leo shrugged. "Suits me. It's up to you if you want to sell Greenwich. I can't think why you haven't gone ahead already. It's not as if I'm there more than the odd night every once in a while. And everything's in your name now, isn't it Archie? Didn't you change things over a year or two back? Mortgage, deeds and all that?"

"More or less," Archie said. "We decided it made more sense and was the practical solution with you being away so much."

"Of course. I'm really not into contracts and all that sort of tedious paperwork, anyway. You know that."

"And I'm always on the spot to deal with things. Like with mother too. If you remember we came to the conclusion that it would be easier since I would be the one who'd have to deal with any big decisions about her care."

Leo nodded, waving his hand as if batting the subject away.

"Oh yes, of course, I'd forgotten all about that Power of Attorney business we sorted with some solicitor in Norwich. You're still happy to handle it, Archie? Be the one with your name on the dotted line? It's all a bit beyond me, quite frankly, these legalities and technicalities."

He stood up, stretched his arms above his head so that his hands grazed the low ceiling. He looked restless as if wanting to move the conversation on from what he viewed as tedious and irrelevant to him.

Archie said, "Of course you can always stay with us when you are in England, can't he, Grace?"

Grace imagined a future of Leo randomly arriving in the middle of the night and assuming a room, a comfortable bed and board for as long as suited him. Then she reminded herself that he was Archie's brother. Without siblings herself, she could hardly quantify the bond. She felt she should feign more warmth towards him.

"Of course you can," she said, "wherever we decide to settle."

Archie smiled at her.

"Perhaps we'll put it on the market in the autumn, then," he said. "The Greenwich house. That would be a plan."

"Makes no difference to me. Autumn, winter, spring, whatever you two decide. Right now, I need a shower," Leo said, heading towards the staircase as if he instinctively knew the geography of the house and assumed his place in it. "Then I'll take you out for a meal. It's the least I can do, landing on you for a few days without even asking."

Leo insisted on the pub a couple of hundred yards away. Grace and Archie had always steered clear of The Boot at Jacob's Bottom. They had been there on their first evening at the house and had felt conspicuous, stared at as if objects of curiosity by the handful of men who had come in to drink. The thatched roof and planted window boxes suggested a comfortable village inn, but the interior was tired with yellow walls seemingly encrusted with the nicotine of past generations. Leo seemed impervious, however, both to the surroundings and to the indifferent food that he ordered lavishly from the limited menu. They drank a bottle of sharp, acidic wine. Over the food and alcohol Leo grew more expansive and fluent, describing in some detail the time he'd spent in Tanzania, working with villagers and other volunteers to build a school. Grace began to warm more towards him, seeing his slight detachment of manner as simply that, a way he had of talking rather than an intended slight. Archie was obviously enjoying his company and she wondered why during Leo's long absences he made so little effort to keep in touch. They walked back to the house under a starless sky and, on Leo's persuasion, sat in the back garden on the uncomfortable wooden bench, talking for some time. Archie went into the kitchen and brought them out mugs of coffee and Leo produced a bottle of brandy. Although a mild night, the August air was damp, harbouring signs that high summer had passed without having made much of an effort to appear.

"The equinox in another month or so," Leo said. "I'd almost forgotten about seasons having spent so much time in places that don't have them."

An owl hooted in a nearby tree. A couple of dogs started barking from a house across the fields. There was a flash of torchlight in the distance as if someone was checking hen houses, barn doors.

"I have to go up to London tomorrow," Archie said abruptly, waving away the proffered brandy bottle, "into the college to sort things."

Grace was surprised. Archie had made no previous mention of needing to interrupt the long summer vacation with a visit into college. He had spent a little time in the room adopted as his study over the past few weeks preparing, she had assumed, for the next academic year or attending to his own studies, but nothing had been said about going up to Aldgate.

"Tomorrow?" Grace said, "why tomorrow? Surely you can put that off with Leo being here. Term doesn't start for another few weeks."

"No, I can't," Archie said. "I can't just rearrange things like that. It's a big meeting and it's been fixed for weeks. It's important I'm there. I can't just fail to turn up."

"You've not said anything about it until now."

"I don't see there's any problem, Grace. You're not working, are you? You said at the beginning of the week that you weren't going in on Friday. Anyway, it can't be helped. It's just one of those things, inconvenient but inevitable. You can take Leo around a bit, go into Fletwell, show him the arts centre or something."

"You forget I don't really do towns, any more. Cities at a pinch, but not small market towns." Leo passed Grace the brandy bottle and she drank some in mild defiance. Archie knew she disliked spirits.

"I don't suppose I'll be late," Archie said. "My meeting's at noon. It shouldn't take long."

"I thought you said it was important. A big meeting."

Archie threw the dregs of his coffee on the grass and stood up.

"It is. I told you. I'm going to bed now," he said. "I have an early start, after all. Are you coming Grace?"

"Not yet," she said, "I'm not tired."

She turned away from Archie, annoyed by what she saw as his awkward, unreasonable decision to go to London. It was not the absence itself, but his apparent impulsiveness and failure to explain that angered her. She swallowed again from the brandy bottle, tolerated the taste. Leo lay down on the damp grass, stretching out his long, thin frame as if he were on a yielding mattress.

"No threat from malarial-carrying insects or venomous snakes," he said. "You have no idea how welcome that is after the places I've been in."

"So why do you go there?" Grace asked. "No one's forcing you. Or is it pure altruism? For the greater good and all that sort of thing."

Leo said nothing. Grace began to wonder if he'd fallen asleep or was annoyed by what he might well see as her flippancy. Eventually, however, he sat up, and turned around to look at her as if he had entirely forgotten she was there.

"What? Oh well, you have to do something with your life, don't you? There's an awful lot of it to fill. It wakes you relentlessly every morning month in, month out. That's an endless amount of time, in fact."

"Well, people do usually have a career or at least a job of some sort," she said. "Ambitions, anyway. And then there's marriage. Or at least a relationship. Children, possibly. Hopefully. They seem to be the sorts of things people find filling up the years. Although," she added hastily, "it's just as well someone's doing such selfless work, I suppose."

"I was going to be married," Leo said. "She was killed. Just like that. So it didn't happen. I didn't get married." He lay down again on the damp grass. A couple of tomcats wailed in the field next to them.

"I didn't know," Grace said inadequately. "I'm so sorry." She remembered now something vague Archie had said about Leo's failed relationship; she had assumed, she supposed, unrequited love, rejection. Certainly not sudden death.

"So there's never seemed a lot of point in trying for the usual things," Leo went on, "not after that. Not when they can be taken away so easily. In minutes, in fact."

"What happened?"

"There was an accident," Leo said, "with a car. Except that Natasha wasn't in it. She was walking. She was just walking along when a car – the driver was drunk, lost control and mounted the pavement. I heard it. She was coming to meet me, you see, at my flat just along the road and I… I still hear it, actually. Brakes, screams, skids. The noise of utter confusion. Or I imagine I do."

Grace picked up the brandy bottle from the grass, passed it to Leo.

"I had no idea. Archie didn't explain."

"It was ten years ago now. It wouldn't be uppermost in his

mind, Grace, so don't blame him. He would find it hard to talk about."

"Why? It's your loss, not his."

"We're not the sort of family to dwell on these things, I suppose. Never been good with… words. Talking. All that sort of thing. I mean, don't get me wrong, he was helpful at the time, invaluable with… the practicalities. Did all he could. The… arrangements. But then we… just moved on. I never talked to him about Natasha again. I got the feeling Archie never really liked her."

"What's that got to do with it?" Grace said in a voice that seemed too loud for the late hour. She glanced up at the house to see if it had disturbed Archie. The windows remained dark. Leo said nothing for a while. She wondered if he'd regretted his confession and whether she was now supposed to consign her knowledge of the event to the far reaches of her mind, the way Archie had obviously done. Eventually, however, Leo stood up, brushed grasses and twigs from where they'd attached to his sweater and came and sat next to her.

"The places I've been to since then," he said, "well, I suppose you could say it puts my loss into some sort of perspective. When you see so much suffering it makes you a bit ashamed of your own grief. It sounds clichéd, but it's true. And Natasha's the one who's lost out, after all. Because of some fucking idiot who fancied his chances at the wheel after downing a few too many in his local. And it's so stupid, that's always seemed the worst part of it, a stupid, inane and unnecessary way to die when you think about it."

"What was she like?"

"Natasha? She was…" He picked up a mug of cold coffee, drained it.

"I'm sorry," Grace said, "I shouldn't have asked."

"No, it's all right. But really it's hard to say. She was… well, just another person, really. To other people, that is. I could have told you then, ten years ago. But now… myth and reality are all a bit mixed up, I suppose. I loved her then, anyway. Loved her dearly. Unconditionally. Isn't that the word? She had nice eyes, kind eyes. Dark hair. Pretty. Just started learning to play the guitar. Had always wanted to and not quite got around to… anyway. She was twenty-seven. Only just. It had been her birthday the weekend before and… there was cake left. The cake was still in the tin."

Grace grappled for appropriate words, for some gesture adequate to express the unimaginable. But none seemed to exist and they sat on for a few moments in silence.

"And there's never been anyone else?" she said eventually. "In ten years you've not met anyone to… well, to be with?"

"No," Leo said decisively, "that just couldn't happen. I wouldn't let it. I'm too much of a coward to try again."

She waited for him to say more, but instead he stood up as if drawing a conclusive line under their conversation, placing it beyond further consideration, yawned loudly and said he needed to sleep, bounding swiftly in the direction of the house. She followed him after a few moments and heard him already upstairs in the bathroom then closing the door of the small spare bedroom, his boots noisy on the bare floorboards.

She lies awake next to Archie, thawing her chilled feet and hands in the warmth of his sleeping body, unable to sleep. She thinks about where to take Leo the next day while Archie is in London. She no longer resents the prospect of time spent alone with him and wonders whether he will talk more about Natasha. Such a haphazard way to die, she thinks, and feels disturbed by her knowledge of it, dredging images into her mind. She imagines the woman, Leo's fiancée, waking that morning, possibly bothered by small details of her day, a late bus, an irritating boss, warmed by the prospect of her evening with Leo, falsely consoled by its reliable ordinariness. And then the unimaginable, the million-to-one outside-chance tragic event; the choice of a particular bit of pavement on a particular city street at the precise second a crazed driver mistook it as an acceptable place to drive. Time, place and event coinciding catastrophically.

No one would even take bets on that as a way of dying.

Grace cannot understand why Archie has not told her. He's deeply asleep now, the alarm clock on the side table next to him set for six so he can make an early start for London. *He so rarely talks to me about Leo*, she thinks. *And when he does it's in a dismissive sort of way almost as if his younger brother is a figure of fun, an eccentric unhinged from the normal responsibilities of adult life, a perpetual adolescent ever rootless and roaming. I suppose I've started to think of him in a similar light*. She begins to look forward to the next day, thinks she'll walk Leo up to Fox Woods and beyond, to the trickle of small hamlets wedged along the ridge above Jacob's Bottom.

But by the time Grace woke up and came downstairs, Leo had left. There was a note on the kitchen table evidently addressed to both of them. 'Thanks for the hospitality. Too good a morning to hang around. Headed off at dawn. Be in touch. Leo'. When Archie got back from London around seven that evening, he seemed unsurprised by his brother's impulsive departure.

"He never hangs around. Just when you're beginning to enjoy his company he behaves like this. He's probably half way across Exmoor by now. Didn't he say something about that? Still, at least it meant you had the day to yourself, Grace." He looked tired as if the day of meetings and travelling had been excessively onerous. He sat at the kitchen table drinking tea, flicking through some post, tearing most of it up and discarding it in the bin before wandering through to his study.

As usual, papers and books were strewn over the floor and she imagined he was making some attempt to tidy them, sorting them into files or onto shelves. She came in an hour later to find him staring out of the window. A couple of neighbours, the man who lived at the converted church and an elderly woman from the thatched cottage by the post box were talking at the bottom of their track. The man's brown Labrador was chasing and fetching a stick with declining enthusiasm. Grace handed Archie a glass of wine and perched in front of him on the deep windowsill.

"Leo told me about Natasha," she said. He looked at her blankly for a moment as if his mind was on a matter too remote to hitch itself swiftly to something else.

"Oh that," he said eventually and sat down next to her, staring across the room as if unsure whether his attempts at bringing order had made any difference. "I'd forgotten all about that business. Her name, even."

"Why hadn't you told me? I felt foolish not knowing."

Archie took a gulp of wine.

"I don't know. I thought I had. I… it was such a long time ago, I suppose, and it's not as if we see a lot of Leo."

The brown Labrador darted down the track leading to the house and barked close to their window. Its owner called him back.

"Leo's obviously never got over it," she said. "No one would. It seems to explain a lot about him, this constant restlessness of his."

"You're probably right."

"He said he was too much of a coward to try again. As if the possibility of loss has become too alarmingly normal."

Archie looked distracted as if unable or unwilling to focus on the conversation. He got up, returned to the morass of books and papers still strewn untouched on the floor, staring down at them for a few moments as if seeking a clue and key to their order, sipping steadily from his glass of wine. Grace watched him, wanting to pull him back to talk about Leo. Wanting to understand why so often he seemed out of reach to her. Neither spoke. She opened the small window behind her. Snatches of conversation from the two neighbours drifted in on the damp, dank evening air. August was producing no more warmth than the earlier months of summer.

"He said something along those lines to me once now I come to think of it," Archie said, staring blankly at an open file. "Something about disaster suddenly seeming to be everywhere or at least the likelihood of it. It was a truly terrible thing to happen, Grace, of course it was."

"You must have known her – Natasha?"

"Not really," Archie said. "Of course I'd met her, but..." He closed the file, tossed it on the floor. "I'm having a bit of a clear-out here, Grace. Can't see the wood for the trees if the truth be told. I need to consolidate it all, I think. Decide what needs keeping. I've been hoarding things for so many years now and... there's a lot of useless stuff here. Utterly useless."

He knelt down on the floor and began to sort papers as if attacking the job methodically and with purpose. Grace felt redundant, the conversation about Leo clearly abandoned. As if, she thought, Archie can choose to shut his mind, discipline it to dismiss matters out of control or distasteful to consider.

"Do you think we'll see him again this summer?" she said. It was some moments before Archie answered, his attention apparently taken by the contents of a bulky cardboard file full of handwritten notes that he was dividing into two piles, one for retaining, the other apparently to discard. She moved towards him, knelt down to offer her help in his task.

"Who?" he said, sitting back on his heels and looking

blankly at her. "Oh Leo, you mean. I doubt it. What did he say last night? Heading off to Africa again?"

"Nigeria, I think. In a month or two. He said something about working with some organisation bringing relief to Aids orphans."

"Well, then, that's probably your answer. We've had our ration of him for the year or more, I should imagine."

***

At the end of August, they went to France for a few days. Crossing to Roscoff, they drove inland from the coast through small towns and villages until reaching the outskirts of Rennes. Archie pulled the car into the side of the road and consulted guidebooks several years out of date.

"These places don't change," he said, "not in rural France. Trust me." He circled the name of an old inn, pointed out the village on the road map propped on Grace's lap and asked her to direct them to it. After an hour or so of driving west, they reached the edge of a vast forest and found the inn, which proved Archie's point. It appeared to be a place little changed in decades. They were shown to a large, dark bedroom furnished with velvet drapes, flock wallpaper and an enormous bed that sagged almost comically as soon as either of them sat on it. In the dining room where they appeared to be the only English guests they were presented with an extensive menu and an extravagant wine list that Archie ordered from freely. His attempts to order in slow, faltering French were met with blank stares.

"I expect it's your lack of a Breton dialect," Grace consoled. She had not expected a holiday and was too grateful for the impromptu trip to choose to be anything other than conciliatory. The weather was little better than in England, but at least it didn't rain and they explored the forest on foot, Archie supplying commentary on the Arthurian legends and myths abounding in the area. Grace was relieved to be away from home, to shelve briefly the concerns she felt she should be confronting more actively. Her work at the arts centre was increasingly hindered by the presence of Giles Meredith who had begun to call in more frequently. In name, he was the director, but as his salary was only nominal and his duties unspecified she had initially understood that he would mainly direct affairs from his home some distance away in Bath. There he ran an antiques shop with his wife or, in Melanie's version of the arrangement, his estranged wife, an expert in Victorian furniture in which their shop specialised. Melanie was an efficient and effective manager and when Grace was working solely alongside her she found the days productive and satisfying. But the presence of Giles disturbed the balance. Melanie became obsequious, sycophantic almost, apparently incapable of making a decision without his approval and reducing Grace's role to little more than the office junior.

"Which I suppose I am," she said to Archie, discussing it as they sat at a pavement café, snatching breakfast on the final day of their short trip, driving back north to catch the ferry for the afternoon crossing. "But it never feels like that when I'm working with Melanie. We just divide up what needs doing or she allocates me certain jobs and lets me get on with them."

"But Giles meddles, does he?"

"He patronises. At least I think that's what he's doing. He reminds me that I'm the unqualified, unskilled member of the team. Not in so many words, of course, but it's how he makes me feel. And then of course there's the fact that they're having an affair. When the two of them are in the office together I feel rather intrusive, as if I'm an embarrassment to them."

"So it's still going on?" Archie ordered coffee.

"I believe it's in its third year so it's standing the test of time. Or perhaps it's the opposite – if Giles hasn't left his marriage by now perhaps he sees Melanie as simply… well…"

"His mistress. A convenient, legitimate arrangement of sorts."

"Something like that. Mind you, Melanie doesn't seem to consider it an affair. She talks of Giles as her partner and ignores the slight inconvenience that he's got a wife."

"And children?"

"Two, girls of ten and twelve, I believe. I think Giles uses them as his excuse for not leaving. At least that's Melanie's side of things. And I'm sure she believes it."

"And I take it you don't particularly like our Giles Meredith?"

The tray of coffee arrived, a basket of bread, a bowl of jam.

"Not really. There's something arrogant about him. He's very knowledgeable, of course, certainly knows what he's talking about where the arts centre is concerned and he has a lot of good contacts. He's pretty astute on the financial side of things as well. But as far as Melanie's concerned, well, she deserves someone nicer, someone for herself alone who's offering her a more certain future. I certainly think that's what she wants."

Grace poured milk into the strong coffee. She wanted to say how she knew that Melanie wanted children. But it was eleven o'clock in the morning and the conversation she really wanted to have with Archie, the one that would develop naturally from such a comment, was inappropriate for the hour and for the place, a sunny pavement café beside the market square in a busy provincial town. The last few hours of their brief holiday should remain just that, untouched by Grace's mounting anxiety. They sat watching the large, bustling open market, the numerous stalls and displays: charcuterie, enormous cheeses, headless poultry, huge carcasses of meat, bread, vats of cider, endless varieties of vegetables and fruit, plums, apples, damsons, blackberries and crab apples. Service was brisk and constant, customers selecting and picking out the choicest and best to load large wicker baskets.

"Actually," said Archie, continuing to stare across at the market square, "while we're on the subject of jobs, there's something I've been meaning to mention about mine. About a change with college, I mean."

Grace put down her cup, turned her attention towards him, anticipating good news. She knew Archie was keen for promotion to Head of Faculty, had said it was only a matter of time before the post fell to him on the eventual retirement of the current holder, but she'd understood that was still to be a few years off.

"I'm leaving," he said and swallowed the remains of his café crème. "In fact, you could say I've already left although of course my salary's paid up until the end of this month." He continued to gaze intently at the busy market as if he were conducting some sort of customer survey that required him not to shift his eyes for a moment.

"I don't understand," Grace said eventually when Archie had offered no more explanation. "What do you mean, you've already left? When… when did all this happen?"

Archie spoke swiftly with the suggestion of something prepared in his fluency as if he was avoiding a conversation with her by simply stating the facts of his departure from the Aldgate college.

"I resigned when I was in London the other week. You remember, the day after Leo came to see us? That's why I went up to London. I just decided that enough was enough. It was quite an impulsive decision, in fact. But all that travelling was getting me down and you know how tired I've been lately.

Then there's the politics of the place, of course, which you wouldn't know anything about. It's getting worse all the time. They're talking about an amalgamation with another college and shifting to another campus even. There are all sorts of changes afoot, evidently, and quite frankly, Grace, I decided I didn't want to be part of it anymore. It's all getting very... well – engineered. Not my kind of thing at all. I simply didn't want to be there any longer."

"But you've said nothing. All this time's gone by and you've not even mentioned it." Grace found herself raising her voice over the street noise. A car was revving as it attempted to pull away into traffic, a baby was crying at the next table. "Not just your resignation, but how you must have been feeling about the place over the past few months. You always seemed so settled there. You've never once discussed things with me, said you were unhappy with the travelling, with the politics, as you call it."

Archie turned towards her, finally pulling his eyes away from the marketplace.

"I didn't want to worry you until everything was sorted out. No point until there was something definite to tell you."

"But we should have talked about it. That's what people do," Grace said, exasperated. "That's what couples do. They talk about this kind of thing together, discuss the problems and the options. They don't just... neither of them just goes and... I can't believe you've kept the whole thing secret from me as if I'm a child. As if I'm incapable of contributing helpfully, being of use to you in coming to some sort of decision about it all. I'm your wife, Archie."

He looked surprised by her reaction, by the irate tone of her voice. She was so rarely angry. Grace, too, felt alarmed by the vehemence of her feeling.

"I thought it was for the best. Grace, you're being unfair.

There was no question of secrecy. Just… well, it's always best to get things sorted, otherwise there's only half the story to tell." He smiled at her suddenly as if expectant of her blessing, awaiting her capitulation. He reached out to take her hand in his, but she got up from the table, suddenly feeling a need to be away from him, from the congested café and milling people for fear of losing her temper uncontrollably in front of them and rashly saying too much. Every table was now taken with a small queue forming and she saw a woman start to move towards theirs as she moved and headed out across the narrow road. She darted rapidly through the marketplace, dodging between countless stalls, aware that Archie was no doubt following at some distance behind, attempting to catch her up. Or perhaps he'd simply wait, expecting her swiftly to calm down, return biddably, even apologetically to his side so that they could find the car and continue their drive north to the coast.

She hurried on. At the other side of the marketplace, a maze of narrow streets and cobbled alleyways wound around the back of a great granite church and she weaved her way mindlessly and without direction amongst them. She suspected Archie would think her melodramatic, her response irrational and uncharacteristic and however much her flight was driven by inflamed anger she knew that sooner or later she would have to retrace her steps; she had only a few francs in her bag, barely enough to buy a drink let alone sustain her through any prolonged absence. Part of her felt like an immature adolescent, acting impulsively instead of talking calmly through their dispute, articulating her feelings so that he could understand. But Archie's behaviour bewildered her and it would be his inability to understand why she felt so isolated by his arbitrary, clandestine actions that most disturbed her. She plunged on, rapidly covering the streets of the preserved medieval quarter of the town, turning corners haphazardly, going right or left with no set purpose or direction in mind.

Then the thin strap of her summer sandal snapped.

She lurched forward and fell onto the cobbled road, causing a cyclist to swear and swerve to avoid her. Her knees stung badly and were beginning to bleed and her hands, which had supported her as she fell, were grazed and smarting with the shock of the impact. Her bag, its contents liberally spilt across the cobbles, and the broken sandal lay a few feet away. She sat there dazed for a moment or two, close to tears, wondering whether she had banged her head as she fell. Then she pulled herself up and leant against the substantial stone wall of a building and watched while a stout, elderly woman in a headscarf and heavy coat put down her large basket of shopping and went to retrieve her bag and its contents. The woman tried to inspect Grace's knees and hands, chattering all the time in rapid French, searching in her pockets as if for something to staunch the bleeding. Grace thanked her, but tried to wave her away, wanting only to be left to inspect her own foolishness, gather herself and her thoughts together, but she was persistent.

And then Archie appeared.

The woman grinned broadly at him, spoke even more rapidly as she patted him on the arm, then picked up her large shopping basket and went on her way.

"Have you hurt yourself?" he asked with concern, rescuing the remains of her sandal and attempting to tie it together sufficiently for her to wear. She shook her head. "You must have done – I was worried you'd banged your head. But your ankle, have you twisted it?" He knelt down on the pavement and gently flexed her foot against his hand. She felt his cold palm against her hot, stinging foot and she shook her head again. "Do you think you can hang onto me, then?" he went on, carefully taking her arm, supporting her. "You've had a shock so we'll move slowly. We'll get you to a chemist and see to these wounds." He slipped his arm around her shoulder and slowly guided her back through the narrow lanes, behind the church and across the marketplace to a pharmacy. Grace sat quietly on a chair, watched silently while her grazed knees and hands were bathed, cleaned and bandaged. Ointment was applied. Large bruises were appearing on her elbow and forearm. She drank the glass of water handed to her. Archie insisted on her swallowing a couple of tablets to help relieve any pain. She felt her anger ebb and tried to retain it, to store it for an hour or two, a day or more, until the moment seemed more appropriate to confront Archie about the manner of his resignation. They drove northwards to the channel port, took the late afternoon ferry crossing back to England and by the time they were home in Jacob's Bottom, the idea of such an abrasive conversation began to seem to Grace vacuous and entirely futile.

***

Archie had taken a job as an English teacher at Court House, a small girls' school some twenty miles from Jacob's Bottom. Unknown to Grace, he had been interviewed during the summer and received the offer of the post the day before they'd left for France. He had remained vague about the exact order of events, leaving Aldgate, applying for the new job, and Grace had seen no point in pursuing him for such details. He appeared content and wholeheartedly convinced that he had made the right decision so it seemed only sensible for her to acquiesce. Just before the start of the autumn term, he drove Grace over to the school, a converted late Georgian mansion set in several hundred acres of verdant pasture land. His duties appeared undemanding, teaching English to small classes of affable girls of average ability. The pupils were mainly affluent farmers' daughters and mostly boarded during the week since there was no feasible transport system within ten miles. Some came from further afield, London even, children with parents content to see them safely removed from assumed urban dangers and distractions. To Grace it appeared a genteel and anachronistic establishment; the school had stables so the girls could bring their horses with them, a pets' corner took care of the needs of their rabbits and hamsters and ballroom dancing lessons were compulsory. It seemed to be an educational environment not so much focused on broadening and extending the vision of its pupils as one set up to satisfy and confirm the limit they already had in place.

"You'll be bored," Grace said to Archie as they drove back to Jacob's Bottom. "Swapping undergraduate teaching for setting punctuation exercises and correcting commas? Whatever are you thinking of?"

Nevertheless, she was by now complacent about Archie's decision. He presented it in such a positive light that her objections had begun to seem rootless.

"It will be a refreshing change," he said, not for the first time. "It will give me so much more time to devote to my own academic studies. Really get the PhD completed at last. Besides, introducing young minds to poetry and great drama, getting them reading really good literature is such a privilege. They've given me a pretty free rein on what I teach. It's all very exciting, really."

Grace hoped Archie would not be disillusioned too soon. He seemed to have the ingenuous belief that his own passions were contagious even to adolescent girls.

"They're lucky to have you," she said. "It can't be every day they get someone of your calibre."

"Thank you, Grace. I think the Headmistress is pleased to swell the number of men in the staff room, that's for sure."

"So you'll be in a minority?"

Archie smiled. "The Classics teacher is male. And the visiting tennis coach."

"In that case, you'll have to watch out for signs of seductive behaviour over the lunch table," Grace said. "Still, it's not my idea of a school. So much for so few. However do they finance it?"

"Exorbitant school fees, no doubt, although some of the land is let as grazing, I believe."

"You could always go back, I suppose," Grace said as they left the main road and turned down towards their hamlet. "I mean, if it doesn't work out at Court House School. If you find it all too dull and constricting. You could go back to Aldgate or somewhere similar. They'd welcome you, surely. Especially once you've got this PhD together."

Archie said nothing.

Grace chooses to see his silence as compliance. *He's not burning any boats*, she thinks. *He's simply trying something different. In fact, if I view all this business as Archie being not so much covert and self-absorbed as adventurous and dynamic, then it's a welcome move. Surely. And I'm glad to think of him feeling settled here, in this part of the world, close to home. He's not going to want to pull us back to London, to the Greenwich house and those dinners with Monica and Bernard and those appalling jobs of mine.* She thinks of how contentment is always just in the future, just out of reach, never quite attainable in the here and now. She finds herself saying so many times 'once we have done this, once we have that'. In the weeks before she married Archie, still living in her damp Earl's Court basement, she viewed the time after as an arrival, as a plateau of perfect happiness. But the wedding came and went and the honeymoon in Florence and still this blithe state seemed to be eluding her. Then there was the move to Jacob's Bottom and the same expectation of shedding all that was indifferent and uncertain for a fixed state of delight. She knows life is hardly as predictable, as controllable as that, yet nevertheless the inclination stays. She cannot help but always see the future as some defined Elysian field, endless, timeless, and wonders if she is alone in such naivety or if it is, in fact, what most people do, an inescapable human trait of perpetual self-delusion. She's like a child on a long journey constantly asking herself, *Are we nearly there?* She wonders if she is perhaps more restless than she has always imagined, less content with the here and now and aspiring after something perpetually just out of reach. At times she is uncertain if she even knows what that is.

Back at Jacob's Bottom, Archie switched off the car engine then stared ahead through the windscreen, his hands firmly holding the steering wheel, as if deep in thought. Then he turned to Grace, looking as if he was surprised to see her still sitting next to him.

"Thank you, Grace," he said and grasped her hand.

"For what?"

"For… never mind. No point in going over why I need to… it's a new start, that's what matters. And a fresh beginning has to be a good thing. For both of us, I'm convinced of it."

# 7

"Archie, what's this absurd news I hear about you becoming a schoolmaster?"

Hester sat back in her chair, held out her glass to be refilled.

"I don't think they call them that anymore," Grace said. "Schoolmasters are all a bit Dickensian and Mr Chips."

Hester ignored her.

"Grace tells me you've exchanged intelligent, gifted students for grubby little schoolchildren," she said. "Whatever could have possessed you?"

"Not so gifted, in fact," Archie said quietly, retreating to the sofa beside Grace. "You'd be surprised by some of the students we had turning up at Aldgate. We were probably the last resort for many of them."

"Even so," Hester said, "what were you thinking, Archie? If the commuting was getting a bit much you could have moved back to London. Or gone to another university. They say Bristol's awfully good these days and that's more this part of the world, surely."

Archie seemed amused rather than offended by Hester. He sipped calmly from his glass of wine and then offered the bland defence that Grace had already used in an attempt to placate her mother. Hester swiftly interrupted.

"Yes, I know all this nonsense about enlightening young adolescent minds and the delight of chalk dust. Grace has already tried me with that excuse, but it simply makes no sense to me. I just hope you don't live to regret it, Archie. A country schoolmaster just sounds so… well, parochial and tedious. Like something out of Chekhov. Turgenev, even."

Grace stood up, anxious to divert the conversation. Hester had promised not to broach the subject with Archie too vigorously, but she found it hard to resist being contentious. Her mother, she knew, enjoyed the occasional combative wrangle.

"Dinner's probably ready now. Shall we eat?" she said and led the way firmly into the kitchen.

Hester had come to stay for a few days in late September, her first visit to the house at Jacob's Bottom. She was finding herself in growing demand as a house-sitter and had squeezed them in between a week in Shropshire and a fortnight on the Isle of Wight. Grace, meeting her at Fletwell station that morning, had taken her to the arts centre where Hester had met both Melanie and Giles.

"A vain man with an inflated ego," was Hester's appraisal of Giles. "He trades on his rather oily old-fashioned good looks. Melanie's pleasant and pretty enough. Although she could do with losing a stone. Middle age will play havoc with those hips if she doesn't do something about her weight before then."

"I hope they're being more complimentary about you," Grace said as they went back to the car.

Hester took her arm. "Take no notice of me, Grace, and my appalling intolerance. Besides, I'm sure they found me charming. I was on my best behaviour with them. I don't want to muddy your patch or whatever the saying is. You've got yourself a nice little niche there, I can see that. You always were such a bookworm, disappearing into your bedroom to read for hours on end, so I imagine you're in your element, dealing constantly with writers and so forth."

"I'm glad you approve," Grace said, fishing car keys out of her bag. "It's very varied work and I'm learning a lot. And we're getting busier all the time. Melanie says they might be able to increase my days to full-time later in the year providing the new sponsors go ahead with their promised support. I do feel guilty, only working three days a week at the moment."

They had driven back to Jacob's Bottom through an autumn countryside of conker-laden horse chestnut trees, acorns and sycamore seeds and fields deep in windfall fruit.

"You seem very settled," Hester said as Grace pointed out various landmarks on the way, made a detour to see a stone Saxon church in a nearby village. They peered at ancient gravestones mostly sunk into the neatly mown turf. "You're obviously contented with a quieter, rural way of life, Grace. It suits you."

"It does," Grace agreed. "And Archie too, of course."

They found the church unlocked and went inside the small building, plain and austere save for two stone-carved angels on the ceiling high above their heads.

"Why only two?" Hester said. "Or possibly carving even two took someone the best part of a lifetime."

"Perhaps there were more and they've been destroyed over time. After all, the place is thought to date from the late $10^{th}$ century."

"Ah yes, the ravages of time. Probably even angels are subjected to its heartlessness."

Back in the car, navigating the narrow lanes heading towards Jacob's Bottom, Grace had told Hester about Archie leaving the Aldgate college, careful not to mention how covert he had been in resigning and applying for the new post. She found herself inevitably defending Archie.

"He was very resolute about it," she said. "I have to admit

I was a bit surprised myself at the time, but he was so sure in his own mind. And it's giving him much more time to work towards his thesis.

"Ah. The ongoing thesis, yes. Coleridge and laudanum and mad, ancient mariners alone on wide, wide seas boring poor, unsuspecting wedding guests."

"It's good to have him working close to home. It's so much less stressful then commuting to London."

"Positively slothful, I would have thought. Surely Archie's got higher aspirations than a small seminary for spoilt young things occupying themselves between childhood and marriage."

"It's just a job," Grace said simply, slowing down as they passed a rider attempting to restrain a traffic-averse horse. "It's just what he does. I don't care where Archie works as long as he's happy. What does it matter?"

Hester said nothing for a moment, waved at the grateful rider, then briefly placed a hand on Grace's arm.

"It doesn't matter," Hester said. "You are right. Absolutely right, Grace. It doesn't matter at all. As long as the two of you are happy and loving each other faithfully. For richer for poorer, isn't that right?"

Hester liked the house.

"It's charming, Grace. Would you buy it if it came up for sale? Once your tenancy is up, I mean."

"Maybe," Grace said, "although Archie would probably prefer something nearer the sea, closer to the beach for swimming, ideally. But it's quieter away from the coast and a lot cheaper too, of course. I'm not sure we could afford the sort of thing he would really like. Anyway, he has to sell the Greenwich house first."

They walked up to Fox Woods and along the Ridgeway above Jacob's Bottom, enjoying each other's company. Back at the house, they drank tea, talked of Hester's sister Ruth in California, of Fergus in Wales.

"I'm glad he came to the wedding," Grace said, "even if it was all so odd, the way he arrived like that out of the blue. I mean I didn't even recognise him. Why would I? He's hardly kept us up to date with photographs."

"He hasn't changed," Hester said. "The fair hair's gone rather grey, of course. And I suppose his face is a bit weather-beaten. But at least all this healthy living on the fruits of the fields and the exercise has kept him trim. Not like so many men of his age who carry their overindulgent lifestyles around their middles."

"What was Alec like? Your first husband. Was he anything like Fergus?"

It was a question that Grace realised she had never asked. There had always seemed sufficient mystery about her own father to bother herself with a man of no consequence to her at all. Now, however, she was suddenly curious. Hester drained her mug of tea.

"Alec was a beautiful young man," she said, "had the classic good looks of the time, in fact. Tall, dark, what you'd call rugged and handsome, I suppose. Of course I hardly knew him."

"What do you mean? You were married to him," Grace said.

"We were married for such a short time, Grace. And I'd only met him a few months before. Really, we were strangers to each other. There'd been some rather glamorous dates, Alec terribly smart in his RAF uniform, me in something I'd borrowed from some actress friend. And that ghastly war, of course. Everything seemed so unreal. I remember thinking, why not marry him? Who knows what the future will hold? No point in thinking long term or being sensible and restrained about things. I wasn't surprised when he was killed. That was the strange thing. Dreadfully sad, of course, but half expecting it, nonetheless. One was surrounded by people suffering such losses. And worse, of course. At least we'd had a few weeks."

She drained her cup, cut herself a small slice from the lemon cake Grace had placed on the table.

"So nothing at all like my father. Fergus sounds very different from Alec Adaire."

"Oh yes," Hester said, "very different. They would have loathed each other, Alec and Fergus. Isn't that strange? I've often thought of it. The one so charming and flirtatious, the other more plainsong and earnest. Yet women can be so wonderfully chameleon-like. Accommodating. Or perhaps I had simply grown up a bit. I was years older when I met your father, after all."

"You must have changed. Circumstance would have done that for you."

Hester looked across the kitchen table at Grace. She had grown her hair longer and it fell now around her shoulders, thin, flat strands the colour of pale butterscotch.

"Yes, losing Alec was certainly… it made me adjust, I suppose. And I loved them both, of course, in different ways. Both times there seemed a sense of an inevitable sort of compulsion as if I had little choice in the matter. It felt how I supposed love should feel. Later, you wonder. I wondered, anyway. Alec Adaire was, possibly, just an infatuation. Who knows what would have happened if we'd had longer? There's nothing static about love, after all. It starts off as quite a precarious business and hopefully along the way evolves into something far deeper, stronger. If the main players have the guts to stay the course, that is. Oh poor, darling Alec. So terribly, terribly young. Such a waste of… of so much."

Grace stood up, her chair noisy in the quiet kitchen,

squeaking on the flagstone floor. She went over to the sink, turned on the tap.

"Let's have more tea. Archie's got a staff meeting after school. He won't be in until gone six."

After dinner Archie lit a fire against the increasing chill of the evening, their first, he noted, since late spring. Hester fetched a black shawl from her suitcase and curled up on the sofa, suitably mellowed by the copious amounts of good wine Archie insisted on pressing upon her. She talked about her house-sitting jobs; Archie asked appropriate questions.

"It's strange how it's suddenly become respectable," she said, holding her hands out to the warmth of the fire's flames. "This caretaking business seems to have lost its subordinate servant status and become an acceptable occupation for the cash-strapped middle classes. Or unemployed actresses, in fact. I qualify on both counts."

"I think you're ideally suited to it," Grace said. "You can play lady of the manor all day long to your heart's content."

"Role-playing and performing again," Hester said wryly. "Yes, I suppose you're right. I tend to relieve something of the boredom by playing fantasy games imagining myself the rightful owner. I've been known to invent a retinue of servants. A butler, of course, and a housemaid named Polly. Well, in another life, perhaps. A second coming. One can but dream."

Archie moved to put another log on the fire, a satisfying hiss from the damp, seasoned wood and the smell of pine filling the room.

"My mother's both a realist and an incurable romantic," Grace explained. "One moment she's threatening to join the women at Greenham Common, the next she's nostalgic for the days of a servant underclass."

"A hopeless case, in other words, a foot in both camps,"

Hester said. "Clearly a woman who doesn't know her own mind."

"You've always been one to swing between extremes. Or that's how it seemed to me when I was growing up. One moment there was only toast for tea and the next you were planning us a weekend in Paris."

"A girl has to see Paris," Hester said firmly, "and we did. Do you remember, Grace? Your fourteenth birthday. The hotel, of course, was appalling. Full of prostitutes."

"Really? I didn't know that."

"I'm relieved to hear it."

"I remember lots of stairs. And our bedroom had a view of rooftops."

"I think you've invented that. Not the numerous stairs, but the rooftop view. You've stolen it from some arty French film. It was more an inner well of dustbins and drug pushers, if I remember it rightly."

"I'll keep the rooftops."

"Wise choice. I would if I were you."

Later, Hester, in the small guest bedroom, stands in the darkened room looking out through the paned window over the wet countryside. *Archie is not entirely at ease in my company*, she thinks. *He struggles with his perception of me, wants to see me as a suitably sedate mother-in-law figure with set views and genteel habits. I rather confound all that for him. I ask questions, I challenge some of his assumptions. But then, of course, I hardly know him. A few polite, set occasions are hardly the foundation for real insight on either side. He strikes me as a man guarded, unwilling, perhaps, to disclose too much about some secret self. But what do I know? Grace loves the man and has surrendered herself to that, body and soul. And she's the steadfast sort and will no doubt accommodate any quirks and flaws she might discover in him along the way.*

*But where are these babies of theirs?*

*Grace needs children or she will go quietly mad. She's not like me. I could have had other lives. I would have embraced various other destinies if they'd insisted on coming my way. The single independent woman harnessed to career and ambition, for example. Or the faithful, keep the home fires burning, salt of the earth sort of wife with a brace of offspring in suburban Solihull. If necessary, I would have adapted to foreign shores in some unstable regime, entertained diplomats and dodgy politicians for my husband's advancement. I might even have coped with the wilderness of a Welsh hillside if I'd been offered the chance. No doubt this exposes me as pliable and shallow, always ready for dissimulation, shape-shifting if the occasion demands it. But Grace is not like me. She is entirely lacking my capacity for artifice, my relish for self-assertion. Good for Grace. She's happier in the margins, on the sidelines, it seems. A home, marriage and children are what she needs to define her. A quiet place. She's a woman not entirely in tune with the times in which she's living. All this current licence for aggressive self-seeking is entirely wasted on her as if she sees it as a burden and an embarrassment, in fact. She's too soft, too self-effacing for it and I've been guilty in the past for trying to draw her out, encourage her to abandon her instincts. Fergus, if only he'd taken the trouble to stay around, would have understood her more easily and sympathised with her temperament. Although he might have been bewildered by this need of hers to love unconditionally, to see such love as the warp and weft of her existence.*

Hester draws the curtains against the night, undresses and gets into the narrow, spare room bed. She feels, suddenly, unusually alone. She thinks of Fergus on his remote hillside. She wonders whether he ever feels any nostalgic desire for what they once had or could have had. The past, after all, has a habit of becoming so much more splendid and extraordinary than it actually was. Those moments no doubt pleasant, but not out of the ordinary become gilded, sublime in recollection. They detach themselves from the matter that surrounded them at the time, the doubts, the anxieties, the aches and pains and irritations of everyday life and lift themselves out of such detritus. Hester remembers a day in Leeds. She's playing weekly rep, juvenile lead in a J.B. Priestley play, and at the curtain call she sees Fergus sitting in one of the cheap seats at the side of the stalls. She's known him just six weeks and he's travelled up from Wembley to surprise her. It is 1952 and there's no possibility of taking him back to her theatrical digs for the night. No possibility at all. So instead, they buy fish and chips and huddle together on a bench near the station, staying up all night so he can catch the early morning train back to London. It is a moment she can now detach from the bleak weather of that February night, from her concern at the time that he might be finding her superficial, insubstantial. Now, thirty-five years on, she remembers only Fergus' young, eager face, his fingers laced through hers, the two of them like some effigy of romantic love. And suddenly she wants, entirely irrationally, desperately, to be young again. To alter the past, reconfigure their destinations.

To have, in fact, another chance. Another go at things.

Archie wakes in the middle of the night. He turns over onto his back, pillows his head on his arms. Somewhere outside an animal is screeching, slaughtering another, no doubt. Voles, field mice, foxes and hens, stoats and weasels lurk and vie for survival. It is the autumn equinox and there's a gibbous moon. He likes the idea of such perfect equilibrium, equal hours of day and night, nature's natural balance. In the room next door, he remembers, his mother-in-law sleeps. He glances sideways at the foetus shape of Grace's sleeping body.

He stops, checks and listens to her even breathing. He wants to wake her, wants to seek some sort of consolation and assurance, an acceptance and understanding for something that he would like to tell her. For so much, in fact, that he would like to confess. But he lacks the words for such a conversation.

And beyond that he lacks clarity in his own mind about what exactly it is he wishes to share. There must have been a time when there was no muddle between what he knew to be true and what, whilst not entire falsehoods, are shades of deception. But the lines have become muddied and no longer clear-cut even to himself. He is like an actor who has begun to adopt the mannerisms and habits of his favourite role to an extent that the character has overtaken the man.

Archie shifts position, rolls onto his side, away from Grace. *No,* he tells himself, *let things go on as they are for the time being. It will all sort itself out in time. Give it all time, the perfect watchword. Head down, maintain the status quo, avoid too much baring of souls and keep looking firmly ahead. That's the thing, really. That's all there is to it.* He thinks of his mother, increasingly confused and timid about everyday events and resolves to visit her more often. These days he can no longer bring easily and quickly to mind the image of his father's face and the fact distresses him. He finds there is still a sense of the young child's panic about being an orphan, rudderless, entirely alone. He turns his mind to South Bay, to the likelihood of another month's swimming before the temperature drops too low. The prospect is cheering and soon he is sliding soundly into a sleep of complicated yet not unpleasant dreams.

Grace, however, at his side, has sensed his restlessness and now lies fully awake herself.

***

A car draws up and the noise, unexpected, pulls Fergus away from the kitchen table, his mug of tea, two fried eggs and the last of the loaf. Jill comes on Fridays. The day is indeterminate to him, Tuesday possibly, Wednesday more like. But certainly not Friday. He stands at the open door and watches as two people get out, cautiously negotiate the mud, the puddles that are constant save in a rare, dry year. It has been a wet winter and an equally damp spring and summer. The woman is wearing dungarees. Not workman dungarees, but a fashionable imitation of the style in primrose-yellow. The man, younger, bearded, wielding some equipment on each shoulder, is dressed entirely in black. Fergus stares at them. He is not entirely surprised by their arrival, but can't quite remember why the couple feature subliminally in his mind. Ah yes, he thinks, there was a letter. A letter from Hess. Jill brought it up one Friday from the post office in the village. It sat on the shelf above the stove for a few days until he got around to reading it. He goes back to the table, sits down and demolishes the remaining eggs, scrapes the scrap of bread around the plate and swills down tea. A figure blocks the doorway, shielding the light. He looks up at the primrose-yellow dungarees, at a proffered hand.

"Fergus Barnes, I presume. My name is Primrose Larrington. I hope we're not intruding."

***

Archie had been persuaded into giving a talk at the Arts Centre in late October. Picking Grace up one day after work, he had been cajoled and coaxed by Melanie who was anxious to fill an evening that had fallen unexpectedly vacant.

"It's one of our freebie evenings and we've already advertised for *Metaphysical Magic*," she said, holding firmly onto his arm. "There's no charge, but we make money by selling refreshments and wine beforehand. Go on, Archie, be our relief academic and say you'll do it. No one will mind if you talk about the Romantics instead – in fact, if they drink enough they'll probably not even notice."

Although initially agreeable to the idea, he had become

increasingly nervous as the date had approached, spending what seemed to Grace to be an inordinate amount of time in preparation.

"I presume there won't be any... well, what is the audience for these kinds of events?" he asked her, restlessly thumbing through sheaves of notes.

Grace reassured him. Free evenings with a strong focus on wine and cheese tended to be socially rather than intellectually driven. The idea was to garner interest in the arts centre, to hook future audiences and he should think of his talk more in the nature of an entertainment. Archie looked unconvinced. Coleridge and his problems, he said to Grace, his laudanum addiction, his bewildering, unfinished *Kubla Khan* were hardly the ingredients for a light-hearted evening. And then there was that mad, glittering eye of *The Ancient Mariner.* Should he throw in Keats' consumptive death, Byron's unsuitable attachment to his sister to give a bit of a gloss on things? Perhaps Melanie should retract her offer and pull some unsuspecting local in to talk about Morris dancing. Grace had rarely seen him so irascible.

In the end, however, the evening was a success and she was overwhelmingly relieved.

"I thought you struck just the right note," Melanie said, embracing him warmly, and even Giles Meredith, who had arrived just as the token audience of twenty or so had been encouraged away from the wine bottles and into their seats, had been complimentary.

"Not too high-brow or self-indulgent, thank God. You kept things to the level of the man in the street, more an open discussion than a formal lecture. Good move that, Archie."

Melanie slipped an arm around Giles' waist, leant in close to him.

"I'm quite converted to poetry, you know," she said. "The

way Archie read that one about the frost and midnight really moved me."

Giles rolled his eyes.

"You're just my little philistine, Melly. No need to try and show off in front of our esteemed intellectual here. Our Professor Archie. Now, how about the four of us head to the pub for some more serious drinking? Or do the two of you have to be sensible and drive soberly home like the dull married couple you no doubt are?"

***

The following Saturday, the first in November, Archie drove into Fletwell and came home in a new car. He walked into the kitchen, handed Grace a single key and beamed broadly at her.

"Early Christmas present," he said, "it's yours. Hope you like the colour." Grace stared out at the small, shiny red car sitting next to the house, looking uncomfortably new and unblemished on the muddy track. "Come on, you can drive me back into Fletwell to collect my car. I left it behind at the car showroom." He looked at her, clearly expectant of gratitude, an enthusiasm she was finding it hard to summon. They had not talked of a second car. They had not discussed the financial implications of running one for Grace alone. She followed Archie out and stared at the newcomer and tried to respond appropriately.

"It's lovely. Of course it is. But it's such a surprise, Archie. Is it a sensible idea? I mean we were managing with only one car."

"Only just managing. It was getting more inconvenient daily, you have to admit," he said, opening and closing the doors, the boot, like an eager salesman. "We need two cars living here. That's what people have, living in the country. It's the only way to cope."

"Some people cope with none," Grace said, thinking of the families living in the tied farm labourers' cottages in Jacob's Bottom, reliant on bikes or the erratic twice daily bus service that was constantly under threat of being cut.

Archie said sharply, "Not people like us, Grace, professional people. Be reasonable. In fact, I can't think why I haven't bought one for you before now. I've certainly been thinking about it."

He slipped into the driver's seat, started the car, revved the engine, appearing pleased with what he heard. Grace cautiously got in next to him.

"I wish you'd asked me," she said quietly, "about buying a second car. Why didn't we even discuss the idea?"

He seemed not to hear. He went on, playing with seat positions, headrests, flashed headlights like a boy with a new toy. Grace persisted. "Of course it's… lovely. But… it's just so… unexpected. And unnecessary, really. Is it brand new?"

"Absolutely," Archie said. "No point in settling for something second-hand and then having maintenance troubles from the start."

"But it's an extravagance all the same. Can we really afford it at the moment? How are we paying for it?"

Again, Archie appeared not to hear, absorbed in flicking indicator switches, trying out sun visors, hazard lights, windscreen wipers. He backed the car out into the lane, got out to change sides.

"Happy?" he said to Grace, catching hold of her hand as she stared at the dashboard, tried out the gears. She nodded, smiled in spite of a sense of worrying unease. She searched for words that expressed caution, but were not unkind.

"Of course," she said, "anyone would be delighted to be

given a brand new car. It's just… I think we should at least have discussed it first. The financial implications of running a second…"

Archie held up his hand to stall her.

"It's a gift, Grace. From me to you. Don't you see? Leave it at that, please. Besides, there are such good credit deals to be found these days so money doesn't really come into it. Now come on, drive me into Fletwell."

Melanie was impressed.

"Not just a dry academic then, our Archie," she said when Grace, a little apologetically, parked her new car on Monday morning. "One thinks of them all being holey pullovers and tweed jackets and behaving like parsimonious old buggers. But Archie's a man with style, evidently. You're a lucky woman, Grace."

"Yes, I suppose I am," Grace said. "Of course I am." She opened her desk drawer, placed the car keys inside and closed it firmly. "Now, are we going ahead with a firm booking for the woman leading the gothic writers' workshop next April? I promised we'd let her know."

Melanie put down her pen, shifted back her office chair and looked at Grace.

"Ah yes, the spring season. It's going to be tough given the current financial situation. Giles says we need to rein in a bit. Anyway, fingers crossed that things start to look a bit brighter on that front by then. One has to be optimistic and just plough on. Onwards and upwards, as my old Headmistress used to say."

***

Primrose Larrington's lips are deep mauve, Fergus notes, something that alarms him at first until he sees a similar mauve imprint around the rim of the mug of tea he's handed her.

"So," she says, peering over the spectacles perched on the bridge of her nose, "it's a sort of 'Week in the Life of…' format. At least that's how I see it. Just a pilot series of four initially to see if the whole thing takes off. If there's an audience for it out there. Of course you would only feature in one of the programmes, possibly the first. We've got other subjects lined up for the subsequent slots. Other 'Alternatives', as I call them, like you. People who've intentionally chosen alternative lifestyles and resisted the lure of financial gain and material comforts, so to speak."

She sneaks a quick look around at his kitchen, managing to look both bewildered and delighted by the deprivation she clearly notes. He wonders if he should lend her a sweater. She looks cold, perished, in fact, and not just because of the mauve lips. Her bony hands are very white, fingers possibly numb. He thinks there's an old Fair Isle of Jill's somewhere about from that time she stayed when her husband was in hospital.

"We've only a working title at the moment," Primrose goes on, "and it's bound to change once we're into production and editing and so forth. Any more questions, Fergus? We do want you to feel entirely happy before we start filming."

Fergus is unaware that he has asked any questions so far and therefore has no idea how to ask more. Primrose Larrington has talked at length, mostly in language and jargon beyond his comprehension. Her silent, black-clad companion called Jake has sat beside her, every now and again excusing himself to go outside to smoke another cigarette. Fergus feels tired. He has slept badly for several nights, an ache in his left knee twitching every time he tried to turn and his lower back beginning to play up again. He had not intended allowing these two to return. When they'd arrived the day before and he'd said brusquely that it was too inconvenient to talk, he'd hoped they'd take the hint and disappear on a permanent basis. But this morning they'd popped up again, evidently refreshed by a night at the Castle Hotel, the woman's primrose-yellow dungarees now replaced by something tight in dark denim, the man still in black. And he appears to have let them in, removed chicken feed and organic fertilisers from the kitchen table and made them tea. Primrose pulls out a notepad and pen and begins to make notes.

"Of course this is just so perfect. As a setting, I mean. It's very… rugged, isn't it? Elemental, I should say. Life in the raw. Just what we're looking for. I can't tell you how pleased we are to have someone who really, genuinely lives… well, like this." She gestures widely. Fergus follows the sweep of her denim arm. He sees not a setting, but a home. An adequate shelter of sorts to which he gives scant consideration. Now he notes the discernible patch of green mould that he's been meaning to deal with for months growing up one wall. The picture calendar for 1983 displaying 'September, Oriel College, Oxford' propped up on the windowsill. A jam jar of loose change. And on the mantelpiece, a small photograph of his only daughter, Grace, on the day of her wedding, hand in hand with a man he supposes he could claim as his son-in-law. Primrose Larrington seems to be waiting for an answer to a question he has not heard. She taps her pen on the table, glances at companion Jake. Jake coughs, pulls out his packet of cigarettes and finds it empty. She clears her throat, raises her voice to repeat her question. "So would you describe yourself as happy? Are you a happy man, Fergus? Living the contented life that eludes so many of us? That's what our audience will want to know."

Fergus stands up, collects empty mugs from the table and places them in the sink. He stares out onto the pile of wood and kindling stacked by the back door. He watches a blackbird chivvy a worm out of the damp earth.

"To tell you the truth," he says quietly, "I've never really thought about it."

# 8

At the end of November, Archie's mother had a fall and broke her hip. A neighbour coming in to prepare her lunch had found her collapsed in the hallway, sprawled helplessly between the toilet and the front door. On her way to hospital she had suffered a stroke followed by a second as she lay in A and E while her fractured hip received attention. The phone had been ringing as Archie had come into the house and Grace had arrived back from the arts centre to find him still standing by it, overcoat and car keys and a pile of exercise books lying discarded on the living room floor.

"I'll have to drive up there," he said. "I need to be there with her." He had scrawled illegible notes on a pad that he passed to Grace as if needing her to verify the details.

"Of course," she said, "I don't suppose it will be possible to reach Leo." They had not heard from him since his abrupt departure in August. "Shall I come with you? We could share the driving if you like. And I'm not needed in the office again until Monday. You shouldn't do such a long drive on your own at this time of night."

Archie said nothing. She went into the kitchen to make tea. When she returned he had moved across to the inglenook fireplace and was fiddling with the ash and burnt-out logs from the night before.

"Do you think she'll die?" he said, more to himself than

to Grace. "I don't think I can bear that. Not right now. I really can't lose her."

There was little she felt she could say in comfort. Ever since she had known Archie she had been told that his mother was vulnerable, confused, elderly, so she imagined that the prognosis after such a fall and a stroke was not good. She went over to him, tried to place her arm around him and pull him close, but his crouched position in front of the cold embers made it awkward and he did not appear to notice her gesture.

"I'm sure they'll do everything they can," she said lamely. "You'll know more when you've talked to the doctors, Archie, there's no point in jumping to conclusions right now."

He left Jacob's Bottom for East Anglia an hour later. She watched him drive away into the bleak winter's evening, having spoken hardly a word to her except to insist repeatedly that he wanted to go alone. At eleven o'clock that evening, however, he rang her from the hospital and again the following morning, sounding far more sanguine and optimistic. His mother had survived an operation on her fractured hip, the strokes were deemed to have been mild and she appeared to be making a steady recovery. There was no imminent danger and, considering her age and her frailty, the immediate outlook was reasonably positive. Living alone with an unreliable pattern of carers, though, was obviously no longer going to be an option. Archie had booked himself into a hotel in Norwich, intent on spending a few days finding a good local residential nursing home where his mother could be moved on discharge from hospital. There was no point in trying to contact Leo, given their mother's relatively stable condition. He was insistent, in fact, that it would be wasting time and a fruitless exercise trying to trace his brother; it was for moments like this, after all, that they had made arrangements for Archie to hold Power of Attorney and be autonomous over their mother's affairs. Grace listened, concurred.

On Monday morning, with Archie still away, Grace sits in the waiting room of her GP's surgery and reads out-of-date magazines, turns the well-thumbed pages with staples loose from having recipes torn out by previous patients. Her doctor, no older than Grace herself, with very evident signs of an advanced pregnancy impeding easy reach of her desk, picks up test results, checks notes.

"Everything's fine," she says briskly, "blood results, hormone levels, the lot. Nothing to prevent conception from your side of things."

Grace stares beyond her at a row of premature Christmas cards lining up on the windowsill. Robins, reindeer, plum puddings and snowy scenes, an ample-bosomed Madonna and child. She looks back at Dr Kate Welbeck's ballooning navy-blue dress, her neat necklace of seed pearls and her narrow, pale-skinned hands holding her pleasing test results. She feels gratitude is in order, expected, even though it is her body rather than Kate Welbeck or some laboratory technician who has engineered such success.

"Thank you," she manages, "that's a relief." And it is, of course, an enormous, overwhelming relief yet she knows there's more to come.

"So we need to see your husband now, Mrs Copeland. Obviously, we only have half the picture here, part of the story as it were, and we should run some routine screening on him. Has he made an appointment yet?"

Involuntarily, one hand moves to the mound of her stomach, rests lightly there for a moment as if responding to some movement.

Grace says, "No. I mean yes, I think so. I'm not quite sure

when, though. You see he's away at the moment, a bit of a family crisis for him so it's not a great time."

Dr Welbeck looks at her with something akin to irritation in her very pale blue eyes. She sees evasion, dodging with the truth, Grace thinks, and she feels inadequate, a foolish child in front of this accomplished, clever, fecund woman.

"Well, it takes two, doesn't it?" she says. "We need to add his results to yours then we can take things from there." She slips Grace's pleasing test results into a thin folder and presses a bell to summon the next patient.

Archie had not refused to see a doctor when she had made the suggestion over dinner one night. Neither had he agreed. She had tried not to implore, tried to keep the desperation she was increasingly feeling out of her voice and place the idea before him as prosaically as she could, the way one might advise a dental check-up, a precautionary X-ray for a swollen ankle. She had swiftly outlined the tests required, adopting the impersonal tone of a medical practitioner for whom such matters are tediously routine. Archie had carefully washed their plates, rinsed glasses and placed them to dry in the wooden rack on the draining board before eventually turning to her and saying something about it all sounding a little excessive, a bit of a fuss, an overreaction to a matter that was taking its own time to sort itself out. He wasn't at all sure, he said, that it was a good idea to interfere with nature. Knowing the reason for things, he added bewilderingly, delving too much into the unknown for explanations was not always the wisest course of action.

"But if I wanted you to have these tests," Grace had pursued, "would you do it for me?"

He had opened the cutlery drawer, neatly slotted in knives and forks, steel striking steel in the quiet kitchen. She had repeated her question. In the living room, the sound of a log shifting in the fire basket, sending shards of burnt wood and ash into the hearth beneath, drew Archie's attention.

"I need to see to that," he'd said, "don't want to let the fire go too low at this time in the evening. Can we talk about all this another time, Grace? I've had a heck of a day and really don't feel up to it right now." He had disappeared through the door into the living room before she could answer. Grace had sat on in the kitchen, confused by his prevarication, by her own lack of protest. She knew she should get up and follow him, confront him directly, but she felt unequal to finding the words required and even more resistant to hearing the explanation he might offer. Increasingly, she found herself thinking of Louise, of Archie's first wife and their marriage of some seven years that had been childless; marrying swiftly a second time, Louise had produced two children in evident quick succession. Grace could choose to see any link between events as spurious. At times, there could be a luxury in ignorance, she thought, or at least a preference for muddied uncertainty. Yet she was aware that her attitude was craven, woefully acquiescent.

Grace leaves Dr Welbeck's surgery with the promise to make another appointment. Kate Welbeck smiles fleetingly and says that since her maternity leave is about to start, any appointments in the near future will be with the locum covering her.

"Good luck," Grace says as she heads out of the surgery door, "with the birth, I mean."

Kate Welbeck looks up from the next patient's notes in some surprise.

"Luck?" she says as if some pagan ritual has been suggested. "I will be leaving as little to luck as possible, I can assure you."

***

Archie stayed on in Norfolk for ten days to see his mother settled into the nursing home he had found for her. On his return, he seemed far more positive. She appeared to be making a good recovery and he visited regularly during December, still insisting that he make the long trips alone.

"I suppose you'll have to sell her house," Grace said, "now there's no chance of her going back to live there."

"I don't think there's any need to rush that quite yet," he said. "One thing at a time. Besides, no one sells houses at this time of year." They had an enormous Christmas tree sitting in the corner of the living room awaiting decoration. Archie had brought it home with him after school one day and had needed to lop off the top to fit it into the low-ceilinged room. "The spring will be soon enough to think of selling. And there are sufficient funds in her various savings accounts to cover the care costs in the meantime."

"Perhaps Leo will be home in the New Year and can help you."

"I don't need his help, Grace. I can cope perfectly well with the business of selling our mother's house without him being here," Archie said sharply then moderated his tone. "After all, that's why we arranged things the way we did, legally, that is. I'm the one with the power to effect things, not Leo. He really has no idea about… well, he's simply not needed for these decisions."

"I was thinking of the emptying and clearing of the house," Grace said, "your mother's possessions, furniture, photographs and so on. That will be quite a job and I just thought if Leo could be there with you, it would make it all so much—"

Archie interrupted her. "Yes… her things. Her… but let's not talk about all that now, Grace. I really don't want to think about it. After all, it's nearly Christmas. What are we going to do with it, who are we going to invite? We could be selfish and just devote it to each other. On the other hand, a houseful of people could be fun. That's what you do when you live in the country, isn't it? Invite down your poor, city-bound friends and relatives for Midnight Mass and the Boxing Day hunt and all that sort of thing." He walked over to the preposterous giant of a tree and began to hook the silver and gold baubles and decorations that he had bought one day from a gallery in Fletwell. Grace handed him an angel with sparkling tutu and wings.

"We don't have hordes of friends and relatives to invite," she said. "We'd have to hire some."

"There's your father, you could invite him."

"He already lives in the country," Grace said. "I think he'd view Jacob's Bottom as almost urban in comparison with his Welsh hillside."

"Then there's Hester. She'll expect an invitation, surely."

"Yes," Grace said, "yes, I am sure she will. I'd like her to be here."

"Cyril and Celia might like to come. Then there's Bernard and Monica. Perhaps just for Boxing Day?"

"We don't have enough rooms," Grace said swiftly. "Not for them to stay if my mother is coming. And she will if she's invited."

Archie reached up to place the extravagant angel on the tree's topmost branch.

"That's settled, then," he said. "You, me and Hester. Our first country Christmas, Grace, I can't wait."

***

In the end, the filming is less tiresome than Fergus anticipated. Initially, there had been constant delays and at one point it seemed as if the project was close to collapse. A couple of months went by when Fergus heard nothing and he had begun to think the idea had been abandoned. Then Primrose Larrington wrote in early December to say the whole thing was to be 'put on hold' until the New Year. He wondered if this was a euphemism used by telly people like Primrose.

But in late January they arrive just as the weather sets into a pattern of bitterly cold, raw days with scant hours of full daylight. Although the lack of light proves to be a practical problem for filming, Primrose Larrington is thrilled by the extremity of the conditions. She is delighted by frozen clods of soil and ice-encrusted spades and hoes as Fergus forages winter cabbage, turnips and swedes. Some interior shots of him lighting the open fire, chopping vegetables for soup, drinking his home-brewed rhubarb wine are added to the shooting schedule. Fergus finds himself making platefuls of bacon sandwiches and brewing constant pots of strong, sweet tea to keep the crew energised. And when they finally leave, the shoot, apparently, complete, he notices the silence, their absence, in a way that surprises him. He returns to the tasks and routine of his days, waiting for the relief that he has always found in his seclusion. In the evenings, he sits close to the wood fire, watching the reflection of flames as shadows on the wall and for the first time he considers whether, as the years inevitably accrue, it becomes more difficult to be alone. Or perhaps not so much difficult as dubious, debatable, as if solitariness is no guaranteed sinecure after all. The thought is unsettling.

***

Hester props herself against the wall of the church hall, scours the room for something or someone to interest her amidst the tangle of early spring symbols, the rabbits and eggs and the heady scent of forced hyacinths. She cannot imagine why she offered to help at the Easter Bazaar, a premature event given that the festival itself is still a month off. Then she remembers a weak moment after the Christmas Carol service when a woman called Frances Babcock had cornered her over mulled wine and mince pies. Hester has an ambiguous relationship with organised religion. She craves the sanctity of places dedicated to devotion; simple country churches, silent chapels, serried rows of wooden pews before an altar. She is comforted by the unfathomable nature of a deity immeasurably greater and more powerful than herself. She is reassured by the language, the structure and cadences of the King James' Bible, the narratives of kings and stars, mangers and miracles for the most deserving. Yet she is repelled by the cosiness of church-going, the social obligations of summer fetes and coffee mornings and jumble sales and Lent lunches. Those self-satisfied congregations gathering each Sunday with their sanctimonious smiles on their well-scrubbed faces are little better. And the sermons, no doubt painstakingly written and rehearsed, earnestly intended and yet for Hester, evasive, couched in metaphor, intentionally vague. A cheat, in fact. As if addressing the central core of every human being's terror, the fears that lurk at the margins of even the best of days, was vulgar, entirely tasteless. She wonders if she should ditch the Church of England and try something else on offer. Roman Catholicism, for example, which appeared to provide more in the way of ritual even after abandoning their services in Latin. All those obligatory Masses and the incense and the importance of the Pope and the Vatican City had a certain appeal. Or perhaps she should be radical in her departure from the established church and seek something eastern or orthodox. She feels quite indifferent to sect or creed, providing there's mysticism, intensity, performance.

And, most crucial of all, an absence of early Easter church bazaars where she is required to preside endlessly over the bric-à-brac stall.

A large woman with a pinched face approaches and picks up items, points out a crack in a pink milk jug, a flaw in a painted butter dish. Hester smiles glacially, reduces the price of each by half, points out that the proceeds are to go towards much needed church funds. The large woman stares back then moves on, heads towards the cake stall. Frances Babcock, treasurer and self-selected chairperson of all charitable church events, is at her side. She counts Hester's meagre takings, sniffs audibly.

"Not exactly stellar," she sighs.

"Nor are the items for sale," says Hester. "I can't imagine who offloaded this junk onto us in the first place."

Frances notes down '£7.49p' in thick black ink.

"Most of it came from collections of mine," she says. "Much loved pieces that I decided to donate to such a good cause, as it happens. Perhaps you wouldn't mind wrapping all unsold pieces carefully in newspaper so I can get them safely home. My husband, I know, will be relieved to see so much returned to its familiar setting." She moves on swiftly to the plant stall and Hester can hear her enthusing over the sales of overpriced begonias and baskets of tight crocus bulbs. She rapidly sets about her task of dismantling her stall, wrapping Frances' sugar bowls and toast racks and decorated vases and commemoration mugs in recent copies of *The Times* and *The Daily Telegraph*. She smoothes out a sheet and places two cheap glass sundae dishes in the middle of the Entertainment section, wrapping them up in a review of a controversial new play containing nudity and bestial acts. She warms to her task and checks other pages for suitably salacious material in which to place a chipped Wedgwood ashtray, a plastic teething beaker. She dispatches a matching pair of egg cups in the shape of hens to an article on the increase of sexually transmitted disease, wraps a cracked jelly mould in a full-page item on the proliferation of call girls in country villages. Her job satisfyingly complete, she waits to be dismissed from her post, her trestle table collapsed so that she can scarper into Oxford and reward herself with a decent cup of coffee and possibly an indulgent cake. She folds up the unused sheets of newspaper then decides to secrete the most recent into her bag as recompense for her morning's service.

Thus it is that, seated in the window of her favoured café in Turl Street, she turns to the television schedules for the coming months and finds herself staring hard at a small photograph of a man with a shock of rather wild, unkempt hair and a hesitant half-smile. She reads the brief article attached then returns again to the photograph, unable to take her eyes away from the image, from the familiarity of the face in the photograph. Fergus Barnes, her estranged husband of some decades, stares uncompromisingly back at her.

***

Fergus has been surprised by the fuss. He owns no television and has little idea of the importance people apparently attach to appearing on it. Jill has been anxious to hear details of the filming and disappointed at his apparent lack of ability to elaborate.

"What about a script?" she wants to know. "Did you have to learn lines?"

He has been taken aback by her interest. Horses, primarily, with a little occasional loud and energetic sex as recreation, have appeared to be her sole concerns. Now she presses him for details.

"You'll have to wait to see the real thing. The transmission, isn't that what they call it? It's going to be in June sometime, I think they said. Or was it in the spring with repeats in June? Or September, even? I didn't take much notice. And I can't imagine what it'll be like. Deadly dull, if you ask me, but then I have no idea what people like to watch." He is uncomfortable with her questioning yet hardly aware why. "They were here far too long and I was pleased to see the back of them if the truth be told."

It is not entirely the truth, but he is still confused by his ambiguous reaction to Primrose Larrington and her team, noisy and intrusive, disruptive to his daily routine. He still finds himself noting the return of silence to the house, the lingering sense of absence when they left.

"It's not every day we have a film crew in these parts, you know," Jill says, removing her navy fisherman's sweater followed by an aertex shirt straining over her large bust. "I'd have given anything to be here, but of course that would never have worked. Just in case word got round, you know."

"Yes," Fergus says. "No. Probably not. Tea? Or afterwards?"

"After," Jill says, shrugging out of her socks, "although I won't have long. My sister's joining me for a hack at four."

Later, Jill gone and a second pot of tea made, Fergus gets out the diaries and record books again. Until the arrival of Primrose Larrington and the *Alternative Lives* crew, he had not looked at them for years. In fact, he had entirely forgotten their existence and had dug them out from under his bed, heavy with dust and general grime. As diaries, they are rudimentary, factual and specific to the point of tedium. But they speak to Fergus. They remind him. And therefore they are of comfort. Some comfort of sorts.

"So how was it at the start?" Primrose Larrington had asked him. "When you first got into this self-sufficiency life? How did you begin?"

"With a bit of land," he had told her, "I leased a bit of land."

"And?" she had said with a note of mild exasperation.

He had stared back at her, feeling suddenly extremely tired. As if he was required to relive the utter exhaustion of those early years in order to satisfy her need for an authentic programme. Then he had remembered the diaries.

"Here," he had said, placing the pile of grubby exercise books, account books, a couple of journals and a cardboard folder or two in front of her on the kitchen table. "It's all in here. Take a look."

Primrose Larrington had quickly glanced through a few then asked to take a couple away with her, to help her get "a real, genuine insight into your world," as she had put it, "share them with our researchers." Fergus had spent the next few evenings wading through those remaining, the rest the history, as it were, of those first few years when he had meticulously recorded every detail. Even his failures and over-ambitious plans were scrawled down in fading pencil or ink so that he had been reminded of the folly of thinking of a herd of cows and several sows alongside a flock of a dozen sheep. Beekeeping, salting and curing pork and working horses had also been part of early, deluded plans that had been judiciously jettisoned. But he had been a younger man then, reasonably optimistic and excessively naïve about farming practice so naturally inclined to impractical, grandiose thoughts. His achievements over the years were recorded there too. The couple of cows he had acquired and found to be such splendidly useful and productive creatures, the grass-guzzling goats and the endless chickens and ducks and geese. And the faithful dogs, of course, Connie, his beloved retriever and then the old sheepdog, Rufus, that he'd taken off the hands of a retiring shepherd. There were endless lists of produce: potatoes and brassica and peas and beans and soft fruits that he'd learnt to turn into jam and apples and pears that had made their way into pickle. He even read accounts of his early cheese-making days and his novice attempts at bread before he mastered, in a roughshod sort of way, a palatable loaf, an edible soft cheese. Primrose Larrington had returned the borrowed records on the first day of filming, commenting that they were all "fascinating, just fascinating," in such a general way that told him she had not even bothered to look.

Fergus wonders who will watch. No doubt the programme will be scheduled for late-night viewing and caught only by insomniacs or invalids seeking diversion from pain and boredom. He is unsure whether he wants either Grace or Hester to see him through the subjective eye of Primrose Larrington and her team. Perhaps he will be made to look faintly ridiculous, an absurd eccentric. For a moment, he allows himself to imagine sitting down next to Grace, and with Hester there too, watching the programme together, pointing out to them its inaccuracies, exaggerations and distortions. Then he snaps out of the absurd idea, reminding himself that he has chosen to be a virtual stranger to his daughter over the past few decades and has not earned the possibility of such collusion. Swiftly, he goes outside, intent on checking some broken fencing before it grows too dark.

***

Archie arrives home to an empty house around five and remembers that Grace is staying late to supervise a dance workshop at the arts centre. He puts on the kettle then, feeling too restless to wait for it to boil, he finds a warm jacket and sets off to walk rapidly up to the ridge above Jacob's Bottom, taking long strides as if he is in some sort of hurry. The season is slowly shifting from winter into early signs of spring and the light will hold on for another half hour. He arrives breathless and turns to stare down at the view of the valley, remembering the first time he brought Grace here little over a year before. It seems far longer. He is wholeheartedly relieved they moved from Greenwich, from the trappings and hooks of that existence. Yet he is not entirely untethered in the way that he had hoped. Shackles persist. Habits pursue. He remembers how, when he was a young boy and his life was apparently orderly and simple, uncomplicated by the errors of maturity, he would wake in the night and list his worries to himself: Monday morning spelling tests, a scratched mudguard on his new bike, the ball he'd lost to the neighbour's garden. Then he would lie in bed, force himself to face each concern so that, mostly reasoned and resolved, he could then ease himself back into sleep.

Such an exercise now, however, only leads to alarming confusion. Resolution recedes.

He turns back, retracing his steps, heading not for home, but for Fox Woods and hopefully some signs of spring although it is still far too early for the bluebells. Perhaps they should move somewhere more remote. Perhaps Jacob's Bottom, initially a haven after Greenwich, is still too connected and tame to give him the sort of refuge he seeks. That's what people do, after all, he reasons, they abandon the past, shrug it off like an ill-fitting coat, and move on. Southern Ireland is supposed to be beautiful, empty roads, a dramatic coastline, endless countryside. Of course there's a lot of rain. Grace wouldn't like the rain. There's the west coast of Scotland, perhaps, more temperate, and no doubt equally spectacular. Yes, that's a definite possibility. He feels cheered by it and walks on into the centre of the woods where the undergrowth remains damp even in a rare arid year. Scotland may well be a feasible plan. It has to be cheaper to live there, surely, the cost of living considerably less and there have to be jobs of sorts. He's a teacher, after all, he can still lay claim to that. He leans against the trunk of a tree and stares up, trying to see the sky. But the woods are so dense at this point that the sky remains entirely shrouded by branches and the thick foliage of spring growth. He feels suddenly overwhelmingly tired, like a man who has been endlessly deprived of sleep through some marathon effort of endurance. He would like to lie down in the dank undergrowth of the woods amongst the thick bed of leaves and give in to the searing fatigue he feels, like a winsome character in a child's fairy tale. But he can't. There are too many matters to see to at home, letters that should be answered, buff-brown envelopes to open, phone calls to be made in order to ward off the harpies, stall those loathsome avenging angels.

And there is Grace. Soon Grace will be home, needing a fire lit, a meal prepared, his arms around her in welcome. Yes, as long as there is Grace, all has to be well.

Archie begins to pick his way back through the trees until he is out of the woods and on the narrow country road that leads down towards Jacob's Bottom. Scotland, he thinks again, with sudden clarity, the west coast by choice, extraordinary beaches, no doubt, excellent swimming and mesmerizing sunsets. A modest, pleasant home for the two of them, a bit of land attached so he can grow things. He picks up his pace now, eager to get back to the house and spend an hour or so poring over a map before Grace's return.

Part Two

# Kronos and England 1988

# 9

She woke each morning around eight. Slipping quietly from bed, she would open the door onto the veranda of their simple white-walled room and stand barefoot, wanting to catch the moment when the mountains to the east turned from pale pink to grey, the overnight ferry pulled into the small port of Kronos Town and the air was still cool on her skin. The sky, opalescent at this hour, would be brilliant blue in an hour or so when Archie was awake and the heat of the day already beginning to build.

"We should get up earlier," Grace said as they sat on the hotel terrace having breakfast. "It's the best time of the day before everyone else is awake. You could be swimming by seven."

Archie pulled a rough loaf apart, handed her a piece.

"We're on holiday," he said. "Give a man a break. But you're right, of course. Perhaps tomorrow."

"That's what you said yesterday," Grace said, "and you'll say it tomorrow too."

He smiled. "I'm still catching up on sleep. It seems easier to sleep here, somehow, just to give into it. Perhaps in a week or so I'll get the urge for an early dip."

Grace spread honey onto bread.

"I've lost track of the days," she said. "I don't want to think in terms of time. Of how much longer we have here. I want to pretend it's endless, that we only have to go back when we're bored."

"And when would that be?" Archie said, looking at her with a deep affection that caught her unexpectedly. It was a regard that she had not seen in his face since their early months together and it touched her profoundly.

"I don't know. But possibly never. That's the trouble. We have to go back."

Archie emptied the remains of the coffee pot into his cup, tore off another piece of bread.

"Don't think about it at the moment. I'm not. What shall we do today? There's a couple of places in the mountains I've been reading about in the guidebook that I'd like to see. Evidence of ancient settlements there. Minoan, of course, and then there's some Roman stuff. Or Venetian, more like. We could drive up there, find somewhere for lunch and… Grace?"

"Yes," she said. "Yes, please. Let's."

***

The letter had arrived halfway through the Easter holidays. Archie, visiting his mother in her nursing home near Norwich, had been away and on his return it had sat neglected for a few more days. Opening it eventually he had read it, handed it silently to Grace then gone out to the garden where she had found him staring at a cluster of late daffodils.

Court House School for Girls had closed.

Grace had read the letter again and again, trawling her way through mitigating phrases about recessionary times, drop in numbers, escalating costs and, ultimately, financial viability. Appropriate profound regrets were, of course, expressed by the Governors of the school, an anonymous body of people charged with the duty of informing the employed staff that they were, in fact, no longer employed and that their services, in the absence of students to teach, were now redundant.

Archie had seemed stunned rather than upset or angry as if the news was failing to penetrate. Did he have any inkling of such a thing about to happen? Grace had stood next to him in the damp chill air of the April morning. What about talk in the staff room, any suggestion that class numbers were falling and that the school was unlikely to survive the bleak financial climate of the past few months? She had plied him with questions, but he had few answers to offer. He had said merely that he had no idea that such a thing could happen, a school closing its doors overnight, throwing staff and students abruptly out into the cold. He had been very quiet for the rest of the day and that evening, eating little dinner.

"You'll get another job easily," she had said the next morning after a night when Archie had been restless and she had heard him wake early and go downstairs to make tea. "Teachers are always in demand, surely?"

"Of course," he'd said emphatically and she had been pleased to see his composure returned. He had seemed buoyant again as if his dark mood of the day before had been an aberration. "It's just a case of scouring the educational press for a new post. You're not to worry, Grace. We'll be all right."

"And if we finally get on and sell the Greenwich house, that's got to help, surely. Realising an asset."

"They're paying me until the end of the month, anyway," he'd said, "and what with your job bringing us a bit in, just to tide us over…"

"Giles might make me full-time next month. With any luck."

But Giles had not made her full-time. Instead, four days later, he had arrived at the arts centre and announced that, most regretfully her job was to be cut down to two days a week. And even that, he had added, would need to be reviewed in another month. The stock market crisis of the previous October had hit several of their donors hard. Their comfortable, profitable investments, permitting them philanthropic gestures, had been devalued in a matter of hours. Too many patrons for comfort had withdrawn their support. Giles, business-like and brusque in his announcement, had nevertheless appeared genuinely sorry and had assured Grace that they would be loath to lose her. The likelihood of her job entirely disappearing, however, could not be discounted.

And then she caught flu. It had been years since she had experienced proper flu with its attendant high temperature, painful limbs, nausea and loss of appetite. She had been amazed by how ill she felt, considering how dismissive people always were when flu was mentioned as if it were just an excuse for malingering. She had floundered for days and nights between fitful sleep and outlandish, feverish dreams and had only been vaguely aware of Archie, hovering with glucose drinks and plates of porridge that had risen up before her aching eyes like grotesque Roman banquets. And then the fatigue afterwards. She had sat at the kitchen table, considering the energy it required to move towards the kettle, onwards to the cold tap in order to complete the task of making a single cup of tea. Archie had been attentive, concerned. He had sat at her side, scanning the papers, skimming page after page in search of an appropriate teaching vacancy. The market, it seemed, was less fertile than he'd anticipated. Still, he had reassured her, things would look up over the next couple of months. There was bound to be a flurry of job advertisements in the summer and he had the advantage of a wealth of wide experience. "Perhaps I'll even please your mother and return to academe and further education," he'd said and Grace, astonished by her pallor in the bathroom mirror, by how thin she'd swiftly become, had been grateful for his constant optimism.

A few days later, Archie had driven into Fletwell and

returned after a couple of hours with flowers for her. She found a pale pink vase, filled it with water at the kitchen sink and arranged the ten white tulips.

"That's not all," he'd said, grinning like a child too excited to contain himself as she placed the vase on the table in the living room. "We're having a holiday. It's all arranged. I've booked the flights and the hotel and everything. It's going to be wonderful, Grace, I just know it is." And he had handed her a thick brown envelope containing two air tickets, two ferry tickets and a confirmed fax booking for a double room at the Hotel Andromache on Kronos, an island in the south-eastern Mediterranean. "I admit it was a spontaneous idea," he went on as she sat down on the sofa and examined the travel documents, "I was just passing the travel agent's on the way to the bank. To be frank, I was only going to have a browse, pick up a couple of brochures, that sort of thing. But then the manager in there started talking about this place, said it was one of his favourite islands and he could particularly recommend the hotel as he'd stayed there only a month or so ago." Grace's protests had been brief and mild. She could not imagine anything she wanted more than to escape the predictably cold and wet late English spring. She imagined Melanie and Giles would be more than happy if she agreed to take unpaid leave from the arts centre and Archie refused even to discuss whether it was financially wise to take a holiday while he was unemployed. Grace had put her arms firmly around him; he had held her close.

"And by the time we're back, I'll be spoilt for choice where jobs are concerned," he'd said. "It will be high summer here and you'll be fully fit and well again and we'll be able to take on the world, Grace. Don't think of it as an extravagance, it's just exactly what you and I need right now."

Grace had given in easily to his persuasion.

They had left Jacob's Bottom less than two weeks later. When they had reached the ferry port on the mainland, they had sat brazenly in the full heat of the early afternoon sun, reluctant to seek the shade like troglodyte creatures long deprived of the light.

"And it's only mid-May," Grace had said, shrugging off her sombre black cardigan which suddenly seemed inappropriately dour, burying it deep in the bottom of her bag. Crossing on the overnight ferry to the island, they had emerged from their stuffy cabin into an early dawn, the port of Kronos Town bustling even at that hour. Owners with available accommodation, taxi drivers, hire car companies, hopeful guides had hovered, waiting for a hesitant tourist, but Archie had already spotted Hotel Andromache. The only hotel of any size, set a couple of hundred yards back from the port area across a narrow road, it was partially screened by a long row of palm trees, a gracious building of Venetian design resembling a large private house or colonial embassy rather than a hotel. To one side was a terrace where one or two early risers sat drinking coffee while a boy watered the brilliant bougainvillea. Archie had picked up their suitcase and taken Grace's hand.

"Come on, this looks like us."

And Grace had willingly followed. Already Jacob's Bottom, the financial troubles of Court House School and Giles Meredith and the arts centre seemed remote and insignificant details in a life that could offer so much more.

Within a few days Grace felt stronger and more resilient than she had in months. At first they did very little, sleeping long and late in the mornings so that breakfast would have finished and they'd walk into the town instead, sit at one of the many cafés on the harbour and order fresh orange juice, bowls of thick yogurt, walnuts and honey. It seemed possible for several hours to slip by easily enough, watching passers-by, reading books, ordering coffee so that late morning would have dissolved through lunchtime into early afternoon and they'd move on to another café for a cold drink, a salad, ice cream. The picturesque harbour side drew locals and visitors alike to the cafés and tavernas stretching arc-like around the bay. In the winding narrow streets and back alleys of the old town there were endless small shops selling leather goods, carved wooden figures, silver jewellery, ceramics and baskets and hand-loomed rugs. They explored the large indoor market with its enormous range of fruit and vegetables, spices, herbs, goats' and sheep's cheeses, fresh fish and meat and jars of deep green olive oil while skinny stray cats with eyes apparently too large for their bony narrow faces skittered amongst their feet. The mountains loured over the town, a dramatic backdrop with patches of snow still clinging to the highest peaks or on plains out of reach of the sun.

They found the town beach on the other side of the harbour on their second afternoon. Although the sea still felt cool to Grace, Archie had immediately returned to the hotel for swimming trunks and towel and was swimming within the hour. She was content to leave him, dipping, diving in the deep blue water while she walked along the beach, picked up pebbles and shells, then returned to sit on the sand, occasionally glimpsing his cavorting shape while she threw her head back and bared her shoulders to the heat of the sun.

"Of course, this is all unreal," she said to him one evening as they sat having dinner at a table set only feet from the sea. "All this lotus-eating we're doing. We're indulging ourselves foolishly whereas we should be back home trudging around employment agencies. We're being highly irresponsible."

Archie poured more of the light local wine into her glass. He took salad from the bowl, ate an olive before replying.

"Perhaps we should stay here. Find work here, I mean. People do, after all. Teachers in particular find work abroad."

Grace waited for him to retract the suggestion, laugh and say he was only being fanciful. But instead he went on eating then paused, as if expectant of some sort of response from her.

"I can't believe you really mean that," she said eventually. "You've always seemed so… well, attached to building us a conventional sort of life at home. You've never even suggested something as radical as moving abroad before."

"You mean I've always seemed stuck in a rut, unimaginative," Archie said. "Incapable of changing direction."

"No, not at all," Grace said swiftly. "After all, you left the Aldgate college on a whim."

"Ah yes, that," he said and seemed about to say more, but the waiter arrived, placed more dishes before them, taking time to ask them about their visit to the island and by the time he left them to attend to another table, their conversation seemed to have shifted on.

In the middle of the night Grace wakes, interrupting a dream in which she appears to be living still in her basement flat on the outer edges of Earl's Court. She lies for a moment, adjusting, ordering her mind, gratified to be here not there, lying next to Archie, her pale yellow dress from the night before tossed haphazardly on the chair, white sandals on the tiled floor. The door leading onto the balcony has been left open and a sudden breeze ruffles the thin cream curtain. Since they have been on the island, in this place, she thinks, Archie has seemed happy. Happier. He has appeared calm and far more content than she can remember since their marriage. And not just because they are on holiday, blissfully detached from the obligations of home, she reasons, for even on their honeymoon in Italy there had been times when he had seemed remote, immured by his own concerns, occupying some region out of reach so that she had felt redundant almost, surplus rather than central to his existence. Here, however, he has let down some guard that so often he projects, that carapace of measured control that deflects intimacy. Grace thinks of the spontaneous affection they have shown each other over the past week, the small gestures and subliminal tokens and signs of love. She wonders if Archie is serious about the idea of staying on the island to work or if it is just some random thought that he will regret even expressing.

It's possible, after all, to live another way.

Archie shifts in his sleep, turns one way then rolls the other, shrugs off the single sheet covering them. Perhaps they could stay here, make another sort of life together, something simpler and less hidebound by the conventions and trappings she's always imagined she seeks. What she has taken for granted, assumed without questioning, that Archie wants too.

They hired a car during their second week and drove up through tortuous passes, around hairpin bends into the mountain range that crossed the island, separated north from south coasts. Often, they would have to halt for five or ten minutes at a time to let herds of goats or hill sheep cross their path. Climbing higher, delving deeper, they would stop in small hamlets, always finding a *kafenion* for a cold drink, a plate of olives and bread, looking back at the spectacular sweep of coastline, the sea limpid, glass-like. Everywhere, it seemed, there were chapels and churches, white-stoned buildings clinging to hillsides, often only a few feet wide and deep so that the two of them would just fit into the ornate small devotional space. Grace lit candles, Archie slipped coins into an offertory box. They began to explore the coast beyond the main port town, driving east, stumbling across small seaside villages with sandy bays and coves. Archie swam constantly, Grace occasionally, finding the water growing pleasantly warmer each day. One of the larger villages, Anixi Bay, boasted a fine, long beach bordered by a few tavernas and there was a small selection of shops in the two streets straddling the narrow beach road. Grace bought postcards, wrote one to Hester, another to Melanie, then peered into the window of an agency advertising houses and apartments to let.

"Are you looking for something?" A voice at her shoulder surprised her and she turned to see a dark-haired woman with a small child, a toddler, hitched to one hip. "Somewhere to stay, I mean. I could help you out."

She was clearly English although there was the suggestion of an accent of some sort, faint Australian, possibly. Canadian at a pinch, Grace thought. The voice of someone who has lived in too many places for the accent anymore to have a firm footing.

"Not exactly," she answered, "we're just on holiday here, staying at the Andromache Hotel in Kronos Town."

The woman raised her eyebrows, the young child made a play for her earring, long and dangling nearly to her shoulder. She shifted him onto the other hip, let him switch his attention to a thin plaited strand of her hair.

"Sky-high prices there. You really don't need to be paying out money like that, you know. I let rooms just as good as theirs any day and at a quarter of the price, I'll bet. I'm just a few kilometres up the road at Aghia Kallida. If ever you're in need, give me a call."

She started to walk away then turned back abruptly, fumbled in her pocket and produced a small notepad and a pencil. Wordlessly, she handed over the child to Grace while she scribbled on a piece of paper, tore it out, tucked it into the pocket of Grace's skirt and retrieved the little boy.

"Thank you," Grace said, pulling out the scrap and reading a name and a telephone number. But the woman, Clea, according to the pencilled scrawl, had disappeared inside a shop.

That evening they sat on their balcony watching the sun set into the sea before going out to find somewhere to have dinner.

"This happens every night at home, the sun setting, it has to. Yet we hardly ever notice," Grace said.

"We're busy doing other things. Like opening bills. Taking out the rubbish. Watching pointless television. Moaning about the weather."

They sat in silence, not wanting to miss the moment when the sun slid down, dissolved into the horizon and the sky turned impossibly orange, scarlet and tangerine, a child's bold effort with poster paints lacking restraint and inhibition.

"Did you really mean what you said the other day?" Grace said eventually. "About working here. Finding a teaching job instead of going home?"

Archie said nothing at first so that Grace felt he had chosen to ignore her, as if being reminded of his random, off-chance remark had been unwelcome. But then he said,

"I don't see why not. Perhaps it's what's needed. And people do things like this, don't they? On a whim, they leave their old life behind and start again. The past can just be the past, after all."

"I suppose we'd have to go back for a while," Grace said tentatively, not wanting to pose negative thoughts, "to sort things out, the house and the furniture. And there's my bit of a job, of course, although it's hardly an impediment, but I'd have to resign. We can't just leave it all, Mary Celeste-like."

"A pity," Archie said. "That is a pity. The idea is so attractive. Simply upping sticks and… but I suppose you're right. There are a few ends that we would need to tie up."

Grace was racing ahead of him, dispatching the rented

house at Jacob's Bottom, selling the cars, the Greenwich house, amassing some capital to tide them over until they both got themselves jobs here on the island. The cost of living would be so much cheaper, renting a house, buying one in time, eating the plentiful, locally grown products, possibly growing their own in the reliable sunny climate. And a grapevine, of course. Everywhere here, even the smallest cottage, appeared to have its own grapevine. She knew she was probably being naïve, imagining an idyllic lifestyle for the two of them. As if the island offered a life absent of worry and responsibility whereas in truth, of course, their same dispositions, their flaws and frailties, so often the cause of the imperfections of their lives, would accompany them wherever they went. But she could not stop herself thinking that this was something they should try. There seemed so little reason not to, so little to lose. Later, over dinner at one of the harbour tavernas, Archie grew more expansive.

"It would have to be English as a Foreign Language, I suppose," he said, pouring a glass of wine from the jug on the table. "But that's all right. I did a bit of that when I was a student. There are always people wanting to learn English wherever you go and there must be language schools around."

"And I could... well, I could find something to do especially in the tourist season. There's always cleaning, waitressing, maybe even working as a tour guide. And we could both learn the language in time."

Grace was not willing to concede any obstacles and Archie seemed convinced. He suddenly looked years younger as if the prospect of such a drastic change in their lives was energising. For once, she thought, for the first time, they were planning something together, nurturing an idea in the way she had always imagined yet had so far eluded her in their marriage. Archie started to write lists on the paper tablecloth with a pencil borrowed from the willing waiter. They'd need somewhere to live, an apartment, a small house, perhaps, at a reasonable rent. Out of town would be cheaper, Grace said. But near the sea, Archie added for in this climate he knew he would swim for much of the year and she agreed. He wrote Home, Sea and she added Jobs, and then Archie began a separate list of things they would need to attend to at Jacob's Bottom before returning to the island.

"A month would be enough time, I would have thought," he said, "perhaps less. We could try and do it all in less. Perhaps just a fortnight or so."

"Really?" Grace said. "Could we really do everything so quickly?" It seemed unlikely to her that they could discard so much of their lives, shift the hooks and trappings and banal details in such a short space of time, but she was very willing to suspend disbelief. The moon was almost full, an enormous bowl of light in the sky reflecting onto the dark sea water of the bay. The waiter placed a flask of *Raki* in front of them, carefully poured out three glasses and raised his.

"*Yammas!*" he said, swallowing the contents swiftly and slapping the glass down on the table. They followed his lead with as little caution.

Grace lies awake in the arc of Archie's arm, unwilling to sleep when she feels something akin to perfect happiness. She shifts marginally away from Archie, now deeply asleep, and feels warm anticipation for the next day and the next in a way that has eluded her for months. Together, they will sit and plan their brief return to Jacob's Bottom, even visit, perhaps, before they leave Kronos, a local agent to ask about homes to rent. She imagines telling Melanie. She thinks of ringing Hester who will be surprised but encouraging, Grace is sure. She suspects that her mother has registered Archie as stubborn and predictable without the flare for such an impulsive act and

Grace is pleased she will be able to disillusion her. Eventually she sleeps and is dreaming of the house in Greenwich, which has incongruously acquired a strip of sand and some sunshades separating it from the busy A2. Then into her dream comes the disturbing sound of knocking, knuckles on wood, a low repetitive rap at a door that becomes louder and more insistent so that Grace sits up in bed, trying to stir herself out of the dream.

But the knocking went on. Archie stirred, woke and sat up for a moment in bed before groping in the darkened room for a towel, a shirt to cover himself. He stubbed his toe on the bedside table, cursing under his breath.

"All right, all right, I'm coming," he said, opening the door onto the dimly lit hotel corridor. A man, the night porter they had seen the previous evening in reception, was standing there, a piece of paper in his hand. He mumbled something apologetic in his limited English, seemed exasperated by his inability to explain. Grace assumed he had mistaken the room for one that required an early morning call. But after a pause as if to gather his limited vocabulary together, concoct some sentences into a cogent order, he went on.

"Mr Copeland, telephone call for you. So sorry, very sorry but a… I… emergency. Your brother. He rings for you. He need to talk with… to you. Now please. Please come. He waits."

The porter stepped away from the door, but hovered as if needing to underline the speed with which he wanted Archie to follow him. Turning on the main overhead light, Archie grappled on the floor for discarded trousers, some shoes and within moments was outside the room, talking in loud whispers to the man. Grace heard their footsteps, resonant in the silence of the hour, swiftly moving along the corridor and down the stone staircase. Within five minutes Archie was back in the room. The phone call had been from Leo. By chance, he had been back in England for a few days, staying with a friend in East Anglia when the nursing home had rung to say that their mother had been admitted to hospital, having suffered another, more major stroke. She was gravely ill and unlikely to recover. Archie moved frantically around the room, opening drawers, finding his passport, his wallet and then going into the bathroom to splash his face with cold water, pull a comb through his hair.

"I need to be on the morning ferry to the mainland," he said, "then I can get an afternoon flight to London. Then a train up to Norwich. I'll be there easily before midnight." He seemed to be talking aloud to himself rather than to Grace. She tried to calm him.

"It's only five o'clock, Archie, the first ferry doesn't leave until eight. We've time to shower and dress and pack properly. And we need to pay the bill at reception, of course."

He looked in the bathroom mirror at her reflection as she hovered behind him.

"No, Grace, there's no need for you to come. I'll go on my own if you don't mind." He collected his razor, his toothbrush and shoved both into the pocket of his jacket that he slipped around his shoulders.

"Of course I'm coming with you," Grace said. "Don't be silly. Why ever would you think I'd stay here alone?" She began to look around her for her clothes, so easily discarded the night before, lying on the floor.

"It makes no sense at all for you to come with me," Archie went on. "There'll be nothing for you to do, Grace. I just don't want you... well, hanging around at a hospital is hardly going to be a pleasant experience. And it's not as if you even know my mother. Leave things to me and Leo."

His voice was determined, resolute, deflecting her concern.

"Then I'll go back to Jacob's Bottom and wait for you there," Grace said. "Then at least I'm on hand, just a few hours' drive away from you when you need me." She moved towards the wardrobe and began taking clothes from hangers, folding them on the bed, but Archie stopped her, firmly took her arm.

"No, Grace, it's not what I want. Please. Let me go on my own. Anyway, I won't be alone. Leo's there. It's better this way, really." He pushed a strand of her uncombed hair away from her face and she caught his hand. He looked very tired, suddenly, as if at the end of a tedious long journey rather than at the beginning. Tension and fear had instantly replaced the relaxation and ease he had shown since their arrival on the island.

Grace reasoned, "But it doesn't seem to make any sense, me being here. I ought to be with you or at least close to hand." She saw that he wasn't listening, seemed anxious to be out of the room and down by the port as if by simply being there he could hasten a departure that was still hours off. She watched him finish some careless packing of a small suitcase. He reached into his wallet, chose one of several credit cards that he handed her.

"Here, use this for the hotel bill if they want paying before I get back. The room's booked for another week so you might as well make use of it. And anyway, this is all probably a lot of fuss and I'll be back within a few days." He attempted a smile, but the effect was unconvincing. "Then we'll be able to forget all about this… well, this interruption and pick up our holiday where we left off, Grace."

She insisted on walking down to the port with him in the half-light of the early morning. The ferry had only just docked so they found their way to the café, busy with customers despite the hour. Archie ordered a small cup of strong coffee, drank it in moments and ordered another, keeping a constant eye on the large vessel that was still disembarking passengers.

"You'll ring me when you know anything, won't you? In fact, just ring me when you arrive and leave a message. I'll keep checking with reception if I go out."

"Of course," he said automatically. "We'll talk very soon, Grace. Don't worry. And as I said, once I know everything's all right and she's on the road to recovery, I'll be back. After all, we've been through an emergency like this before with mother and I expect Leo is just being dramatic and exaggerating how things are."

"Perhaps," Grace said doubtfully as he fussed with checking his passport, his wallet, the ticket he had collected from the ferry office just ten minutes before. "And if you change your mind and need me back home with you, you've only just to ring and say. Please."

He said nothing, checked his watch again. Grace signalled to the waiter, asked for tea.

"And you'll get yourself some breakfast on board? There might be no time at the airport before your flight, after all."

"Yes. Yes, of course, Grace. I'll be fine."

"I know. I know you will. Sorry to fuss so, but..."

"No, it's all right, I understand. You're just being..."

"Concerned."

"You're just being Grace. And thank you for that. I don't know what... but you're not to worry."

He slipped his arm around her shoulder, kissed the top of her head, held her close. Eventually, they could see passengers beginning to move towards the ferry to embark. Archie stood up, reached into his pocket and fumbled a handful of notes into Grace's lap.

"Here, you'll need some money. I almost forgot. Just to keep you going until I'm back."

"I've got some money, Archie," Grace said, "and a few travellers' cheques to cash. Really, there's no need."

"And you'll wait for me here, Grace, all right?" he said, ignoring her protest as if he had not heard. She folded the notes into her bag. "Here on the island. That's what I want you to do. None of this nonsense of following me back to England, all right? I've told you already that it makes far more sense for you to stay here." He took her hand, squeezed it so that it almost hurt. He looked so anxious for her to agree that she found herself acquiescing simply to calm him. "And I'll be back to join you," he went on. "It will be something for me to look forward to, you see, and the thought of you here… well, it will really help me, Grace."

She walked with him down to the ferry and watched as he joined the throng of foot passengers making their way onto the large vessel. Soon, however, she'd lost sight of him, thought for a moment a figure stopping to turn and wave was Archie, but then, uncertain, turned away herself and walked slowly back to the hotel.

She slept until late morning, tired by the interrupted night. Showering and dressing swiftly to shrug off the lethargy she still felt, she walked into town and found a café in one of the backstreets. It was strange to be alone yet she was surprised at not feeling particularly lonely or concerned. By now, she knew the streets well and felt quite at ease wandering among them, filling up the afternoon by browsing in the old quarter, among the narrow alleyways no wider than an arm's span. Archie would not ring until he was in England. He would not ring until he had made his way from the airport up to East Anglia, to the hospital near Norwich, and that would no doubt not be until the early hours of the following morning. Even so, that evening she chose to stay in the hotel just in case. She ate dinner late at a small table at the side of the terrace, absorbed by her book to avoid any curious stares. But no one seemed to take any particular notice of her solitary state. People continued to arrive and order food and wine until nearly midnight. An extended family party, familiar with the hotel staff and waiters, took over a large circular table for the evening. Small children ran around the garden until they grew fractious then nestled into the arms and laps of parents, aunts, grandmas where they grew heavy-eyed and fell asleep. Just before she went up to bed, Grace checked at reception to see if a message had been left for her. "*Ohi*," the man behind the desk swiftly said, the same man who had summoned Archie to the phone in the early hours. Then he smiled and said in English, "No, there has been no message. Not yet. Tomorrow, perhaps. In the morning, Mrs Copeland."

But the next morning, Thursday morning, there was still nothing. Grace turned away from the reception desk, hesitant about the day, then remembered the hired car. It was years since she had driven abroad, but in Archie's absence there was no reason to waste the remaining days of rental. Cautiously, she drove out of the town, taking whichever route looked simplest to follow until she had left the outskirts behind her and was driving through empty roads endlessly bordered by olive groves. She drove slowly, but met little traffic to trouble her; the occasional goat escaped from his herd, a couple of dogs frisked alarmingly at her wheels. The last of the spring's wild flowers dotted the fields before the intense heat of high summer withered them. The road climbed gradually so that she was unaware of how high she had driven until, pulling into a small village, parking by the church in the shade, she realised that she was in the foothills of the mountain range that hung as a backdrop over Kronos Town. She drank coffee in the village *kafenion* and attempted conversation with her six or so words of the language. At another table three old men sat talking with each other, worry beads constantly jostling from hand to hand. Two small children, three or four years of age, played with a mother cat and her kitten, a surprisingly confident bundle of fur that soon decided to nestle its soft warm body on Grace's knee. Lizards skittered across the stone wall behind her. Cicadas hummed. Grace felt suspended, timeless. She rummaged in her bag for a book and sat on for another half hour, reading a chapter or two. A few more people arrived, villagers evidently, since they knew the two children, embracing them warmly, letting them clamber across their laps before settling down to eat and drink.

Eventually, she pulled herself away and walked back to the car, now exposed to the midday sun so that the steering wheel burnt at her touch. The road grew narrower and more precipitous as she drove on and there was evidence of rock fall spilling onto the tarmac. Even in this apparently remote area there were occasional mountain sheep and goats for company and several times she had to steer to avoid them. Then suddenly, an enormous coach rounded the bend coming towards her and she rammed on her brakes, heard the tyres screech on the stony road. The coach was empty and when she had recovered from the shock sufficiently to drive on, she took the road at a snail's pace and soon found herself in a village square at the top of a gorge along with a large party of walkers in caps and climbing boots emerging from a taverna, checking cameras for film, smothering on layers of sun protection ahead of their excursion. Grace felt conspicuous in her thin cotton skirt and skimpy T-shirt next to the uniform sturdy shorts, shirts and thick socks as if she had failed to understand some implied dress code for the day and she was relieved when their guide appeared and marshalled the walkers away from the square. She retreated to the shade of the taverna, feeling somewhat guilty at her slothfulness compared with their activity. Soon the village was peaceful again, punctuated only by the barking of a couple of dogs, the clatter of glasses and plates being collected from the abandoned tables.

"Too hot to start at this time," the young waitress said scornfully, gesturing in the direction the walkers had taken. "You want to start at six, maybe seven. That's when you walk the gorge. Not now. You want to order something?"

She was not hungry, but she wanted to prolong her time in the village, avoiding a return too soon to Kronos Town and her silent hotel room. Suddenly, it seemed far longer than thirty hours or so since Archie had left the island and she felt his absence keenly. She missed the sound of his voice, his reassuring physical presence next to her, the ease of his company. Since they had arrived a week or two before, there had been such a sense of equilibrium, of perfect harmony between them that Grace resented now its interruption, however temporary. Even in the last hour or two before he had caught the ferry to the mainland, she had felt that state slipping away from them and Archie retreating back into himself, the way he so often had before, as if wary of her beside him, reluctant even for her concern. The waitress, barely seventeen or eighteen, long dark hair tied back in a scarlet ribbon, brought a white plate of salad, a glass of orange juice.

"Our own," she said, "everything. The cheese. My mother makes it. And the olives. From our trees, dried on the trees. So not too salty."

"You speak good English," Grace said. The girl shrugged, dismissively.

"Not so good. But I am learning. We have… we get a lot of tourists. The walkers, for the gorge, you know. So I try to talk to them. Like to you now. Then I get better. I get… I grow more fluent."

"You are lucky to grow up in a place like this. I can't

imagine anywhere more perfect to live." Grace looked out at the mountainous terrain, the sweep of rugged landscape forming a dramatic backdrop to the peaceful, somnolent village.

"Yes, it is very beautiful, it is true. The mountains and the… scenes?"

"The scenery," Grace prompted. "And the perfect weather, of course."

"The sun is not always… In the winter we have snow. High up, not so much in this village here, but in villages above us. A lot of snow in the mountains. And storms, sometimes, and rain, there can be days when there is lots of rain. But that is good. Rain is good for… for the growing."

"I'd like to see the mountains in snow," Grace said.

The girl smiled. "Then you must come back. See the island in the winter. In all the seasons."

"I hope to. In fact…" Grace began, but the girl's attention was caught by a couple at another table. A car pulled up across the square and a family headed towards the taverna. Grace was left to her lunch.

Back at the hotel, there was still no message from Archie. Mechanically, she collected the key for her room, went upstairs and opened the shutters that were always drawn when the room was cleaned each morning, lay down on the bed in a shaft of sunlight from the late afternoon. It was easy to reason his failure to phone. Hospitals were unwieldy, awkward places with wards possibly remote from access to public phones, let alone phones that would allow him to make a continental call. And she had no idea of what he had found. In spite of Archie's attempt to be optimistic, Grace could not imagine that his brother would have resorted to calling him back unnecessarily. It was simply not the sort of thing that Leo would do.

Again, she ate dinner on the hotel terrace within reach of

reception. Only three other tables were occupied and Grace was not the only person alone. An American woman who had arrived that morning was ordering in a clear, resonant voice and they exchanged discreet smiles before both retreating into books as if to avoid the necessity for possibly unwanted conversation. It was some time later when Grace, her meal finished, but reluctant to return to her room so early in the warm evening, caught her eye again.

"Excuse me," the woman said, pausing as she passed close to Grace's table, "tell me to get lost, but I just wondered if you would like to take a stroll with me into the town. Get some coffee, perhaps? That's if you're on your own like me."

She was considerably older than Grace and exceptionally tall. Her height gave her a somewhat imposing appearance as she stood close yet there was warmth in her smile, an openness of manner that was appealing.

"Joan Whitford," she said, holding out a hand in greeting. "Now I will disappear this moment if you're waiting for some nice young man to come and join you."

"Nothing like that at all," Grace said and briefly explained the reason for Archie's sudden departure, her reluctance to leave the hotel in case he should ring. Joan sat down in the spare chair next to her as if invited.

"Well, that's too bad," she said. "But how sensible to stay on here without your husband. No point in two of you spoiling your visit."

"Archie rather insisted. I wondered at the time whether… but he was adamant."

Joan patted Grace's hand.

"Good for him. You're lucky to have found yourself a man who lets you live a little. Doesn't parcel you up and carry you in his top pocket. My second husband, Frank, was like that, dear soul. My first was the possessive type and that's no life being with someone like that, I can tell you. So we'll stay in tonight and wait for this phone call for you. How does that sound, Grace? Would you mind if I borrowed your company for the next couple of hours?"

They sat on the hotel terrace until nearly midnight. Joan Whitford was on a tour of Europe with a party of other women from her hometown in northern California. They had already spent a fortnight travelling by coach, visiting major cities and staying only a night or two before moving on. When the group of thirty had reached the capital on the mainland with a programme of organised sightseeing set for the subsequent seven days, Joan had rebelled. Leaving a note for the earnest tour guide to say she would re-join them the following week, she had impulsively taken the ferry to Kronos.

"They are a good bunch of people, Grace," she said, "don't misunderstand me. But I dislike being so… herded. Counted on and off that coach several times a day as if I'm seven years of age again. I needed to feel like a grown up once more, capable of making my own decisions about when to take dinner, what time to go to bed."

She was an easy companion. Suspended and detached from their normal lives, in the way of travellers everywhere, they were open and candid about each other. Joan had been a widow for some years and, after a period of being unwilling to travel, seeking only the limits of her small town, the company of her daughters, family and close friends, she had decided that extended mourning ill-suited her. She had become restless and curious.

"I've always been an inquisitive woman, Grace. Wanting to know what lies beneath the surface of things. And I wasn't going to find that out by visiting the mall twice a week or taking up bridge. And time's never on our side, you have to remember that. Especially at my stage of life." She had sold her house, bought an apartment and begun to travel. "Infant steps at first, a guided tour of England and Scotland, trying to dig up ancestors none of us actually had. You know the kind of thing, Grace, twelve cities in as many days with hardly a moment even to buy a postcard or take your nose out of the guidebook. But it was what I needed. My first trip without dear Frank. With a bunch of strangers, in fact, doing something he would never have considered."

"He didn't like to travel?"

"Not like that. He would never have agreed to be the stereotypical American abroad. Far too many stout matrons in cream Polyester pant suits for his tastes." She signalled to the waiter, asked for tea. "He was a very private man, Frank. Quiet habits. He liked… his music. His books. He'd have loathed those dawn rises to dash off to do Stonehenge and Stratford-upon-Avon before breakfast. Especially in the company of a bunch of compatriots. But that trip gave me the confidence to do things for myself again, Grace. To make decisions, even small ones. You know, after Frank died, it took me some time to realise I had few tastes or opinions of my own anymore. I'd even lost touch with what made me happy, gave me pleasure. Women spend so much of their lives worrying about other people's happiness, scenting signs of disquiet among the family, the children, and trying to swaddle it all with a bland sort of kindness, small acts of selflessness. Then suddenly, you turn round and realise that they're all perfectly fine, they're swanning off living their indulgent, pampered lives and you're left reeling, just a little. Unsure how to put yourself in the centre of things anymore."

The tea arrived. Joan poured, pushed a cup towards Grace. "Don't mind me talking so much. I'm nearly an old woman, on the home stretch, at least, and have to take a final fling at life before the knees or the hips give up. You just tell me if I'm being a bore and I'll take myself off and bother someone else."

Grace protested. Her company was welcome, she assured her. She had begun to wonder how to spend another day alone and now, in possession of the hire car, perhaps Joan would like to join her. Joan produced the guidebook that she'd been reading over dinner and showed Grace a few well-thumbed pages of places she planned to visit. Had she already been to any of them? With her husband, perhaps, before his unfortunate call back to England? No, she and Archie had intended to go to one of the monasteries and to visit the archaeological museum, but had managed neither. Grace felt comforted by the prospect of sharing some time with Joan as if the older woman's direction and enthusiasm were contagious. Spreading out a map on the table, they traced a route along the coast to the far western tip of the island and were engrossed in working out distances from the kilometre scale so that it took Grace a moment or two to notice that her attention was being sought by the waiter.

Archie's voice on the line from his hotel near Norwich was clear, but subdued as if he were trying to control emotion, rendering essential information. His mother had died before he had arrived back in England. She had failed to recover consciousness fully after the major stroke and had slipped away in the late morning when Archie was still on his way to the mainland. Leo had been with her, but it was doubtful that she had been aware of him. Or, indeed, capable of noting that Archie was not, Grace pointed out into the silence that fell on the phone line between them.

"I am so sorry, Archie," she said inadequately, twisting the cord of the phone around her fingers. The hotel foyer felt humid and stuffy after the fresh evening air of the garden terrace. She pushed strands of hair off her face with her spare hand. "I'll come home at once. Or at least, first thing tomorrow morning. I am sure the manager here would see to a ferry booking for me and I can get an afternoon flight to London."

"No," Archie said, his voice suddenly firm. "No, absolutely not, Grace. There's no point in you being here at all."

"But there must be so much to arrange, things to see to. The funeral, for a start," she said, "I want to be with you for that. I should be there."

"Really, there's no need. Anyway, it's on Monday and arrangements are all in place. No, Grace, Leo is here with me and we've seen to everything. Or will have done in a day or two. Of course I won't be able to rush back straight after the funeral. There'll be… well, one or two things to see to. The will for a start. And essential paperwork. It seems to be a complicated business these days. Dying, that is. All sorts of forms to fill in."

"I could help you if I was there," Grace persisted. There was a silence for a moment as if he had changed his mind, was about to agree, but there was irritation rather than warmth in his tone when he answered.

"No, Grace. I've said that I don't want you here right now. The best thing is for you to stay put and wait for me to come back."

"But that could be over a week away, longer no doubt. Surely the best thing is for me to come home to be with you. I don't like to think of you alone." She felt slighted, as if he viewed her presence as a hindrance rather than a support.

"I'm not alone, Grace. I've told you." He spoke deliberately as if attempting to retain his patience. "Leo's with me and he's seeing to so much. And then there's the solicitor, of course. We have to go and see him. There's already a meeting sorted for early next week. So you see there's really no need for you to be here. Absolutely nothing for you to do."

Across the hall, out of the glass doors onto the terrace, Grace could just see Joan Whitford, absorbed still by the map of the island, making notes on a pad, referring every now and again to the guidebook. She thought of Archie, ringing from some nondescript, utilitarian room at the hotel chain where he was staying. Plastic pots of UHT milk on a cheap plastic tray, hard pillows, cracked bathroom tiles.

"Archie, I just feel wrong being here without you. We were intending to go home in a week or so, anyway. We knew we had to go back to sort things whatever our plans were for… well, whatever we decided about the future."

It seemed insensitive now to mention the idea about moving to the island when he had just suffered the shock and loss of his mother. Archie, however, finally seemed placated.

"It's so good to hear your voice, Grace. And I… I miss you. I… of course I do. But stay put, stay on the island and wait for me there. That's really what I want you to do right now. You do understand, don't you? You will be helping me so much by doing just that."

Grace mumbled some sort of agreement.

"And you'll ring again if you change your mind, won't you? And let me know when you'll be arriving back here on the island, the exact day when I can expect you?"

There was sudden static on the line then a gabble of a foreign language, two voices, as if a line had crossed and entangled with theirs for a moment. When she heard Archie again, it was as if midway through a sentence that she had only half-heard. But when she asked him to repeat it, he had gone and the line was vacant, absent of his voice.

# 10

Hester stares at the menu in the Italian restaurant in Walton Street, trying to summon up an appetite. Out of the corner of her eye, she sees Kenneth Harper looking at her across the red tablecloth, too presumptuously for comfort; a hunter assuming he can reel in his prey. She cannot imagine now why she accepted this invitation. What possessed her to think she would find an evening with this appalling man, scarlet shirt straining severely over his indulged stomach, his nose damp, his eyebrows too bushy, an agreeable notion? In honest truth, of course, she has been flattered by the attention. It has been a long time since she has been the object of another's pursuit and although she admits to finding the pursuer faintly repellent, his moral viewpoint suspect, she has succumbed. At least to this dinner in Walton Street, to a shared bottle of Valpolicella and trite talk about the seasons, the students. Bicycle theft and house prices and tourist coaches cluttering St Giles. She intends to make her way home alone after the syllabub or, in fact, skip straight along following the risotto di mare she's now ordering. Kenneth Harper is an unattractive bore, but since he's a bore who's made a lot of money in property development and has a side-line as a sleeping partner in a second-hand car business somewhere near Northampton, he assumes he's God's gift. To women in general and, in particular, to those of Hester's age and standing. After all, she has to admit to being somewhere north of sixty and has spent a good deal of the past three decades, through little fault of her own, as, effectively, a single woman. She can understand why the Kenneth Harpers of the world would see her as fair game. She takes too large a gulp of her red wine and coughs extravagantly. He looks momentarily embarrassed as if she has committed some social faux pas that risks lowering his reputation in this restaurant. "Let me take you to my new restaurant find," he'd said to her, "the Italian place in Walton Street that everyone's talking about. But don't worry, I can always get a table even at the last minute. Luigi's the Chef – you know Luigi?"

Of course Hester does not know Luigi. Of course she has no idea that everyone is talking about a new Oxford restaurant that no doubt charges exorbitantly inflated prices for a simple plate of pasta that could be acquired for half the price and far less pretence at the small neighbourhood family-run establishment in Summertown. Still, she has foolishly accepted this dinner invitation and knows she must endure, graciously, to the bitter end.

"So," Kenneth Harper says, offering her a bread stick. The signet ring on his small finger digs into his skin, causing whorls of flesh to spread either side. "Tell me about your divorce. Did it cost an arm and a leg? They all do these days. Mind you, I took care to steer clear of Oxford lawyers, found myself a sharp chap from Leytonstone. Really knew how to play with the figures, dodging and diving with evidence of the investments and so forth. Otherwise, Margaret and her camp would have had a field day. Margaret's my ex, by the way," he added unnecessarily.

"I'm not," Hester says. "Divorced, that is."

Kenneth Harper refills her glass.

"Not playing away from home, surely! Although there's a lot of that about in Oxford and the Cotswolds, so they tell me.

Wife-swapping too, evidently. It's all the rage in some areas, quite an epidemic."

The waiter places a dish of calamari in front of him. The man eats with greed, thinks Hester, watching him shovelling in the small rubbery fish without a pause. A trickle of something oily runs down his chin and drops onto his hectically patterned tie.

"No," she says, "I am neither a divorced woman nor a philandering wife." She knows she sounds pompous, but she is beginning to cultivate and enjoy her performance. "Nor, in fact, in case the possibility had not occurred to you, a grieving widow. My husband and I have simply chosen to… live apart. To pursue our own chosen paths, as it were. We were anxious not to inhibit the other's ambitions."

Kenneth Harper breaks off a piece of bread, wipes it liberally around his garlicky plate and eats it. She hopes he will not ask her how long she and Fergus have lived in this state of agreeable separation that she has claimed. She enjoys elaborating, feigning facts a little, but she is loath to lie outright.

"So let me get this straight," Kenneth Harper says. "The two of you live apart, separate lives and all that and the marriage bit is just a label left from some event in the dim and distant past. It sounds to me as if you just haven't got around to getting divorced, dealing with the paperwork and so forth. Would you like the name of my man in Leytonstone? He'd sort you out in no time."

Hester looks down at her mozzarella and avocado salad. She has lost all appetite. She thinks of her silent flat, her quietly welcoming sitting room, the Elgar recording – *Serenade for Strings* – she was playing before she left to meet this dreadful man. She thinks of the postcard that arrived from Grace that morning, propped up now on the Victorian pine dresser in the kitchen. She sounded deliriously happy, extolling the beauties of the island, the climate, the sea. And she sees Fergus' face again, staring out incongruously from the television screen the night before. *Green Shoots,* the first of a four-part series, featuring, curiously, her estranged husband. She pulls her chair back from the table, causing it to screech on the ceramic-tiled floor.

"I am so sorry," she says to Kenneth Harper, interrupting his account of limiting his former wife's access to his pension, "but this has all been something of a mistake. My error entirely in accepting your invitation. I should have known better. We are desperately unsuited even to spending two hours in each other's company." And she stands up, takes her jacket from the back of her chair, turns and heads for the door, not even bothering to take note of the amazed, disgruntled face of Kenneth Harper. She is aware of other mildly interested diners turning to look, first at her figure disappearing swiftly through the glass restaurant door, then back to stare at her abandoned companion. In a moment, he swaps his plate, now cleared of calamari, for her untouched dish of mozzarella and avocado salad and swiftly starts to wade in.

Back home she pours herself a glass of wine, slips Elgar out of his sleeve and turns up the volume on the record player. It is not entirely dark, the light of the long June evening clinging still in the sky as she sits down at her table in the window to write.

*North Oxford – June 1988*
*My dear Fergus,*
*Congratulations! I have to say that it feels extraordinary to be the one writing to you, dear man, to comment on your performance. All right, so it's been more than a few years since the proverbial boot was on the other foot and I was in a position to be on the receiving end of praise for my thespian efforts. Well over twenty years, in fact, when I got a walk-on at the Playhouse here during a Sheridan season.*

*But Fergus, back to you.*

*And the screening of your episode in this earnest little series, Green Shoots or Green Routes or some such title. I have to give it to you; you came over well. It was a natural and sincere performance and you had quite a presence. (You always had a presence, of course.) In fact, you almost convinced me that living halfway up a hill in deepest Wales with only cold running water and a most rudimentary method of heating hearth and home was a viable proposition. You have a good face for telly, Fergus. It's that strong jawline of yours and the broad shoulders. And you're lean to the point of emaciation, which the screen flatters. If ever I were fortunate enough to be offered your opportunity of a prime-time slot on national television, I'd have to lose at least ten pounds. Even though I'm only an ounce or two over nine stone, the camera does love unfairly piling on the spare tyres. However, Fergus, I would advise you not to lose any more weight at our age we can't afford to be too thin, you know.*

*But, grudgingly, I have to admit that I admire you. I admire your skills, your resilience, your ability to dig potatoes out of the hardened ground, bake your own bread, chivvy your hens into laying perfect brown eggs and darn your own woollen socks. I had no idea anyone still darned. I am sure it's an art long lost from north Oxford. And you got good reviews, did you know? The national press loved the programme, seem to want more from this lone wolf of the Welsh hills. Next week they're moving on to some hermit in the Hebrides, a woman crofter or some such, which doesn't have the romantic allure that Fergus Barnes managed to conjure. And you did, you know, effortlessly, unconsciously, that slightly bewildered, enigmatic half-smile of yours, your spare frame, no doubt capturing the hearts of middle England's late middle-aged women. For in spite of your self-sufficient and solitary pose, you looked so in need of consolation, protection even.*

*There, I've said it, Fergus.*

*I've admitted that even now, after all these years of undeserved abandonment, my emotional equilibrium can still be affected by you. You can still manage to touch my foolish heart, the vacuum of need that seems to lurk there, unbidden. Goodness, I really shouldn't have written this letter so clearly under the influence of a couple of large glasses of decent Italian red. Perhaps I'll reread it in the morning and dispatch it to the bin along with the teabags and potato peelings.*

*I do worry about you in the cold. And you did look, so very cold a lot of the time. In spite of the trusty layers of holey pullovers and the aforementioned well-darned thick socks. An electric blanket would do such wonders on those bleak, frostbitten nights and early mornings. Do let me know if I can send you anything, Fergus, to ward against those incessant winds and gales. In spite of everything I don't want to see you suffer and perhaps a couple of Shetland sweaters and a padded anorak wouldn't go amiss. After all, neither of us is getting any younger and it does well to keep flesh and bones insulated against the ravages of climate.*

*Well, no doubt I'll be catching you profiled in some smart Sunday magazine or even interviewed for Radio 4. You never know, Fergus, you could become the hot media property of the late 80s, the relevant Man of the Moment, now we appear to be regretting the decadence and self-indulgences of the decade. No more popping of champagne corks and orders of gravlax in city wine bars; instead, dandelion and burdock and a decent dish of kippers.*

*I remain, as always,*

*Ever yours*

*Hester*

Elgar has finished his serenade, Hester her wine. Grace should be back from her holiday by now, she thinks. That postcard probably took weeks to wend its way across various seas and although she had been uncertain about the date of their return before they left, she's probably already home, settling back into her chosen life at Jacob's Bottom. Although, of course, Hester thinks, where life is concerned, choice is a rather misleading term. There are, after all, only a very limited number of options thrust right under one's nose, strewn in one's path. Most women match up with men they conveniently meet at the tennis club. Or succumb to the sweet chap who chats over the photocopier in the office or on the station platform every night, waiting for the crowded commuter train home. It's all very pragmatic, really. Most simply settle for what is readily and easily available and make a go of it for good or ill. She sits back in her chair, stares out of the window at the narrow strip of front garden and at the road beyond.

"Most do," she says aloud. "But not me. And not Grace either, I suspect. For whatever I may think of my son-in-law, Archie, whatever ambiguous feelings I may harbour about the man, it's clear that Grace loves him unconditionally and has surrendered willingly to that. Like me for Fergus. And before him, of course, to poor, darling Alec." Hester glances back at her letter, at the four sheets of blue writing paper sitting on the table, covered in her strong cursive hand. *I am a hopeless case*, she thinks, *I am my own worst enemy in the stakes of love and the affairs of the heart. I have squandered the best part of thirty-odd years thinking sentimentally about Fergus. I could have had others. God knows, there were chances; several sensible chances that I let pass me by. And why? I hardly knew then and can only suspect now that it was in the excessively unlikely belief that, sooner or later, Fergus would steer his sailing ship home to resume his conjugal rights, shove his slippers back under the bed and once more hang his red muffler from a hook in the hall. And was that really what I wanted? Would I have taken him back, regarded his prolonged abandonment as some sort of mild aberration to be treated with Christian forgiveness or female stoicism? Like some medieval paragon of wifely virtue, poor old patient Griselda enduring appalling suffering to satisfy her deathly dull clerk of a husband.*

Hester shoves the sheets of writing paper in an envelope, hastily addresses it and walks out into the late evening to post the letter in the box at the corner of the Banbury Road. In a week or so she's heading for Cornwall, to Fowey, where she's house-sitting for a couple of opera singers off for a season at Glyndebourne. Perhaps she'll call in on Grace and Archie on the way, grab a night's stay and hear all about the holiday. Admire the photographs, the suntans, note the increased sense of well-being that the two of them will no doubt have acquired.

But the next morning, when Hester picks up the phone and rings the house at Jacob's Bottom, the line is dead. Unobtainable. Out of order. She stands for some moments listening pointlessly to the long piercing, continuous sound then redials, finds the operator to report a fault. Only to be told that there is, in fact, no fault on that particular number at all.

The line has, simply, been disconnected.

# 11

On Thursday morning, as Grace sat on the terrace drinking coffee, the hotel manager brought her a message.

"Mr Copeland, he is to arrive here tomorrow. On the ferry. Friday morning. The girl, Rania, she took the phone message just now and he said to tell you. But if you need to speak to him we could perhaps reach him again for you and…"

"No, that's all right," Grace said and felt flooded with a sense of relief as if she had spent the past nine days suspended, in anticipation of such news. "I don't need to speak to him. Thank you so much. You must have been wondering… it's been – well, over a week now since my husband was called home and…"

The manager waved his hand as if to indicate that such detail was irrelevant. He hovered, however, looking a little awkward. Grace put down her cup.

"You have stayed longer than you planned," he said, "than the booking that was first made from England for your room. And, of course, it has been a pleasure to accommodate you and your husband, but… well, the season, it is now June and we have bookings soon for the whole summer."

"Of course," Grace said, "I am so sorry. You have been very kind to let us extend our stay. I am sure that as soon as Archie… as soon as my husband arrives we'll make other plans."

"And the bill… he will settle it when he comes tomorrow?"

The manager was young, younger than Grace, she thought, and seemed embarrassed by the conversation as if it were a confrontation that he would rather not be having.

"Let me pay you now," Grace said, standing up and reaching for her bag. The credit card that Archie had handed to her the morning he had left had been tucked into a side pocket since. "If you can prepare an invoice for me, please, for all our costs so far?"

The manager smiled.

"Not so much hurry," he said, "perhaps this evening? I can give it to you this evening. That would be most kind."

Grace found Joan Whitford choosing postcards at the stand in Reception and gave her the news. She was due to leave herself the next day, return to Athens to pick up her tour group and fly to Paris for a final weekend before returning to California. The older woman took Grace's hand, squeezed it warmly in hers.

"I am so pleased I won't be leaving you here alone and uncertain," she said. "I have a little shopping to do today, but we must meet this evening for dinner. There's a place at the end of the harbour I would like to try before I go. It's supposed to serve the best fish on the island or so the guidebooks say. You will join me, won't you?"

The day was humid, unusually so as there was generally a light breeze blowing over the island to dissipate the heat. By lunchtime the sky was opaque and the air oppressive. The mountains were so shrouded with dense cloud that it was as if they had disappeared entirely, sucked into oblivion. It seemed any moment as if it would rain, but the temperature kept rising through the day and the streets remained dry. Showering at six o'clock, Grace lay in the relative cool of the shuttered room until just before seven when she put on a thin ankle-length cotton dress and went downstairs. The manager handed her a detailed invoice of the charges that had built up during their stay and, giving it a cursory glance, Grace gave him Archie's credit card and waited while he made the standard phone call to check for verification. A scrawny cat sauntered up the hotel steps and into the entrance hall, only to be chased out by a barman with a tray of drinks on his way to the terrace. An elderly couple, the man holding heavily to the arm of his wife, slender and elegant, silver hair upswept to reveal a long neck, emerged from the lift and smiled at her as they passed. Grace waited. She chased an ant across the glass top of the reception desk with her thumb. The manager coughed. She looked up.

"I am so sorry," he said, looking not at her, but at the small card that he held in the palm of his hand. "But there is… a mistake. No, a problem. It seems that it is not acceptable. This card… perhaps it is the wrong one? Perhaps you have another? I am afraid that I cannot take payment from this. It is… the bank will not allow it."

Grace said, "That can't be right. There must be an error with the bank. Something wrong. I don't understand how this could happen." She pushed her hand through her hair, felt it matt and damp with the humidity of the day. "Could you try again?"

The manager placed the credit card down on the glass top, pushed it slowly across to her.

"I am sorry," he said again. "Like you, I thought some error at first. So I tried a second time. But no. The account, it is without credit."

Grace felt someone touch her shoulder. Joan Whitford stood at her side, a faint smell of citrus eau-de-Cologne, her powdered face.

"Can I help? Please, let me," and she started to search in her large shoulder bag before Grace began to protest. The manager stepped back, held up his hand as if he wanted to dispel the awkwardness of the moment.

"No, please. Mrs Copeland, your husband, he arrives with us tomorrow. So perhaps then..."

"Yes, of course," Grace said, "Archie will sort things. Really, it's just a muddle. I am sure he will be able to ring the bank and everything will be – well, arranged."

"If you're sure," Joan said, taking her arm and pulling her away from the desk. "But really, if you need a loan, Grace, I am only too happy to help out. We all have times when finances can be an embarrassment. Believe me, I've had moments when I've wanted to wash the dishes to pay for my dinner!"

"It's so kind of you," Grace said, "but really, I couldn't ask such a thing of someone I hardly know."

Joan smiled, shrugged and led the way down the steps of the hotel and out into the steaming evening.

"It's just a commodity, money, that's how I think of it. Either you have it or you don't. And at the moment, I don't have to worry about it too much. I have a little surplus. Like having too much food in the refrigerator."

They walked down to the harbour and along to the old port. Within ten minutes of settling at the taverna, there was a crack of thunder and rain began to fall so rapidly and densely that even their table, nestled under a large awning, received a drenching. The waiter rapidly reseated them, brought them a fresh basket of bread, another jug of wine. Grace let Joan order fish for the two of them, distracted still by the experience at the hotel. It was irrational to feel anxious; the refusal of the credit card was no doubt an administrative error, a confusion that Archie would sort out instantly and calmly on his arrival. But she could not shake off the sense that there was something wrong. The fish arrived and Grace tried to eat, slipping the white flesh from the bone, but her appetite was gone. Joan appeared not to notice.

"I would like to keep in touch with you, Grace," she said, piling mixed salad from a bowl onto a side plate, "I know that's what people always say when they meet on holiday, then years later discover a scrawled address on a scrap of white napkin tucked into the pocket of a suitcase and can't remember why it's there. But I do mean it. I would like to know what you are doing. From time to time, that is."

Grace drank some wine and tried to return to her plate of food. The storm had stilled as swiftly as it had arrived, the torrent of rain thinned to a few drops and already the air was clearer, lighter, after the heavy humidity of the day.

"I am not entirely sure where we'll be living," she said, "I could give our address at Jacob's Bottom, but we might only be there for a short time. Everything is… well, I suppose you could say we're in a state of flux at the moment." She thought of Archie talking enthusiastically only ten days ago about moving to the island. Already, the conversation seemed remote, as if she had dreamt it or conjured it out of some wishful state of mind. Joan Whitford reached into her large bag and rummaged for a notebook and pencil.

"Once you're settled anywhere," she said, handing Grace a sheet of paper on which she'd written her address in northern California, "just drop me a card. And if you're ever in the neighbourhood as we Americans like to say, there's always bed for you and a good warm welcome. You never know where life is going to take you in the next decade or so, Grace, so don't rule it out."

"I won't," Grace said, slipping the piece of paper into her bag. She glanced at her watch, thought of Archie on the mainland by now, possibly even at the port for the overnight ferry to Kronos. She ate more fish, some salad. They finished the half litre of wine. Joan insisted on paying the bill.

"Really, it's nothing," she said, "a few notes which will be foreign and worthless to me once I fly out of the country in a couple of days. I'm planning on my next trip being a little closer to home in the fall, some friends who live in Vermont and a cousin in Maine, perhaps. That's some coastline, you know."

They walked back along the harbour towards the hotel. The storm was now entirely spent, the sky clear and star-studded once more. Lights from the string of tavernas along the waterfront spilled over the deep dark water.

"Thank you for keeping me company this past week or two," Grace said as they reached the hotel. "It's made it a lot easier for me. I still don't quite understand why Archie didn't want me with him for the funeral, but I am sure he had his reasons."

"People have ways of dealing with these things, Grace. Don't forget that. Grief, loss, those rites of passage we all have to go through test us differently. Perhaps your husband simply found it easier alone. I wouldn't think too much about it, if I were you."

"No," Grace said, "you're right. It's not as if his mother even knew me. He probably found it easier simply to be with his brother, with Leo."

She slept sporadically and woke before the alarm. Leaving the hotel unnecessarily early, dawn only just broken, she glimpsed Joan Whitford in the queue of foot passengers waiting close to the embarkation point, ready to take the return ferry to the mainland. She sat at the café where she and Archie had waited for his departure nearly a fortnight before, ordered tea that she failed to drink. As soon as the large vessel docked she was on her feet, joining the group awaiting the stream of passengers who soon began to appear, looking for a face to greet them, a taxi to transport them to a home or village. A coach pulled into the port, then another, and a third, all parking in a symmetrical line and blocking Grace's view for a few moments so that she worried she had missed Archie, that he might have headed straight for their hotel thinking it too early in the morning for her to be there to meet him. But she dodged between the large buses and saw that passengers were still disembarking although the process was slower now and more intermittent. Two or three minutes would go by without a figure appearing and then suddenly a small surge of half a dozen. Her attention was caught suddenly by a screech of brakes behind her and she turned to see two cars in a near collision, their drivers irate, gesticulating and exchanging a torrent of rapid conversation. When she turned back to the straggle of passengers, now a thin trickle of one or two at a time, she saw a tall shape that was vaguely familiar, not Archie certainly, yet nevertheless a man whose bearing she recognised. She stood motionless, watching the man advancing, a backpack hitched on one shoulder. She watched the way he scanned the remaining few taxis, the last of the coaches to leave, as if only half expectant of a face he knew. Then he saw Grace. Quickening his pace, he strode towards her and was at her side in a moment.

"Grace," he said, "Grace, I thought you might be here. I'm so sorry about all this."

Archie's younger brother, Leo, touched her shoulder, leant down and kissed her briefly on one cheek. "But the truth is, I have absolutely no idea where Archie is."

***

Grace sits on the hotel terrace, watching two very young boys negotiate four steep steps down to the garden. They hold hands, which appears to make their attempt more precarious, each capable of throwing the other off balance, but eventually they reach the bottom step and jump the final hurdle. She has no idea how long she has been sitting here. People have come and gone, ordered breakfast, coffee, met, departed and still she resists the thought of moving, of going upstairs to her room and confronting some sort of idea of a plan. If she stays here, she tells herself, there is some absurd possibility of finding out that this has all been an appalling practical joke. If she resists Leo's encouragement to go and pack, to pull herself together sufficiently to make arrangements for the journey home, she imagines that Archie will suddenly appear, slip through the garden entrance or the main doors of the hotel, and settle down in the chair beside her. She remembers now saying to Leo, over and over again, "What do you mean, you don't know where Archie is?" and the more Leo had shrugged and repeated, "I've told you, Grace, I have absolutely no idea," the more frustrated she became at the inadequacy of his answer. There are no available rooms for him at the hotel so he has gone into Kronos Town to find somewhere to stay for a couple of nights to give Grace, as he puts it, "time to come to terms with things as they are". "I'm here to help," he has said to her more than once, sensing, no doubt, an unfair hostility from her. And he has left her, out on the hotel terrace, signalling to the waiter to bring her breakfast, which she has left, uneaten, although she has managed to drink a considerable amount of strong coffee. She looks around for something else to distract her attention now that the two small boys are climbing over the laps of their mother, their father, who attempt to settle them with a snack and a drink. But eventually she gives in, lets the information that she has been stalling, the facts and account that Leo has delivered to her, flood her mind, gradually sorting it chronologically, so that she can begin to absorb it the way she might the text of a bewildering, confusing narrative.

They had been due at the solicitor's office, Jervis and Jervis, in Norwich on Tuesday morning at ten o'clock. The previous day, their mother's funeral had been brief, perfunctory. "A couple of elderly neighbours from her old house, the matron from the nursing home and us," Leo had said bleakly. Afterwards, the two brothers had shared a couple of drinks, a lunch of sorts at a nearby pub and made arrangements for meeting the following day. "Then I went back to my friend's house in Lowestoft, Archie to his hotel. He said he wanted to be on his own, Grace, which sounded reasonable."

Archie failed to arrive for the solicitor's meeting.

"After about half an hour, we went ahead," Leo had told her. "No point in wasting the meeting, you know what these legal fellows charge. Besides, it was all to be quite straightforward, reading the will, talking about the few assets, sorting out probate, that sort of thing. Or so I thought." The solicitor had assumed Leo knew. Mr Jervis had been very surprised that his older brother had not told him about the constant releasing of equity from their mother's home; the countless re-mortgaging arrangements; the sale of the house earlier that year which had realised only sufficient capital to meet accruing interest. Even their mother's few modest shares, inherited from her husband, a number of premium bonds, small deposits in a post office saving scheme, were gone. Of course, wielding Power of Attorney, Archie had been within his rights. There was no question of illegality in his actions or in his failure to inform Leo. "Nevertheless," Mr Jervis had added quietly, calling his secretary to bring in coffee. "Nevertheless."

Grace gives in to the waiter's concern and orders a bottle of water. She pours herself a glass and drinks it straight down, pours a second and swallows that. So far she is able to follow Leo's related account, justify, even, Archie's actions. Leo is always away. There were expenses, care home fees, no doubt other factors driving Archie to siphon money, exploit assets.

She feels it is just possible to mitigate his conduct at this point in the story although has had to admit that she, too, has been entirely unaware of it. Then, of course, Leo went on in his account, pushed further in an attempt to present the full facts before Grace. The full state of affairs.

When Leo had spent a day failing to find Archie in Norwich, he had gone back to stay with his friend in Lowestoft, leaving early the next morning to drive down to Jacob's Bottom.

The house had been empty.

He had peered through the ground floor windows onto bare rooms, noted an agent's 'To Let' sign in the front garden. "We were planning to stay here on the island," Grace had jumped at Leo on hearing this. "It's obvious what's happened, he's cleared the house and is on his way back here!" She knew her claim was lame, a weak defence with no substance that Leo did not even bother to counter. In Fletwell, he had tracked down the agent's office. Yes, the manager had admitted, the house at Jacob's Bottom had become untenanted at short notice. Mr Copeland had rung on Monday afternoon to cancel the agreement and to say that he had instructed a storage company to empty the house immediately. No, there was no forwarding address, but there was the matter of two months' unpaid rent, cheques that the bank had returned and perhaps Mr Copeland's brother… Leo had dismissed Grace's concern. "Money," he had said, "bills, debts, don't worry, Grace, I can sort out anything outstanding for the time being." Grace had been pulled back to the house. "Empty? Entirely empty? Of all the furniture? All our things, our possessions?" And Leo had said somewhat indifferently, "I shouldn't worry, they're just objects, after all. Just things." And she had said, "No, of course, you're right. They're all of no consequence." But even so, she had thought of specific books, a particular picture, a certain dress, a pair of shoes, as reflections and confirmation of herself and the knowledge of their sudden disappearance was disorientating. Grace thinks suddenly of Joan Whitford. She is overwhelmingly gratified that she is no longer here, that there is no need to come up with some sort of explanation for Archie's failure to arrive, to lie, in fact, as she knows she would have done. For what else was there to do? The truth was hardly palatable to herself, let alone a virtual stranger. "My husband appears to have left me, simply walked off with no trace. Oh, and by the way, there seems to be a problem with money too. Debts. Deception, you could say, where finances are concerned. You'll remember the problem with the credit card, of course. Well, it seems that was just the tip of the iceberg, a timely warning of more, so much more, to come." Grace pours the last of the bottle of water into her glass, swallows it too swiftly and starts to cough. And for the first time since Leo's arrival she finds her throat clogged, the possibility of tears too close to risk, sitting visibly exposed on the hotel terrace. She gets up, turns and goes inside, unintentionally catching the eye of the receptionist.

"Mrs Copeland," he says and smiles. "It is all settled. All sorted out. Mr Leo Copeland has paid the bill. I am so sorry for troubling you yesterday. All is now well."

Upstairs in her room she feels a tight band of pain fasten around her head as if pincers have been applied and she lies down on the bed, feeling suddenly inordinately tired as if she has not slept for days. Yet sleep is impossible, she knows. Her mind hovers between extremes; one moment, her natural instinct is to rationalise events, grasp confidently at tissue-thin explanations for Archie's behaviour; the next, she is thwarted, frail, childlike in her sense of abandonment. She stares up at the ceiling, at tiny cracks in the white paint running in directions like tributaries of a river and she concentrates on tracing one to its source. Something nudges. There is some germ of familiarity in what Leo has told her that is not entirely foreign or surprising as if Leo has simply dredged up to the surface a confirmation of some latent knowledge she has long suppressed. As if she has chosen, not so much to overlook evidence, as to fail to interpret given signs. She shuts her eyes, allows uncontrollable tears to drench her face, soak into the white pillowcase, matt her unruly hair.

Leo had found a place to stay in a narrow side street back from the harbour.

"Your room's paid for until Monday so that will give you enough time to make plans," he said, sitting across from her at one of the waterside tavernas. "The hire car's returned, hotel bill settled so that's all sorted. I'll take care of some travel arrangements for you, the ferry and flight back to England, best if you fly back with me, really. And then I can help you with whatever you might need the other end, back in London."

"That's kind," Grace said, "I really am very grateful, Leo. But I can't let you do all this." Even as she said the words she knew her objection was invalid. She had only a handful of notes in her purse, a few travellers' cheques to cash, but insufficient to pay the large bill and support her beyond a few economical days. She despised her sense of powerlessness. She was angry at not protecting herself from such exposure yet at the same time she knew she had willingly surrendered her autonomy to Archie's care. "You'll think I'm foolish," she said, dredging up a shred of dwindling resilience. "But I still feel it's possible that there's been some mistake. An enormous muddle. Not about the money and the house and everything, of course. But about Archie simply disappearing. He might still just… well, contact me. Or just arrive. I mean… we can't be sure of anything."

Leo said nothing, ordered wine from the waiter. In silence, they drank for some minutes and Grace sensed his exasperation with her. He rapidly ate from a bowl of olives, threw stones accurately into the sea.

"You need to make plans, Grace," Leo eventually said again. "Do you have anyone you can stay with back in England? Obviously, now Jacob's Bottom has gone, you'll be…"

"Homeless. Destitute. On the streets. Yes, Leo, I understand that." She resented his tone, paternal, patronising, although she suspected he was trying to be kind.

"I'm just saying… look, Grace, this is difficult for me too. Archie's my brother so naturally I feel a degree of responsibility for you."

"That's quite unnecessary," Grace said, "and I will pay you back. I am, of course, very grateful for your help right now, Leo, but it's just a loan. As soon as I can…"

Leo gestured with his hand as if the sums involved were too insignificant to consider. A waiter arrived bringing a basket of bread, a menu. Leo ordered swiftly without consulting her then pulled off a chunk of bread and placed it on her plate.

"Eat," he said.

She shook her head, but let him refill her glass.

"Let's go back to the last time you saw Archie," she said. "How did he seem?"

"At that dreadful pub near the crematorium? Quiet. Withdrawn. A bit miserable if I'm honest, but we'd just been to our mother's funeral, Grace. His behaviour seemed… well, normal given the circumstances, I suppose."

"And he didn't even hint about money problems? I mean, why didn't he tell you then about selling your mother's house?"

Leo shrugged, leant back in his chair and stared out at the sea.

"I imagine he was still in some sort of denial about the whole thing. He must have realised that, once that bit of information came out, there would inevitably be an unstacking of all the bricks, all the lies and deceptions would come out."

"So there's more?" Grace declared too loudly so that a woman at the next table looked over at them. Leo turned back, stared at her as if assessing how much he should tell. "I need to know everything."

"It's more of the same, Grace. Mostly financial. I suspect Archie was running several credit cards to their limits. The house in Greenwich has gone too, of course, sometime last winter. Again, any profits were soaked up by mortgage arrears."

"But I just don't understand. Why was there such need for so much money? Why didn't he tell me things were difficult? You said this morning that borrowing against your mother's house has been going on for years, before I even met him."

"I don't really have any answers, Grace. I'm not sure if I even know my brother particularly well. We've never been that close. All I can say is that Archie always seemed to live very comfortably. Considering he earned his living as a lecturer, that is. I mean his salary would have been adequate, but hardly sufficient to fund any sort of sophisticated city lifestyle. And when I think back, he's probably been living beyond his means for years. You know, nothing wildly ostentatious, but just constant outgoings in excess of income. He always used to insist on taking me to the smartest, most talked about new restaurants when I happened to be home, for example. As if he felt a need to impress me. And then there was his choice of friends, the ones he invited round to the Greenwich house, at least. Clearly all well-heeled types with ludicrously inflated salaries and no doubt private family incomes as well. I often used to think he'd quite consciously constructed some sort of image for himself that he tried to live up to – you know the sort of thing, the quietly cultured and affluent man of the 80s, seen in the right places, doing the right things. And I couldn't ever quite work out, when I bothered to give it much thought, how he was funding it."

"Didn't you ever ask him about it? Confront him?" Grace asked.

"Did you?"

The waiter arrived, unloaded several small dishes from a heavy tray. Leo began to eat, Grace crumbled a piece of bread between her fingers.

"Archie always gave the impression that financially there was some sort of cushion. Always, from the beginning, I got the idea that there was more money than just his salary. I expect you think I'm very foolish for not asking more."

"Not really," Leo said, "you're probably an honest person, Grace, who doesn't try to see what isn't obviously there. And even if you had pressed for answers, there's no reason to believe he would have told you the truth."

"Even so. I've been too complacent. Too… acquiescent."

"There was that business with the college, of course, the Aldgate place. Clearly he was sacked from there. Well, asked to leave, shall we say?"

Grace said nothing. Even a defence against Leo's claim seemed vacuous. Again, she had the sense that random, abstract strands from the past were beginning to coalesce into a discernible pattern. It had been convenient to think of Archie's somewhat clandestine and spontaneous actions as reflections of his personality; now she saw them as pragmatic steps to deceive and maintain an illusion. For a moment, she despised him. Then she let herself think of the idea of losing him, considering the future as a place where she would have to move on without him and she was flooded with unhappiness. Leo was talking about some phone calls he had made just before leaving England. "Hospitals," he said, hesitantly. "I checked with hospitals near Fletwell and in Norwich. Just in case…" he said. Grace did not bother to tell him that she had spent a couple of hours that afternoon making similar calls, connections arranged by the receptionist at the Andromache. And that she had also already rung the London friends, Celia and Cyril and Monica and Bernard, no doubt causing them to gossip endlessly amongst themselves, just in case they had seen him or offered him a bed for the night. She had learnt nothing.

"Where do you think he is, Leo? What do you think has happened to him? I'd like you to be honest with me. Even if you think there's someone else. Another… I need you to tell me."

Leo went on eating, emptying dishes onto his plate and pouring more wine for both of them. Grace stared out at the harbour. A pleasure boat pulled in, dispersing a cargo of day trippers still dressed in swimsuits and sunhats, clutching inflatables and snorkelling equipment. They looked out of place next to the mid-evening strollers and diners, showered and changed out of their sandy beachwear.

"There are three possibilities as I see it, Grace," Leo said eventually. "And none of them, you'll be pleased to hear, involves another woman. Archie may well have decided to take himself off somewhere. Abroad, even, if he can push enough money together. Seeking some sort of new start, leaving the past entirely behind him, in… oh, I don't know, Spain, Portugal, perhaps? That's what I would have done in his position. Or, alternatively, he's just lying low for a while, confused, getting by as best he can, and sleeping rough, probably, until he decides whether he wants to come back to you. No doubt based on whether he thinks you'd take him, of course."

"Of course I'd take him back," Grace said, "that's not even… I mean, it's not as if he's even been gone for… But what do you see as the other possibility?"

Leo looked down at his plate, avoiding her gaze.

"Well, he might have decided it was all too much for him to face. Hitting rock bottom means a hell of a climb up again, Grace. You have to concede that."

"Archie wouldn't take his own life," Grace said automatically, "I just know... At least... I think that's the least likely option."

She was unsure whether she was as convinced as she claimed or whether the idea was simply too intolerable to consider. Leo was silent. He yawned, stretched his arms above his head, muttered something about having had little sleep for two days.

"You think our marriage is over, don't you?" she went on. "You think this is all about Archie leaving me. No doubt you see his actions, his deceit, his... lying about his job at the college, all the hidden money problems, as symptoms of a breakdown between us."

"You're wrong, Grace," Leo replied, sounding now wearier than she did. "Or at least you're wrong if you think I see things as clear-cut and simple as that. I have no idea why Archie has lied to you. I don't understand why he felt he couldn't talk to me. And I have absolutely no inkling why he should feel the need to create some absurd, cost-heavy image of the ideal life for the two of you. He became a fantasist. Perhaps rather a tame, domestic one in terms of material gain for we haven't uncovered leased yachts and penthouse suites yet. But nevertheless, the man has lied to you over and over and with intention, Grace. And now he's left you. Those are the facts. It's up to you to decide how to respond to them. But I would have thought a heavy dose of disgust would be a healthy start."

He signalled for the bill. The taverna had become very busy and it was at least ten minutes before the waiter produced it. Grace found herself drawn to watching the table next to them, a large family party apparently celebrating a birthday or an anniversary and exchanging constant hugs as new members arrived to join them. Their happiness seemed almost tangible and Grace felt she wanted to reach out and immerse herself in it as if it could infect and transform her own bleakness. Leo walked her back to the Andromache.

"I'll call in tomorrow evening around six," he said, "confirm arrangements for your journey back on Monday. And if you need me before for anything at all, you can leave a message at the Eleni Rooms above the café."

"Thank you, Leo. I'm grateful for everything you're doing. And really, I'll… I'll be fine."

He looked for a moment as if he was going to embrace her, but then stepped back, awkward, as if the gesture had been checked.

Upstairs, Grace sits upright on the bed, resistant to the possibility of sleep. She goes over the evening's conversation with Leo, seeking some sort of comfort from thinking of Archie, pulling him closer to her as she sits alone. Her own loneliness is bearable if she considers Archie's state. She can only imagine how desolate and bereft he must feel, shorn of his own illusions, and although she still feels anger towards him, it is too tempered with anxiety and fear to wield much heat. She goes over the two weeks spent together on the island, thinking of the shift in his mood, a lifting of some indefinable barrier between them as if, away from home with its attendant troubles, he was invigorated again by a belief in the two of them and their love. Of course this, too, was an illusory place since accruing debts and empty bank accounts worm their way into every setting; yet it was as if he could at last see beyond his empty material dreams, his pathetic deceits and recognise the possibility and goodness of another way. Suddenly, Grace feels as if she cannot bear Archie's absence another second.

The visceral physical need of his arms around her, his skin close to hers, the familiarity and comfort of him overwhelm her so that she starts to weep, loud, unguarded sobs that shake her whole body, disturb even her own sense of propriety. She crawls under the crisp white bed sheet and burrows her head into the pillow. *This is no help at all,* she thinks to herself, *it's entirely disproportionate to events. Archie is not dead. There's really no need for me to cry like this.* But each time she tries resolutely to stop, she dissolves helplessly again as if her unhappiness needs to be spent with such tears. Eventually, she sleeps or at least dozes heavily for around four in the morning she realises that the bedside light is still on and she has not undressed, her skirt creased and twisted around her. In the bathroom she splashes water over her face, bathes her sore eyes then stares at her reflection as a memory, lurking hazily at the side of her mind since Leo's arrival, clarifies itself. *Archie told me to stay here. On Kronos. He was most insistent,* she thinks. *He kept saying that I wasn't to follow him back. That he would be the one to come back here.* She chooses to grab on to his instruction, however straw-like and sentimental it sounds.

Besides, the alternative really offers no contest.

She has no particular attachment to Fletwell and now no home there. The prospect of returning to find some sort of job and flat share in a city, London or Oxford, spending her spare hours alert only to searching crowds for a sighting of Archie, is unimaginable. If Archie wants to find her, he will come here, to Kronos. She is strengthened suddenly by the thought of staying, of trying to find a way of managing to remain on the island.

It was the following morning, dulled by sleeping only fitfully, drinking strong coffee in the hotel garden to offset her exhaustion, that she remembered her meeting in the seaside village along the coast. Back in her room she searched through her bag, her purse, half-heartedly at first, then with more urgency as she thought of the casual warmth of the woman with the young child, the directness of her approach. Eventually, she found the scrap of paper folded in the pocket of the white skirt she'd been wearing that day. 'Clea Kolomiets', she read, then a phone number with several digits. That was all. It was worth a try. Even if Clea Kolomiets was not able to help her directly, she might be able and willing to point her in a suitable direction. It was preferable to trawling through the town from one place to the next, possibly attracting attention and curiosity. Buses travelled frequently along the coast road and within the hour she found herself on one of them, heading east in the direction of the seaside village of Anixi Bay.

***

There was no need to leave him a message. Grace found Leo sitting at the Elena Café reading when she arrived there mid-afternoon. She pulled out a chair, sat down and let him order her some tea.

"I've made some arrangements," she said. "It means I won't need an air ticket home. I won't be going back with you on Monday, Leo. I am staying here on Kronos." Her voice sounded more assured than she felt although her resolution was secure.

"That's impossible," Leo said, "the hotel's only paid up until Monday morning."

She shook her head, poured pale tea into the thick white cup.

"I've found somewhere else to stay. It's all… well, in fact, I'm moving out of the hotel today. There seems no point in delaying things and really I don't feel comfortable there any longer. Besides, I've found a job." She found herself relishing the surprise on Leo's face. She reached into her bag, pulled out a postcard and handed it to him. "This is my address where I'll be staying. And working, in fact. There's a phone number too so if you hear anything at all about Archie – when you hear something – you can contact me. I'd be very grateful, Leo. Of course, I'll do everything from this end that I can, keep making phone calls, writing to anyone who might know anything. It's… well, it's still such a shock at the moment, but in time, names will occur to me, I'm sure."

Leo swallowed the remains of his glass, stared at the postcard Grace had given him.

"This is nonsense, you know," he said irritably. "I can't just leave you here to… well, not like this. Not on your own."

Grace was glad of his tone; it made it easier to resist his persuasion.

"Leaving a woman on her own?" Grace said, "I'll manage, Leo. I'm not entirely helpless, you know."

"I didn't mean that," Leo said, "but Archie would expect me to… I feel responsible for you."

"You are not," Grace said quietly. "But I do need your help back in England. There are certain organisations, I believe, who help find people and…"

"Missing Persons," Leo interrupted, "yes, of course I'll contact them. And the Salvation Army are supposed to be – they do this sort of work, I know. And naturally I'll report his disappearance to the police."

"Please."

"Not that I imagine anything much happens when an adult man disappears. Especially with… well, let's just say that the circumstances surrounding Archie going missing will seem reason enough to the relevant authorities. I'm sure debt is a very common denominator among those on their records."

Grace rushed on. She was anxious to retain a composure in front of Leo that she did not fully feel.

"I'm going to contact the college in Aldgate. Even if he did, as you think, lose his job there they might have some information on him. And if you're wrong and he simply chose to leave as he told me, well, he may very well have approached them for work and be back on their staff by now."

She had, however, no belief in such a claim; and she saw again his study at Jacob's Bottom, endlessly chaotic with scattered sheets of typed and handwritten notes and the constant sense of prevarication with his thesis. Then there was that impromptu visit to London on the day of Leo's summer visit. Now it was all so easy to see it as a formal summons, a final reckoning at his inadequacy. Leo flapped a fly away from the brim of Grace's cup.

"I'm really not happy about leaving you here, Grace," he said. "It seems a mad idea. Entirely unconsidered."

"To you, perhaps. I've given it a lot of thought."

"Although I do have to concede it's a wonderful island. Great climate, beautiful scenery. But surely you'd be better off back home among friends at a time like this."

"Friends have their own lives," Grace said simply. "I don't want to be at the edge of theirs. I need to find a way of living my own. Besides, Archie will expect to find me here. We talked about it, you see. And when he's ready, he'll..."

"Ah, Grace, you really have to shake off such a romantic notion, if only for your own sanity," Leo interrupted. "No doubt it will wear off in a few weeks and you'll finally accept that you are now on your own. And when you change your mind about leaving, want some help getting back and sorting yourself out, well, this will find me." He fished out a small notebook and pencil from a pocket, wrote on it an address in Lowestoft, added a phone number. "This is where I stay when

I'm in England, on the whole. Which isn't that much as you know. But you can always leave a message with Antoinette. She's an old friend and she'll always know how to reach me wherever I am."

He tore out the page, placed it on the table. Grace looked at it for a moment or two then placed it in her pocket to placate him. He stretched out his long arms above his head as if feeling restless and constrained by their conversation.

"I have to go," Grace said. "There's still some things to pack back at the hotel and… someone is picking me up around six."

Leo looked for a moment as if he was going to object again to her plans, but instead he reached for his wallet in his shirt pocket and pulled out a substantial wad of notes.

"Here, take this as something to tide you over," he said without counting them. "It's not a great deal, but as you're being so stubborn about staying here, it might prove useful until you find your feet." Grace started to refuse, but he was adamant.

"It's very generous of you, Leo. One day, I'm sure we'll be able to pay you back for everything. And I'm sorry if you think I am being stubborn and ungrateful. I really am very appreciative of all you've done, for coming here to tell me in the first place."

He shrugged dismissively.

"As I see it, Grace, there's no happy ending to this story and you're deluding yourself if you think there is. Even if he does come back, Archie's clearly not the man you thought you'd married. Entirely untrustworthy for a start and that's no basis for any relationship."

Grace said nothing. Any defence would sound trite and hopelessly naive. More importantly, she was unprepared to admit to Leo that undercurrents of concern, forewarnings of disquiet had been whispering to her for three years. It would serve no purpose and simply drip-feed into his assessment of their marriage. He seemed, however, to be waiting for her answer. She drained her cup; the tea was now cold.

"I love him, Leo," she said firmly, "however inadequate or foolish that may sound to you. I knew I loved him even if I felt I couldn't always reach him. It's possible, you know, to love someone without feeling entirely and utterly close on every level. And now that I understand the reason for any distance between us… well, I find myself feeling closer to him than ever before. Loving him even more."

Leo threw a few coins onto the table of the Café Elena and stood up.

"If you ever find him," he said, "you'll be able to tell him that. If he ever comes back."

"As you say, Leo, if he comes back." She moved swiftly away from him and had reached the end of the narrow street when she remembered something she had forgotten to ask. "Just one last thing, Leo, before you go. The cars. I meant to ask about the cars."

"Cars?" he looked at her blankly.

"At Jacob's Bottom," she said. "Did you see our two cars parked outside the house?"

"No," he said. "There was nothing there to connect either of you with the place any more. I've told you that, Grace."

"Yes, I know," she said. "Yes, you did. I just wanted to check, Leo. Thank you."

She walked away from him slowly, unable to suppress the idea of Archie driving away from Jacob's Bottom and heading, not into Fletwell as she had always supposed, but towards South Bay. To the beach where he always swam.

# 12

Adonis House in the village of Aghia Kallida was a fine old stone building, white-walled with wooden shutters, set a couple of hundred yards outside the village at the side of a narrow country road. The heavy front door opened onto an outer courtyard and beyond that, through an arch, was the entrance into the main house. The thick walls kept the place cool in the mounting heat of the summer. Even so, by midday in late June, the rooms were close and the garden offered little shade. The guests, occupying the four letting bedrooms, took themselves off to the coast at Anixi Bay a couple of miles down the road or set off exploring the island's rich interior soon after breakfast, rarely returning before seven o'clock in the evening. Usually, they ate dinner at the village taverna, but once a week, Clea would host a barbecue and then the guests, mostly couples, the occasional single traveller, would stay and eat and drink copious amounts of local wine together under the densely star-filled sky. Usually, Grace would be the first to leave, retreating quite exhausted to her room, falling asleep almost before she had undressed, a single sheet pulled over her on the narrow bed. The cockerel from a nearby farm usually woke her around dawn when the light was grey, the mountains pink from the reflection of the rising sun and, after a brief glimpse of the early morning from her small balcony, she would retreat to bed for another couple of hours' sleep before waking a second time to wash, dress swiftly and go down to the kitchen to help prepare breakfast.

Clea Kolomiets had come up with the proposition. Grace had taken the bus to Anixi Bay, where she had met her ten days or so before and only had to ask in the first shop she came to before being directed to Aghia Kallida, to Adonis House and to Clea. She had not seemed particularly surprised to see Grace and had immediately poured her a cold drink and sat her down in the outer courtyard while she continued to work at a table, deftly filling vine leaves with spoonfuls of rice mixture. She wanted a room, Grace said. Somewhere reasonably priced to stay for an indefinite amount of time. Clea had said nothing for a while, gone on spooning and folding and nestling neat parcels of leaves into a large earthenware dish. The young child Grace had seen when they had first met outside a shop played with sand and stones across the courtyard. Every now and again, Clea said something to him, either in English or in the local language. Eventually, just as Grace had begun to feel that she had made a mistake in coming, that her presence was awkward and unwanted, Clea had said,

"You want more than a room. You need a job, don't you? And somewhere to live. I mean really settle for a while and sort yourself out a bit."

Grace had begun to mutter something about plans changing, about her husband being called back to England unexpectedly, but Clea had stopped her abruptly.

"You can explain everything if you want. But not right now. You don't know me well enough yet and I'd prefer to have the truth when you do tell. How it actually is, Grace, not some prettified version you've invented for convenience. But you were right to come and find me. I could do with a hand here, you see, running this place for the summer. Possibly longer. We could work out something between us, I'm sure. Bed, board and enough cash to give you a bit to spend on your day off. Not that there will be an entire day off until the autumn, of course. We've hit high season already and I've a pretty full house here until late August. And that's good news since this is only our second year letting rooms. We've a few return bookings from last year so whatever it is we're doing seems to be working. And we're picking up some casual trade, people who are just drifting for a while with no planned itinerary. So things are moving in the right direction. But the plan is to build, possibly staying open for much of the year if the demand is there."

Grace had felt events were overtaking her, but the sensation was consoling. Clea's long trailing skirt, peasant blouse and ringed toes belied her efficiency and briskness of purpose. "What would I have to do?" Grace had asked. "I mean, I don't have any experience in catering or… well, hotel management. Or training for that matter."

Clea had thrown back her head and laughed, her loose pile of chestnut hair tumbling down to her shoulders and showering the courtyard paving stones with pins.

"Nor did I until a year or so ago. But I'm sure you're capable of changing sheets, washing down bathrooms and serving a breakfast of rolls and coffee to our guests. We're hardly the Savoy, Grace. People come and stay here for simple pleasures. We're the alternative to places like the Andromache where you've been staying. Come on, let me show you around. Then you can decide whether you think you'll fit in. But you will. I can tell. And I'm never wrong about people. My instinct is almost witch-like, Grace, I promise you."

By the time Grace had left, she found that she had agreed to work alongside Clea running Adonis House for the summer season. There seemed no reason not to accept. In fact, Clea's assumption that she would take the job made it easy for her to acquiesce. She had followed her into the cool interior, to the large, high-ceilinged sitting room leading from the hallway and up one of two staircases to the room that would be hers. A single bed, washbasin, wardrobe, small table and upright chair, its simplicity felt appropriate to her. The guests' rooms were on the lower ground floor with direct access to the garden. The other staircase led to three rooms where Clea and her children slept.

"I hope you're all right with kids," she had said as they had come back downstairs, "I seem to have acquired four. But they're all interesting people. And this one here's the youngest." She had tweaked the cheek of the small boy who had been balanced on her hip. "And the last, I might add or at least that's the idea. But knowing me, well, I tend to let nature take its course where procreation is concerned so there's no guarantee of that plan working. New life will find its way, it seems, and who am I to stand in its path? My oldest is almost off my hands now, of course," she went on, "or will be very shortly. That's Tara who's seventeen and then there's Venus who's almost twelve and Alara's eight next week. This little one, Mercury, is just fifteen months."

At the back of the house the garden stretched for some distance, partly cultivated, partly overgrown with dense undergrowth. There were numerous carob trees, apricot, citrus and olive trees and some beds clearly prepared for growing crops. The idea, Clea told Grace, waving her hand in the direction of the planned vegetable crops, was to become as self-sufficient as possible. She wanted goats, some chickens.

"But you can't do all this by yourself, surely," Grace had said, "or do you have other help?"

Clea wore rings on every finger so it was impossible to tell whether she was married and she had offered no such clarification. Her kind reticence to Grace's own situation had inhibited her from asking too much.

"I'm looking ahead," Clea had said, "I have plans for what I would like to establish in time. A centre for yoga, perhaps, alternative therapies, creative arts, that sort of thing, but first things first. No point in running before we're fully up and marching. You are going to help me get the bed and board side of things really established this summer, Grace. Good impressions this season will bring follow-up bookings and recommendations for next, you see. It's the best publicity and free which is always a bonus. I'm not into glossy brochures and fancy advertising, that's not what this place is about. But we have to survive, cover the rent, pay the bills and live."

Clea had picked her up from the Hotel Andromache late the following afternoon and by the evening, she had unpacked, settled her few belongings into the single wardrobe, placed her books on the small table and had gone downstairs to the garden of Adonis House to watch the sun set behind the mountains. Already, Hotel Andromache and Leo's visit seemed remote, events far removed from the necessity of the moment she now inhabited.

The routine of the days suited her. She found that she did not need to mark the passing of the weeks, separate weekdays from weekends or even be particularly aware of dates. In this way it was possible to remain detached from a clear sense of how long it had been since Archie had disappeared. She worked alongside Clea for the first few days, preparing and serving breakfast, cleaning the guest rooms and accompanying her on trips to buy bread from the baker's in the square so that she began to be familiar with the faces and smiles of the locals. Clea was obviously well known and liked, an adopted villager who was helping to bring business to the place with her small, but steady stream of visitors.

"It's low-key tourism we're after," she said as they walked down the narrow, stony lanes towards the village square.

"Enough guests to keep the local tavernas going, to spend a bit in the *kafenions* and cafes. But nothing to disturb or change the way of things here. After all, that's why people come to a place like this, to Adonis House and the village. It's not for discos and fancy international cuisine, that's for sure. But injecting a steady stream of income into the area will help to preserve it, keep the younger generation on the island rather than losing them to jobs on the mainland."

"What brought you here?" Grace asked.

"Chance," Clea said ambiguously, "like everything else that happens to me. Just chance. Like you turning up at my front door looking for somewhere to stay."

They went into the baker's and bought loaves still warm from the enormous oven, a box of pastries sticky and oozing honey and nuts. Grace wished she could join in the rapid conversation between Clea and the woman who served them and wondered how long it would take to acquire even a smattering of the language. In the small general shop they bought large ripe peaches and oranges, plums and a melon, soft white cheese and coffee beans. Back at the house Grace prepared rooms for the new visitors arriving in the early evening. She replaced the used sheets with clean crisp white linen from the large cupboard on the landing, changed towels and swept and washed the tiled floors. The work was repetitive yet strangely satisfying, she found.

She had heard nothing from Leo since his departure from Kronos. For the first few days at Adonis House, she had started each time the phone had rung, expectant of a message from him. She had even found herself harbouring the idea of Archie simply arriving as if, however foolish the notion, it was impossible entirely to squander hope. In the absence of any news, she persevered with her own attempts, however futile the gestures. She wrote letters. To police forces, to charities for the homeless, to hospitals; Jervis and Jervis, the solicitors in Norwich, Monica and Bernard, Celia and Cyril, even to Louise, Archie's former wife. Someone, after all, might have heard or seen something of Archie. His former college in Aldgate had been brusque when she had rung, spoke curtly of Archie leaving and had made it very clear that his departure was permanent.

There were scant replies to her correspondence; she had expected few.

She rang Melanie in Fletwell. It was a difficult phone call, Melanie's sympathy and shock at Archie's disappearance distressing her so that she found herself breaking down in a way that she had managed to control since arriving at Adonis House. With Clea and the children, the guests, French-speaking, Scandinavians, Dutch, a couple from Ireland, she was able to detach herself from her profound unhappiness for hours at a time for they knew nothing of her recent history and she managed to project a neutral, bland persona to get her through the working day. Melanie had nothing of comfort to offer her; there had been the chance that Archie, after all, was still in the area, renting something modest in Fletwell, trying for jobs, even. But again, Grace was confronted with an absence of news. Leo, no doubt, after some perfunctory enquiries, had headed abroad again somewhere too remote, too stricken to concern himself overly about his absent brother. He seemed to accept personal loss as inevitable, a calculable part of human experience that simply needed to be borne stoically. Grace began to accept that she would not hear from Leo again.

Hester was another matter.

She knew she had to tell her mother about events, but was consciously delaying. The day after she had moved into Adonis House, she had sent an inadequate postcard. Hester, she was aware, would not easily accept its bland message about an extended holiday and Grace felt unkind at shielding her from the truth. Yet she dreaded the outcome. She felt weary at the prospect of her mother's arrival on the island, intent on taking her home. She could imagine Hester structuring and organising for her an alternative life; a bedsit in some south Oxford suburb, a flat share in High Wycombe or Reading, a substitute for the infrastructure of her marriage that had imploded.

Only when she thought of such an alternative life did she feel close to desperation.

Day to day, she managed, carefully living in something of a constant present, refusing to look more than twenty-four hours or so ahead. Clea lent her the car so that she could go further afield, collect guests from the ferry port or bus station, undertake shopping in Kronos Town. She became a familiar face in the village and in Anixi Bay, the small seaside resort five minutes' drive away. She began to feel that she belonged to the fabric of the place, walking at the edge of the beach, drinking tea at one of the cafés, and was further convinced that she was right to have stayed, to have resisted Leo's coercion to return to England. Sometimes, she would be so entirely overwhelmed by the beauty of her surroundings, the rugged mountain backdrop, the dense green terrain of the valley, the sweep of the shore on the coastal road, that she would find herself experiencing moments of intense happiness detached from rational thought. Then, almost guiltily, she'd hitch herself once more to the truth of her situation with a consequent swift shift in her mood.

During the first couple of weeks of June, Clea's oldest three children were still in school and left early each morning to catch the bus from the square, reappearing in the early afternoon when the younger two would play with other children in the narrow streets of the village and Tara, the eldest, would go to her room to study or head down to the beach with friends. When the school year came to an end and the children were more in evidence, Grace noticed how independent and self-reliant they were. The reliably hot, fine days meant they were never confined to the house as English children would be and the intimacy of village life left them free to wander safely. Often she would come across Venus or Alara in the kitchen mid-morning, finding bread, a couple of tomatoes, some peaches, putting them in a bag and disappearing out to the courtyard or down the lane where some friends would be waiting with an old bike or two, a scooter, some balls.

"All my four have different fathers, of course," Clea said suddenly to Grace one day as they sat in the shade of the courtyard, going through bookings for the following week. Tara had just relieved her of Mercury, tucking him under one arm and taking him down to a neighbour's house. "A result of my wanderlust, I suppose, never in one place long enough to settle down. Tara was born in Nepal when I was travelling there, soon after my marriage ended." She poured them glasses of iced mint tea from the large jug that Tara had made them. "It was a good place to go to sort myself out for a year or two. Although, as it happened, I ended up staying for four. Have you been? Everyone should, you know."

Grace shook her head, feeling faintly inadequate.

"So your surname is your maiden name? And the children share it?"

"God, no!" Clea said, "Kolomiets was my married name. I was married very briefly to a brilliant Russian artist. He was a beautiful man, but entirely unpredictable. Dangerous too, in his way. Sexually, he was quite sadistic. So I left him after six months. But I kept his name. There was no chance of me going back to being little Christine Clark from Romford. I left her long behind, believe you me, when I married Andrei in Paris."

"So four years in Nepal and then where did you go?"

"Oh here and there, I forget all the details now. It's not as if we exactly had a planned itinerary, me and Tara. And you know how it can be, you arrive somewhere intending to stay only a month then you meet people, move in with them, find a job and suddenly another year's gone by. I do remember celebrating Tara's fifth birthday in New Mexico. But it was time for us to come back by then. There was a pull, you see, I distinctly knew we were supposed to be in Europe."

"Not Romford, I presume?"

"Never Romford," Clea said. "No, it was Rome, at first. I'd met someone briefly in New York where Tara and I had spent a few cold months staying with friends while I got some money together. Luca was a singer in one of the bars where I worked. A singer in the evenings, anyway. I was never too clear what he did during the day. Anyway, we needed to leave – New York was not a good place for us."

"So you went to Rome. You and Tara moved to Italy?"

"With Luca, yes. It's an extraordinary city, Grace. But extremely hectic. Frenetic all the time. Luca's family owned a hotel at the bottom of the Spanish Steps so we always had a roof over our heads. Quite a palatial roof, in fact. It was one of those luxury places with high ceilings and marble staircases. I picked up some Italian while we were there and Tara too, of course. Although she's forgotten it all now or so she claims. And I got to know the insides of running a business, picked up some idea of the hotel trade, in fact. It's proved useful. Then Venus came along, of course."

"Venus is Luca's son?"

Clea nodded. "But we left when he was about six months old. Rome is not the sort of place you want to bring up a child. And Luca needed to be free of us. He was a remarkably talented singer, you know, and I didn't want to feel responsible for stifling his ambition. He got himself an agent, wanted to go to Milan and then onto London for auditions. It was time we parted." She turned to the file sitting on the table that held the bookings and confirmations for the guest rooms, picked up a pen. "We've a Danish couple arriving Sunday and an English woman on Tuesday so there's a bit of availability unless we can pick up some passing trade. I really don't want spare capacity at this point in the season so it's important to put the word about when you're in the village or down at the bay, Grace."

Grace wanted to pull Clea back to her account before she moved onto her next task of the day. Although she appeared languid, as if time was never of relevance, refusing to have clocks in the house, Clea was surprisingly productive.

"So after Rome?" she prompted. "By now there was Venus as well as Tara. It can't have been easy, moving from place to place with small children's needs in mind."

"Why? There were three of us to feed rather than one, but their needs are very few when they're young. And strangers are kind to children and very forgiving. We found generosity everywhere we went, Grace."

"So you came here, to the island?"

Clea shook her head, put down her pen and pushed the file of bookings to one side.

"We went to the mainland first. As usual, there wasn't any particular plan. But we got on a train in Rome, headed south to Brindisi and made our way to the port, taking the first ferry that left that evening. It was the right thing to do. I knew it as soon as I woke up in the early morning and went out on deck and saw the mountains. Funny how often your body senses these things, your base instincts, ahead of your mind. Minds can be very unreliable in guiding us into what we should be doing, you know."

There had been a series of jobs in tavernas and hotels, Clea said. She had made friends with a household of students and moved herself and the children into two rooms on the top floor of the shared house. But once winter came, Clea's constant supply of jobs dried up, the students became more serious about their studies and were less available to mind Tara and Venus and spend endless hours playing with them on the beach. Again, it was chance that brought her to Kronos, she said. She had met an elderly English woman, Edith, and her companion, Rosa, staying in one of the hotels where she cleaned. Rosa had been engaged to assist Edith on an extensive cultural European tour and they were due to leave for the island the next day. Rosa, however, had just had an urgent phone call about her father who was seriously ill and had already booked a flight back to England. Clea offered to take her place, to accompany Edith to Kronos so that she could complete the final stage in her itinerary.

"And once we were here, well, it just seemed as if the place was telling us to stay. Edith went back to England after a couple of weeks and then I realised that I was pregnant again. Or at least I was a few months later. Alara's father had left the island by then and anyway, I wouldn't have troubled him with the information. Things ended rather stormily between us. He was a very self-obsessed, troubled young man and not meant to be part of our lives, I am sure of that."

Clea emptied the last of the iced tea into her glass. She shielded her eyes from the sun that was beginning to flood the courtyard with heat. Between midday and four o'clock in the afternoon there was little shade except at the far corner of the garden by the jacaranda tree.

"And Adonis House? You said you'd been here just a couple of years."

"I've been running it as a guest house for two seasons, but the children and I rented rooms here before that. In fact, it's been home for most of the time we've been on the island. Then the chance came up to take over the lease. The place had got quite shabby and we were the only long-term tenants so something needed to happen. I met the owner, put a proposition to him and he was happy to give me a long lease on the house. Of course it was all a bit more complicated than that, tedious paperwork and licences needed, that sort of thing. But essentially, I got what I wanted. A home and a business for me and the children."

"So after years of being nomadic, you're finally settled?"

Clea collected the glasses, the emptied jug, put them on the tray and pulled the bookings file towards her.

"Oh I don't know about that," she said, "I'm not sure I believe in ever being finally settled. Sounds too complacent. But for the time being at least this life will suit us. While the kids are young and dependent on me."

Grace realised that Mercury's arrival was still unexplained. She asked. Clea smiled.

"He was one of my first guests, Lars. A lovely man from Sweden. Mercury is the gift, you could say, that he left behind when he went home. And Mercury seems to have his gentle disposition, I'm pleased to say. Lars had booked a room for a week and ended up staying three months. But eventually, he needed to…" She shifted the numerous silver bracelets on her arm then pulled them off, placed them jangling onto the tray. "Now Grace, back to work, we need to get on before the kids are back and under our feet again."

***

One evening, when she had been at Adonis House for a month, Grace talked to Clea about Archie's absence. It was a relief, she found, to be open and honest at last, yet she was glad she had waited so long. Clea knew her by now. She had proved herself, working effectively in the house and contributing to the success of the family enterprise. It would not be out of pity that Clea continued to employ her. Clea listened, making little comment and no judgement as Grace trawled back over the past few years, providing more detail than she had intended.

"Do you think I'm mad? In believing Archie still to be alive? Waiting here for him, certain he'll return?" she said eventually. "His brother, Leo does, I can tell. Leo thinks he's deserted me intentionally, I'm sure of it. And there are times when I even wonder myself. Whether I'm simply fooling myself, clutching at hope to avoid thinking the unimaginable."

Clea put a hand lightly on Grace's shoulder for a moment, but said nothing. Tara came out to the courtyard with Mercury, looking tearstained and hot in her arms.

"He can't sleep," she said, "I'm taking him for a walk down to the village. It usually helps. He likes to see the lights in the taverna."

They watched her go.

"She's a good girl," Clea said. "Mature and grounded beyond her years. She's too maternal for her own good, of course. Still, there are worse things and we all have to be what we are. That's the most important thing. I'm sorry, Grace, we were interrupted."

Grace shook her head. She felt suddenly exhausted and although it was only ten o'clock she longed for her quiet bedroom, for the prospect of lying down and closing her eyes until early morning. She stood up, muttered something about going inside to get a drink, about needing an early night. Clea followed her into the kitchen, watched while she filled a pitcher with water then moved to the fridge and took out a large chunk of watermelon, placing it on a board to cut.

"Here, take some of this up with you too, Grace. It's very refreshing." She placed slivers of the rosy flesh onto two small white plates, handed one to Grace. She found a tumbler, poured herself a glass of ouzo, offered one to Grace who shook her head.

"You know what, Grace?" she said. "Trust yourself. You are doing what feels right for you at this moment. Don't bother yourself about other people's opinions because they're of no concern to you at all. You have a very difficult situation that you could not possibly have foreseen, so don't beat yourself up about it. But clearly you love your husband and believe in him. Believe he's worthy of your love. That's all that matters right now. What I think about the whole matter is entirely irrelevant, by the way. I've never met Archie so can have no view that's worth considering. Go with your instincts. And of course, this is a good place to be, this island. I am sure you were guided here for a reason and you did the right thing in staying. I am sure of that." She reached as far as the hall then turned back and called out, "Oh Grace, I forgot to say that the Danish couple are leaving very early tomorrow so they won't want breakfast. They'll see themselves off around four and the other guests are booked on some all-day trip with an early call. So sleep on in the morning, please, you'll not be needed. You've been looking very tired lately."

Grace fell to sleep easily almost as soon as she kicked off her sandals and shrugged her dress over her head. But she woke later around three, a pattern that had appeared over the past few nights when suddenly she would be wide awake and wishing it was morning yet at the same time knowing that she would be weary and sleep-deprived by eleven. It was always at such an hour that her thoughts of Archie were most bleak. There was nothing to distract her from dwelling on entirely negative possibilities and even the consolation of Clea was insufficient armour against pessimism. *Now, I must write properly to my mother*, she thinks, batting away a mosquito from its intended route towards her face. *No more fraudulent postcard messages about extended holidays. And writing will be easier. I can simply state the fact. If I ring, the inevitable concern in her voice, her sympathies, could well be my undoing.* Yet when she finally sits down to write to Hester the following day, she finds it harder than she thought and nearly resorts to a phone call after all. Twice she tears up her efforts, thinking the tone too desperate or, worse, too casual and unconcerned. Eventually, she covers a couple of sheets of paper, firmly folds them into an envelope and asks Clea if she can borrow the car to deliver it to the main post office in Kronos Town. That way, she knows there is a chance of her letter reaching Hester within a week.

# 13

Hester sits staring at the darkened space of the stage at the Oxford Playhouse. She has no idea what she has just watched. But something, evidently, has run the course of an hour or two for there is now a trio of dishevelled-looking young actors standing on the stage, receiving tepid applause. They slink off into the wings and the small matinee audience gathers itself together to depart. Hester sits on, apparently transfixed.

"Quite a powerful performance, most affecting, I thought. Wouldn't you agree?"

"I'm sorry?"

Hester becomes aware that a man is speaking to her, possibly out of a need to shift her from her place so that he can reach the aisle. She stands up swiftly, letting her bag slide onto the floor, spilling its contents, so that she has to grovel in the small space retrieving articles, delaying the man still more.

"But then Beckett always has that impact on me, I find. Disturbing yet somehow compelling. That existential angst that is somehow always present in our lives."

"Disturbing, yes," Hester says, "compelling, as you say. And Beckett. It was definitely Beckett. I remember now."

The man stares at her, faintly alarmed, then quickly moves away.

The letter from Grace had been reassuring at first. Her daughter was alive and well and Hester had been able to dismiss all the deep concerns she had been harbouring during the weeks of her absence. Grace was not suffering from some appalling, terminal illness that she was too fearful to disclose. She had not disappeared from Somerset because she had committed a heinous crime. She was on a southern Mediterranean island by choice. But after initial relief, twenty minutes or so in which Hester had found her mind relatively more at ease than it had been for weeks, had been able to make a pot of tea, sit eating toast and marmalade and listen absently to the news on the radio, she had returned to Grace's letter and reread it with increasing concern. 'We don't know where Archie is,' she had written. 'He seems to have disappeared. It appears that there have been financial problems that I had not been aware of, that he had not felt able to share with me.' The letter went on to give a mainly factual, chronological account of events as if at pains to avoid inducing panic. 'I am staying here as long as I can. Because this is where I believe he will expect to find me,' Grace had written. 'Besides, I have found work and feel as settled as it is possible to feel at the moment. And I am coping.' Archie had returned to England on 24th May and had evidently not been seen since the last day of the month when he had been supposed to meet his brother, Leo. It was now the second week of July. Hester had stood, letter in hand in her neat, cream kitchen, looking out unseeing at the picket fence, the blighted, unwieldy rambling rose and had tried not to feel bereft that Grace had taken so long to contact her. She had suppressed with difficulty an overwhelming desire to walk straight down to the nearest travel agent to make arrangements to go out to the island so that she could see Grace, take her in her arms without further delay. She suspected, however, that such a gesture would be most unwelcome. So instead, she had left the flat, ignored the bus stop and walked the two miles and a bit into the city and wasted a couple of hours mindlessly.

Arriving in Beaumont Street, footsore and with no appetite to take refuge in a restaurant, she had randomly bought a ticket for the matinee at the Playhouse conveniently due to start within ten minutes.

"Beckett," she had said out loud again, this time to herself and possibly the girl collecting up discarded programmes and sweet wrappers from the stalls, "I never have liked Beckett. Too bloody bleak."

Later, Hester is having supper with a friend who has recently moved to a house in Woodstock, a woman she has known for years and whose life appears to have been lived on an emotional high trapeze. They sit in her cottage garden in the mild air of the July evening.

"How's Grace?" Lydia asks, handing Hester a substantial glass of white wine. "Still enjoying life with that husband of hers... Arnold, isn't it? Or Arthur?"

"Archie," Hester says and looks away at the array of summer flowers. "I love honeysuckle. And stocks and hollyhocks and aren't those night-scented phlox? You're lucky to have inherited such an established garden, Lydia, and so much space. I've only a pocket handkerchief to speak of as you know."

Lydia looks at the garden as if at a tiresome eyesore.

"It's a bind, makes demands on me I'd rather ignore. Weeding and such like. Not my thing at all, Hester, I'd swap it for a couple of tubs and some evergreens any day. But I suppose concreting it all over would bring the wrath of the neighbours so better not risk that especially as I'm the new girl on the block. Rather good this," Lydia says, tipping her glass. "Met up with an old flame of mine the other day and he gave me a couple of bottles to take home. He's got a bit of an import business going, just a side-line, you know, since Henry's a boring, but exceedingly affluent accountant the rest of the time. I hope you don't mind cold, by the way. I've got us a smoked chicken and salad. It is summer, after all."

Hester has no appetite, but agrees that smoked chicken sounds splendid. Lydia pushes a bowl of nuts in her direction.

"Of course no one expects marriage to be for life anymore," she goes on. "What are the latest statistics about divorce? Not that I'd put your Grace into that category. She's always been the steady type, almost old fashioned in her way. Not like my two girls at all. Not when they were in their wild adolescent phase and Grace stayed so… well, so nice. Civilised. But quite frankly, I can't imagine why anyone bothers to get married these days when cohabitation is so much easier. All that legal wrangling when the thing breaks up. It would have made my life a lot simpler in the past if there'd been no need to involve lawyers and courts and such like, I can tell you. Any babies yet, by the way? For Grace and Arnie… I mean Archie?"

"No," Hester says. "Not that I… no babies. Not yet."

"Perhaps that's the modern way, childless by choice. I must say if I had my time again – not that I'd be without my two for anything, naturally – even so, once you've given birth your fate is rather decided, isn't it? No more purely selfish gestures. They're always part of the scenario of your life. An inescapable burden and source of constant worry and anxiety. Yet also, of course, of absolute joy and enormous, overwhelming pride and adoration." Lydia refills Hester's glass, splashes more wine into her own. She leans forward in her blue-and-white-striped garden chair, forages for a crisp.

"How much do you think one should interfere with their lives?" Hester says, "I mean when our children are children no more, when they're adults and ostensibly in charge of things themselves?"

Lydia looks sideways at Hester. They have known each other too many years for Lydia not to suspect some underlying reason for the question. Hester flicks away the fly teetering on the brink of drowning in her wine glass, waits for a response.

"No more and no less than is wanted or required," Lydia eventually says.

"But how do you know what that is?"

"Pick up on the cues, read between the lines and watch out for the signs."

"That's considerably easier said than done," Hester says. "Especially from a distance."

"Of course it is. But then who said parenthood was easy? From the moment of conception, it seems to me it's one anxiety after another. Remember when all we had to worry about was sleepless nights and the possibility of blocked milk ducts? Then there was teething and the trauma of not being able to soothe our beloved red-cheeked little souls at four in the morning. And then the toddler tantrums in the middle of the high street, when all our adult rationality in the world wouldn't shift our determined, stony-faced offspring. We used to delude ourselves that once we were on to the next stage the drama would let up a bit, the sources of worry and apprehension would lift like some temporary storm clouds. But of course they never did. Because around the corner was always a new concern. Learning to ride a bike, crossing a road alone, the raging temperature that always seemed to start in the lonely hours of the night when it seemed impossible to tell the difference between imminent meningitis and a mild case of the common cold. Then later, there were the unsuitable, perfectly ghastly friends and their even more ghastly parents. And don't even get me started on the fear of teenage pregnancy, sexual predators, abduction, rape, drugs and the like. Then just as you think you can hand responsibilities over to a sensible son-in-law and withdraw to the wings for a quiet life, that very same individual proves himself to be shifty and unfaithful and by this time there are grandchildren on board so the whole damn cycle starts again. And believe me, Hester, if you think you and I had it hard when our brood were small, there's been an epidemic of worries released since then so that grand parenting is bringing a new level of stress and responsibility, I'll have you know. Nowadays, there's cot death, overheated nurseries, the wrong sort of car seats, the right sort of educational toys to tangle with. We had it light by the terrifyingly stringent standards of today." Lydia shades her eyes with one hand to look at Hester to avoid the direct glare of the sun setting onto her west-facing garden.

"I'm not sure you're helping," Hester says.

"Sorry. I like a little rant every now and again. But seriously, Hester, all you can do when they're adults is to keep the channels of communication open. It's not your place to go barging in on your child's life without an invitation. Just make sure they know, make sure Grace knows that you're there to help if she needs you. And if the summons comes, give her as much or as little advice as she asks for."

Inside the house the phone rings. Lydia ignores it. It stops then starts again a few moments later.

"Shouldn't you answer that?" Hester says, thinking of Lydia's two daughters, one living in Preston, the other in Kew.

"It will be the old flame," Lydia says, "Henry. The French wine importing accountant. He's been pestering me every evening since the present of the Chablis. Seems to be expecting something in return and I really can't be bothered with that whole business of sex, anymore. I've announced my retirement from the habit. Let's go inside, Hester, and find this smoked chicken. Evidently, it's the latest thing to be seen eating at smart picnics this summer."

The next morning Hester picks up the phone and dials the number given in Grace's letter. She listens to the long, unfamiliar foreign peal on the line and is about to replace the receiver when it is answered. She leaves a message. "Just tell Grace I am thinking of her," she says to someone who calls herself Tara Kolomiets. "If there's anything she wants she only has to let me know. Tell her… just that. Thank you. And give her my love. Send her a great deal of love." The person called Tara says, "Sure, of course, she's not here right now, but she'll be back soon. Should she ring you?" Hester hears voices in the background and she is floored for a moment when Tara says something indecipherable to her. Then she realises that she is speaking in another language addressing someone else and for a moment she feels suspended from her north Oxford sitting room, the plump sofa and fitted carpet and sash windows and imagines a cool, high-ceilinged hall with filtered sunlight, ceramic tiles, rough stone walls. "No," she says, "no need for Grace to ring unless… whenever she would like to." Tara says, "I understand," and Hester senses that somehow this young woman does indeed understand.

That afternoon she writes two letters. In spite of her phone call she feels she must reply to Grace in writing. She says little, elaborating merely on what she has said to Tara, aiming to sound concerned yet at the same time expressing support and confidence for whatever Grace decides to do. It is only in her second letter of the day that she pours out her conviction that Archie is either dead or has no intention at all of returning to Grace. She writes at some length about her fears and sense of hopelessness for the situation. She suspects she sounds a little hysterical, but sees no reason to curb her tone. Addressing the first letter to Grace at Adonis House and the second to her erstwhile husband and Grace's father, Fergus Barnes, in the Welsh hills, she leaves the flat just before five o'clock in order to catch the sub-post office in the Banbury Road before closing time.

***

Fergus Barnes sits uncomfortably in the stuffy waiting room, attempting to pass the time by reading dog-eared copies of old magazines. He cannot remember the last time he visited the place. When he had finally decided to delay no longer and had made his way down to the village, waited for the bus to take him into town and had pushed open the door to the surgery he had been taken aback by what he found. Orderly rows of plastic orange seats, an officious receptionist, forms to fill, leaflets to read as if he was seeking employment rather than a chat with a doctor. No, he had told the woman partly submerged behind a hatch, he did not have an appointment. Nor did he know who he wanted to see. He did not know there was a choice. He searched his mind for the name of someone he'd seen on a previous visit, possibly some fifteen or twenty years before. Dr Hughes, the submerged woman told him crisply, had retired a decade ago. She had handed him a sheaf of papers, a clipboard and pen and sent him off to fill in extensive personal details. Eventually, he finds himself sitting in front of a young man with thick blonde hair who introduces himself as Dr Jones. Fergus feels inclined to ask to see his birth certificate, to verify his qualifications before removing his shirt. He is prodded with fingers, with a stethoscope and asked to breathe in and out several times. He coughs involuntarily and Dr Jones steps back as if affronted by the noise. "Just a cough," Fergus says and attempts to laugh, but finds himself coughing again. "Sorry to bother you with just a cough. But I'd quite like to shift it before the winter begins again." Fergus is far more concerned than he is willing to admit. It is early August and his chest feels as tight, tighter, in fact, than it did in early February when this wretched coughing began. Dr Jones retreats behind his desk, looks at Fergus' notes which are sparse; an infected knee in

June 1966 which responded to a short course of antibiotics followed three years later by a septic thumb similarly treated. The man appears either immune to illness or an excellent example of the masculine habit of dismissing suspect physical symptoms.

Fergus coughs some more. Dr Jones scribbles on a pad. "I want you to have a chest X-ray," he says, and Fergus nods, intending to ignore the advice. "As soon as possible," the young doctor adds and passes over a form. "You can go to the cottage hospital, they'll look after you. Today would be ideal. Now, in fact." Fergus stands up, slips the form for the hospital in his pocket. He had planned on mentioning the increasing pains he has been getting in his limbs, the dull, thudding ache in his knees and wrists. But he has had enough medical advice for one day. Now all he wants to do is head to the bus stop, wait for the midday service back to the village, take his time walking up the hill, his hill as he thinks of it, an hour at a quick pace, more like two the way he has been feeling since late spring.

But something nags. Enough to make him leave the surgery building, the flimsy 1970s squat box of a place incongruously set next to a terrace of slate-roofed cottages, and head for the main road and the bus into the nearest sizeable town. As it happens, he doesn't need to wait for the unreliable service. A car slows down and a woman throws open the passenger door and offers him and another man a lift. He takes the back seat next to a yapping spaniel, gives the front over to the elderly man with a stick who has been muttering to himself in Welsh at the bus stop. At the hospital, he waits more than an hour before pictures are taken of his chest by a young woman who addresses him as if he is frail and vulnerable. He has never thought of himself as being of any particular age. He has intentionally sidestepped labels and categories by his very way of life. He is aware, naturally, that he used to be a young man, a man with his entire future lying ahead of him, marriage, parenthood, career prospects. But for the past thirty or so years he has been more conscious of the cyclical pattern of the year, the changing seasons and their implication upon his daily routine than of the passing of time.

His time.

Now he sees himself through the eyes of others, the eyes of his youthful GP, the woman who stopped her car, this fresh-faced radiographer and he is alarmed. He is shocked by the stacked up years as if he has only just realised that they are spent, expended and that what lies ahead is limited and, very probably, diminished. He can no longer afford to be so dismissive about the passing of the months and years, behaving as if his existence is limitless and the nature of it entirely of his own choosing.

Instead of going straight home he walks from the hospital into the town, which he has visited only a handful of times since he arrived in the area decades before. He hardly recognises it and is not impressed by what he sees. On the outskirts, he passes a strip of shops each offering cut-price goods and cheap clothes, a betting shop, a baker's displaying buns iced in garish colours. Opposite, a large petrol station, a tyre depot and a furniture warehouse selling sofas covered in stretched nylon, neighbour each other. At the end of the street he turns into what was no doubt once the centre of the old market town with some red-bricked 19th century buildings, originally municipal and now requisitioned as a library, the post office, a small tourist office. He finds a café, sits in the window and waits to be served. The bright young radiographer has assured him that his GP will be in touch about his X-ray results. By phone, she says, and looks confused when he says he has none. "You should ring, then," she says, "tomorrow, please ring your surgery tomorrow." He tries to dismiss his concern at her sense of urgency and is surprised when he can't. He has hardly considered his health in years. In fact, he has never considered it, dismissing colds, wading through the odd spell of flu, the rare stomach upset as if mind over matter is the obvious solution to all ailments.

When he had turned his back on suburban Pinner and headed for the Welsh hills, he had taken out a contract with himself that had stipulated supreme physical fitness. It had been the only way to survive, to defy the doubters. In the early days of getting the smallholding off the ground, he had learnt by his mistakes, muddled along in ignorance and stoically refused to admit any defeat. Alongside he had taken on any casual farm labouring jobs he could find and had soon discovered that, however low the wages paid, it would be this work that put regular money in his pocket, money he became dependent upon in a way he disliked admitting. Sheer exhaustion had sustained him in the first few years, eighteen-hour days when he had scarcely gone to bed since he had usually fallen asleep at the kitchen table over a mug of tea and chunk of cheese around midnight. He had rarely been lonely and loneliness had been something he had been prepared to face, had expected even and had viewed more as an indulgence than a disadvantage. After all, he had chosen isolation, a dislocation from company and companionship and easy consolation when he had turned his back on his superannuated position at the bank, his wife and small child. There were, after all, so many worse things to endure than a touch of loneliness. Like the alternative, the slow grind down through the years, watching his erosion towards retirement, nudged into the margins of his own life. He had seen it happen to others. He had been to the farewell parties, contributed to the leaving gifts of gold watches and clocks and cut-glass tumblers, laughed too loudly at the weak jokes of the departing employees who now had only their declining faculties, their slack bodies and unremarkable achievements to show for their service. It had been what had ultimately convinced him, sitting in that dentist's surgery in Eastcote, reading about another way of life in the crofter's cottage, thinking about the huge skies, the endless horizons. It had convinced him that it was possible to escape such a bleak, inevitable destiny.

But of course he had been fooling himself.

He had been a naïve, very stupid young man who seemed to think that he, Fergus Barnes, could be different. Deserving of more. Immortal, immutable, a sort of Faustian figure who had made a pastoral pact with the sods of the earth. He wonders if it is an accident of birth that had made him so convinced of his ability to escape what snared others. Born in the summer of 1927, the war had conveniently drawn to a close just as he would have been required to participate. A fortunate man, people had said, as he had joined the celebrations in Trafalgar Square. Then there had been Hester. He had met her at a party he had stumbled upon by chance, passing the open door to the flat on the floor below his own bedsit in Colet Gardens. His loose engagement to a girl called Daphne, a sweet, shy, fresh-faced virgin with whom an understanding appeared to have been construed by her parents and his, lifelong friends and close neighbours in Coventry, had been jettisoned instantly and they had married in six months. Four years older than him, Hester had been captivating. He had never known an actress before, had never made love to a woman who knew far more about the business than he did and had been happy to experiment and instruct. His parents' disapproval, Daphne's tears, simply served to swell his ardour. Yet he had known that his greatest triumph in marrying Hester, in abandoning sweet, fair Daphne, had been in escaping the fate that had been outlined for him by her parents and endorsed by his; a stake in her family's business, the small building concern that had lain painfully dormant during the War, but was emerging phoenix-like out of Coventry's very discernible ashes. Fergus had understood, at the age of twenty-five, that his life was being ordered for him, prescribed and defined so that it had not taken a great deal of imagination to see himself forty years on, a successful local businessman heading towards old age, handing things on to his eldest son, a daughter, even, who would be urging him into retirement, dispatching him to senility and oblivion. In marrying Hester, attaching himself to this beautiful, vibrant woman who swore, wore black stockings and drank whisky, he had been in flight. Like a parachutist leaping from the safety of a plane into free fall he had felt untethered, loosed from a life of claustrophobic certainty.

But within two or three years it had begun again.

That sense of gnawing dread at the inevitability of what lay ahead. For it seemed that even his enchanting Hester and darling Grace had needs that could only be served by a lengthy mortgage, savings schemes, life insurance and deferential chats to bank managers who all wanted to talk in precise, depressing terms about budgets and investments and pensions. In that dentist's waiting room in Eastcote, he had experienced something akin to a religious conversion, a calling, you could say. And it had sustained him on the whole; he had held fast to his belief in his choice and way of life. In as much, of course, as he had ever allowed himself even to consider consciously the wisdom and sense of it all.

It had been that woman, Primrose Larrington, and the camera crew and the fuss over the programme that had been the beginning of all this. She had asked too many questions. She had made him think too much. "Do you have regrets?" She had tested him and hadn't been satisfied when he had quipped, "Doesn't everyone?" She had dug further, terrier-like, scenting his dodging, fixing her sharp, narrow eyes upon him, pencil poised to note down every shuffling evasion. "You must look at your contemporaries," she'd said, "at what they've achieved, what they've acquired. And ask yourself, has it all been worth it?" He had been able to answer candidly that no, he did not look at other people and envy them their smart, shiny cars, their large houses with double garages, their extravagant dinner parties and golf club memberships and pompous influential friends. He had been able to say honestly to the Larrington woman that he had never yearned for excessive materialistic gain nor seen it as a worthwhile aspiration. Still, after she had gone, after they'd all gone, the bearded cameraman, the silent fellow on sound, the young assistant who fussed around with combs and cries for coffee and complained endlessly about the cold, after they'd all packed up and disappeared down the hill, back to their congenial, cushioned lives, he had sat and wondered whether she'd had a point. Whether, in fact, it had all been the most appalling waste of time, of his very precious time.

After all, there was so little of it.

He wished that he had been able to say with absolute certainty to Primrose Larrington with her short uncompromising haircut and globs of enormous rings on most fingers, that yes, of course, if he'd known then what he knew now he'd willingly do it all over again, dispensing with the solace of unconditional love from his wife and child, in order to forge his own unfettered life in the wilderness of the Welsh hills. But he had found himself unable to say to her anything quite so clear-cut and finite with any profound conviction. Because he simply had no idea of the truth of the matter anymore.

Fergus stares down at the cooling cup of coffee that he does not remember ordering. Suddenly, he is hungry, ravenously hungry as if he has not eaten properly for days. Perhaps he hasn't. It is entirely possible that he has not cooked himself an adequate meal for weeks, has made do with his doorstep sandwiches, fried bread, too many eggs. He gets up, walks over to the counter and, reading from the blackboard on the wall, orders soup, dish of the day, vegetables. The price sounds exorbitant, but he hands over adequate notes to the young man behind the counter, returns to his table.

He had never thought about growing old. That had always been part of the deal of choosing to live the way he had. He had lived, or so he told himself, day by day, in the present moment that took note of the future only as far as crop growth, seed sowing, harvesting had been concerned. Stubbornly, irritatingly for the few people with whom he had come into regular contact, he had always refused to look ahead, mapping out his life only in small immediate spoonfuls of time. And on the whole, it had served his situation. The casual farm labouring jobs he had undertaken to supplement his income had been just that, seasonal, random, responding to immediate need. For a while he had taken on evening milking at a farm a mile down the hill and had done holiday relief herd work elsewhere. Otherwise, he had woken each morning and had done what had to be done: feeding the hens, collecting eggs, milking the goat, digging up root vegetables, mending fences and the roof leak, turning over earth, coaxing blackfly off lettuces, picking berries and currants, turning fruit into jam, vegetables into pickle. No day had ever hung upon his hands, lingered long enough for him to wonder what lay ahead in ten years, in twenty, when he might not be able or willing to get up before a cold dawn, to coax his declining body into strenuous tasks and return at the end of a long, physically exhausting day to silence.

Emptiness. An absence of company and consolation.

A bowl of vegetable soup is put down in front of him and a large hunk of soft white bread. Fergus breaks off chunks of the cotton wool-like substance, spreads it liberally with butter and eats it slowly, relishing its bland, easy texture, the way it dissolves on his tongue. He has been eating his own rough homemade bread for over thirty years and has forgotten the sensation of such softness. A plate of steaming steak and kidney follows with creamed potato and peas sitting in rich gravy. He has not eaten a meal away from his own spartan kitchen since Grace's wedding over three years ago and he feels self-conscious at first, as if as a lone diner he is a curiosity. But no one appears to be taking any notice. The three women at the table nearest to him are talking intimately, heads close together as if sharing something clandestine. A young man eats a pie rapidly, newspaper propped up against a sauce bottle. An elderly lady orders a pot of tea and a poached egg. He has forgotten when the pains in his knees started, when his back refused to recover completely from that fall in the mud by the outhouse. Not that he is in excruciating pain or unable to carry out essential day-to-day tasks; nevertheless, nothing is as easy as it once was. He is aware too often of his body's resistance to unrelieved activity. The way muscles seem to stiffen, joints ache. And the cold. For the first time he is noticing the cold and feeling unable, unwilling almost, to endure it. It is only August and already he has dug out his thick winter sweater, put an extra blanket on the bed. He has never before noticed the absence of comfort in his surroundings, but now wonders if the place could do with a bit of attention. No wall-to-wall carpets or plush three-piece suites, of course, but perhaps a few touches to lift the starkness, soften the edges as it were. What he really wants, if he's honest with himself, is simply to make things easier. He would like each day to be less of a long haul of concerted effort to get through, combatting fatigue at every turn. In fact, Fergus admits to himself, he is ready to do more than simply endure.

That woman, the Primrose television woman, had tried to wheedle personal stuff out of him, of course. As he knew she would. Not that any of it got recorded for the programme, she'd assured him. "Strictly off the record!" she'd said and fixated him with her toothy smile, smoothed the back of that cropped auburn hair. "Any partners in your life? Surely there's someone with whom you've shared the past thirty years." What she had meant was sex, of course. She had wanted to know whether he had led a monastic existence, a chaste life since departing Pinner and Hester and Grace. He had hedged. He had been unwilling to divulge anything so compromising and intimate to this stranger. For a start, her claim to keep such matters 'off the record' could not be trusted. And the prospect of Hester sitting down to watch a television programme about her estranged husband and hearing in some sort of voice-over about his various sexual entanglements was unthinkable. Yet he had no reason to have qualms about the matter. After all, Hester must have had numerous relationships since he had left; he had not been deluded enough to think of her living as a celibate. In fact, each time the occasional letter had arrived from her over the years he had always expected it to contain a demand for a divorce, a finite declaration of the state in which they appeared already to live. He could not imagine why she had failed to ask him for one. And continued to be, for some unfathomable reason, overwhelmingly grateful that she had not.

So he had said little. He had not mentioned Nancy, the young woman from the large arable farm down in the valley with whom he'd had a truculent casual relationship for some years. Nor Pauline, the rather rapacious music teacher he'd met when her car had careered into his bicycle one icy December day. Pauline had been more trouble than the sex had been worth, ever expectant of more than Fergus had been willing to give of his time and affections. In the end, she had taken herself off to Dublin, much to his relief, soon falling in love and moving in with a saxophonist psychotherapist poet. Jill, therefore, had come as something of a reprieve. Jill had wanted no more than a couple of hours of his company every other Friday or so when her academic husband had been in Swansea supervising his PhD students on matters of theological complexity. Jill was a practical, forceful woman who had no illusions about Fergus' regard for her. He admired her ability to detach herself so cleanly, adeptly from the murky subterranean world of emotions. She appeared to have no guilt about betraying her husband nor did she expect Fergus to treat her as anything other than a convenience. They were, as she frequently said, of use to each other. He sensed that she quite liked him, found his company congenial and bore him some mild affection, but no more than was required to go to bed with him and depart with equanimity an hour or two later. She seemed indifferent to knowing too much about his estranged wife, his only child. Her husband, evidently, had long since shown a disinclination for sex in favour of steeping himself in ancient languages and matters of original sin and Jill had apparently accepted his choice, calmly turned elsewhere for physical satisfaction and acquired a horse. Fergus thinks of making love to Jill as a functional exercise in which both of them obey the rules and achieve an outcome of sorts. It is a satisfactory matter, a procedure in which they are both competent and accomplished in a controlled and measured way. Afterwards, he is often astounded by the speed with which she leaps from his side, clambers back into her indifferent clothing and starts talking about the exorbitant price of horse feed. Straw. Barley. And he finds himself, occasionally, yearning for more, an experience less rooted in the prosaic practical world

– where he could lose himself, momentarily touch for even a split second something of the sublime. Then he reminds himself of his age. His thinning hair, his troublesome knees, the pale flesh that reflects back at him each morning as he stares in the bathroom mirror. He has lost all rights and claims to states of ecstasy, he reminds himself, and is fortunate in knowing the obliging Jill.

He spreads the last mound of kidney with English mustard, swallows and pushes the empty plate away from him. He feels sleepy, a mild slanting sun catching the corner of the table where he sits so that he wants to close his eyes and doze in the warmth of the early afternoon. He wonders whether a portion of the plum crumble he's noticed on the chalkboard would be unwise given his already heavy intake of food. Yet the thought of more comfort, an excess of indulgence, is irresistible. He feels like a penitent breaking a self-imposed fast as he calls over to the boy who brought him his soup, the steak and kidney. The dish of crumble sits in a sea of bright yellow custard, a purple pool of plum juice seeping through its surface. It reminds him of the watercolour of a sunset he once saw at an amateur art show in the village. He has surprised himself that he still has such an appetite, an ability to eat a solid, square meal, and is comforted by it. After all, he can't be a seriously sick man, that chest X-ray is unlikely to reveal anything too sinister. No tumours, surely, or worrying lumps and shadows requiring further investigation. He feels distinctly more cheerful at the thought and smiles benevolently at a middle-aged woman whose eye he happens to catch as she walks past his table. She looks at him as if trying to place his face, settles at the neighbouring table and continues to stare. Suddenly she smiles broadly, leans over towards him. "It's you off that telly programme, isn't it? Knew I knew you. Was it all for real or just a bunch of actors pretending?"

There is no bus until five o'clock.

Fergus hangs hopelessly around the bus stop for a while, hoping for a repeat of his earlier luck when he found a lift, but a constant stream of cars passes him by and he begins to walk. After an hour he is tired, his cough is troubling him, his chest tight, his knees aching and he takes refuge on the grass bank beside the road. When the bus finally approaches, he waves it down and steps inside with relief. There is no empty seat. He wedges himself awkwardly in the aisle, between loud teenagers and an elderly woman muttering to herself. It has begun to rain, light, fine rain at first that soon turns into the drenching, incessant sort that the bus windscreen wipers have difficulty repelling. He dreads the next stage of his journey, leaving the relative shelter of his aisle and waiting for the local bus that will take him to the village and drop him at the bottom of the hill for his steep, wet climb up to home. And it is only now that he remembers the letter that has sat in the centre of the kitchen table since Jill brought it up the previous Friday. Or was it even the Friday before? It has been his habit of years to postpone opening the rare letters that are clearly from Hester and he tends to steal up on them days or even weeks after their arrival. Now, however, as he leaves the first bus and waits for the second, feeling the rain drip insistently down his neck, finding a place that his windproof jacket manages to expose, he feels an urgency to get back to his kitchen, to Hester's letter patiently awaiting his attention.

# 14

A letter finally arrived from Leo one morning in mid-August. Grace delayed opening it all day for fear of what she might find, waiting until she was free and could drive down to Anixi Bay to sit at a café to read it alone.

In the event, there was little revealed and nothing to surprise her.

Leo's enquiries appeared to have mostly mirrored her own. He, too, had been in touch with the college in Aldgate and received a similarly brusque response. He had then followed various procedures, informing the police of a missing person, checking hospitals, hostels, cheap hotels and boarding houses in Norfolk, in Somerset, in Greenwich. He had tracked down friends from their childhood, a couple of very remote cousins, only to find everywhere bewilderment and a lack of information. Calling at the Greenwich house on an impulse in the unlikely event of finding a forwarding address, he had been met by the mildly affronted new owners who said they had bought the house the previous spring and had little knowledge of the former owner. 'It appears to be,' Leo had written, 'not so much that Archie has been careful to cover his tracks as that there are no tracks to follow.' Grace folded over the single page of his letter, tucked it into the pocket of her skirt, threw a few coins onto the café table to pay for the coffee that she had not managed to drink and began to walk along the beach.

It was early evening, but the sands were still active with people making the most of the cooler part of the day. Gaggles of young children busied themselves building elaborate sandcastles, a couple of boys played bat and ball, calling out their climbing score until one lunged too far, slipped and fell almost at Grace's feet. Walking further along the beach, past the emptying sun loungers and piles of folded umbrellas and chairs neatly stacked for the night, she reached the far end where steps led up onto a small promontory projecting out into the sea, providing an anchoring for a few sailing boats and a place for some desultory fishing. It had become a favourite spot for her to sit, either in the early morning when the air was cool and clear or at this time of day, awaiting the sunset and the moment when the mountains changed from grey to pink and quickly dissolved into darkness. She sat now, trying to order and quantify her response to Leo's bland letter that had neither advanced nor stalled her search for Archie.

She had resigned from the arts centre soon after her first phone call to Melanie. Writing to Giles Meredith she had been evasive, saying that she had made an impulsive decision to stay on the island and was expectant of staying for some time. Melanie had possibly been more expansive to Giles, but Grace doubted whether he would show any spurious interest in her fortunes. In fact, her last conversation with Melanie had revealed some disquiet and unease about his increasing absences from the centre, leaving her to cope with the bulk of the organisation alone. "Don't be surprised if I turn up on your doorstep one day soon, seeking a sunny refuge and a diet of local plonk and vine leaves," she'd said. "I could do with a decent holiday and am owed masses of leave. Some local Lotharios thrown into the mix wouldn't go amiss either and would serve Giles right for his neglect of me."

Grace watched a lizard dart its way across the ground close

to her bare toes, disappear between two large stones. Two children, one in scarlet shorts, the other in a turquoise sun dress, scampered past where she sat, evidently in some sort of race with each other, chattering and giggling breathlessly as they ran. A call from the beach checked them and they stopped and turned back to retrace their steps more soberly. Grace turned and saw a woman folding towels and collecting stray sandals from the sand, a man screening his eyes against the light as he watched the two children return. Other families and couples were gathering up belongings, dusting sand off bags and soles of feet, packing up after their day at the beach, ready for the evening. Grace consciously turned away to concentrate on the setting sun sinking its way inevitably into the horizon. Most of the time she managed to bury herself in the routine of her work at Adonis House, which gave her little chance to feel anything other than exhausted at the end of every day. It was now high season, the house fully booked into late September and even with Clea's two older children available as additional practical help, she was constantly busy and occupied. So a chance to note her loneliness, to confront fully her situation, was thankfully rare. But every now and again, something trivial, insignificant, caught her off guard. Like these people now on the beach, the man hefting the small boy onto his shoulders, the woman grabbing the hand of the little girl. The young couple next to them collapsing sun umbrellas, planting large hats on each other's heads, laughing, jostling, a kiss on the cheek, one hand slipping easily into the other. Such moments of ordinary, casual affection would assault her and cause her to feel acutely alone, desperate for easy intimacy, another's flesh close to hers as if to confirm her humanity.

And she finds herself thinking of Hester, of her mother, and wonders how ever she coped when Fergus left them. It has never really occurred to her quite how young she was, little older than Grace is now. She has always admired her mother, of course. As a child she had felt sheltered by her apparent confidence and forthright attitude as if the evils of the world would always halt at their front door, make a hasty retreat on encountering Hester's brazen assurance. Growing up she had even felt somewhat overshadowed by her indomitable spirit and dogged independence. But it occurs to her now that Hester was like that not out of choice but out of necessity. *Perhaps we become the people we need to become*, Grace thinks, *in order to cope with the consequences of whatever happens to befall us. Sink or swim, by hell or high water. Or something like that.* She gets up, brushes grains of sand and small stones from her skirt, slips her feet back into her discarded sandals and feels suddenly as if she is going to faint. She feels light-headed, nauseous and overwhelmingly weak as if in need of a strong pair of arms to support her. She crouches down for a moment to recover herself and remembers that she has hardly eaten all day. A bit of bread at breakfast, no appetite for lunch, then a banana mid-afternoon that had tasted unbearably sweet, overripe, so that she'd thrown most of it away. No doubt she's insufficiently hydrated too. She sits for a while longer then slowly starts to make her way back along the promontory, skirts the beach and walks along the road, returning into the centre of Anixi Bay. She drives back to the village, retreats into the cool of Adonis House, to her darkened room, drinks two glasses of water, and begins to feel better.

***

A week later, Clea came out to find Grace sitting in the courtyard, making up accounts for two couples leaving later that day.

"Do we charge the lovely Danish people for that meal we gave them the night they arrived? Their flight was delayed, remember, and they didn't get here until midnight."

Clea pulled up a chair, sat down and peered at the paperwork Grace was studying.

"No, don't charge them, but make a point of telling them that we're not. That way we're quietly drawing attention to our goodwill and they leave with a positive impression. They're already talking about coming back next year for Easter."

"Will you open that early? I thought you said there was too little business before mid-May to make it worth your while."

"Up until now," Clea said, pulling off the countless bangles on her arm in her usual way and placing them on the table in a neat pile. "But you know my long-term plan is to extend our season and we have to start sometime. Even if it's slow for the first year and we're hardly breaking even. Anyway, we can talk about that another time. I've been meaning to catch you all morning, but I had to drop the kids off in various places then I'd promised Mercury a paddle down on the beach. And that turned into a bit of sand-digging and shell-collecting as these things tend to do. Consequently, he's fast asleep now and looks like staying that way for a couple of hours. And that means we can have a chat about things."

Clea placed her arm lightly on Grace's. "I'm growing impatient, you see. When are you going to tell me about your pregnancy?"

Grace looked up, attempted a half-hearted laugh then stared at Clea as if trying to grasp a coherent meaning in her words. The idea was so absurd, so remote from possibility that she knew she must contradict her straight away.

"No, you're entirely wrong, I'm afraid. It's ridiculous. I'm not pregnant. There's no chance of such a thing," she said. "I can't think why you're even saying it." She was aware that she sounded angry, almost defiant, which had not been her intention. Clea said nothing for a few moments. A dog barked in the lane outside the house, then another as if in conversation with each other. A couple of ants crawled their way across the Danish couple's account lying on the table.

"I hadn't realised it would come as such a surprise," Clea said eventually. "It can be hard to allow yourself to accept such an idea in the early stages. I thought, perhaps, you were just waiting for the right moment to tell me."

Grace shook her head.

"Sorry if I sounded… annoyed. That's not how it is at all. Not at all. But you see, it's something I've so wanted… we've both wanted. Children. And… it simply hasn't happened. That's how it is. And Archie… he seemed to find it difficult to talk about. As if by avoiding the subject, we'd… and now he's not even around to… well, it's just absurd. Just… there's simply no possibility of me being pregnant."

She picked up her pen, bent her head over the accounts again as if dispatching the subject.

Inside the house, the phone rang a long, pealing noise from the black handset in the lofty hallway. Clea moved swiftly inside and Grace heard her answering in the local language then switching to a few halting words of French before transferring to English. Clea was being absurd with her notion of a pregnancy, as if Grace was as vulnerable to the fecundity that appeared to fall to her with her four unplanned, delightful children, living lives comfortably unconcerned by their paternity. And yet at the same time it seemed unlikely she would make such an assertion without good reason. Grace stared at the paperwork in front of her, made a couple of attempts to add up figures, which insisted on darting and confounding her efforts. She threw down her pen, concentrated instead on the bees, busy with the bougainvillea and hibiscus, the increasing volume of the cicadas. After ten minutes, Clea was outside again, car keys in hand, her large fabric beach bag slung around one shoulder.

"I'm off for a swim before the kids get back and Mercury wakes from his nap. You'll watch him for me, Grace? I'll be under an hour. I just need some time alone."

"Of course," Grace said.

"And by the way, I knew there was one more thing to tell you. I spoke to Hester this morning. She's coming over for a visit. I said I thought it would be a good idea. She sounds like a nice woman, Grace, you're lucky. My mother was a reactionary bigot, bless her."

"My mother?" Grace was confounded. "But she hasn't said anything. To me, I mean. Why would she suddenly decide to come and see me?"

"You wrote, evidently," Clea said, pushing open the gate into the lane where a couple of tabby cats were sunbathing on the bonnet of her old car. "Naturally, she was concerned by your changed circumstances. She wants to come and see you. Reassure herself, I expect, that you're coping without Archie. I told her I thought it was just what you needed right now. And don't worry, I didn't mention the latest development – I thought that should come from you. News of a baby is hardly the sort of thing your mother would want delivered over a crackling phone line from a stranger."

She shooed the cats, got into the car, pumped the accelerator and disappeared down the lane, leaving a spray of dust and small stones in her wake.

Mercury slept on. Grace went upstairs and sat in his small, darkened room, listening to his steady breathing although she knew there was no need to be so vigilant. Every time she tried to occupy herself by doing something else around the house, however, she ended up staring into space, kitchen knife or mop or duster tense in her hand. It was true that she had felt unlike herself for the past few weeks, exhausted, either without appetite or suddenly ravenous, emotional and easily prone to tears. But Archie's unexplained absence was surely reason enough for such symptoms. Her husband was missing. He had either abandoned her voluntarily or something catastrophic had prevented his return; it was impossible to find any more comforting explanation. No wonder she felt ill, sometimes nauseous and light-headed, her body reacting to the stress of her situation. Yet as she watched Mercury twist and turn in his sleep, sucking first one thumb then another, a scrap of white blanket first grasped in his hand then tossed aside onto the floor, she began to believe that it could be true. For however distraught she had felt at times by Archie's continued absence, she had never felt entirely hopeless, without direction, as if there were something unconsciously driving and propelling her on. Clea was closer to two hours at the beach. By the time she finally came back, Grace had given Mercury a snack and set him down to play with piles of coloured bricks in a cool corner of the courtyard. Clea brought out a tray of bread, olives and cheese, a jug of the homemade lemonade that Tara had made the previous evening.

"Have you sorted out dates in your mind?" she asked, pushing a plate of food towards Grace. She had been doing little else since Clea left, but was reluctant to admit it.

"What makes you so sure?" She took some cheese and bread, poured a glass of lemonade.

"I have a sense for these things," Clea said. "I could have told you weeks ago. Only you wouldn't have believed me."

"I'm not certain I believe you now," Grace swiftly countered.

"I think you do, but it's the hardest actuality to accept until you have a burgeoning stomach as proof. I would say you're fourteen weeks or so along. Does that sound right?"

"I suppose so," she conceded. "After all, Archie went back to England over three months ago. And I certainly wasn't pregnant when we arrived on the island."

"And I take it that you're pleased?"

"Yes," Grace said, "yes, of course. If it's really true." She found herself unconsciously tracing a finger over the front of her dress. "I just find it hard to accept that this could be happening now when it's what we've both wanted for so long. When it's the most inappropriate time imaginable and I can't even share the news with Archie."

Clea crawled across to Mercury to retrieve a brick that he'd lost under a chair, stilling his distress in a moment.

"There's no such thing as an inappropriate time where a baby is concerned," she said firmly. "They don't arrive according to timetables and the convenience of the moment, you know. But the gift is yours for the taking."

Grace broke off a piece of bread, dipped it in the bowl of dark green olive oil as if suddenly acknowledging she was hungry.

"But how will I cope? On my own, I mean. Of course, there's every chance that Archie might simply turn up one day, but even so."

"You're not on your own, Grace. You're in a good place, here on the island, and with me and the kids and the village all to support you. You mustn't even think of leaving. You belong here more than ever now. I hope you know that."

"But I can't think of staying. How could I presume on your kindness in such a way? I mean if I really am pregnant… well, I shall have to make plans."

Yet even as she spoke Grace knew she had no more desire to leave Kronos than before; in fact, her resolve to stay seemed even more rational, confronted with Clea's goodness and generosity. Daily, her link with her life back in England loosened, receded as if no longer of relevance to her. Clea went on as if she had not even heard Grace's mild protest.

"I have a good doctor here who was wonderful when I had Mercury and I'm familiar with how things work, of course, so there's nothing to worry about. Giving birth is the most natural thing in the world, Grace, remember that. You're a healthy young woman so any complications are extremely unlikely. And you'll find you've got a ready-made baby-minder in Tara. As for the other three, they'll be thrilled to have another little one around."

Clea's certainty was contagious. Grace found herself moving from a state of profound disbelief into one of utter conviction as if she was finally permitting her mind to accept the truth that her body harboured.

"And my mother?" she said, remembering the other news of the morning. "You spoke to her, to Hester?"

"She'll be arriving Friday morning on the ferry," Clea said. "Of course, I explained that we have no vacancies for her to stay here. But I'm sure we'll find her a room close by. There may well be someone with space in the village or a last-minute cancellation at one of the hotels in Anixi Bay. I'll ask around."

Grace found herself suddenly longing to see Hester. She dreaded an inquisition on Archie's behaviour, of course, her mother's hot-headed response to his disappearance. But she knew such reactions stemmed only from her love and could accommodate them, understand their foundation.

"Did she say how long she was planning to stay?"

Clea shook her head.

"I got the feeling it was dependent on how she found things with you. No doubt she'll be expecting to sweep you off back home with her. But don't worry, I'll make it clear you have responsibilities here with me at Adonis House. And you can convince her it's best for the child too. A pregnant woman has right of veto about where she wishes to give birth, remember that, Grace."

Mercury toddled over with an armful of bricks that he toppled onto Clea's lap and into the folds of her voluminous skirt.

"I hope I'm not going to be a liability for you," Grace said, watching the child, the way he clung with absolute trust to her knee.

"Nonsense," Clea said briskly, "you haven't changed into an invalid just because you're expecting a child. I've always worked right up until labour and neither I nor any of my babes have been any the worse for it. As long as you eat well and rest well, you'll sail through the next few months."

On Friday morning, Grace left for the ferry port in Kronos Town before it was entirely light and pulled into the car park in the early pink light of the dawn. Hester, one of the first passengers to disembark, was dressed in a pale blue trouser suit and emerged from the overnight ferry looking fresh and alert. Grace surprised herself at feeling close to tears at the first sight of her mother and swiftly went forward to retrieve her from the scrum of cars and taxis. They drove back to Adonis House on quiet roads, Hester talking constantly, outlining her journey since leaving Oxford the morning before at the same time as looking out of the window and admiring the sweep of the coast road that plunged down to the shore. Grace concentrated on the early traffic of the occasional goatherd, a couple of motorbikes roaring unexpectedly around a corner, the local bus, and wished they could perpetuate such inconsequential talk for a day or two. It was consoling listening to her mother's familiar voice, her habitual expansive turn of phrase and only now did Grace realise how much she had missed her, how in need she was of someone so close to sustain her. Back at the house Clea and Tara were already busy with the guests' breakfasts and after brief introductions, Grace prepared a tray of juice, coffee, fresh figs and bread for the two of them and led Hester down to the bottom of the garden under the jacaranda tree which still had an hour or so of shade to offer. Hester drank two cups of coffee and ate several figs.

"I'd forgotten they didn't just come out of tins sticky with syrup," she said and sat back in her chair, pushing sunglasses on top of her head and bathing her face in the warmth of the sun. "And I'd forgotten how muted and pathetic our English sun is," she added, "compared with this southern Mediterranean heat. What deprived lives we live! And how foolish of us when this is available virtually on our doorstep. And the light! It's like walking onto a fully lit stage, footlights blazing, rather than living under a forty-watt bulb. By the way, Grace," Hester sat up again, replaced her glasses and took the final fig, "I've brought you a few books. I've no idea whether they're your sort of thing, but I thought you might be feeling a bit deprived. I know what you're like, always a book on the go so I made a swift foray to Blackwell's the day before I came away. There was a sweet young man in there and I placed myself, so to speak, in his hands as far as selection was concerned."

"Thank you," Grace said, "you've no idea how much that helps me. I'm always begging any unwanted books off the guests when they leave, but so few of them are in English and I've been feeling bereft without something new to read."

"Ever the bookworm, Grace. You put me to shame."

They sat for a few moments in silence eating breakfast until Hester turned to look at Grace in a way that brooked no more evasion.

"So tell me. I need to know everything your letter didn't say."

Grace spoke slowly, deliberately. "There's really little more to tell than what you already know. I still have absolutely no idea where Archie is. Or if… I mean when he's going to come back. I've tried to find out, done everything I can think of, contacted anyone who might have a clue about where he is."

Hester waved her hand as if in impatience.

"Yes, yes, I know all that. I'm sure you haven't simply been sitting here indolent in the sun, Grace. And your letter gave me the facts. But they were pretty scant, I must say, and unconvincing too. I mean the man loses his mother, attends her funeral then disappears into the blue. My darling girl, do you have any inkling why he should choose to do such a thing? Was there a huge row between the two of you? A major disagreement?"

"No, of course not!" Grace said. "That's not the way things were between us. It just wasn't like that. And anyway…"

"You don't do rows. No, I know that, Grace, you're the least combative, confrontational person alive. Not that it's always a wise option to be quite so passive. Even so, that's the way you are, your natural, benign disposition always choosing to see the best and positive aspects of fellow human beings. A sort of moral choice of yours, I suppose, and I've always envied you for it. But surely that's all the more reason why Archie wouldn't simply abandon you."

Grace poured herself more juice.

"Evidently, there were problems. Financial problems," she said carefully, trying to avoid Hester's intense gaze. "I think I mentioned that in my letter, but not quite the extent to which… well, there were debts. Considerable debts that had built up over quite a long time. It was all a bit out of control, quite frankly. And Archie had lost his job. Not just when the school closed down, but before. The college at Aldgate had evidently… They'd asked him to leave. I had no idea. About any of it, in fact. I mean he always spoke as if there was enough money to fall back on. A safety net, you could say. And he seemed to be so in control that it never occurred to me to doubt that things were… well, very different. I expect you think I'm very foolish not to have known. Not to have asked more questions. Essentially, he was letting us live way beyond our means. Like people with substantial savings and lucrative salaries. Why couldn't I see that?"

Hester took her hand.

"We see what's presented to us. And, after a while, we see what we want to see. What seems to make sense or that we can convince ourselves makes sense. You mustn't blame yourself, Grace. That's nonsense. And I don't suppose even Archie had any idea what he intended to do when he left here to go back to see his mother. No doubt it was just a spontaneous decision, a response to his loss. He panicked, felt rootless and very alone, perhaps."

"But why couldn't he talk to me? And he wasn't rootless! He had me. Has me," Grace corrected herself. "We have a life together and he knows how much I love him. Surely he does."

Hester said nothing for several minutes. She drained the pot of coffee, drinking it thick and black. Grace shifted in her chair, searching for the last strip of shade as the sun filtered its way through the branches of the tree. Then she began to recount in more detail, went through the litany of discoveries that Leo had found, expectant at any moment of her mother's interruption, her exasperation at such behaviour. She shared the little she knew about his suspension from the college at Aldgate, her suspicions that his failure to complete his PhD in his ten years of employment had been influential. Hester listened patiently, her face attentive yet neutral in expression. Eventually, she said,

"Perhaps it was a measure of his love for you that he chose to disappear. In his eyes, he had let you down so badly, Grace. On every level."

"How? That makes no sense to me."

"Well, think about it. When you first met, he was indulging you. Nothing seemed to be beyond him, financially. Plush seats at the ballet, tables at all those smart new restaurants, and those rather ghastly, affluent friends of his to complete the picture. As if he felt he needed to provide you with all that to believe in him. Or to let him believe in himself."

"That wasn't what I fell in love with," Grace said, "not at all."

Hester went on as if she had not spoken.

"Then there was the business about a rural existence in Somerset, a husband supporting you and pursuing his academic studies while you toiled over jam-making, a spot of patchwork, possibly joining the WI. All a sort of fantasy of his own making."

"You're being too harsh. I wanted those things too. Well, the rural life, anyway. I certainly wanted to leave London. It was a joint decision."

"Was it? Did you really discuss it? Of course there's nothing wrong with his decision to move you both to the country, but it strikes me that Archie had created some sort of preposterous image of what he saw as a perfect life. First of all, he tried the cash-rich, materialistic lifestyle of the capital and when that failed or was proving too costly to pursue, it was to be the rural idyll, complete with kitchen Aga and chocolate-box-pretty country house. But he couldn't deliver that either. Financially, the whole thing was combusting around him. Like some exploding volcano or gushing geyser, a mass of froth and lava or something equally insubstantial and unsustainable."

"You make it sound so false. As if our marriage was a lie, built on some false premise of Archie's."

"Nonsense, Grace, don't be so melodramatic. Clearly the man loved you. Otherwise why would he go to the lengths he obviously has to give you what he imagined you wanted? What you deserved, as he saw it."

"I don't understand why he couldn't talk to me," Grace said, running her hands through her hair, limp with the heat, gathering it on top of her head and pinning it with a clasp she found in the pocket of her skirt. "That's what hurts most. The fact that he was being secretive about… so much. Everything, in fact. At times it simply makes me very angry with him."

"Good," Hester said, "anger is healthy. He has behaved appallingly badly, you know."

"I try to see it like that," Grace said, "really, I do. Because logically it's true."

"The man has clearly been a victim of his own self-delusion. And you have been implicated cruelly in it all."

"No," Grace said firmly. "He thought… of course I have no idea what he thought, but…"

A car drew up in the road outside, a taxi, and Grace was pulled back to the other events of the morning, a couple arriving from the mainland to stay for a week and she needed to welcome them.

"Go," Hester said, waving Grace away, "I don't want to keep you from your work when you've so clearly landed on your feet here. I'm quite content to occupy myself, you know, and settle in. Self-reliance is the role I've learned to play best, after all."

Clea had been unable to find accommodation for Hester either in the village or at one of the two small hotels at Anixi Bay. But a *kafenion* that let a couple of rooms had a single that Dimitri, the owner, could let her have for as long as she wanted. Grace had been concerned that her mother would find it basic, too plain, but its simplicity seemed to delight her. That evening, she found her sitting out on her small balcony overlooking the beach, changed into a vibrant yellow skirt and floral shirt, having accommodated herself with alacrity to the room's small, neat space. They walked along to the far end of the beach to have dinner at one of the tavernas perched within splashing distance of the waves, ordered several dishes to share and a large salad of tomatoes, cucumber and feta. Grace talked about Clea and her children. About Adonis House, the village and the island and how attached she had grown to the place in spite of the reasons for her prolonged stay. Hester talked briefly of Fergus and the documentary, the curiosity of seeing his familiar face on the small screen in her living room, reading favourable reviews in the press the next day. Grace felt the strangeness of her absent, remote father suddenly becoming the focus for an entire television audience. Pools of light from the taverna spotted the glassy sea as the last of the day's sandcastles were sucked and swallowed by the waves.

"I am expecting a child," Grace said suddenly, unable to restrain her need to share the news any longer. She watched her mother's face, wary of seeing concern, unease with the prospect, but saw only delight, spontaneous joy. "I was afraid of your reaction, that you'd think the timing so... well, unfortunate. It's not what I'd imagined or planned. Discovering that I am pregnant with Archie absent is hardly ideal."

Hester took her hand across the table, held it warmly.

"This is right for you, Grace, so right. I can't tell you how happy I am. As for the timing being less than perfect, I've long grown out of the idea that everything is comfortably within one's control. A well-planned life is an illusion that only the cowardly and unimaginative believe in."

"Even before I knew, I think it's what has stopped me feeling entirely desolate. As if subconsciously I sensed a reason for feeling positive about the future. Of course there are still times when the outlook seems pretty bleak, but... well, Clea is an enormous help. I'm not quite sure what I would have done without her."

"You were very fortunate to come across her just when you were most in need. She seems to be a very resourceful woman. Unconventional people so often are."

"But I'm not leaving the island, you know," Grace went on hurriedly to stall what she expected her mother to say next. "If you have any thoughts of persuading me to go back with you, you can forget that. Even now I've discovered that I'm pregnant. In fact, to me, there seems even more reason to stay."

The waitress, a young girl in white shorts and a scarlet T-shirt, removed their used plates, replaced them with a dish of watermelon, a small stoppered glass jug of spirit and two thimble glasses.

"I assume this stuff is lethal," Hester said, pouring herself a measure and tossing it back swiftly with a grimace. "On the other hand, it possibly does great things for one's digestion. For mine, that is. No doubt you're sensibly avoiding alcohol right now." She poured a refill, repeated her rapid swallowing and put the glass firmly down on the table. "I might as well drink your measure rather than see it go to waste."

Grace ate a piece of pink watermelon flesh. She waited for Hester to summon up arguments, begin a persuasive entreaty to take her home, but instead she simply asked for dates, details, talked about symptoms, signs, heartburn and hormones as if this was a pregnancy in the most normal and expected of circumstances. They walked slowly back along the seafront, still alive with diners and strollers enjoying the temperate warmth of the late evening air.

"I could very easily get used to this climate," Hester said as they stopped in front of her *kafenion*. She pulled Grace close to her for a moment then held her at arm's length. "Grace, I wouldn't presume to tell you what to do at a time like this if that's what's worrying you. Of course part of me wants to drag you back to Oxford straight away, but what use is that to you? You don't want to be an appendage to my quiet and really rather dull life."

"I have to stay," Grace said. "You see, I promised Archie I'd stay."

Hester started to speak as if to object, but Dimitri, sitting on the terrace of the *kafenion*, called out for her to join him and his wife, Anna, and swiftly ushered her onto the terrace, settled her down with a glass of wine. Grace, resisting their entreaties to join them, drove back along the dark, twisting road towards the village and Adonis House.

She wakes up in the night and thinks of Hester's calm acceptance of her situation. Hester has been all she could hope for. Even her reaction to Archie's disappearance has been surprisingly without judgement. Grace pulls up the single sheet from where it has crowded itself around her feet. The day before her mother's arrival, she had visited Clea's obstetrician, had her pregnancy confirmed by the quiet, attentive doctor. She can expect to give birth around the middle of February, she has been told. If all goes to plan. Grace dates conception to sometime over the days just prior to Archie's departure. She turns over in the bed, traces her fingers on the rough, whitewashed wall of her room and wonders how he would respond if he knew of her pregnancy. It occurs to her now that her apparent inability to conceive before could have added to his sense of failure, further loaded the burden of stress he must have been feeling. Yet the knowledge of responsibility for a new life could weigh equally with him if he knew of it. She closes her eyes, tries to go back to sleep. In the morning she needs to be up early to prepare for two new arrivals, two guest rooms to clean and she is on the early breakfast rota with Tara.

Hester stands on the small balcony of her room, stares up

at the stars, at the moon which is only a day or two away from being full. She cannot imagine that this splendid custardy yellow orb is the same one as in the sky over north Oxford. It is gone one o'clock in the morning, but earlier tiredness has deserted her. She has possibly drunk too much alcohol to allow her to sleep although her mind feels clear, alert rather than stupefied. She has spent the last two hours sitting amongst strangers yet has felt embraced and included in a way that too often eludes her at home. An enormous surge of happiness overwhelms her suddenly. How marvellous life is, she thinks. How spectacularly miraculous it can be with its sudden, unsought surprises and delights. I must live to be at least a hundred and ten to make the most of all there can be on offer! Granted, there are the fallow times, the wading through encrusted thick loam and mud times when the angels of mercy, the wretched fates, seem set against one for their merriment. But then, all of a sudden, the gothic mists clear, opportunity thrusts out a welcoming hand and you are off again on some enticing adventure. *I am to be a grandmother*, she thinks, *God willing*. And takes a cautious step back into her room in case her mildly inebriated state causes an ill-timed topple onto the street below. *This is absolutely no time to abandon ship*, Hester cautions herself. She senses a shift, a discernible awareness that things are changing. *It could be My New Chapter*, Hester thinks, and is delighted by the notion. She is ready for it. Perhaps her sister, Ruth, over in San Diego, is right and she's grown rather provincial, too devoted to the church flower rota, too bothered by the lack of litter bins in the Banbury Road. She was beginning to think it was a matter of age, an inevitable slipping into genteel decline where days and seasons were prescribed by careful routine: the single slice of brown toast and Seville marmalade for breakfast, the welcome pot of Earl Grey at four, glass of Sauvignon at seven. As if it were enough to be mildly relieved by signs of the first snowdrops in January and hosts of golden daffodils in March. As if this were all she could now expect or feel entitled to, a life hovering around the margins, in the wings, as it were, instead of centre stage.

Hester knows that she belongs always centre stage.

And, of course, for Grace too, extraordinary change is now rapid and irrepressible. Hester had imagined arriving on the island to find her daughter bereft and inconsolable; instead, she is resolute and determined. She finds it hard, of course, to share Grace's conviction that Archie will return, is more inclined to think that he has given up on his marriage. Or, of course, on life itself. *But naturally*, Hester thinks, *I'll keep those thoughts to myself.* She slips off her shirt, the yellow skirt, leaves them in a heap on the floor and cannot be bothered to find the nightdress she has not yet unpacked from her case. Switching off the stark overhead light she climbs into the narrow bed, feels the sheets pleasantly crisp and cool on her bare skin. Open-eyed, her mind too active for sleep, she stares at the ceiling. *This child*, she thinks, *Grace's child, will take her forward regardless of the actions of an erstwhile husband. New life. There is nothing as potent with hope and regeneration.*

She needs to tell Fergus.

In spite of his patent neglect of parental duties and obligations over the past decades, he, too, is inextricably a part of this; a grandfather-in-waiting, no less. And, to give him his due, his recent resurge of interest and concern for his daughter – his resort to calls from public phone boxes, even – when he had sounded most anxious about Grace, merit that he is kept up to date. "I am a forgiving woman," Hester says aloud to the white ceiling, "or at least I am not a bitter one." Car headlights reflect into the room, two or three voices and laughter reach her from the *kafenion* terrace below. She discards one pillow from under her head, rearranges a second to suit, turns over onto her side and is swiftly asleep.

***

A couple of days later, Grace arrived at the *kafenion* to find Hester holding a tray of drinks, chatting to some customers on the terrace.

"Dimitri's morning girl is sick," she said to Grace by way of greeting. "So I offered to help out. I'm rather enjoying myself, actually. Reminds me of when I played the maid in a Feydeau farce many moons ago. Although, of course, that was all black uniform dress and lacy apron and cap." She had bought herself a couple of long, cool cotton dresses from a small local shop and, dressed now in one of them, a striking sapphire-blue, she looked transformed from the neat, trouser-suited woman of her arrival. Carefully, she offloaded the contents of her tray and returned it to the bar, calling through to the kitchen that she was off for a couple of hours. Dimitri's wife, Anna, appeared, thanked her warmly. "Any time," Hester said. "I mean that, Anna. I can't sit around in the sun reading flighty novels all day long and Grace has a job to do. She can't be wasting too much time with her aged mother."

They walked down to the western end of the beach and found shade at the beach café. Hester rummaged in her bag for postcards, a pen.

"Now I must be a proper tourist and send a few of these off to people. Ruth, for a start. It will make a change for me to send her a missive from somewhere hot and interesting instead of being on the receiving end of her messages from Florida and the rest."

"What will you say? That you had to come and rescue your

abandoned pregnant daughter who's apparently run out of sense and judgement?" Grace said.

"No such thing," Hester said, "I'll just say something enigmatic and evasive about taking an impulsive holiday. Anyway, you've never lacked common sense, Grace. Judgement, possibly. But I'm hardly one to be casting stones."

"You mean about Archie? When you first met him, that time we drove up to Oxford, you seemed to like him. To approve, as it were."

"He made a good first impression, I'll give him that. Suitable marriage material for a dear daughter. By which I mean he was nicely dressed, had good manners, appeared to adore you and seemed financially secure."

"And after that? After the first impression?"

Hester said nothing for a while. She stared at a couple, stretched out on sunbeds, fondling and embracing each other as if oblivious of anyone else on the beach. A child dug a spade firmly into the sand and let out a cry of anguish when the handle broke. She ordered an iced coffee for herself, lemon tea for Grace.

"I don't feel I ever knew Archie," she said eventually. "He seemed hard to reach. As if he was hidden behind rather a lot of smokescreens that he was keen no one should penetrate. But then I am only the mother-in-law. No reason in the world for him to open up to me."

Hester wrote a postcard to Ruth, one to her neighbour in north Oxford, another to an old actress friend living in Hull. They drank, nibbled at almond biscuits.

"What about my father?" Grace said abruptly. "When he left us, did you accept that it would be forever?"

"Of course not," Hester said. "I gave it six months. For the novelty to wear off and the cold and discomfort of his rural retreat to get to him. Then I gave it a year. To get it all out of his system, as it were."

"And then? When did you admit that he was never coming back?"

"That's not how it works," Hester said. "One doesn't deal with 'nevers' in life. There are few absolutes. You deal with bits of time. We get through days, the weeks, a month goes by. A season or two. You think of planting some spring bulbs for the following year. You think of buying the cards for sending in December. You don't think of thirty years. How can you? It's always impossible to imagine ourselves more than a year or so ahead, after all. I suppose there were some mornings, after Fergus had been gone for ten years or so, when I would wake up and think about divorcing him. Or in the night, even. I'd wake and think, whatever am I doing, clinging on to this preposterous man who hasn't had the time of day for me and Grace since forever. I'd suddenly turn and look at you and realise you were an adorable twelve or thirteen-year-old who wouldn't be recognised in the street by your own father. You deserved something better. But I don't know. I couldn't give you better. Your father was Fergus and, as such, irreplaceable. And it wasn't as if he was a bad man. He was simply… what, eccentric, selfish, disinclined to conform? They're hardly venal sins. And I loved him. Or rather I had loved him dearly and you were a product of that love. So when it came to it, I never felt capable of intentionally severing our connection. It didn't feel right."

"And you never met anyone else, another man you wanted to be with?"

Hester briskly tidied her small stack of postcards, slipped them into her bag.

"Oh, there are always men available," she said, "plenty of men around for the taking. And of course I haven't lived a celibate life since your father left, Grace. Give me some credit. But these men always seemed… well, superfluous, unnecessary as it were. Fine for a little distraction from time to time, to serve an appetite, but in the end always easy to discard. And they wanted too much of me, more than I was capable of giving. I suppose they wanted the part that I had already given to Fergus."

"I think you're more of a romantic than you'll admit."

"Of course I'm a romantic," Hester said, "which means that I am all too aware that life rarely lives up to my romantic ideals."

"And you never entirely gave up on the idea that Fergus might come back one day."

Hester laughed loudly. The woman at the next table, who was berating her son for slurping his drink, glanced round.

"I don't know about that," Hester said. "Perhaps you're right."

"Like Penelope waiting for her Odysseus."

"I always get that Penelope woman mixed up with Pandora."

"Pandora was the one with the box although it was, in fact, a large jar," Grace said. "Penelope was the patient wife."

"Oh yes, of course," Hester said, "and Pandora was tempted to open the lid and let out the contents, spreading evil all around the world. Silly girl."

"Leaving only one thing in there, don't forget."

"Ah yes," Hester said, "the twist at the end of the tale – the spirit of hope."

***

Hester was due to stay on the island for ten days. After a week, however, she was reluctant even to think about going home.

Clea encouraged her to stay on; Grace wanted her to delay her return. At the *kafenion* she had been doing more shifts to help out since the absent waitress had broken her wrist and was little use with serving. Dimitri proposed reducing the cost of Hester's room by over half as well as offering her a generous share of the tips.

"And I'm enjoying myself so much!" she said to Clea at the midweek barbecue at Adonis House. "I'd work for nothing if it came to it. Mind you, I think Dimitri is missing a trick. He really could extend his menu and find the custom. Only today a couple were asking me if we did breakfast. Something more than the basket of bread and apricot jam he offers at the moment." She moved on to offer a dish of olives, replenish glasses and introduce herself to a solitary woman guest who was staring fixedly at the mountains.

"Hester appears to be at ease," Clea said to Grace, "as if she finds this life suiting her. She's adaptable, I admire that in people."

Grace looked across at her mother who was attempting to draw the solitary woman from Sweden into conversation with the man who had arrived at Adonis House that morning, an ornithologist from Roehampton who had come to study the eagles and buzzards of the area.

"My mother is a shape-shifter," she said. "Endlessly capable of reinventing herself. But you're right, she seems very happy."

"Encourage her to stay," Clea said, moving toward the barbecue where Tara was turning chops and chicken. "At least until the end of September. I think it does you good to have her close."

In the end, Hester's ten-day visit turned into nearly five weeks. The season was drawing to a close by the time Grace drove her back early one morning for the ferry crossing to the mainland. The intense heat of high summer was beginning to give way to temperate days, the occasional rain shower and cooler, shorter evenings. The village children were back at school, sleepily walking down the narrow lanes with heavy bags early each morning to wait for the bus that delivered them to the nearby town. The routine of the days was shifting, one season sliding into the next. Grace was now noticeably pregnant. She had felt the first stirrings of movement.

"Not so much a kick as the feeling of a trapped butterfly fluttering its wings," she said as Hester pulled her suitcase out of the boot of the car. She held Grace's face in her hands for a moment, pulled her close.

"I expect you to take great care of my fledgling grandchild," she said. "Now disappear, drive yourself back to the village so we don't stage one of those appalling departure scenes with endless tears on both sides. And make sure you keep in touch. I shall expect bi-monthly updates, you know. Or I may just descend on you again uninvited."

Grace hesitated, fiddled with the single car key in her hand.

"I know it's a lot to ask. And I don't even know where you'll start," she said, "but if you can think of anything you could do to help me find Archie, I'd be… well, it would be good to think someone was still doing something. All the letters I've written, phone calls, the lot, in fact, have come to nothing. I'm sure Leo tried his best, but no doubt he's abroad now."

"Archie may be too, of course," Hester said, "or choosing not to be found. You do know that, don't you Grace? You might have to accept that one day. The man may foolishly and inexplicably have chosen to walk out on you permanently."

"One day, perhaps," Grace said, "but I'm not ready to believe that now. Not yet. I simply can't."

Hester grabbed her suitcase in one hand.

"You sound as stubborn as me," she said, "but I'll try, of course I'll try and do whatever I can for you, my darling girl."

She turned and walked resolutely away towards the queue waiting to embark.

# 15

Melanie Babbington arrived the last week of October. After a couple of weeks of changeable, windy weather, the heat of late summer seemed to return as if anxious for a final emblazon before winter.

"I simply have to get away," she had said to Grace, ringing just ten days before. "Any chance you'd have room for me?"

There was only one reservation, a similarly late booking, for that week and Clea was delighted to let another room so late in the season.

"Now," she said firmly as Grace drove her back from the ferry to Aghia Kallida, "the name Giles Meredith is not going to pass my lips all week. This is a break from him, from all that ghastly situation as much as anything."

Grace concurred. In turn, Melanie was circumspect about Archie after a fleeting enquiry for any news.

By now Grace's working day at Adonis House had diminished considerably and Clea suggested she should view the week with Melanie as something of a well-earned holiday. So there was the opportunity to drive her first to some familiar spots, mountain villages and seaside coves, a remote monastery she had first visited with Archie, a spectacular gorge she had discovered with Hester. Exploring further afield, they found a freshwater lake where Melanie braved the cool water for a brief swim, a restored amphitheatre, endless small white churches, some so precariously clinging to rugged, exposed hillsides that it was hard to understand how they had ever been constructed. Although Grace loved the intense heat of the summer months, the mild, temperate climate of late October brought its own consolation with clarity of air, empty roads and beaches and the sense of a peaceful hiatus between seasons when the days were cool enough to complete jobs ahead of winter. Some small shops dependent upon tourists were closing their doors until spring, garden tavernas moving chairs and tables indoors, barbecues disbanded. Bonfire smoke was evident everywhere across the lush valleys, permitted again now the fire risk of high summer was past. Logs were cut and piled neatly in readiness to fill the large, open fireplaces of the village houses. Even the ubiquitous cats seemed to sense that winter was on its way as they lost their summer sleekness, became fatter, furrier creatures.

Melanie was an easy companion, delighting in all she saw and as happy to sightsee as to sit talking for hours at cafés or in the garden of Adonis House so that Grace felt she grew to know her far better than their snatched conversations at the arts centre had ever allowed. Towards the end of her week's visit, they sat out in the courtyard one night after dinner, convincing themselves there was still enough warmth in the air although Tara brought them out shawls to offset the inevitable dampness of the autumn evening. For the first time, Melanie allowed herself to talk about the arts centre.

"Things have changed quite a bit as far as staffing is concerned," she said. "We've drafted in a team of volunteers which is helping a bit with the cash flow problem. There's a couple of retired women, ex-civil service and appallingly bossy, but nevertheless efficient around the office and frightfully intelligent. Quite scare the pants off me, in fact. But they have time on their hands and organisational skills to boot, so I shouldn't complain. Then we've got some rather sweet school leavers who are happy to fill a few hours before they go off to university next year. Seem to think it will stand them in good stead to have some work experience under their very slender belts even if it's basically leaflet distribution. So we've not actually replaced you, Grace, and we've no doubt lost the budget for your salary if you did ever think of coming back."

"I don't think there's a chance of that," Grace said swiftly. "Whatever happens next, I can't see myself back in Fletwell."

"No," Melanie said, "I rather gathered that. And I can't say I blame you. Seeing you here… well, it's a world away from Fletwell, isn't it?"

"Yes, it is," Grace said, "and yet it seems like…"

"A good fit. As if the place accommodates you."

"Something like that. In fact, exactly that. And yet if it hadn't been for Archie not coming back, I would never have… well, I suppose it's pointless to think in that way. What has happened has happened and…"

The sentence was left incomplete. They sat in silence for some time, drinking tea, nibbling at some pastries that Melanie had bought in the village bakery that afternoon, layers of tissue-thin filo pastry filled with honey and nuts. The only other guest that week, a quiet, seemingly self-absorbed man of about fifty, stepped out into the courtyard, but on seeing Grace and Melanie, furtively retreated. The two women exchanged glances.

"Are we that off-putting?" Melanie said. "Poor man, I expect he thinks we're discussing stretch marks and pregnancy piles. Shall we call him back? He's a bit of a dish in an unassuming sort of way. I'd like to get to know him better."

"I can't tell you much about him," Grace said, "except that he was a last-minute booking like you. Tara might know more, I expect, as she's been serving him at breakfast this week."

"There you are," Melanie said, "it's meant! Two late

bookers obviously destined to meet, both in need of a new start. Serendipity, isn't that what they call it?"

Grace felt Peter Merritt, quiet to the point of withdrawn and clearly content with his own company, would be a challenge even for Melanie. Each morning he left the house early in the company of only a small backpack, a pair of binoculars hanging from his neck, and returned mid-evening to retreat to his room. She could not imagine Melanie would be able to breach his guard. Their conversation drifted.

"You know, I nearly went into midwifery," Melanie said suddenly, cupping her hands around her mug of lemon tea, "then I got distracted by school nursing instead. Actually, I'm thinking of going back into nursing of some sort. That's if I can manage to rescue my medical knowledge and qualifications from the meaningless flotsam of artistic admin, of course. I'm ready for a move, geographically as much as anything."

Grace was surprised and very aware of the implication for Melanie of leaving Fletwell. She went on, as if in confirmation of the thought. "Of course, it's partly a means to an end. If I leave the arts centre I can get away from Giles. If I take myself off somewhere, at least a hundred miles from Fletwell and return, possibly, to nursing, it will be easier to resist. He, the man himself, will be easier to resist. Like a dieter chucking out the chocolates or an alcoholic disposing of the gin. It's the only way I'll wean myself off him, I can see that now."

"I thought you believed there was a future for you with Giles."

Melanie pulled a face. She took the last piece of pastry, licked fingers sticky with trailing honey.

"That's what I've always told myself, believed it even, for a long while. But it's all nonsense, just a pathetic fiction, and I've finally allowed myself to realise it. If Giles had wanted us to be together, it would have happened by now. He's not a particularly patient man. He gets what he wants, when he wants it." She leant her head back, stared up at the dark star-streaked sky. "And anyway, such a thing would come at too high a price ever to bring complete happiness."

"You mean because of his children."

"The collateral damage, yes. And then there's his wife, Beth. She does have a legal claim on the bastard and has every right to stride the moral high ground if she chooses. Whereas I... well, guilt becomes increasingly difficult to handle as you get older, I find, and I'm not so sure I'm entirely happy with the role of culpable mistress, after all. Oh, there's simply so much ugliness involved in this marriage break-up business. You think it will be easier once the kids are out of childhood, but if anything it probably makes it even trickier. The hard-edged judgement of a couple of pubescent teens is not for the faint-hearted, I imagine. And, quite frankly Grace, I'm growing just a little tired of it all. Of coming way down the list of Giles' priorities, being unable to plan, look ahead, a hostage, if you like, to his whims and obligations. It's not that I love him any less. If only I did it would make a split all the easier. But I'm beginning to dislike myself, for my involvement, my rather sad situation in the sorry mess. And, of course, in my saner moments, I have to admit to acknowledging the fact that a man who can betray once can betray again. Perhaps I am beginning to lose just the teeniest bit of respect for him."

They were interrupted by Tara who came out looking for a book she'd mislaid and Melanie, immediately abandoning her mood of introspection, asked about the quiet guest, Peter Merritt.

"Single, evidently," Tara said, "or at least I know he is now although I get the feeling there was a wife somewhere in his past. Even a child, a boy. Lives in... I'm not very good with English places so I forget the names. Something like... no, that's it – he lived near Cambridge for years, but he's recently moved to London. Or near London. You'll have to ask him."

"Oh I will, Tara, thank you, thank you so much!" Melanie enthused. "And clearly the man is not as socially inept as he suggests if he's been sharing so much with Tara. Just a little shy and reserved, no doubt."

"Go gently with him, Melanie," Grace said. "We don't want the poor man frightened off homeward before the end of his stay."

Tara found her book. She rubbed her bare arms, shivered visibly.

"It's autumn now," she said, "too cold to be outside at night. Stop pretending, you two, and come inside. There's a fire lit." She turned to go then stopped as if suddenly remembering something she needed to share. "And another thing I found out, talking to Peter Merritt. Apart from the fact that he's a keen ornithologist." She smiled broadly at Melanie. "He used to be a vicar."

***

Hester watches her neighbour sweep leaves in his back garden into five neat piles, parcels of amber and russet and gold that he will later consign to a smouldering bonfire. She dislikes city garden bonfires in autumn when they seem an unnecessary dispatch of nature's final colour of the year. *Let the leaves mulch, compost, decompose at their own leisure,* she thinks, and is pleased when she sees him casting a disparaging eye over the fence at her own unkempt foliage. She leaves the neighbour to his desecration and takes herself into the living room to stare out of the front window at the Sunday evening traffic on the Banbury Road. She is restless and bored and is impatient with herself for harbouring such feelings. She has always been intolerant of people who express such attitudes and has been known to upbraid such complainants with a list of the books they could be reading, the languages available to learn, the activities and societies and organisations available to them to allay such ennui. But now she admits to her own sense of dissatisfaction. She watches a young man pausing to allow his spaniel to sniff at her gate, an elderly woman, Bible in one hand, black handbag in the other, hurrying past. A man in a purple Mini pulls up in the curb to consult a map. Two cyclists ride slowly by as if with nowhere in particular to get to. Hester rearranges the cushions on her cream sofa, draws the curtains on a street that still harbours early evening light. "I am lonely," she says aloud to her pale walls, and is shocked by her confession. Hester is a woman who has never allowed herself to admit to such a state. She has always seen loneliness as an affliction of the weak, the spineless, and has firmly steered clear of association with either camp. Now, although she knows she has an address book of friends she can ring and is in possession of the social skills to invite in a neighbour or two to share a bottle of wine, she knows neither will satisfy some deeper yearning for company. For companionship.

She blames it on the island. On Kronos. Now, instead of feeling accommodated by her quiet, tasteful flat, her genteel evenings of light classical recordings, a little jazz, a simple cheese omelette and perhaps a ripe pear, she feels estranged, repelled even, by such solitariness. By the order and predictability and restraint of such living. Leaving Grace behind, pregnant and composed in spite of the débâcle of Archie's disappearance, was naturally difficult. But her disaffection stems from more than maternal feeling. At least she thinks it does. She imagines the place now, the island, the village, the *kafenion* at Anixi Bay where she worked alongside

Dimitri and his wife, Anna. She sees the old men sitting for hours over a glass of local spirit, worry beads endlessly passing from one hand to the other, children scampering in the safe streets, large families gathered around long tables eating late and deep into the night. Hester has never thought of herself as someone dependent upon the company of others, has always prided herself on her independence. Now, however, she suspects it has been necessity rather than choice that has schooled her in such habits. She thinks of her week ahead, the planned events adorning her wall calendar in the kitchen and knows she cannot complain of isolation when she has so much arranged to occupy her days. But it all feels contrived; it lacks spontaneity. Within a day or two of staying on the island she had felt sufficiently at ease with the place to sit and talk and drink on the terrace of the *kafenion*, to wander quiet village lanes at night or walk to catch the sun rising on the beach in the early morning. Her behaviour was unconstrained by convention and custom. Contrarily, it was easier on the island to be both alone and in the company of others. There appeared to be no need to create a web of purposeful activity to justify rising from bed each day the way she did at home; the wretched church flowers, her cinema visits, cheap matinees at the Playhouse to see some appalling student production. *And another thing,* Hester thinks, walking back to the kitchen to ferret in the fridge for the chilling bottle of Frascati, *I wore no labels there. Unlike here. Here I am a single woman well beyond middle age, a woman reputedly separated from her husband and thus with a marital status vague if not downright suspect. I am ripe for pity and therefore for patronage or avoidance. Certainly for exclusion. I don't quite fit into cosy invitations to dinner with other contented couples. I am of no financial significance to merit being included at fundraising bashes. I am not known to be learned or terribly intellectual which would accord me a status, a certain regard in this city of erudite minds.*

*In fact, I am, to all intents and purposes, a* persona non grata. *One of the dispossessed. A bit of an oddity.*

*But not there. Not on the island, on Kronos. My dubious marital history, my career implosion failed to render me a social pariah, unsuited to civilised circles. The events of my past life were simply that, stories about myself that I could choose to tell or not. And everyone I met had some sort of story. I can see why Grace wants to stay. I can even see why Archie, no doubt tinkering on the brink, sensing the inevitable collapse of all his fabrications, chose to take Grace there, talked of staying permanently. If only the fool had not lost courage and run away altogether, they could have picked themselves up from the débris he had strewn and pieced and patched themselves a new and decent sort of existence.*

She glares out of the kitchen window as she sips steadily at her Frascati, glowers at the neighbour's bonfire, which is swelling smoke and flames as he stokes it with a broken broom handle and throws on some paraffin for good measure. Swiftly, she draws down the blind, returns to the sitting room, makes a short phone call to confirm the arrangements for a few days of house-sitting in Burford. Then sits staring at the phone wanting, illogically, to ring Fergus.

At this moment, the only person she wants to talk to is Fergus.

She wants to talk inconsequentially about impending grandparenthood. She would like to tell him that she spoke briefly to Grace that morning and that she is well, 'blooming', as the women's magazines would put it, with just an occasional touch of indigestion, which is only to be expected at twenty-six weeks. But it is not only Fergus' lack of a phone line that inhibits her. It is far more than this. Hester feels herself being trawled back, as if accessing again a feeling, a certain emotion that she has long thought irrelevant and redundant to her. Once she loved Fergus. She loved him profoundly.

In all the years she has spent without him, she has known other men, grown fond of some of them, briefly become besotted with one or two. But she has always weaned herself easily away, irritated by certain habits, infuriated by particular traits. For each time she has found that she cared about these men insufficiently to view any of them as anything other than transient diversions. And, in spite of his betrayal, his cruel and unmerited departure to deepest Wales, during the decades of his absence, she has never managed entirely to stop herself from caring about Fergus. Loving the man, even. "Damn, damn, damn, damn!" Hester declares aloud to the Rodin print on her wall then switches on the television in an effort to find some distraction. Early Sunday evening programming, however, offers little relief and she abandons *Songs of Praise,* her near-empty glass of Frascati, finds a jacket, changes her shoes and takes herself off for a walk into the city.

She had written to Fergus as soon as she was home from her stay on the island. At first there had been no reply, a response which had annoyed but hardly surprised her given his negligent attitude towards communicating. Then he had surprised her with a phone call, apologising even, for the delay, explaining that he had been ill, briefly in hospital. Hester had found herself gripping the receiver hard, trying to suppress a sense of anxiety as she had asked him more. He had paused, mumbled something about his chest, a bad cough, shortness of breath, sounding embarrassed to share his symptoms and only when pressed admitted to "a touch of pneumonia". When Hester pursued for more detail he agreed that he had been foolish to ignore a course of antibiotics prescribed in the wake of an X-ray in August and that the consequent emergency admission into hospital a few weeks later had been chiefly of his own making. "So you're all right now?" she found herself needing to know. "Right as rain," Fergus had said, "fighting fit," before adding, "just the usual aches and pains, of course." Then Hester had told him that Grace was pregnant. There had been another long pause during which she had begun to wonder whether he had run out of coins to feed the public phone box in the hamlet below his hill. Eventually, Fergus had said, in his low, measured way, "I am beyond delighted, Hess, this is very good news." And Hester had found herself inexplicably close to tears.

Walking briskly, before long she is into St Giles, passing a restaurant, a couple of pubs, endless ranks of bicycles and a narrow strip of shops. She slows down as she passes the Randolph Hotel, feeling flushed by the energetic pace of exercise, realising that she's covered a couple of miles in under forty minutes. Impulsively, she slips into the thickly carpeted reception hall, finds one of the large lounges where she knows she can sit mostly unobserved for an hour or so. Two or three couples occupy other areas of the room; a large woman in a red dress sits with a man who pays her lavish attention, stroking her hand, whispering into her ear; a younger couple walk in, hand in hand, head for the sofa by the window, where they sit quite silently, staring out of the plate glass windows onto Beaumont Street.

And Hester wonders about attraction.

About the irrational and often arbitrary lure one has for another. *How easy it would be,* she thinks, *if one could choose to fall in love with the sensible choice, select the kind, the available, the propitious partner to ensure a steady path through life. Instead, we so often seem propelled to love perversely. And what is it that we love in one another, anyway? The first time I saw Fergus,* she remembers, *he was pouring himself a drink in the kitchen of that squalid little flat in Baron's Court. Something about him, a certainty of purpose, the way he turned and leaned against the wall simply watching, how he chose his moment to walk calmly across the room and talk to me. And then, of course, the voice, his voice attracted me from the start, low, measured yet clear and confident so I was drawn to listen to him. Is it possible that one really falls in love with such insignificant details in another? And contrarily, can it be the minor, irritating yet innocuous mannerisms and habits that can stand in the way of passion?*

A waiter sweeps past, hovers in front of Hester and she orders a pot of coffee to allow her to sit on in her comfortable lounge seat. She has to do more to try and find Archie. After all, the man may well still be alive. They have to do more, she and Fergus, to help Grace who, for better or worse, richer and certainly poorer, unquestionably loves the man. Hester has already rung hospitals. She has contacted the worthy souls of the Salvation Army, but so far has drawn similar blanks to Grace in her pursuit of answers. She must speak to Fergus again. The two of them should sit across a table from each other and plan a campaign of sorts. It is the least Fergus can do after decades of paternal neglect. The waiter brings her coffee and, energised, she asks him if he can fetch her writing paper, a pen. Within half an hour she has written a short letter to Fergus, insisting that he meet her somewhere mutually convenient. Cardiff, she suggests, Swansea even, thinking of a city railway station and an assignation under a big clock. Then she swiftly drinks her cooled coffee, bothers the man at reception for a stamp and entrusts her letter to the hotel post box. She is home by nine and gives over the rest of the evening to the remnants of the bottle of Frascati and a plate of scrambled egg.

***

The first snow fell over the mountains at the end of November. Grace woke one morning to find a white-capped backdrop to

Aghia Kallida, even though the courtyard at Adonis House still provided a couple of hours of heat most days.

"I'd never imagined snow in this part of the world," she said to Clea that morning as they sorted linen after the departure of the last guests of the year. "People just associate islands like this with sun-drenched beaches."

"That's where they're wrong, Grace. And there's a market there I would like to tap, if I knew how to reach it. There's no reason why we shouldn't operate in the winter as a place for people who want to see the snow, possibly ski on short runs, walk in the mountains, that sort of thing. It's unproductive to think of us as only a destination for sun-seekers."

Grace handed Clea the last of the pile of neatly folded sheets, crisply laundered and ironed pillowcases, and watched her place them in the large linen cupboard on the landing of the guest bedrooms. Since Melanie's visit at the end of October and Peter Merritt's departure a week later, there had only been three guests, a middle-aged couple from Belgium and a single woman from Paris, a linguist who had gratified Grace by leaving behind copies of English novels she had been reading; Jean Rhys and Muriel Spark paperbacks were now stowed away in her room, feasts for famine days.

Melanie had approached Peter Merritt at breakfast on her final full day at Adonis House. Grace had left them talking, clearing away around them and discreetly bringing them more coffee two hours later. That evening, Tara's birthday, Clea had thrown an impromptu barbecue party, the last of the year, inviting villagers and friends as well as Peter and Melanie. Grace had noticed Peter's apparent ease with Melanie's monopoly of him throughout the evening. Early the next morning, she had driven her to catch the ferry.

"Peter's a lovely man," Melanie had said as if a conversation had been interrupted. "Not shy at all once he relaxes. A little reserved, of course, but then he has been a vicar. That would rather go with the territory, I would have thought."

"Why do vicars stop being vicars?" Grace had asked as she drove them out of the village towards the coast road. "Why did Peter Merritt?"

"His wife left him. Evidently, she had an affair with one of the parishioners. Can you imagine such a thing? Poor Peter, it left him devastated. And it turned out that he wasn't the first, this particular parishioner. She'd been making quite a reputation for herself, straying from the vicarage and Peter was the last to find out. Of course he wanted to get away, couldn't face staying with all the tittle-tattle going on. And also he had serious doubts about continuing in the church at all, standing up in the pulpit and preaching moral truths to others when he'd been so compromised himself."

"So are you planning on staying in touch?" Grace had asked. Melanie ferreted in her handbag for a small scrap of paper, producing it as if it was a winning ticket.

"I have his address and phone number right here," she had said, beaming.

"And he has yours?"

"Of course, although I suspect that I shall have to make the first move. He's a little lacking in self-esteem at the moment. Well, you would be, wouldn't you? What with his whole life being turned upside down."

Melanie had talked rapidly on while she drove. There was a child involved, a boy of eight, and a custody case ongoing that Peter Merritt had every hope of winning. Grace had sensed Melanie's need to steep herself in a complex domestic issue that could provide her with a cause, a crusade of sorts. At the port, they had stood beside Melanie's large suitcase, waiting for embarkation to start.

"Thanks, Grace, for putting up with me when I thought

I was coming out here to support you. But the week's given me a chance to think, get it all in perspective, as they say, and see things as they really are. It's not going to be easy, ditching Giles and moving on, of course. But it has to be done. I see that now."

"And I suppose you think Peter Merritt could help sweeten the severance? However beleaguered and confused the poor man must be at the moment."

Melanie had smiled, hugged Grace warmly.

"I think we might be able to help each other a bit," she had said, "offer some mutual consolation. I am fond of the man already. Very fond. And that's a promising start."

★★★

The olive harvest began in early December during a dry, mild spell and straddled Christmas, and into the New Year. The roads around the village were busy again now, not with holiday coaches and tourists' hire cars, but with vehicles of every shape, size and condition trundling sacks of picked olives to the factory to be turned into oil. Grace felt redundant. It seemed as if the whole island was involved in some way with the harvest and it was valuable employment for seasonal workers from the hotels and bars. Tara, Alara and Venus spent any free days from school helping out friends with large olive groves and Clea taxied sacks for villagers without transport, returning from the mill each night to deliver litres of rich, dark green olive oil. They paid her in kind so that the larder store at Adonis House was already well stocked for the coming year. At seven months pregnant, Grace felt fit and well, if prone to light-headedness and fatigue. There was so little demanding her attention that she felt pangs of guilt when watching Clea constantly moving from one task to another, painting jobs around the house, repairs, gardening and she contributed as much as she could to the household by cooking for the family most evenings. She tried hard not to allow herself to think of what would happen once the baby was born. She was aware of existing in a defined span of time, letting the rhythms of her pregnancy take over, allowing herself to focus only on the weeks that counted down to her due date.

Beyond that, it was impossible to imagine.

She had no idea whether it was her unique situation, the absence of Archie, her impulsive decision to stay on the island that made it so hard to believe in the truth of this child. In the reality of impending motherhood. Or whether a state of disbelief attended all women expectant for the first time, the everyday miracle of conception and creation. So for the most part, the present was sufficient, her attention focused on the squirming, prodding, jabbing, nudging movements she watched as she lay on her bed, her hand lightly resting on her splendidly rounded abdomen. Her body seemed to her miraculous, a fully functioning, efficient machine that had unlocked and tapped into a wealth of mechanisms that had lain dormant, ready, on a given signal, to develop a creative marvel. She had expected only nominal interest from Clea who had, after all, experienced four pregnancies, but she had misjudged her. Clea was constantly curious, ever ready to talk as if gaining some vicarious pleasure from this imminent new life. She dug out baby clothes and blankets and shawls and found the rough-hewn wicker crib that she had used for Mercury.

"Best to be ready," she said to Grace, carrying it to her room and placing it in the small space available under the window.

"But there's still ten weeks to go," Grace protested yet found herself infinitely moved by the sight of the small crib as if it defined something that still felt remote and amorphous.

She placed the washed, neatly folded and aired baby clothes in the bottom drawer of the chest and each day was drawn to taking them out as if these tiny, soft garments were some talisman of good fortune.

Most days, in the late afternoon, a log fire was lit in the large open fireplace of the sitting room of Adonis House. Clea took out brightly coloured woven rugs and spread them over the stone floors. She filled the house with hurricane lanterns that could offer candlelight in preference to the glare of light bulbs. Grace liked to sit with Tara, Alara and Venus as they completed homework for school, listening to their conversation to try and improve her own grasp of the language. They were bilingual and often their exchanges would be an intriguing mix, the most suitable word being grabbed from either vocabulary to suit the purpose. Grace craved their ability and began to make a more concerted effort to learn. Methodically, she worked her way through the pages of the phrase books she found around the house, intended for the use of eager guests, and tried hard with mastering the challenges of the alphabet. Clea, seeing her sitting one evening studying and silently moving her mouth in an attempt to grasp pronunciation, suggested she might like to help the children improve their written English and Grace was relieved to feel useful. She soon found that although Alara and Venus could talk effortlessly enough they were far more limited in their ability to write confidently and even Tara was grateful for her support. In turn, Tara helped her slowly master a little more conversation so that she could begin to feel more integrated into the place. Although communication was no problem with most people having at least a smattering of English, Grace felt it was lazy of her to rely on this and was gratified when villagers encouraged and responded to her tentative efforts.

Near Christmas, she contacted Leo at the address in East

Anglia he had given her before leaving the island in June. He knew nothing, she realised, of her pregnancy. Her message, a brief couple of lines in a card, was factual and posted with little thought of a response. She was touched, therefore, to receive by return, a short letter thanking her for her news and enclosing travellers' cheques to the worth of five hundred pounds. 'For costs incurred,' he wrote, 'for the birth of my niece/nephew.'

# 16

Hester arrives early. She has told Fergus that she will meet him at twelve o'clock by the ticket office in case there is no central clock at Cardiff station that they can rely upon as a meeting place. She has nearly twenty minutes to compose herself, inspect her reflection in the cracked mirror of the ladies' toilet, straighten her skewed silk scarf. The day is cold, bleak, with an unremitting sense of darkness about it to tempt sluggishness and indolence. She has feared Fergus will cancel. After all, climbing down his Welsh hillside and making his way to a bus stop to travel to a town to switch buses to catch a second to reach another town that will provide him with a national coach to bring him to Cardiff to meet his estranged wife of some thirty years who has recently become a more insistent force in his life, are, to say the least, challenging obstacles.

And it is December with the suggestion of sleet in the biting air to further confound the day.

But he is here. Hester sees him first, his tall, gangly figure, still youthful from a distance, his hair resolutely thick and only greying sporadically, standing amongst the discarded cigarette butts and random litter of the forecourt, a still presence in the midst of the constant comings and goings of the place. Fergus has always managed detachment as if he is never quite of the moment, but a step or two outside it, a voyeur almost. *Like Grace,* Hester thinks, *a little like Grace.* And Grace has, of course, taken on also the shape of his face, his long limbs and spare physique. Hester sees this now as if the knowledge has been long lodged, but only just revealed. She walks towards him, waiting for him to turn from the queue of passengers apparently holding his attention and is gratified to see his impulsive smile, notes how his hand involuntarily moves to the collar of his coat as if adjusting any misalignment. She is unsure whether to kiss his cheek, offers her gloved hands instead and they attempt an awkward embrace.

"Coffee," Hester says in an inappropriately loud voice so that a woman close by turns in surprise. "Dear God, I need a cup of coffee, Fergus. Do you think there's anything decent to be had at the station?"

"I doubt it," he says, "shall we walk a bit? Bound to be something preferable to a British Rail cafeteria."

Hester peers up at the leaden sky, feels the raw air like sharp splinters in her skin.

"It could snow," she says, "it might very well snow."

"Not yet," Fergus says, taking her arm, heading her towards the station exit. "Later. It will probably snow by five. We've hours before that."

They find a quiet café in a backstreet, take a table in the window. Coffee arrives promptly in large, thick white cups.

"I seem to remember being here before," Hester says, staring out at the pavement, across the road at the narrow row of small shops. "The city, I mean. Oh, decades ago, before Grace was born. I think I was in a third-rate production of… of something."

"Rattigan," Fergus says, "*The Deep Blue Sea,* and it wasn't third rate. At least you weren't. You made me cry, I remember. That moment when the husband throws the shilling for the gas meter."

"I'd forgotten," Hester says, "I'd forgotten you saw it."

"Hester playing Hester," Fergus says and spoons brown sugar into his cup.

"Pardon?" she says. "Oh, yes, of course. Hester and Freddie and… whatever the husband's called. A small cast – very popular with managements in those days."

And she remembers clearly now; the theatrical digs on the outskirts of the city, the smell of frying that had seemed steeped into the fabric of the place, into the faded wallpaper and thin sheets and hard pillows. She remembers waking in the night, so cold that her fingers and toes were numb and in the morning sheets of ice covered the insides of the narrow windowpanes. She picks up her cup, drains it. She looks across the table at Fergus who is looking back at her as if having just noticed a particular feature in her face, her eyes, nose or cheekbones, something that suddenly surprises his expectation. Self-consciously, she finds herself turning aside, looking out at the winter day, passers-by shrouded in thick coats and muffling scarves. Heads are down against the bitter wind that is picking up and skittering litter, empty crisp packets and discarded cigarette boxes and stray sheets of newspaper.

"Grace," Fergus says after a moment or two, "we're here to talk about Grace. How is she?"

Hester shrugs, flexes her fingers as if inspecting her painted nails.

"Resilient. Robust. Impervious to negative thoughts."

"About the husband, you mean?"

"Archie, yes. She… well, Grace sees goodness in every human heart, of course. I used to think of it as a failing in her. Saw it as a naïve lack of judgement. These days, though, I'm not so sure. Perhaps it's the only way to live peaceably, equably, alongside one another. Anyway, she's resolved to wait for him."

"So she definitely wants him back? If, that is, he is – well, shall we say able and willing to return?"

"Oh yes. There's no doubt about that. Forgiveness is Grace's stock-in-trade, after all. Besides, she loves him. Loves him unconditionally, it would seem. And Grace does appear to have an enormous capacity for love. Most women would have given such behaviour as Archie's short shrift, I can tell you."

Fergus takes Hester's hand in his for a moment then withdraws swiftly as if uncertain of the propriety of the gesture. She feels an irrational urge to pull him close, to reach across the narrow café table and bury her head into his neck, let her fingers roam through his unkempt hair, feel the roughness of his bottle-green woollen sweater against her cheek. She is close to tears, feels her throat thickening and knotting with the emotion she has suppressed now for weeks. And she has no idea whether the cause of such foolish tears is solely her anxiety for Grace's state or relief at being able to share it at last with Fergus. With Grace's father. She forages in her handbag for a tissue, mutters something about a cold. Fergus sees her empty coffee cup, signals to the waitress to bring another. He has allowed his to grow cold and he glances down at it now, a skin formed on its surface, and swallows it at a gulp. Hester begins a rambling account of her futile attempts over the past couple of months to find news of Archie. She has, she admits, in desperation even taken the coach from Gloucester Green to Victoria on one or two occasions and spent the day furtively checking the underpass at Waterloo, benches along the Embankment, around St Martin-in-the-Fields, returning home each time overwhelmingly relieved not to have spotted her son-in-law amongst the beleaguered and bereft yet also at a loss for where else to seek. Fergus listens, his face grave even when Hester attempts a self-deprecating remark about her uneasiness amongst the dispossessed; their rancid smell, their skinny, despondent dogs, their cardboard constructions attempting faux domestic comfort. Of course it's also occurred to her, she goes on rapidly, that she is looking in entirely the wrong place, that destitution is the opposite of Archie's current state and that he has, in fact, taken up with an affluent woman who is showering him with extravagance and excess. She should, perhaps, be striding the pavements of Chelsea and Knightsbridge, peering through the windows of champagne bars and fancy restaurants for her chance sightings.

"It's all hopeless, I know," she says eventually. "Proverbial needles in proverbial haystacks and all that. And if it was just Grace rather than Grace and her unborn child that was the issue, well, I wouldn't be lifting a finger to search for the renegade, I can tell you that."

Hester finishes her coffee, replaces the cup more firmly than she intends so that the spoon spins across the table towards Fergus. He picks it up, replaces it.

"You know that's not true, Hess," he says softly. "You would use every last breath in your body to help Grace, whatever her situation."

Hester fiddles with the neck of her grey polo-neck sweater, straightens the silver chain that has caught in the weave of the wool. She feels suddenly very tired. The café's subdued lighting and warmth, the comforting smell of toast and teacakes and ground coffee beans have lulled her into a not unpleasant state of lethargy where she feels ill-suited to strategic thought and planning. She could so easily put her head down on the table, pillow it on her folded arms and doze the rest of the day away. December is a somnolent month, she thinks, too scant of daylight to even bother with the exertions of rising, washing and dressing each morning when darkness begins to encroach again within hours. And she cannot imagine now why she suggested this meeting with Fergus in the first place, what she thought it could possibly resolve in the light of her waning campaign. She glances at her watch, wonders whether an earlier train home would be advisable.

Fergus reaches into his pocket, produces a small notebook and pushes it across the table to her. Silently, she turns over the pages, filled with his careful cursive script detailing letters written, phone calls and enquiries made.

"No doubt I've been following in your path a lot of the time, Hess, and Grace's too, of course, but I have invoked the advice of those television people. You know, the ones who made that preposterous series featuring me in the opening programme. That woman – Pauline Larrington or Primrose or some such – she's been quite helpful, actually. I have to give her that."

Hester is astounded.

"You contacted her? That woman who… of course, she was at their wedding. Why didn't I think of her?"

"Not that she knew Archie particularly well, I understand. In fact, her being at the wedding was just chance – she happened to be staying with friends of his, err… Margaret and Bertie, would it be?"

"Monica and Bernard," Hester prompts.

"That's right, rather a terrifying woman, that Monica, I seem to remember. She insisted on cornering me just before I left that restaurant wanting to talk about Dylan Thomas. Did I live anywhere near Laugharne, she wanted to know. Very odd. I think she'd been overdoing the red wine, if truth be told. Anyway, the Larrington woman was staying with them, with these Monica and Bernard people, while her place was being built or renovated or the like and so evidently she ended up with an invite to the wedding. No doubt it was felt she couldn't be left out. But as it happens, she's proving invaluable. A resourceful woman, there's no doubt about it."

Hester feels wrong-footed. She has imagined coming here today to galvanise Fergus into some sort of piecemeal action; instead, she finds him leading, herself crawling a little in awe behind. She watches him flick through the pages of the notebook, propelling pencil in one slim hand, his eyes scanning swiftly through his careful notes looking for the essential details to share. And she is aware of the slightest stir of unease within her, such an irrational and therefore redundant emotion that she tries to suppress it. But as Fergus takes her through his dealings with Primrose Larrington, outlining the contacts and networks she has suggested in his search for Archie, some methods he could employ, Hester concedes to herself the root of her disquiet; she feels jealous, disarmed by their association, disquieted by his exploitation of the connection.

Yet at the same time she is immeasurably consoled by it as if this gesture from Fergus, his profound concern for Grace, is a reaffirmation of his paternal love in which she wants to believe.

Eventually, Fergus closes his notebook, slips it back into his pocket and suggests they should order something more in order to justify their occupation of the table. Soup and a cheese roll arrive for Fergus. Hester drinks more coffee, attempts a mince pie. There is silence between them for a while; the café shifts over the busy lunchtime trade and gradually empties around them until they are one of only two occupied tables. Hester sees Fergus covertly checking his watch.

"You have a train to catch," she says.

"A coach, actually, or rather two coaches. So yes. And you too. A train, that is."

Hester shrugs.

"It's an easy journey back to Oxford. Yours is more complicated, I imagine. And no doubt hens to house and dogs to feed and cats to placate when you eventually get there."

Fergus smiles. He reaches out and touches the back of her hand for a moment, starts to say something then turns and shrugs his arms into his large coat instead. They walk back to the station together. The scant light of the day is already receding, cars turning on headlights although it is barely three o'clock. The air is raw, a sharp wind tunnelling down the side streets and Hester fumbles for gloves. On the station forecourt, a group of young carol singers, all bobble hats and long knitted scarves, launch enthusiastically into 'Hark the Herald Angels Sing'.

"I'll be in touch, Hess," Fergus says as they arrive at the station, check the time of the Oxford train. "News or no news, I'll be sure to keep you up to date."

"It would make life a lot easier if you overcame your outmoded reluctance to the telephone, you know, Fergus," Hester says, feeling curiously reluctant now to see him disappear to the coach station to begin his arduous trek back to his remote hillside. "We're only a dozen or so years away from the 21st century, after all."

"You're probably right," he says after a pause, "actually, I did start to look into it when I was ill in the summer. I thought it might be… well, sensible. So I have moved in that direction. Of a phone line, that is."

Hester places a gloved hand on his shoulder, leans towards him, brushes his cheek with a kiss.

"Happy Christmas, Fergus."

She moves swiftly away into the thick throng of passengers and turns only when she is too far away to hear any reply. But Fergus is already gone. For a moment she thinks she glimpses him by the carol singers, succumbing to the rattled collecting box, but it is someone else entirely, shorter, slighter, and of no significance to her at all.

★★★

On the morning of 25th December, Grace opened gifts from Hester that had arrived a few days before. On the island no one else would be opening presents until 1st January, St Basil's Day, but Grace could not resist ingrained habit and woke early to unwrap a soft, pale blue loose sweater that easily accommodated her expanding shape and a silver necklace. She had anticipated a sense of strangeness and dislocation over Christmas, but found herself easily caught up in the different celebrations. Besides, as she told Hester when they spoke on the phone later in the morning, every day for the past six months had presented the unusual and unknown; simply experiencing the season in alternative style was inconsequential.

"How are you?"

"Enormous. I can't remember what it's like to see my toes."

"That sounds normal. I hope you're looking after yourself, Grace."

"I'm being spoilt. And I feel as if I'm the centre of attention for the whole village. An old lady came up to me yesterday in the baker's and insisted on buying me a pastry. I couldn't understand a word she said, but she placed a hand on my stomach and mumbled something very fervently."

"Well, you certainly wouldn't find that here in north Oxford," Hester said, "so perhaps you are in the right place for this birth, after all."

"I am," Grace said, "I know I am."

She had received a Christmas card from Melanie together with a long letter which expanded on events since her return from the island. 'I have been getting to know Peter over the past month or two,' she wrote, 'spending most weekends with him in north London. I resigned from the arts centre as soon as I was back from holiday and left at the end of November. Giles was very surprised, but, I suspect, also a little relieved.

And that's very hard for me to admit. He is not an easy man for me to forget, but I am being Melanie Sensible and moving on. Peter is kind and in need of shoring up. His little boy is a delight! And I'm used to small boys after my boarding school experience and feel I've got the makings of an ideal stepmother, (although, of course, I'm keeping those thoughts to myself for the time being.) Meeting Peter couldn't have come at a better time for me – and him, of course – and I have to thank Adonis House for that! Anyway, will keep you up to date with progress, dear Grace, and I expect no less of you. I hope the New Year will bring you much happiness and allow you to feel that you are getting on with your life, in whatever shape or form that will need to take.'

***

"I hope you don't mind," Primrose Larrington said to Fergus, settling herself beside the log fire in the kitchen. "It's just that, when I looked at the map, I realised that a small detour – well, quite a considerable detour, as it turned out – would bring me virtually to your doorstep. I've just spent Christmas with friends somewhere far north of here near Bala. Do you know it? Breathtakingly beautiful, Lake Bala, and very Welsh. I mean, they all speak it, in the shops and… it's just a country place of theirs, of course, these friends, a second home. They've renovated this old farmhouse and really, it's quite exquisite, all done in the best of taste, kept up the ambience of the place, that sort of thing. Although I have to say it's not the warmest of buildings. Hard to heat, I suppose, and the draughts… well, you can imagine."

Fergus hands her a mug of coffee. She is wearing scarlet suede boots under a loose black woollen dress that appears to be smocked or embroidered with motifs of animals. The effect is curious; a child's dress in an adult size or an adult who has failed to put childish ways behind her. He is unsure why she is here. Or rather he wonders why she found it necessary to arrive without warning when they have so far communicated by letter. She curls her scarlet suede legs underneath her and looks around as if with some astonishment.

"I must say, Fergus, this place is looking much better than when we were here for the shoot. You've definitely done a bit of work, haven't you? It's… well, cosier. More habitable. In fact, charming in a rustic sort of way."

Fergus sits down opposite her, irritated. He wishes she would get to the point. There is something faintly coquettish and coy in her manner which he finds disarming. She is probably at least twenty years younger than he is and would no doubt rebuff any advances made towards her, but she behaves as if expecting such an approach. He finds her deeply unattractive. She is too strident, too controlled, blatantly self-possessed and manipulative as if she has consciously cultivated a persona that is impervious to chance.

However, she might prove to be of use to him.

Fergus is unpractised in exploiting connections, but he has fathomed that, these days, this is what people do.

"I've done a bit of decorating," he says vaguely, avoiding her gaze, the way she is smiling at him with a familiarity that the nature of their acquaintance does not merit. "Thought the place could do with cheering up. And I bought a few pieces. A couple of comfy chairs, a new table. That pine dresser. There was some money from the filming, of course. I spent some of it." He swallows the contents of his mug and sets it down on the stone floor. "Presumably you have quite a drive ahead of you today, back to London, so perhaps we could get down to things. Anything you might have found out."

Primrose Larrington shifts slightly in her chair as if

adjusting her angular body to its shape, testing its comfort. One of the two cats that Fergus has acquired, Flossie, the maternal ginger who has an extensive family of offspring spread across the valley, leaps onto her lap and burrows her way into the animal smocking on her chest. Primrose strokes the furry body for a moment or two, then suddenly glances at her watch, swigs back the contents of her mug and sits up, as if wrenched back to the point of something that has temporarily eluded her. Flossie objects, snarls and streaks away across the floor.

"Actually," Primrose Larrington says precisely, taking the word and pulling out its syllables as if stretching a piece of elastic, "this whole business of Archie Copeland's disappearance has opened up a can of worms for me. I mean it's got me thinking. There are so many people, you know, who simply disappear. For no apparent reason. Or so it appears to the people they leave behind. I've been doing quite a lot of digging into this area since you contacted me, Fergus. I have to say that I didn't think it would be my thing at first. Couldn't see the mileage in it as far as a project was concerned. But now, well… I think I have enough material for easily one documentary if not an entire series. Human interest is where it's all at right now so I am sure I could get the funding. And the stories I've heard already, you'd be amazed. You wouldn't think it was so easy for people simply to disappear, go, vanish, *finito* with life, as it were. But it is. They do. Scores of them every week evaporate into thin air."

Fergus gets up from his chair, takes the empty mug that she still holds in her hand and puts it on the draining board next to his. He turns back to her, controlling exasperation.

"This is all fascinating, I'm sure, from your point of view. And I hate to sound selfish, but there's only one missing person I'm interested in. And that's Archie Copeland, my son-in-law, Grace's husband," he says firmly. "Any news of him?"

Primrose Larrington stands up, stretches her arms above her head, grazing fingertips on the low ceiling. She runs a hand through her cropped hair, picks off some cat hairs that have attached themselves to the front of her smocked dress.

"Oh yes," she says, "yes, of course, Fergus. That's why I'm here. So sorry, I get rather manic when I feel I'm on to something."

"So?" he says.

"So? I think I've got a few leads for you," she says and turns to her large black bag sitting on the flagstone floor. She rummages through the contents, spilling keys, tissues, wallet, lipsticks and comb before retrieving a piece of paper. Fergus takes it, reads.

"Thank you," he says. "Thank you very much. I really am very grateful.

Part Three

# England and Kronos

# 17

There was no plan at first. In fact, even after months, a plan eluded him. It surprised him to realise how spontaneous he could be, how unconcerned he was to have no strategy. He simply edged forward, hours at a time, occasionally a day or two if a journey was involved. But even destinations tended to be random. Spur of the moment decisions made out of expediency. The offer of a lift to a particular motorway junction; a bargain coach fare; the necessity to reach somewhere before nightfall.

So there was no plan.

No overarching aim or intention to avoid detection. Which was, possibly, foolhardy, unwise. Considering. Even on that first day, that Monday morning back in late May or was it early June, he hadn't consciously run away. He'd simply decided he needed time to gather himself together, compose himself, come up with a reasonable story, an explanation of sorts to present to them. To Leo, to the solicitor, to letting agents and credit card companies.

And most of all, of course, to Grace. He had no idea what he was to say to Grace.

So he needed time. That's what he told himself. Simply a bit of time to think and to work something out. A few days was all it would take, surely, to get his head into gear, his mind fully conscious of the implications of his actions. He needed to sit himself down somewhere quiet, away from the distractions of grief at his mother's death, resist the diversion of guilt at his devious conduct. What was done was done, after all. Practicalities were obviously called for. There was no point now indulging in endless sessions of self-reproach at his profound foolishness.

Except that there was.

As he drove south-westwards, turning deliberately in the opposite direction from Norwich and the solicitor's office, he acknowledged for the first time that he had chosen to lose touch with rational, reasonable living. And it wasn't even as if his gestures had been particularly lavish or grandiose; there had been, after all, no Ferraris or Fabergé jewels; no Parisian pied-à-terre or arcane art collections. Certainly no adultery or desire for it. Such signals could at least have been judged audacious, bold. And that, possibly, would have been something; or at least, less than nothing.

But no.

He had merely been underhand, duplicitous, evasive and two-faced in his desire to impress, trying to emulate those who, naturally, had more, pretending to belong. Trying, in fact, to be a cleverer, smarter, sharper man than he really was. As if his own self was too inadequate, too ordinary to make a mark. But at least he'd made a start. He was owning up to himself, after all, seeing the folly of his delusions, the vanity of his conduct. Next, he needed to begin to see a way out of this appalling mess of his own making. And he would manage that, of course he would. In a few days or so, a few weeks, even, he would get things straight in his mind, be able to talk it all through with Grace, with Leo, sort things out with the various creditors and start again.

So that was a plan of sorts, wasn't it?

He even said it out loud to himself, to the empty car as he drove towards Jacob's Bottom. "One thing at a time. First, let's hand back Grace's car. There's a huge loan on that and everything's going to help, after all. Then the house, the rented house. I'll get our stuff out of there, into storage, cancel that financial obligation which will be the next relief. After that, I'll think again. One thing at a time. If I can just focus on the task in hand, rid myself from all these monthly erosions into my bank account, marauding magpies that seem forever on the job, then I can see things more clearly. And this car, too. My car. We don't need it. It's several years old now, won't fetch much, but it will give me some cash to be going on with. It's all there is now, anyway. Current account up to its maximum overdraft level, nothing remaining on the credit cards, no doubt. I daren't chance them at any rate. Think there might still be a few premium bonds I could cash. Or did they all go to pay for the fares out to the island? Yes, I'd forgotten that. Still, it was money well spent, getting us out of this place, finding somewhere new. There's hope for us there, I feel, a new start. A clean slate, all that sort of thing. So that's the next two or three days sorted then I'll think again. See about getting back to Grace. Give Leo a ring. Explain. I'll have things in hand by then."

But always it felt as if he was at the bottom of an enormously steep, demanding hill, breathless even with the prospect of climbing it.

The first day was straightforward. Arranging storage for the contents of the house, giving notice on their tenancy, even the matter of the cars were tasks that he carried out with relative ease. After all, he told himself, it was what they had talked about just days before. Grace had seemed as enthusiastic as he had about moving to Kronos, trying their luck in a different place and he was careful to pack a few of her clothes in his small suitcase, a favourite dress, a jacket she often wore as well as a necklace and a locket he found in her drawer. By ten o'clock that night he felt a slight sense of triumph at having achieved so much so swiftly, shrugging off Jacob's Bottom and the trappings and obligations of their life there and he went to the station in Fletwell and caught a late train that took him to Bristol. Tomorrow, he thought, checking in to a cheap hotel in a backstreet near the station, carefully counting out notes to pay for the basic accommodation, he would contact Leo, leave a message for Grace, once he'd slept and cleared his mind of all that was still clouding it.

Except that the next day he felt his mind not cleared, but as dense and fogged as if he were suffering from a serious bout of flu or an excess of alcohol. He found himself incapable of facing a phone call to Leo, leaving the intended message for Grace, for he had no idea what he would say. The enormous apologies, the extensive explanations they deserved would require more clarity of understanding about his actions than he possessed.

So instead he walked.

He walked endlessly around the city that he hardly knew, losing himself among streets strange to him, asking passers-by for directions to places he thought he might need to reach: the park, the suspension bridge, the coach station, police station, a hospital. It made him feel he had a purpose by such interactions with strangers, comforted him to hear his voice capable of forming logical questions that received logical replies. He stayed another night at his cheap hotel, a bed and breakfast place used, he suspected, by the local council to house deserving homeless.

He began to lose track of days. Was it two or three days since the aborted appointment with the solicitor? Or a week, perhaps? Had Leo given up hope of hearing from him and headed back to Africa or Namibia or Mongolia or wherever else he was taking his philanthropic mission next? He admired him, of course. He admired his brother's selflessness in diverting his energies in the service of others. Or perhaps it was an easy choice, a get-out from the responsibilities of functioning in the ordinary world, of the expectations of sensible adulthood. He had never asked him why he did it, why he continued to live such a nomadic existence now that all that Natasha business, the lost fiancée, was so long in the past. Leo had always been a bit of an outsider, happy to follow his own path rather than negotiate a conventional route. Their parents used to say he was unique, an original, they'd say, and with some awe as if this was a gift rather than a deviation. Even without the Natasha tragedy Leo would no doubt have shunned a life like others tend to choose. He was clever, could have done anything he liked if he'd put his mind to it, but he'd dropped out halfway through university, said he couldn't see the point of graduating in something that didn't interest him. It was a relief in a way, left the field free for Archie to be the academic and Leo to be labelled alternative. *At least that's how our parents saw us. Or perhaps it was me. Perhaps I was the one who needed to invent the labels.*

He counted the notes in his wallet carefully and constantly. Even living so frugally, they disappeared at an alarming rate and after a few days in his cheap hotel room he found a hostel with dormitory accommodation that charged less than half. He needed little food; it was summer, after all, and if he ate badly he found his appetite diminished. A plate of chips, mugs of sweet tea and dry Swiss roll in the late afternoon made him feel sufficiently nauseous that he did not want to eat again until the next day.

And of course all this was temporary.

Very temporary, he told himself. He tried to think of it as a sort of experiment, the way he was living, like research for a book, a kind of autobiography of a super tramp for contemporary times. He would look back at his experiences and be grateful for the material they were giving him for something that he would no doubt want to write in the future. Soon, after all, he would get a job. That was the thing. He needed to get a teaching job swiftly, get a regular salary, pay off the debts, set things right with Leo, pave the foundations financially for the next stage of his life. All this was a mere setback, a brief period of dislocation caused by… by what?

At times, he wondered if he was having a breakdown.

Often, in fact, he wondered if this was a breakdown of sorts. But he could still think. However muddily or hazily, his mind still operated on a level of vaguely lucid thought so he dismissed this idea, disliked its whiff of self-indulgence.

He went to London. One day, a Sunday possibly, but it may have been a Monday, he found his way to the coach station and picked out notes sufficient to take him on the cheapest fare to Victoria. That morning he had seen a fight take place in the dormitory of his hostel; two men fighting over a packet of cigarettes that each claimed as his own. He was frightened by their anger, by the speed with which their disagreement turned to physical violence and he grabbed his jacket and left. He did not belong in such a place, could not imagine how he had come to be staying there amongst people so volatile and unpredictable. Besides, London made more sense. He knew London, he belonged, could find work and an adequate income easily. He sat on the coach considering his options with reasonable optimism. There was always supply teaching; he could sign himself up with a local authority and be working by the next day, no doubt. Then there was the possibility of his old college at Aldgate. All right, so they hadn't parted on particularly good terms, his resignation being demanded in no uncertain terms, but that was only because he had failed to show any progress on the wretched PhD, a condition of his original employment. Surely they'd find a bit of work for him, not a regular lectureship, but some casual classes, perhaps, those vacation courses they ran for students new to study.

There must be something. It was only when the coach pulled into Victoria bus station that afternoon that he remembered, in his haste to get away from the explosive situation at the Bristol hostel, he had forgotten to take his suitcase and with it the things he'd carefully packed when he'd left the house at Jacob's Bottom. All that remained in his possession was his wallet, his passport, his redundant bank cards and a small photograph of Grace. Suddenly, he felt overwhelmed by exhaustion, too tired even to register his distress. In the station buffet bar, he drank several mugs of coffee, ate a couple of greasy sausage rolls and tried to keep himself awake by reading discarded copies of the day's papers. *Tomorrow,* he thought, *tomorrow or the next day or the day after I'll go back to Bristol, collect the case. After all, I can't lose Grace's things, that jacket, her necklace. I'll go back in a few days and sort out the suitcase.*

He liked the anonymity of the city. He liked the fact that he could endlessly pass people by without any eye contact and that, even if he inadvertently bumped into someone, the collision would be ignored. As if he wasn't really there or of so little import that his presence was overlooked. After a while, he imagined that even if he saw someone he knew, there would be no recognition because he felt he had taken on a shadowy definition, his features no longer individual and personal, but merely those of a thousand other random people concentrated into the crammed city. It was a relief, at first, this sense of being swallowed up as if he no longer mattered or entirely existed. And it was extraordinary how easy it was to get through a day without any particular structure or purpose. The vast city absorbed him for it seemed to be peopled by faces and figures as rootless as his own and the endless spaces, the parks, precincts, churchyards, cemeteries, cathedrals and clogged, congested streets appeared to accommodate him with ease. And while there was still a bit of money, the dwindling cash from the sale of his car, to pay for a bed of sorts to sleep in each night, he could ward off, delay, as it were, that moment when he would have to confront finally the hopelessness of his situation.

It came, eventually.

One day, after a summer that most people spoke of as poor, complaining throughout the dull days of June, the wet, sunless days of July and the indifferent August, he rescued a scrap of *Evening Standard* that was heading towards the Serpentine and was astonished to realise that it was now September. The summer had, apparently, gone. It was the expanse of time he had given himself to come up with a plan. A solution. A resolution, in fact, that would allow him to absolve himself of his appalling conduct, make good and return to Grace. Now, sitting on a bench in Hyde Park, he felt the inadequacy of his clothes against the cooler air of early autumn, the thin soles of his shoes. A young couple sat down, sharing their lunchtime sandwiches, oblivious of him at first, talking of their weekend, their ongoing flat-hunting in Fulham.

Until he started to cry.

That's when they noticed him. When the man sitting at the other end of the bench began to make a noise like that of a distressed, wounded animal, quiet yet desperate, suppressed, but impossible to ignore. The woman looked at her partner who shrugged, went on eating and began to talk in a loud voice about endowment policies and mortgage rates. But she put up her hand as if to quiet him and turned to face the man, reached out and touched his shoulder.

"Is there anything we can do?" she said, "do you need help

of some kind? Someone we can fetch for you? There must be someone."

Her voice was mild, gentle. He had forgotten the sound of concern and tenderness. He looked up into her face, embarrassed now by his demonstrative behaviour yet unable to staunch his tears as if shed by a mechanism beyond his control. The woman's partner was agitating to move. He saw him stand up, try to take the woman's arm and pull her away. It was what he would have done, had Grace displayed similar sympathies to a distressed, dishevelled man. He shook his head, wanting them to go, wanting her, in particular, to go for he knew such evident sign of empathy would only feed his weeping. By now two or three other people were staring; he was aware of a woman pulling her child swiftly past, talking loudly as if in distraction; a dog-walker let his spaniel nose the turf around his feet. He heard his voice aiming to reassure them, shuffling to his feet, trying to adopt a sense of purpose in moving away swiftly as if he had somewhere to get to, a destination in mind. He made sure he did not look back.

At Marble Arch, he stood for some time watching the dense traffic, the endless stream of buses and taxis then negotiated his way across the road and began to walk north, turning east once he reached the Marylebone Road. By now he was used to endless walking; in spite of months of an inadequate diet he was capable of daily, mindless treks that would once have defeated him. He bought a bar of chocolate from a kiosk at Euston station, found the cloakroom and washed his face and hands thoroughly, staring back unwillingly at his reflection in the mirror, the dullness of his eyes. Finding a cheap barber in one of the side streets behind King's Cross, he spent a valuable few pounds on a shave and a haircut.

"Any plans for the weekend, Sir?" the barber asked in a strong Scottish accent. He shrugged, muttered something vague about a trip, a visit north, perhaps. To relatives, he threw in for authenticity. The barber settled a towel around his shoulders, picked up a comb from an array on the shelf and nodded. "Get yourself out of the city for a couple of days, find some fresh air, that's the stuff," he said. "See your family. I envy you, you know that? Would swap places with you at the drop of a hat."

Cars queued on the approach roads to reach the roundabout then queued again to leave it, to funnel into the slip roads and join the traffic moving north, north-east or south. It was a good place, he'd heard, as likely place as any to get a lift. Even so, he waited over an hour before a driver signalled to him thumbs up and he found himself darting between semi-stationary cars to climb into the passenger seat.

"Leeds any good to you?" the driver said, "I'll not be stopping before that."

Archie fastened his seat belt, leant back against the headrest and closed his eyes for a moment.

"Leeds," he said, "Leeds sounds all right."

# 18

Hester despises New Year's Eve.

Such a foolish reason to celebrate, she thinks, but doesn't admit to the small gathering at a neighbour's house, some hour or so before midnight. She sips from a glass of unpleasant punch and wishes she'd turned down the invitation. Tomorrow's simply another day, after all, the first day of a bleak, dark month and hardly worthy of marking with a night of enforced jollity. She has become wedged against the wall of the large sitting room next to the ornate fireplace and is only half-listening to the conversation of the irritating woman who insists she knows her from another time, another decade and seems intent on rekindling the acquaintance. The woman, Angela Somebody or other, starts to say something about finding New Year's Eve parties light relief after the obligations of the turkey, the endless entertaining and the string of visiting relations then breaks off suddenly.

"Primary school playground, that's it!" she says, shrieks, in fact, so that two or three people look round. She grabs Hester's shoulder as if in forceful arrest. "You and your little girl, of course! She was a bit younger than my two, just a year or so. Andrew and Martin, the twins, everyone knew them, as like as two peas in the proverbial in those days. Not now, of course. Not once adolescence hit them, in fact. And of course I rather lost touch with people once they'd left the state primary and we went private. Well, you just want to do the best for them, don't you? But I remember those days so well and how sorry I used to feel for you. We all did, naturally. I mean, it was quite rare then to see someone on their own and it just seemed so… well, sad. We really felt for you. And now Andrew's well on his way to a consultancy here at the Radcliffe and Martin's a merchant banker. Hardly seems possible, does it?" She laughs loudly, grabs from a bowl of nuts on a nearby table and feeds the handful rapidly into her mouth.

"Why?" Hester says. She remembers the woman now and her husband too, a flush-faced, stout, self-important man who grinned too easily and once made a pass at her at a school social event, placing his large flaccid hand on her knee and letting it roam upwards before she forcefully removed it.

"Why medicine and banking?" Angela says, "Well, why not? Financially, they are good career choices and of course we've always told them to aim high and…"

"No," Hester cuts in, "why did you feel sorry for me and Grace?"

"Well, you know," Angela says, edging a peanut from her front tooth with her tongue, "I mean clearly you were putting on a brave show and doing a marvellous job, but… well, it can't have been easy."

Hester stares at the woman's neat face, her neat, navy dress, her carefully curled hair.

"Easy? I wasn't aware that life was supposed to be easy," she says, "for any of us. Not part of the bargain, as it were. But in what particular way was my situation not easy? More difficult than yours, would you say?"

Angela looks confused, confounded, like a contestant on a quiz show finding questions unexpectedly obtuse. She looks around her as if for support.

"Well," she says, turning back rather reluctantly, "you know. A woman alone. I mean, when all's said and done, it's not the usual... it certainly wasn't back then, anyway. Not here in Oxford. And clearly we could tell that you were... you are the sort one would expect to see with... I mean you were such an attractive woman. Still are, naturally. And your little girl. Such a pity, that's all. No... no support. No one to lean on. At least as far as we could see."

"Ah," Hester says, "so I was something of an enigma to all of you in the playground, was I? Me and Grace?"

"I wouldn't say that, I mean it was all such a long time ago, but we were simply..."

"Curious. Judgemental. Disparaging," Hester says.

"Oh no, that's not fair, not that at all. Of course not. For all I knew you could have been a widow." Angela looks hopeful.

"I was," Hester says.

"Ah! Well, there you are then, I knew..."

"But Grace's father was my second husband. Is, in fact, still my second husband."

Angela fondles her empty punch glass; Hester swallows the remaining contents of hers. A man next to them is consulting his watch, telling others to check theirs so that there can be a consensus over the appropriate moment to launch into 'Auld Lang Syne'.

"Good," Angela says weakly. "That's good to hear."

"Now, if you'll excuse me, I really have to go," Hester says, edging away, crossing the room in the direction of the hall, ducking around various couples and into the kitchen. She resists misguided efforts to refill her empty glass with floating pineapple from the large punchbowl and grabs the bottle of good red wine she brought with her, still sitting unopened on the table.

"Can I help you with that?" a man asks, attempting to wrestle the bottle from her grasp. Hester clings on.

"No, thank you," she says, heading for the door, "I've

been opening my own bottles for the past thirty years with apparent success and am not about to relinquish the privilege and pleasure right now."

Back home, she flicks through the television channels devoted to celebrating the night either with bagpipes and Scottish dancing or retrospectives on the year's news. Neither appeals. She pours out a substantial measure of wine from her rescued bottle and wonders whether her premature departure from her neighbour's party will be judged rude. Or whether she still occupies a place in people's minds that evokes sympathy, even pity. *Shall we invite poor Hester? Alone as always on New Year's Eve, what a shame. Still, she must have brought it upon herself. Perhaps she's difficult, too temperamental to live with. Used to be an actress, after all.* People so like slick, satisfying explanations to define an aberration. *Which is what I suppose I am*, Hester thinks, *an aberration. An anomaly. A bit of a misfit. At least as far as the respectable middle class burghers of the city of Oxford are concerned.* She wishes she could ring Grace, but the island of Kronos is already two hours into 1989 and she has no wish to wake the household. She thinks of ringing her sister, Ruth, then remembers that her Christmas card said something about a trip to Las Vegas for the New Year. So she sits, steadily sipping her wine, contemplating the pattern of her beige William Morris curtains in the bay window, feeling not lonely, but certainly very aware of being alone.

When the phone rings.

"Hess? Is it too late? I'm not sure how late one is supposed to ring people."

"I don't think there's a law about it, Fergus," Hester answers and holds herself back from saying how good it is to hear from him. "Especially tonight. I would say there's a certain dispensation about time tonight."

"Really?" he says, "I see. Well, that's a relief. Now I don't have to go down the hill and queue for the phone box by the pub I feel there's a whole decorum to learn about phoning people. I thought I'd start with you, Hess, because you'd understand if I got things wrong. I mean it's what you probably expect of me after all these years."

"Fergus, you don't mean to say that you actually have a phone connection at last? That you are ringing me from the comfort of your own home?"

"It took them long enough to sort it out. I've been waiting since the summer. Then suddenly, they turned up this morning, the engineer people, fiddled around for hours with wires and so on and left me with… well, with this, rather smart-looking cream phone affair. And a number, of course, and a fat directory."

"It's the best news I've heard today, Fergus," Hester says. "Congratulations. So I'm your virgin call, as it were? Your first tentative step into the modern method of communication in the late $20^{th}$ century?"

"Oh no," Fergus says, "well, you're my first evening call, that's what I meant. But I spoke to Primrose earlier today. You remember, Primrose Larrington from the TV production people?"

Hester notes how swiftly her mood can deflate. And registers also the absurdity of it. It is, after all, neither appropriate nor fitting to feel anything other than mild curiosity at Fergus' mention of a woman's name. He's talking on and it takes a while for her to focus again, distracted both by self-reproach and the need for more wine. She asks him to break off for a moment while she reaches for the bottle, refills her glass. When she at last settles down to listen to what he has to say, she is too astounded to believe his words and asks him to repeat himself to make sure she has not misheard.

"We must tell Grace," she says eventually, "right now. Or I

can ring her first thing tomorrow. But perhaps tonight would be… the sooner the better, surely."

"No," Fergus says firmly, "absolutely not. Things are still far too uncertain."

"But surely…"

"There's nothing to be gained from it at this stage and everything to be lost. It's a delicate situation, to say the least."

"You're right, of course," Hester says. The strength of his opinion is heartening. "And with the baby due so soon, only weeks away now…"

"Exactly. She needs to focus solely on that, not be distracted by some slender hope that could so easily dissolve."

"Yes, that makes complete sense. But still…"

"That's for us to do, Hess, to try to push things forward now, very, very slowly. Strategically, you could say. So no phone calls to Grace. That would be far too premature. After all, we have no idea what he's planning. We don't want to – well, false hopes and all that, Hess."

There's a silence on the line for a few moments and Hester wonders why Fergus is the only person she has ever allowed to shorten her name, is warmed, even, by his use of it. Outside, there is noise, mildly drunken cries, general merriment and she glances at the clock over the mantelpiece.

"It's midnight. It's next year, Fergus," she says.

"What? Is it really New Year's Eve? Well, I suppose it must be. I hadn't really noticed."

"Fergus, you're impossible, do you know that?"

"Very probably, Hess."

"So 1989 it is. Dear God, only eleven years left of this century, just think of that."

"Of the millennium," Fergus says. "We are in its waning years."

"How poetic that sounds. Or possibly unbearably

significant. Portentous, would you say? So no wild parties for you tonight, Fergus? No alcohol-fuelled happening down in the valley?"

"Oh, I am sure there is," he says, "but I am happier here with a glass of single malt whisky in hand. Does that sound very dull? Too ordinary for words, Hess?"

"No," Hester says, "or at least..."

"Yes?"

"So often the extraordinary is simply a lot of pretentiousness. A lot of noise and pomposity. Give me the perfect contentment of ordinariness any day. Don't you agree?" She tilts her glass to the armchair opposite, as if someone, as if Fergus, possibly, is sitting in it, nestling his glass of single malt. She thinks of the sweet smell of alcohol on his breath, of the roughness of his thick woollen sweater smelling of wood smoke. "Happy New Year to you," she says.

"And a very Happy New Year to you too, Hess," he says and adds, after a pause, "and may it be exactly that. For all of us."

***

He found work. Employment of sorts to fill his vacant days and provide him with a meagre means of support. 'No Questions Asked' sort of jobs, no forms to fill in or references to provide. Cash in hand at the end of a day of clearing an overgrown garden, digging over an abandoned allotment. Newspaper rounds, morning and evening, one of each, for two small newsagents who soon found him more reliable than schoolboys who arrived late or failed to turn up at all when it rained. Their windows were rich sources with numerous handwritten postcards seeking heavy labour hands, leaflet distributors, assistance with local removals, house clearance, casual gardening. On some days, he worked fourteen hours and clutched a wedge of notes in his hand at the end of it; on others, he spent the time between the morning and evening paper deliveries in libraries, moving between shelves and sections constantly to avoid attracting attention. Some mornings, he woke to find himself surprised that he was still alive and alert to the possibilities of the day; he would leave the hostel or his temporary board at a bed and breakfast and head to the newsagent's to mark up the papers for the first delivery. The proprietor appeared to begrudge the effort of conversation, usually nodded and dispatched him with minimal exchange. It suited him. At least, he supposed it did. He seemed of little curiosity and, after initial concerns that the newsagent would ask awkward questions, enquire about his situation, he realised that his existence, his being, was of absolutely no consequence or concern at all to the taciturn man; he mattered to him solely in his function to deliver newspapers efficiently. It was the same with all the jobs he did; he was a cog in a wheel, a part in a process, his role limited and easily defined.

As an individual, he was irrelevant.

At first, the manual work was hard. He was used to gardening, but heavy digging and turning unturned soil strained his back and his shoulders so that when he woke his whole body ached and groaned and he felt like a man twice his age. Gradually, however, he became more accustomed to it and could bear more although he was uncertain whether he was growing physically stronger or simply learning to endure. The season was against him, the hours of daylight diminishing and he worried whether he would find enough work to occupy him once winter got a firm hold. And the cold was depressing. He wondered suddenly why he had decided to travel north, whether it had been foolish to imagine some sort of functional alternative life, as if such a destination would provide him with a structure and a feasible means of survival. He suspected he had acquired too romantic a vision of the shiftless, dispossessed traveller from reading Kerouac as a student. The map of England, in contrast to the endless swathes of states and regions, anonymous cities and never-ending routes of American literature, seemed to him claustrophobic, confining, the options so few. He had, after all, tried the south, turned his back on the south-west and the east was flatly, alarmingly redolent of his recent escape from Leo and the dreadful, desolate funeral. That prospective meeting with the solicitor. So the north had seemed all that had remained. And he could adjust to colder, rainier days, move on further, over the border into Scotland and onto the west coast, perhaps. Didn't people say it was milder there? Wasn't it reputed to be one of the most beautiful places in the United Kingdom and somewhere he had once considered for the two of them? In the days when there had still seemed some point in believing and planning for a rational, legitimate future with Grace. But of course even then the notion had been fraudulent, built on sand rather than firm foundation. Concealment had stolen up on him over the years, a habit at first, a desire to please and gratify more than an intended gesture to deceive. Even with his first wife, with Louise, he had failed to be entirely frank and open. He had allowed her to conjure blithely a lifestyle he could not possibly satisfy, aspirations he did not share. If they'd managed to have children things might have muddled along for them, but that apparent inability had been the start of her discontent, the catalyst, as it were, for her excuse to seek fulfilment elsewhere. He had, in many ways, been relieved by her voluntary departure.

And then Grace.

His overwhelming joy at finding her, sensing in her a

capacity for love that he could both receive and reciprocate should have been enough. He should have believed that it was enough, that Grace did not need something more than she found in him, his essential self. But he could not stop himself. Out of fear of losing her if she really confronted his inadequacies, his very average achievements, he tried to be more. As if ordinariness was some sort of sin instead of what he saw it for now: a blithe happiness, a catching of something sublime, as simple and reliable and delightful as a sky shot with the light of early morning, a sun setting in a pale, opalescent sky.

He knew he must, indirectly, contact Grace. No doubt she had been back in England for months, in London or Oxford or even in Fletwell if she'd returned to her job. He flinched, however, from the thought of her arriving at the house at Jacob's Bottom, expectant of some normality there only to find their connection with the place severed. Curiously, it was hard for him to imagine her anywhere other than on Kronos. It was easier to see her in strong sunlight, her feet in flat sandals, a thin skirt skimming bare legs the way she had looked in the days before he'd left. Now he looked back at their time on the island and considered it as a sort of precious borrowed happiness, a charmed interlude, as if Kronos had provided him with an amnesty from his actions.

He had always loved Grace.

Of course he had always loved her deeply, from the moment he had first seen her looking bereft and confused in the foyer of the opera house, fumbling in vain for her lost ticket. From that instant he had wanted to console her, support her, supply her with every kindness and tenderness he felt she deserved. Yet he knew he had often failed, detached himself from her, hurt her even in his attempt to maintain – what? A fabrication of a life, a construction of tissue-thin lies and half-truths in order to go on with his foolish dissembling. But for those couple of weeks or so on the island, he had felt liberated as if permitted to offer her at last a love unblemished by any guilt or clandestine dealings. He had felt closer to her than ever before.

And now she must despise him.

For he had abandoned her, that's how she must see it. (Although the truth to him felt very different.) How could she now think of him with anything other than contempt?

One day, wasting long hours in the reference section of the library, the frozen ground and bitter wind chill causing an afternoon's gardening job to be unfeasible, he found the telephone directory for Oxford and searched fruitlessly for details of Hester Barnes. There was no listing. Even though he had little idea of what he would do with anything he came across, a phone number, an address, the absence of information was depressing. Perhaps she was listed under an old stage name; perhaps she was ex-directory. Or maybe she had moved. Always at the back of his mind he had held onto the thought that he would be able to reach Grace through her mother. To use her, he supposed, as some sort of intermediary when Grace needed the divorce, the formal separation, or whatever else would be required for her to dissolve their union, as she would inevitably want to do. He flicked through the pages of the Oxford directory again, running his grimed fingernail down all the entries under B as if he expected suddenly to fall upon her name. But there was nothing. He closed the book, returned it to its shelf and stood looking across the floor of the reference library at the chairs occupied by slumped, drowsy figures, several familiar to him after frequent visits over the past couple of months although they had never spoken. One or two of them made the pretence of reading newspapers, but most simply arrived each morning and took up a place as inconspicuously as possible, to sleep the day away in warmth and relative comfort. The librarians turned a blind eye, on the whole; only if the stench of urine or spirits – methylated or otherwise – was too pungent did they move the men on and out to the street.

It was two days later that he saw the programme. Not the entire programme, but the final ten minutes or so of the repeat of a series that had been on earlier in the year. He learnt this from the owner of the boarding house where he'd had a small room for a couple of weeks, a large, genial woman who seemed to welcome company in the downstairs living room where she was always to be found when television was on air. "Just repeats at this time," she told him as he hovered in the doorway late one afternoon with cash in hand to pay the following week's rent. "They don't waste the good stuff at this hour and it's what's coming later that I want. My serial, you know. Wouldn't miss it." He stepped into the room to place the notes on the table and was about to retreat, out of the smell of stale cigarette smoke and gas fire fumes, when he caught sight of the close-up of a man's face on the small screen. He stared at it and although he recognised instantly its shape, picked up on something familiar in the way the man spoke, he could not make a clear connection with anyone he knew in the world he now inhabited. It required him to trawl back in his mind to something once experienced, a state previously known and now little more than a memory. His landlady made inconsequential conversation as he continued to stand by the door, staring at the screen. At the end of the programme he watched the countless credits, felt for a pencil in his pocket, a scrap of paper and rapidly wrote down a couple of names.

He took the room for another month, securing a reduced rent by paying in advance. He had little work now and low expectations of gaining much until the New Year. But he wanted a fixed address for a few weeks at least; an address he could put at the top of a letter in hope of a reply. And the place was better than most as somewhere to spend the festive season. She insisted he share their Christmas lunch with them, the landlady, Rosa, and her husband, Stan, a morose man who said little throughout a prolonged meal that had started with sherry at midday and appeared to be carefully timed to terminate ready for the Queen at three. Afterwards, he escaped for a long walk, mindlessly striding out along deserted pavements and along canal and river paths, aiming for an obliteration of sorts. Later, he spent a couple of hours in a city pub, the garish paper chains and faux snow decorating the windows seeming at odds with the solitary, discreet drinkers quietly inhabiting the place.

He woke late the next morning, relieved to have endured the previous day with relative equanimity, and asked Rosa if he could borrow the bike from the hall. "Take it," she said cheerfully. "Get it out of my way. It was one of Stan's fancies awhile back and hasn't left the place in living memory." Although he hadn't cycled in years, his recent labouring work had built up his strength and stamina so that he soon found himself out of the city, leaving straggling suburbs and heading into open countryside. It was what he'd first intended, when he had waited for a lift at the side of the North Circular, suddenly eager to shrug off London and try somewhere less populous. He would find a remote, rural existence that would offer a simple lifestyle, an honest living that would sustain. But the city had again pulled him in and he'd been frightened to venture further. There was, after all, always work of a kind in the city. And shelter and shops and cheap cafés and parks and pavements and endless streams of people, no doubt as desperate and forlorn as he was. So he had stayed. But now, as he cycled through hamlets and villages, pressed on deeper into the dale so that the landscape softened, the views became more spectacular, he felt consoled and comforted, as if solace emanated from the fields and drystone walls. He had a bowl of soup at a village pub, drank half a pint of lager and reluctantly pulled himself away from the snug saloon bar to begin to retrace his route back to the city. It would be dark long before he arrived; already, the sky was streaked with the winter sunset, extraordinary shades of scarlet on the horizon. He walked the last two or three miles, his legs finally failing him, and felt the drag of the streets and the densely-packed terraced houses pressing down on him in a way he had not noticed before.

The letter arrived a week later.

Brief, to the point, but containing the information he had sought. He carried it around in the inside pocket of his padded windcheater, uncertain now what use he wanted to make of it yet reluctant to risk its loss. The newsagent was open again and he picked up a couple of extra delivery routes, covering for holidays. He found a temporary job collecting and washing glasses at an insalubrious pub that had a reputation for violent disputes. The year had turned; the letter, creased and grimed now by regular scanning, took on an importance he judged to be foolish. There was, after all, no redemption available to him.

Nevertheless. Even so.

In the middle of January, he left the pub at the end of a lunchtime shift and walked through a heavy sleet storm to the reference library. After two hours or so of map-reading and route-planning, he went back to his landlady, Rosa and her silent husband, Stan, gave notice on his room and gathered his spare belongings into a backpack ready for an early departure the next day. He had decided it would be pragmatic to spend money on an initial coach fare to get him well out of Leeds and on his way; otherwise, in the face of an inadequate lift and poor weather, there would be the temptation to abandon the plan and go back. So by late morning he was in Manchester, Chester by the afternoon and Shrewsbury before six. It had been unwise, no doubt, to risk being stranded in such a place for the night. He walked from the bus stop down the main high street, feeling conspicuous in the quiet, genteel city streets. But he was lucky. In a fish and chip shop on the outskirts of town, eating a large portion of chips and batter bits, he got into conversation with a lorry driver heading south and was soon listening to his life story as they covered the miles to Hereford. After that, his progress was far slower. He had only really thought ahead as far as Hereford, leaving the reality of the rest of the journey to happenstance, chance. But by now, he had come so far, committed himself so entirely to the idea, that turning back was not an option. And the weather could have been worse. For the most part, it was dry, cold, but not intolerable and snow was restricted to high ground, to the mountains to the north whereas he was heading to the middle of the region. He had, of course, a phone number, but was reluctant to ring. A spontaneous arrival, though, seemed no wiser and he occupied his mind for hours trying to decide the best approach. Either way, there really was so little to lose.

A week after leaving Leeds, he arrived in the Welsh town with the unpronounceable name that he had first traced on the map in the reference section at the library and spent his final few pounds on accommodation for one night. He lay on a narrow, hard bed, listening to the noise from the bar below, planning the final miles of his journey. Too tired to concern himself with the absurdity of the whole notion, he was soon asleep and did not wake until the proprietor knocked harshly on his door the next morning at nine, anxious to serve him the obligatory breakfast and be rid of him.

# 19

Hester rang Grace in late January.

"Now obviously I'd come over to the island for this birth if I thought I'd be of any use to you. But quite frankly, you're better off having me out of the way. I'd only fuss and worry and send your blood pressure sky high which is quite the opposite of what you want."

"Everything's in hand," Grace said, "and I'm far from alone here. I think most of the village seem anxious to have a hand in the birth of this child."

"But you're not thinking of being an earth mother and opting for a communal confinement in the village square, surely?"

Grace reassured her. The birth would be a conventional event at the hospital in Kronos Town. Clea or Tara would drive her there at the appropriate time.

"I'd rather you came to see us later. Once… once the baby is here. It makes far more sense for you to leave a visit until March, perhaps. When the weather is better."

It seemed to have rained nearly every day since the middle of the month. Most weeks, however, there was one day when the sun stridently appeared as if insistent upon reminding people of its existence. The temperature would rise sharply and it would be possible to sit outside for a few hours, feeling heat on deprived skin. Halcyon days, Clea said, a gift in the midst of winter. Bookings at Adonis House for the forthcoming season were vibrant.

"You could do with an additional room, couldn't you?" Grace said one morning as she sat with Clea, working their way through correspondence and confirming deposits. "You're already turning people down for high season which makes no sense."

"We're supposed to be small," Clea said. "That's what we sell."

"Another room, though, would help. Be honest. My room, in fact."

Clea put down her pen.

"In time, Grace, yes, if I'm honest. One more single room to let would be ideal. But that's not a concern for now. It's something to review in the months ahead when you're settled and more certain about your immediate future."

Already, Grace had begun to covet more space. Although never less than overwhelmed with gratitude for Clea's generosity, there were days when she would have liked to be able to retreat from Adonis House into a place of her own. However small, the desire for a space that reflected her and offered some privacy and occasional solitude, was growing. Besides, she could not see how it would be possible to live with a baby in a room that measured no more than the width of two single beds. Already, the clothing and bedding, sheets and shawls and soft quilts and blankets and small toys that Clea and Tara had insisted on shifting from deep cupboards into her care were spilling out onto every surface. And although in the early days of her pregnancy, during her first months alone on the island, she had found it impossible to imagine staying without the family's support, now she felt not only capable of living separately from them, but eager to establish such independence. Her grasp of the language was still rudimentary, but growing, and she was able to exchange greetings in the village, shop adequately and understand considerably more.

Her informal sessions of helping the children with their English had made her consider whether she would be able to train one day to teach students learning the language. To her surprise, she found she enjoyed teaching and appeared to have a natural inclination and patience for the task. Unconsciously, she realised that she was beginning to think of a future that extended beyond the immediate birth of the child and was negotiating and sculpting some sort of life for the two of them. And part of her yearned for it, for a routine normality, to wake each morning to an ordinary, prescribed day unblemished by vain hopes and false expectations.

Archie, after all, was gone.

His disappearance, out of choice or by chance, was a fact that she would have to accept eventually. Sometimes she would wake in the night, disturbed by restless kicking close to her ribcage, and her thoughts would attach themselves instantly to Archie; a sick fear for his welfare, a vision of his immediate circumstance would render her tense and tearful. Yet perversely, she had begun almost to resent such intrusion. She wanted now only to think of the welfare of the unborn child, to rid herself of morbid thoughts and sentiments that were somehow counter to the creative force of this new life. Gradually, she realised that she wished to turn away from all uncertainties and precarious states. At first, believing in Archie's eventual return had seemed to provide her with a crutch essential to get through each day with some equilibrium. But as the child had grown within her, making its presence more tangible with each passing week, Grace had shifted her perspective so that, contrarily, abandoning hope of his return had been the more consoling choice. It hurt less. It left her free to focus energies on protecting and nurturing this slip of potential humanity that had obligingly assigned itself to her care. She loved Archie. She had loved Archie deeply and she doubted whether she would ever love a man again with the same passion and conviction. But it was possible that she might.

Whereas, this baby. Her child.

How was it credible to love unconditionally something unknown, unseen, with such a driven force and instinct that at times she felt almost light-headed with joy? Yet as powerfully strong was the anxiety to protect and safeguard so that she wanted to place the two of them far out of reach of any negative thought or influence.

One day in late January, she walked to the top of the village, a steep climb up a couple of narrow winding lanes where she had often noticed an empty, small, single-storey pale pink stone house. Peering through the windows, she saw simple, clean white walls, a wooden ceiling, a large corner fireplace and a traditional central archway separating the space into two main rooms. Grace was immediately taken by the potential of the modest space. This would do. This would provide an adequate and welcoming home for her and the child. Surely she could manage, patch together a sufficient living to support the two of them here, a life entirely unhitched to the recent past. The idea of leaving the island now seemed absurd and it felt more as if Kronos was a destination intended for her rather than a chance discovery. Besides, it was what Archie had wanted, what he had tentatively started to talk about before he had disappeared. She pulled herself away, slowly retraced her steps back to the village square, avoiding the skittish kittens that strayed into her path and walked back to Adonis House. She felt heavy and cumbersome and counted on her fingers the days left until her delivery date. The thought of once more being able to slip into a pair of jeans, of turning in bed at night without the sensation of heaving a precious cargo alongside her, was welcome. Yet at the same time she knew she would miss this sense of suspended time, of extraordinary expectation, like holding one's breath before a revelation of great beauty, awaiting the inevitable rhapsodic climax of a piece of music. Birth was so commonplace yet at the same time impossibly miraculous. She found the paradox astonishing.

Clea was helpful when she broached the idea of the pink-stoned house.

"I can ask around. There are quite a few small properties in these villages that are not lived in. Some have fallen into ruin, of course, and no one's quite sure who owns them anymore. Or all the family members have moved to the cities on the mainland and just like to keep hold of a place on the island for some future use. And if there's a bit of land attached, even a small strip to grow some vegetables or to keep some chickens, so much the better. And you're really sure this is what you want, Grace?"

"It is," she said firmly. "Maybe not immediately, but certainly before the summer starts."

"Right," Clea said. "It makes sense, I suppose."

"I wouldn't want to leave Aghia Kallida. Being close to Adonis House is important, naturally. In fact, I'll need as much work as possible if I'm really going to manage to stay on the island."

"There's work for you here, of course there is. Our numbers are increasing, our season's starting earlier and going on longer. And babies can be very adaptable, you know, Grace. Mine always were. They'll sleep in any convenient corner and through any cacophonous noise, babies will. In fact, the more that's going on around them, the more contented they're likely to be."

A few days later, Clea came back from the village with a bunch of keys and walked with Grace up the hill to the single-storey house. It belonged, evidently, to the family who ran the taverna, or at least to someone in their extended family, a cousin or a nephew who had not used it since moving to the mainland for work a year before. They opened the front door with some difficulty, the wood swollen into the frame, but once inside the place felt dry, its thick walls cleanly whitewashed, the floor covered with a thin film of dust that could be easily swept. A pile of logs lay neatly stacked by the fireplace. The central archway provided a natural divide between living and sleeping areas and behind a smaller arch was a basic kitchen leading on to a small bathroom. Some rudimentary pieces of furniture, a well-scrubbed wooden table, a couple of upright chairs, a bed and a small settle scattered with cushions offered the place the semblance of a home. The back door led out onto a square patch of land that had obviously once been cultivated. Two trees, an olive and an apricot, partially shielded the view of the neighbouring house. Nothing, however, could interfere with the spectacular sweep of the distant mountains, encrusted with dense snow after recent falls and, closer at hand, the bowl of the village like a large pudding basin, suspended in the valley below.

"It's small," Clea said, following Grace out into the garden. "Really, it's just one large room and a bathroom. You're sure it's going to be adequate?"

"It's ideal," Grace said. "After all, it's just for me and the baby and… well, it gives me what I need. What I can manage."

"And you can see Adonis House from here. Look, trace your eye down to that narrow road and between those trees. Just beyond there's a turning to the left, the white house and then next to it, set back, you can just get a glimpse of the roof and the garden."

Grace followed Clea's direction, made out several landmarks of the village, and felt how curiously familiar this landscape was to her now. The narrow, stony paths, meandering goat tracks, crumbling stone dwellings with shutters hanging as if at half-mast, felt as sympathetic and familiar as if she had been living in Aghia Kallida for a decade or so. It was hard to believe she had arrived on the island scarcely nine months before.

And she looks back at herself, stepping off the early morning ferry in Kronos Town with Archie at her side, following him to the Andromache Hotel, as if at someone else, or at least at a shadow of the woman she is now, standing beside Clea, heavy in the final days of her pregnancy and relishing the discovery of somewhere she can think of as home. Suddenly, she wishes she could take possession of the pink stone house immediately. She wants to go back to Adonis House and fetch her clothes, her few books, the growing collection of items for the baby, the blue jug that she and Archie bought in a backstreet in Kronos Town the day before he left for England. She could gather together a few sticks of essential furniture, beg and borrow from Clea, from one or two friends she's made in the village, and set to work cleaning and dusting and sorting the place. She wants to feel the walls and cupboards and shelves of her stone house shifting to accommodate her, reflecting back familiarly. She craves, suddenly, such roots; the protection of these walls, the solid stone floor and high wooden ceiling. She wants to wake each morning to that enormous sky and extraordinary vista of mountains and feel she has some claim on it, some right to share in its magnificence. She feels the baby kick sharply and move as if with impatience to find a more comfortable position. A mermaid waiting to come ashore, beach itself permanently. And is reminded that she is being impractical with her small domestic concerns for cushions and cupboards and chairs when there is something more immediate requiring her attention. First things first. A birth, in fact. New life.

Clea is saying something about considering other places in the village, but Grace's mind is made up and she has no wish to look elsewhere. Clea knows it too, smiles, takes her arm and suggests they ask at the taverna about terms and conditions for a tenancy, settle on a mutually convenient date to start. "After Easter, Grace," she says firmly, "that will be soon enough for the pair of you." Grace acquiesces. However impatient she feels to move into the house and find some tranquillity and independence, Clea's wisdom has so far proved infallible. She has no idea, after all, whether the conviction and certainty she feels now about living alone will desert her after the child is born. Yet she cannot imagine suddenly being assailed by a need for dependency. From the moment she had become certain that she was, indeed, pregnant with Archie's child, her loneliness at his disappearance had shifted into a loss that, whilst still painful, could be borne if necessary. Instinctively, she knows now that she will never feel entirely alone again. Clea produces the front door key from her pocket, locks the stone house up again firmly.

"Time to get back. Tara's minding Mercury and I said we'd only be an hour or so."

***

In the end, he didn't ring ahead. He'd resolved to get to the nearest village, find a phone box and ring the number that had been given in the letter. It made sense. After all, he was unlikely to be welcome, turning up, out of the blue, disturbing the man's peace and isolation. But when it came to it, the only phone box he found was vandalised. So he walked on, choice removed from the situation, and tried to prepare himself for his impromptu appearance, come up with an appropriate greeting to match the dramatic gesture.

Yet, as it happened, the meeting lacked drama.

Late afternoon, the winter sun already low and the temperature close to freezing, he stood by the open front door for some moments before noticing a figure some distance away, repairing, it appeared, fencing or a gate.

"Grab hold of this," he was told, reaching the man's side, "keep it firm for me. I've been meaning to see to this for weeks now. And if the wind's bad again tonight..."

The job took thirty minutes or so before the repair was considered adequate. By this time his fingers and hands were frozen, his feet numb in inadequate shoes. He was exhausted beyond the point of civility; if shelter was not forthcoming he was prepared to beg for it. But that proved unnecessary. Collecting his tools, giving the fence a final inspection, Fergus turned and headed towards the open front door.

"Come on. Let's warm ourselves up by the fire. And a pot of tea. In fact, you look as if you could do with something a bit stronger than that."

Archie could not remember falling asleep. Halfway through the night he woke briefly to find himself lying on a mattress next to the fire, a couple of rough blankets covering him, but he was soon pulled back into an almost unconscious state of exhaustion that prevented thought. He slept intermittently through the next day too, only vaguely aware of Fergus coming in and out of the house, pushing mugs of milky coffee in front of him every now and again, a plate of buttered toast. In spite of a sense of profound hunger, he found it hard to eat more than a couple of mouthfuls as if eating expended too much energy. Around six o'clock, he made his way to the bathroom, found the towel, soap and razor left out for him and slowly removed the grime and stain of days of travelling. He sat across the kitchen table from Fergus and, with his encouragement, managed to eat a plate of minced beef and potatoes. That night they pulled the mattress to the side of the room, found sheets, a pillow, and made a more adequate bed for him to sleep on. He awoke the next morning as Fergus was making tea and followed him outside, wearing an old jacket and some boots that had been dug out from the back of the kitchen cupboard.

"Potatoes," Fergus said, "and the last of the swede. A few leeks. Winter cabbage. See what you can find. There should be enough for a few more stews."

"Stews?"

"Stews. Throw in some lentils. Haricot beans. It'll keep us going for a few days."

Archie worked. Fergus finished the fence-mending, saw to the hens and by mid-morning was in the greenhouse sowing tomato and cucumber seeds. They sat over a lunch of his rough bread and thick soup and talked about composts and clay soil and slugs and pests. Then they were outside again, Archie taking more instructions and carrying out tasks and Fergus dividing his time between the greenhouse and the shed. By six o'clock they were both back inside and Fergus found Archie a change of clothes from his muddy work gear. They ate a dinner of vegetable stew and potatoes. Fergus found the last of his bottle of malt whisky bought at Christmas.

"This needs finishing," he said, pouring a substantial draught into Archie's tumbler. The fire spluttered with wet wood, sent curls of smoke into the room. The men left the kitchen table, settled in chairs in front of the hearth. Fergus picked up a newspaper two or three days old and started to read.

"I won't stay long," Archie said, after a silence of ten minutes or so. "Just long enough to... to sort things. To... decide."

Fergus shrugged.

"I'm not going anywhere. Take as long as you like."

"I thought I should, you see. Make contact. But I'm not expecting anything. Don't think that. I just thought I should… can't go on forever pretending." He shifted in his chair and looked around the room as if noticing for the first time the simple, neat kitchen, the stone walls, flagstone floor, red chair covers and cushions. "This place," he said, "it's a haven." He was close to tears and buried his face in his glass, swallowed and felt the warm burn of the liquid run down his throat. Fergus said nothing. He leant forward, shoved a large log more firmly into the centre of the fire. It crackled and sparked, sending shards of hot embers onto the floor. He reached for the bottle of whisky, emptied the remains into their glasses.

***

Hester is perplexed.

"What do you mean you haven't talked to him yet? He's been with you for weeks now."

"A slight exaggeration, barely two weeks, in fact," Fergus says and sits down to deal with Hester's phone call more comfortably. "And of course we talk. But not about Grace. We haven't actually touched on the whole business of… well, the whole business, as it were. Apart from a few vague comments he made early on when I thought it was too soon for him to handle much."

"But surely that's why the man's come to you in the first place. To confess his wrongdoings, seek your advice, find out if there's any way back into his marriage."

"I think that's simplifying things a little, Hess. Quite frankly, I don't think he knows why he's here. He's obviously had a rough ride these past few months and needs time to recover."

"*He's* had a rough ride!" Hester's exasperation explodes

forcefully from her Oxford sitting room. "There's poor Grace, pregnant and abandoned, desperate and alone..."

"Hardly that," Fergus says mildly of her histrionic response. "Although I agree he has behaved appallingly towards her. Leaving her like he did, simply running away."

"So? When are you going to confront him? You can't go on living side by side indefinitely, sidestepping the most important conversation you are ever going to have, Fergus. There's rather a lot riding on this, if I may remind you. Not only your daughter's well-being and future, but that of your imminent grandchild."

"Timing," Fergus says, "is crucial. The man arrived in a broken state. I am just allowing him to recover somewhat, find some equilibrium and strength before talking. When he's ready, he'll initiate the conversation, I'm sure."

"Would you like me there?" Hester says. "Perhaps with the two of us..."

"No," Fergus says sharply, "I think that would be a very bad idea. He would feel cornered."

He can imagine Hester's performance in front of Archie, rehearsed, emotional and intense, with shades of Victorian melodrama. He can think of nothing less likely to appeal to the nervous, fragile man who spends his days quietly and methodically carrying out the tasks given him on the smallholding and seems content to sit in silence most evenings, reading or staring into the firelight.

"Where is he now?" Hester asks. "I hope you've got him on hard labour or the rural equivalent of sewing mailbags."

"He's gone down the hill into the village this morning," Fergus says. "The mobile library calls on a Thursday and he's already read his way twice through my few books. But he's not afraid of hard work, if that's what you mean. He's been a real asset, in fact. Taken a lot of the usual load off me."

Fergus does not say that he has been surprised to find Archie's company, if not congenial then certainly acceptable. He has waited to feel constrained and oppressed by another presence in his small home, irritated by the need to explain slowly how to carry out jobs that he does without thinking; but instead he has felt relief. The experience is a novelty, of course, and no doubt he will soon be restless for a return to solitariness. For the time being, however, he is content and he even finds himself waking each morning relieved at the prospect of having some of the day's physical burden lifted from him by the younger man. Hester is anxious to know more.

"So you really have no idea what he's been doing for the past nine months? In any real detail, I mean? And he honestly hasn't even mentioned Grace's name? I mean why has he even bothered to dig you out if it's not to ask whether she'll take him back? Or do you think he wants a divorce? Surely you've some idea of what's in the man's head? He must have given something away by now. Be straight with me, Fergus, I give you my word I won't beat a path to your windswept door to berate the man."

Fergus thinks how the days pass in a routine that permits them to avoid any real conversation. How he had been at first alert and anxious each time Archie had started to speak in case he had found himself reacting in anger at his son-in-law's justification of his actions. But there has been no such dialogue and he senses that the two men are parrying, negotiating their way towards some sort of respect and understanding that will allow them eventually to talk.

"There's little to tell you at the moment, Hess," he says, shifting forwards in his chair and imagining her doing something similar more than a hundred miles away. "I have no information at all to give you other than he's been living in the north for a while. He'd come from Yorkshire, I believe. That slipped out the other night. Oh, and he said something brief about contacting the television woman, Primrose, and getting my address. But then we knew about that already, didn't we? Relax, Hess, if you can; in time I'm sure we'll hear his whole story. Just be patient."

"But supposing he simply takes off and disappears again? You might just wake up one morning and find him gone."

"I don't think so," Fergus says. "Just trust me, Hess, to get this right. Leave it to me."

There is a silence down the line. Fergus imagines Hester adjusting an earring, tweaking a strand of beads at her neck. Amber ones, possibly. He remembers she once owned a string of amber beads.

"All right," she says eventually, "I'll leave this to your inimitable judgement, Fergus, and I'll try and stop nagging you. But things better hurry up soon or this baby will be born fatherless into the world. Or to all intents and purposes."

He waits until he hears her put down the receiver then replaces his, sets the phone back on the table next to his bed. For a moment, he imagines the smell of Hester's perfume in the room, mingled with the scent of wood smoke still lingering from the fire of the night before. Then he gathers himself, thinks of hen feed and barley stubble, shrugs his arms into his thick jacket and heads to the outhouse.

Hester replaces her earring from the table beside the phone, moves towards the window and stares out at the sky, leaden and dense with unshed snow. She feels restless, too confined by Fergus' sensible caution. She thinks of Macbeth and declares aloud to the Banbury Road that they have scorched the snake, not killed it. Restraint, she admits, is not in her nature and the idea of Archie Copeland knowingly living a quiet rural existence, going about his mundane jobs with some equanimity, inflames her. She is all for confrontation. As soon as the man had stepped over Fergus' threshold she knows she would have taken him prisoner, arraigned him, interrogated him, demanded a full and penitent explanation for his conduct and subjected him to any punishment within her limited means to deliver.

And she is aware that such action would have been futile.

She has to accede to Fergus' wisdom in delay. She wishes she had been more gracious in admitting it.

Sleet begins to fall. Such a disappointment, Hester feels, puny, slimy sleet instead of majestic feathers of snow, like seeing the understudy rather than the leading lady. She enjoys walking in snow, defying the car-bound, either skidding helplessly or stuck at snails' pace, grim faces staring out from their futile cages of steel. She likes to stride out in her sturdy, substantial boots, relishing the sight of the city's ancient buildings undergoing an instant transformation, white frosting and fondant icing remodelling medieval colleges into princesses' palaces, a scenic film set rather than an esteemed seat of learning. But sleet merely soaks and lacks any such enchantment. She hopes it is falling in rural Wales too, causing her son-in-law to suffer frozen hands and numbed toes as he deals with brassica and turnips and hoes and plants and mends in what she sees as some sort of frenzied avoidance activity. Fergus sounded so… Hester grapples for a word, turns away from the window and straightens the Pissarro print hanging over the fireplace. She wrestles with her reason for feeling at the same time frustrated yet calmed by Fergus' handling of affairs; by his delicacy and diplomacy, his measured and most intelligent judgement. It is, after all, more familiar for her to rebuke Fergus' behaviour. In fact, it has been a fail-safe place for her to resort to for the past thirty years or so. As if stereotyping her estranged husband as hopeless, irresponsible, ineffectual, has allowed her to label and view his absence from her life as a gift, a rich alternative to spending it with him. "I am rattled," she says aloud, and turns away from Pissarro's print to plump unnecessarily the sofa cushions. *And it isn't as if I have nothing else to do apart from worry about strategic negotiations in deepest Wales*, Hester reminds herself. *No. I am an independent woman with varying demands on my time.*

As if to prove it to herself she returns to the table by the phone and picks up the list of people she is supposed to be ringing that day; the woman from the house-sitting agency to check on the following week's job at the place in Stow; her friend, Lydia, recovering from her bunion operation at home in Woodstock; the plumber about the persistent blockage of the kitchen sink. But just as she is about to start the obligatory calls, the phone rings, startling her. The Stow house-sitting is cancelled, she hears, a broken foot or arm or some such limb causing the couple to forgo their ski trip to Verbier. Hester feigns disappointment, feels relief; she is beginning to tire of spending so much time in other people's affluently appointed homes, furnished with what she generally views as dubious taste, although she can't deny that the income is useful. Now, stirred out of her lethargy, she is about to ring the plumber to attend to the kitchen blockage when impulsively she grabs her address book and finds the phone number for Adonis House. It is almost a week since she has spoken to Grace and she knows she will be calmed by hearing her voice. The phone in the distant hall rings and rings and Hester is about to give up when the long, foreign tone is interrupted and an indistinct, very young voice says something incomprehensible to Hester. Then there's a pause and the speaker switches to English. It is not Clea or Grace or even Tara, who often answers the phone, and Hester searches in her mind for the name of Clea's other daughter, but is quickly aided. Alara announces herself. No, she is told after some hesitation, Grace is not there. "Clea, perhaps, your mother?" Hester suggests. "Perhaps I could speak to her?" There is another pause and she can hear Alara speaking to someone else who seems to have just come in. Then there's the noise of a young child, the little boy with that curious name of Mercury, no doubt, followed by a rapid and excited exchange in a mixture of languages so that Hester picks up the odd word or two. She waits, coils the cream phone cord around her ring finger. Outside, the sleet appears to be giving in to more convincing thick slices of snowflake.

"Hallo? I am so sorry. Is it Grace's mother?" Tara speaks calmly. "Alara is unused to answering the phone."

Hester assures her that the call was admirably handled. And finds herself holding her breath, sensing what Tara is going to tell her next. "Yes, they left for the hospital just an hour or so ago," Tara says. "No news yet, of course." And after all, only a week before the due delivery date. Quite normal, her mother has assured them all, quite to be expected in a first delivery.

Hester puts down the phone and for the second time that morning finds herself feeling restless and constrained by the four walls of the flat. There is absolutely no point in spending the next few hours staring expectantly and fruitlessly at the phone, striding her fitted carpet like the parody of an expectant father. Resolutely, she goes into the hall, pulls on her heavy boots, envelops herself in thick coat, scarf and gloves and heads out into the increasingly snowy streets.

# 20

He woke up one night, glanced at the clock on the mantelpiece and decided to leave. He had been planning a furtive departure for some days now, but somehow had always slept until gone seven and been woken by the sound of the kettle boiling, Fergus moving plates and cups from the draining board to the table. He had not taken note of how long he had been staying. Days drifted from one to the next without the need for particular markers. He had, he supposed, fallen into a routine of sorts that was dully pleasant; he feared disturbing it. Daylight hours were still limited although winter was beginning to shift towards something less oppressive with light in the sky until beyond five in the afternoon. Even so, by six o'clock the chores and outdoor duties of the smallholding were done. The fire was lit, supper cooked and eaten in front of it and the ensuing hours spent reading, twitching radio dials, making occasional conversation solely concerning plans for the following day.

He felt suspended from time, staying with Fergus, as if granted a sequence of days and nights that were not part of the ordinary calendar that dictated the year's length. It reminded him of how, some fifteen years or so before, he had spent a couple of weeks in hospital undergoing an emergency appendix operation that had been complicated by a post-operative infection. He had experienced then a similar sense of detachment, as if inhabiting a parallel universe with its own unique and binding obligations; the rigid timetable of doctors' ward rounds, medicine trolleys, arbitrary mealtimes, visiting hours and endless temperature and blood pressure taking that conveniently cut the day into tolerable portions of time so that descent into stultifying boredom was avoided. And whilst each day had seemed endless, the passage from early breakfast in the morning to lowered lights and cocoa at night, a challenge of endurance even the most sanguine would find stark, there had been at the same time a comfort to be found in such an absolute structure; solace, almost, in relinquishing responsibility for one's own survival. Like a small child, acquiescence was all that was required to gain approval and earn praise. The underpaid nurses, the overworked doctors liked submission. All it took to please, it seemed, was to abide by the routine of the place, lie still, lick one's wounds and wait for eventual deliverance. Grace's father, Fergus Barnes, seemed to be a naturally quiet, private man. On that first day when he had reached his front door, weary beyond expression, he had been accommodated without question. Fergus had fed him, found him a bed, provided him with shelter, warmth, clean clothes. For the first few days, the kindness of such gestures had overwhelmed him constantly to the point of tears for he had spent the previous seven or eight months or so surviving in a sort of underworld where acts of generosity were either entirely absent or intensely suspicious. He had not even justified his abrupt arrival at Fergus' remote hillside home nor given his name.

His name.

He had played so fast and loose with his name over the past few months that, at times, he had been forced to remind himself of what it really was. At first, it had seemed pragmatic to adopt some sort of pseudonym. At the various hostels and bed and breakfasts and boarding houses, for the random, temporary jobs, he had come up with something other than his own name to call himself. After all, he never stayed long, was never required to produce anything formal or legal to prove his identity. He had quite enjoyed, in fact, plucking out a name that had seemed to suit the place or the role that he was filling. In Bristol, he'd been Ed, he remembered, Ed Hawkins; in London, Charlie Wren. Reaching Leeds, for some reason he'd resorted to his father's name of Jim and had impulsively coupled it with his mother's maiden name of Grey as if from some instinctive filial obligation. So he had developed a curious relationship with names as if they were nothing more than transitory labels attached to whatever particular identity was required to suit the moment. It was like shedding a skin each time he changed one for another; like chrysalis into moth, frogspawn to tadpole, a new stage or at least a paltry attempt to define one.

With Fergus, of course, it had been different.

Even though his father-in-law had diplomatically avoided calling him anything at all for the past few weeks. And they had got along all right, in this evasive fashion. After all, there were only the two of them so confusion was unlikely. If Fergus called out an instruction or asked a question, he was the only one there to respond. And he himself spoke rarely. Only in answer to Fergus, in fact, or on a purely practical matter about a job in hand. The absence of a need to talk, to suspend the necessity for caution and restraint in what he divulged and shared was an extraordinary respite. He could not remember a time when he had last felt so liberated from his own pretence.

But it could not go on, this sabbatical from reality, from the truth of his situation. And Fergus' kindness, his acceptance and tolerance of him, was shaming. He asked so little, had expressed not one vociferous word of anger or fury as if waiting patiently for the propitious moment. And it was what, after all, he had travelled so far to face, confrontation with Fergus, a grovelling, inadequate explanation for his conduct, an attempt to bring the whole sad saga to some sort of definitive conclusion. Except that now he lacked the courage; even the words strung into some semblance of relevant conversation eluded him. So it was easier to go, to leave without warning or gratitude. That way at least, Fergus' opinion of his son-in-law's worthlessness would be confirmed.

He dressed. It was only three o'clock and there would be little light before six. He could not afford to wait, however, and in the kitchen he made himself a thick sandwich of cheese, stuffed it in the pocket of his jacket and moved towards his heavy shoes sitting in the alcove by the front door.

The phone rang.

The sharp peal of sound in the silence of the night jarred him and he dropped one of his shoes, fumbled for it and lost his balance in the darkness, falling awkwardly against the door. Fergus' voice, low and indistinct, came from his bedroom. There was still a chance to leave. Fergus appeared occupied with answering the early call and may not have heard his stumble. When he tried to undo the door, however, he realised his hand was bleeding, a minor cut from the day before now exacerbated by colliding with the heavy iron latch. At the sink in the kitchen he washed it as best he could, but the cut was deep and beginning to sting badly. The overhead light was turned on, harsh and sudden; he felt guilt as if he were an intruder and began to stammer something about having been woken by a noise, but Fergus seemed oblivious.

"That's a nasty cut," he said. "There's some stuff to bind it with in the bathroom cabinet and I'd put on a bit of disinfectant too. Can't be too careful with cuts. Then we'll have some tea, shall we? Come to think of it, an early breakfast wouldn't be a bad idea. Toast, at least. I'll see if I can get the fire going. The embers from last night should still catch if they're coaxed a bit."

By the time Archie came back from the bathroom, his hand clumsily bandaged, the fire had a decent flame and there was a tray of tea and pile of toast set out in front of it. They settled themselves in the two chairs close to the hearth and drained the earthenware pot, ate two slices apiece in silence. The clock on the kitchen wall shifted to half past the hour then marked fifteen minutes to four.

"Let's talk, shall we?" Fergus eventually said, throwing another log onto the fire and concentrating on the resultant spits and sparks of the wood in the grate.

And Archie began to talk.

At first, the account was muddled, lacking chronology as if he had lost touch with sequencing. Gradually, however, he found a narrative that hooked itself adequately to dates, specific months and years. And he felt, as he talked, as if he was relating a tale that belonged to someone else; as if sharing the story of a foolish relation or acquaintance who so confused illusion with reality that the essence of this person dissolved almost entirely. So that this unfortunate wretch no longer knew or could trust in the truth of his ambitions, his actions. "If you lie long enough," Archie said, "it's very hard to know what is a lie, a wish fulfilment, you could call it, and what actually is. What you have actually achieved. There are times," Archie said, "moments in each day when I even wonder if I ever met Grace. Fell in love with her. Married her. Cared desperately about her. If she, too, is part of my fantasy." Fergus listened. He interrupted occasionally, a low prompt rather than a question, to verify a place, a time. But on the whole, he simply sat and absorbed all Archie had to tell him without comment.

Later, around dawn, he fell asleep in the chair where he

sat and dozed intermittently through the morning. Each time he woke, his intention to get up and go outside to join in the usual routine tasks of the day was snatched from him by an overriding weariness and he would sleep again. When he eventually woke fully, he felt curiously light and unfettered, like someone emerging from a form of detention or a paralysing illness who wants to make up for lost time. In the bathroom, he washed, shaved, changed his clothes then went out to find Fergus. An entire day, it seemed, had almost passed for the light was disappearing again and Fergus was occupied with the final jobs of the late afternoon.

"Do you want me to go now?" he said. "Otherwise, in the morning. First thing. I was intending to, anyway."

Fergus went on feeding the hens. Light rain began to fall. Eventually, he turned to Archie and said,

"How's that hand of yours? If you can manage, you finish here and I'll get some dinner on. A bit of stew. Do something with the last of the swede. It's going to be a wet night by the looks of things so check the cover on the firewood before you come in, would you? I meant to do that earlier."

***

A week later, after some milder weather that had seemed to hint at an early spring, there was a heavy snowfall.

"No point in trying to get down into the village," Fergus said, seeing Archie pull on boots and shove books in his pocket. "Even if you make it down the hill, there'll be no lending library van today. It's not like urban snow, you know. They'll clear the roads leading to the farms so the milk can get through, but we're pretty much stranded up here for a day."

Fergus made bread. He sent Archie outside to chop more wood, a job he had been happy to delegate since his arrival.

The phone rang mid-morning. By now, Fergus had grown accustomed to Hester's conspiratorial greeting.

"Can you talk?"

"Briefly."

"Well? Does he know?"

Fergus looked out of the window at the snow-encrusted landscape. He felt suddenly tired, the sort of profound fatigue that even a good night's sleep would not shift. For a moment he was tempted to give into Hester, to ask her to make her way to Cardiff by train, find her way onwards by coach, change to the local bus and finally walk the distance up the hill so that she could be the one to deliver the news to Archie. And he knew she would not flinch from the prospect. Even thick snow would be unlikely to deter her if he granted her the licence. But he was resolved.

"Today," he said simply. "I'll talk to him today. It's the right moment. It's time, I think."

"Time?" Hester said. "I should say it's time. If you don't tell him soon, this child of his will be—"

"Yes, all right," Fergus said more forcefully than he had intended. And he realised that his procrastination had been more than delicate diplomacy. Again, he yearned for Hester to be at his side to share this conversation, to take over entirely, in fact, for words so often eluded him, remained stubbornly unspoken as if thoughts refused to form and attach themselves to appropriate phrases. He wondered now how different his life might have been, its insignificant course and curve, if he had only managed to grapple with the words required to explain himself. Hester was talking, hurrying on, providing possible scenarios for the events of the coming months, in which both a reunion and an absolute rupture were considered as if this was some sort of script meeting for a popular soap opera that needed to find its focus. He cut her short. Archie was heading back towards the house, wielding a basket of logs. He heard the stiff latch of the front door lift, boots on the flagstone floor. Back in the kitchen, he put the proved loaves into the oven, made mugs of coffee and handed one to Archie. The two men stared out of the window at the sky, now a brittle blue, the sun, absent of warmth, starkly striking the whitened valley. Fergus pulled a chair out from the kitchen table and indicated for Archie to do the same with the other.

"Grace," he said simply as Archie sat down opposite him, setting down his mug with the motion of a man expecting a long interview, "I need to tell you about Grace."

***

Hester puts down the phone. She wishes she were at Fergus' side in his remote, draughty and inhospitable lair. It's how she has always thought of it although, of course, she has no evidence that the place Fergus calls home is quite so rudimentary. She hopes to God he's capable of handling the whole matter. Perhaps she should have insisted on being there, ignored his protestations that Archie was better confronted alone. But maybe he's right. Hester suspects she is too angry with her son-in-law to allow for a rational exchange. Fergus has patience. He has always been a measured man. He is pathologically incapable of losing his temper whereas she has always rather relished the occasional rant and tirade at a hapless subject. She goes into the kitchen and makes herself a sandwich that she forgets to eat. She checks the wall calendar and realises that she is supposed to be going to Cirencester in two days to house-sit an elaborate thatched cottage and a couple of spaniels in their owners' absence. She has no wish to go. She feels a sudden dread at the prospect of waking up in the spare room of someone else's silent home, passing the hours looking at a stranger's framed family photos, walking their pampered pets; gathering other people's mail from their mat, piling it teasingly unopened on their mantelpiece to await their return. In fact, she realises that she no longer has any desire to live at the edge of other people's lives, hover in their shadows as if grateful for the opportunity. She goes back to the living room, grabs the phone before mercenary reasons stall her. She is resigning, she tells the affronted woman at the house-sitting agency that has employed her for the past few years. She wishes her details to be removed from their books. And no, she is giving no notice, nor proffering any excuse for leaving them in the lurch over the imminent booking in Cirencester. She is neither ill nor dissatisfied with the terms that are on offer. She simply wants to stop doing what she has been doing. She wants a change. She listens fleetingly to the objections to her behaviour then plonks down the phone with some satisfaction and waits for the sense of regret that so often has greeted her impulsive gestures over the years. And finds no such feeling; more a reassurance of shrugging off the irrelevant and unwanted.

Of moving on.

She has told Grace that she will visit the following month. In late March or even early April. But she cannot contain herself any longer. She needs to go now. And surely she can be of some practical use, deliver in person whatever news there is to deliver after Fergus has, eventually, belatedly, talked to Archie. She has no wish to speak to Grace about such a poignant matter over a phone line spanning its way across most of Europe. She's justifying an impulsive visit to Kronos, of course. In truth, she simply needs to go sooner rather than later because she wants to hold in her arms this sliver of new life. Marvel foolishly at the miracle of minute, perfectly formed limbs. "As if I have never seen a new-born child before," Hester says aloud, attempting to mock her own sense of wonder, suppress clichéd sentiments. But she fails and manages only to weep, tears that seem to insist on falling in spite of her efforts to curb them. Eventually, she goes to the bathroom, washes rigorously and methodically mends eyes and face. She stares for a moment at her repaired reflection in the bevelled wall mirror as if not quite trusting in the swift adjustment, in the mask she's just imposed. *Perhaps I've hidden my tears too often*, she thinks. *Adopted a carapace of capability and calm out of too much foolish pride. Maybe things would have been different if I'd been more honest and displayed my spots of vulnerability. Shown how much I needed, from time to time, shoring up and defending. Instead, I have no doubt appeared to others to have sailed through the days and decades as if entirely and comfortably in charge. Even Fergus has probably thought… but no, probably not. Probably not a single thought about me has flickered through that rural landscape of his mind since departing from our erstwhile life in safe, suburban Pinner.*

Abruptly, she turns away from the mirror, leaves the bathroom and finds her abandoned ham sandwich on the kitchen table. She eats rapidly, feeling suddenly exasperated by her own introspection, the indulgence of it. She has no tolerance for such vanity and spurs herself into action to forestall temptation. She spends two hours cleaning the flat then rings her friend Lydia in Woodstock, issues an invitation for dinner and devotes herself to a complicated recipe for a French provençale-style daube for the rest of the day.

***

He had become a familiar figure in the mobile library van that parked at the end of the main village road once a week. But there was little conversation, the business of browsing and borrowing taking place in a subdued atmosphere as if mimicking somewhere more hallowed than a local authority vehicle. Archie returned his books, resisted taking out more. The woman at the improvised librarian's desk raised an eyebrow.

"Nothing for you today? Well, you know where to find us if you need us next week."

Archie smiled, said nothing. A thaw had set in the evening before and although snow was still dense on high ground, around Fergus' home and outbuildings, the village roads and pavements had turned to unpleasant grey slush. The day was raw, the northerly wind penetrating. He walked to the end of the long main street as if with purpose. A cluster of cottages, some squat bungalows, lined the road for fifty yards or so beyond the village then the pavement petered out and a steep bank was the only way to follow the narrow, twisting road as it headed south, eventually meeting up with a major arterial route. He walked back a few paces to the bus stop, sat down on the bench for some minutes then got up again, headed back towards the village. He was supposed to be buying something. Fergus had handed him a list with a couple of items when he'd seen him gather his books together and he'd shoved it into his pocket mechanically. Now it seemed to have disappeared and for a moment he felt concern and wondered whether he should go back to the library and search for it.

Then he remembered that he had left his father-in-law's home an hour earlier with a clear intention of not returning. At least he thought he had. He had sat listening to what Fergus had to tell him, the day before. About Grace still on the island, about the birth of a child, his child, and had found the enormity of such news utterly bewildering. He had for months now accepted the loss of his marriage, forced himself to confront that his own stupidity and misplaced pride had cost him Grace. Now, the knowledge of losing more, so much more, felt intolerable. At first, he had resisted even believing that such a thing was possible, that in the same expanse of time that to him had been barren, utterly desolate, had been so very other for Grace. He had needed Fergus to repeat himself, to relate events two or three times before he could be sure of having absorbed them. Even then, it had been hard to believe in their truth. Fergus had refrained from judgement or advice. He had simply delivered the news then he had left him alone. They had hardly spoken for the rest of the day and had eaten supper in silence. Just before going to bed, however, Fergus had asked him calmly what he intended to do now. To Archie, the question had been futile. As a husband, he had managed with ease to prove his worthlessness; his unsuitability as a father was therefore self-evident. Grace was fortunate to be free of him. In her wisdom she would see she had the better bargain alone. To Fergus, he had said nothing. Behaved as if he had not even heard the question. He had hardly slept.

He passed the library van again, headed towards the other end of the village street and wished there was a café where he could sit and spend an hour or two attempting to think. For it was the same old trouble, the inability of his mind to order his thoughts, construe them into some sort of understanding and certainty. Or perhaps it would be easier if he could channel himself beyond thought, into a zone absent of conscience and reason. The hardware store next to the Baptist church prompted him to remember items on Fergus' list and he went inside and collected what was required. The warmth of the shop was comforting and he lingered among the shelves as if interested in the contents of numerous boxes and drawers of screws and nails, tacks, pins, pegs and picture hooks. He inspected pots of emulsion paint and whitewash, tubes of filler and adhesives and undercoats and topcoats until he began to think his prolonged stay in the shop would look suspicious. But the owner and his assistant, father and older daughter, were talking to a customer at the counter, clearly catching up on local news, and seemed oblivious of him. A woman came in pushing a large pram and there was a disruption to hold open the door, find space, move boxes to accommodate her. Archie concentrated on a colour chart of exterior, weatherproof distempers. The conversation at the counter changed to include the woman and as he turned to move to another aisle he saw her lift something out from the pram, little more than a bundle of white blanket, it seemed at first, until the strong sound of a newly born baby emerged, the cry echoing around the shop with the clarity of a bell. He stood for a moment or two, arrested by the group, the woman and her child, the onlookers cooing and fussing as if with an object of unparalleled beauty and joy.

Then he swiftly searched his pocket for coins to pay for his purchase, slapped them on the counter and slipped silently out of the shop.

# 21

They walked up the hill to the pink stone house, Hester carrying the baby in the multi-coloured sling Clea had given Grace as a present.

"It's charming," Hester said, peering through the windows, following Grace around to the back of the house to stand in the spring sunshine. After two days of rain, the air was sweet and fresh with a discernible warmth. "But small. Will there be enough room for you?"

"There's only me and this one," Grace said, stroking the cheek of the sleeping child. "We don't need a lot of space."

"No, but… well, it's quite isolated, isn't it?"

"Not really," Grace said, "it's still within the village boundaries and there are a couple of neighbours down the track. And after all, I'm still going to be working for Clea, remember, so I'll be backwards and forwards to Adonis House most days."

"If it's what you want," Hester said, her arms cradled around the shape of the child.

"It is. It feels right."

Snuffling sounds, small, infinitesimal movements that gradually grew into more determined prods and nudges of tiny limbs came from the sling strapped to Hester. Grace sat down on a large stone under the olive tree and held out her arms. Hester left her feeding the baby and walked a little way further up the hill beyond the last of the village houses until she could gain a view of the sweeping coastline a couple of miles away. She had not yet been to Anixi Bay where she had stayed the previous summer. Since arriving on Kronos three days before, she had stayed close to Adonis House, disinclined to pull herself away from Aghia Kallida, from Grace and the baby. Now she stood, absorbing the beauty of the extensive bay displayed in one direction, turning her head only marginally to take in the dramatic mountain range, snow peaks glistening in the strong sunlight. It was easy to understand Grace's attachment to the place and she admired, envied even, her resolve to stay. Even so. The walk back to Adonis House was slowed down by meeting several villagers all eager to admire the baby and talk to Grace. Just before they went through the open front door to the outer courtyard she turned to her and said, "If it's pride that's stopping you, don't make that mistake."

"I don't know what you mean," Grace said automatically, shifting the weight of the child as a reflex distraction. "If you're saying that… I can assure you it's nothing to do with pride."

"I often think," Hester went on, ignoring her evasive response, "of how different things might have been if I'd asked him. Insisted. Fergus, I mean. If I'd shown him how much I wanted him to come back. It would have only taken the words, after all. If I could have found the words and the courage to do it."

The baby began to whimper. Grace kissed the top of the soft head, rocked gently from side to side in an effort to soothe.

"It's all so different now," she said eventually, turning to look at Hester. "I thought before that… that I needed Archie. Depended on him. Life without him seemed an impossibly bleak prospect. As if I couldn't manage alone. But now…"

The baby's cries increased. Grace turned away, headed in through the door.

"I can't talk about it all at the moment," she said firmly.

"It's too hard. It... complicates things. Please... I'm fine with just the two of us."

Hester watched her go upstairs with the baby. She stood for a minute or two in the hall, wondering whether to follow her then, hearing voices from the kitchen, went in to find Clea and Tara drinking coffee at the large table. She pulled up a chair.

"So what did you think of the house?" Clea said, pouring a cup for Hester. "Grace is very taken with it."

"The house?" Hester said, feeling suddenly weary. "Oh, yes, the pink stone house. Nice. Very nice. Ideal for the two of them, I'm sure."

***

Grace remembers every moment of the birth and the hours and days immediately after. Even now when over two weeks have passed, nearly three, she constantly replays the events in her mind, rather like someone who has fallen in love and wants to hold on to the first time such knowledge was evident. She hardly slept the first night. In spite of a day spent in labour, she found the oblivion of sleep almost anathema to her. Her mind would not calm itself sufficiently to give in to rest. And when, around six in the morning, her baby was placed in her arms to feed, she experienced all over again that extraordinary joy and ecstasy she had felt at the moment of birth; the first sight of her child, perfectly formed, detached and separate yet entirely dependent and reliant upon her. "A baby, my baby," she remembered saying foolishly as if she were expecting to deliver some other creature and this human form was a surprise. Yet at the same time there was a familiarity as if this meeting between the two of them was inevitable, certain, and simply long in arrival. She waited to feel exhaustion, a sudden withdrawal of such euphoria after a couple of days, the way she had heard other women speak. But it failed to arrive, her mood refused to shift from a sense of elation, and she wanted only to gaze at the child whether sleeping in the crib next to her bed or feeding easily at her breast. The small limbs seemed both surprisingly sturdy and active yet vulnerably delicate and she gazed with fascination at the tiny lines on the hands, perfect fingernails and knuckles as if the wonder of creation had only just occurred to her. A clean sheet, she thought, a flawless, unblemished being, new-minted and utterly unique. At first, she was terrified to bathe the baby, fearful of the proximity of a little water, of handling the gentle flesh and hearing mild cries of protest. But very soon she grew more confident, wanting no one but her to perform such duties, relishing her ability to discover swiftly the skills as if by instinct rather than instruction.

Back at Adonis House she finds herself the focus for constant visitors. Even virtual strangers seem anxious for a glimpse of the baby as if new life is some sort of talisman of joy and good fortune. Tara is indispensable. She makes her drinks, small snacks, keeps her company while she feeds, fetches clean nappies, clean towels, and seems to have delegated herself to be constantly at Grace's call. Grace thinks of Archie. She tries to see his reflection in the baby's face, wonders if the shape of the mouth, the nose, in any way resembles his. She cannot see any defining connection. But nor can she claim any particular link with her own physiognomy; the baby's eyes are still new-born-blue and even if Clea says that she can see Grace's colouring in the soft, pale cheeks, the few tufts of downy hair, she is unconvinced. The baby is an original, she says firmly, a brand new person who has no need to share parental features; yet wonders if she would sound quite so defiant if she could afford the lure of sentimentality. For she feels strong now, so strong with the baby at her side, and she does not want even to consider how different things could have been. She holds the baby against her, head nestling into her shoulder, soft and fragile and warm on her skin and smells the particular sweetness of the new-born. She has always been a deep sleeper, someone who could remain unaware of thunderstorms and strong winds, yet now she wakes at the first whimper, stumbles out of bed and gathers the baby in her arms before there is the chance for a full-hearted cry. She wants to relish every moment. People tell her constantly to make the most of this stage as if there is within her reach the power to slow it down, to interfere with the natural pattern of day and night, the inevitable growth and development of her child. She nods at them, promises that she will for she cannot imagine ever feeling as contented and fulfilled as she does now. Even when she is tired, in need of more consecutive hours of sleep than the two or three currently on offer, she is charged with a sense of capability, of success, as if she has just completed a lifetime challenge, a feat of extraordinary endeavour.

And she has, of course, she tells herself, staring at the sleeping child in her arms. She has.

"You are magnificent," Grace says aloud, and the baby stirs for a moment, opens wide blue eyes and stares straight back at her, holding her gaze as if to say, "Ah, it's you – you are my mother."

***

"I can't talk for long, Fergus, I have no idea how much these international calls cost." Hester settles herself at the small desk in the hall of Adonis House. She is grateful for Clea's suggestion. Grace, Tara and the baby are out, the coast clear, as Clea has put it, for Hester to bring Fergus up to date. And to check on events the Welsh side of things, Hester thinks to herself, but holds herself back from saying. She has been a little cavalier in the version of events she has presented to Clea. Or evasive, at least. *But then*, Hester thinks to herself, *I really am at a loss to know exactly where we all are at present. Human beings are incalculably unpredictable, it seems.*

"So? The baby is..."

"Beautiful. Ecstatically lovely. Oh, don't get me started, Fergus."

"I'm not. I just wanted to know..."

"Perfect. You have a wonderful grandchild. And Grace is... well, she's happy. Besotted. As is only normal and right, of course."

"Yes. And you've told her? About..."

"Oh yes," Hester says. "I've told her. And I have to say that I think it was the most restrained and subtle performance of my life, Fergus. When you think how over the top I could have been. Was entitled to be in fact."

"And?"

Hester pauses. She wants to give a predictable response. She wants to tell Fergus that Grace collapsed into tears of gratitude and relief and is already planning her flight home ready for reconciliation and a resumption of her marriage to Archie. But she can't.

"At first," she begins slowly, "she seemed... overwhelmed with relief. Grace, that is. For a moment or two. But then... it was as if she wasn't particularly interested in the news. As if I was talking about someone else's husband. But of course it wasn't that at all."

"It was a shock, no doubt. Not what she was expecting to hear."

Hester thinks over the conversation two days before. She

had spent a considerable amount of time on the journey to Kronos trying to work out how to give Grace the news when there was still no certainty about the outcome of, at last, finding Archie. She had tossed aside the magazine she had bought at the airport, found it impossible to concentrate on the contents of the novel she had intended reading on the ferry when the reality of life itself was taking on the substance of fiction. In the end, she had waited only an hour after arriving at Adonis House before saying simply and quietly to Grace, "Archie is alive and reasonably well. Your father, Fergus – Archie is temporarily living with him. For the time being, at least." Now she thinks it might have been her choice of words that had confused Grace and wonders whether she should have been a little lax with the truth. She says as much to Fergus.

"I think I should have fibbed a bit, told her that Archie was desperate to see her, overjoyed about the baby and full of contrition, utterly penitent and all that stuff."

"He is, in his own way, I am sure. All those things you say, Hess. But you have to be honest with Grace about… well, his present state. You can't go writing a script and the speech that he hasn't made."

"It's the habit of a lifetime," Hester says wryly then swiftly moves on. She needs to bring herself up to date with any developments since her last phone call to Fergus a couple of days before she left for Kronos.

"He's said little," Fergus says. "Just after I gave him the news about Grace, just a couple of hours afterwards, he left, disappeared for a whole day."

"How could you let him go like that? Fergus, really! After all that's happened—"

"Archie is not my prisoner, Hess. He has to make up his own mind about what he's going to do next. What he wants for his future."

"But it's not just about his future – this is about Grace and their child. The man is not a lone traveller in the world." Hester is exasperated. She fiddles with the neat line of pencils on the desk, letting one roll onto the floor where its lead breaks.

"To all intents and purposes, that is exactly what he is. What all of us are, Hess."

"Oh, for goodness sake! Damn all this philosophical claptrap about the freedom of the individual, Fergus," she exclaims so loudly that Clea comes out from the kitchen, looking concerned. Hester waves her away. "Archie married Grace. Now they have a child. That child is hardly your lone traveller in the world, I'll have you know, and won't be for another eighteen years at least. And one's parents are always one's parents; they cling leach-like to one's identity throughout life. Not so easy to shrug off as an irresponsible husband."

Fergus says nothing for a moment or two. Then he starts to cough, apologises to Hester and turns away from the phone as if in search of a handkerchief, a glass of water. Hester is annoyed with herself for feeling mildly alarmed. She doesn't want to clutter her mind with concerns for Fergus when there are far more important matters to occupy it.

"Sorry, Hess, just started this morning, a bit of a head cold, that's all."

"Not a return of that pneumonia nonsense you had last year?" she says. "We really could do without you getting ill at this point, Fergus."

He reassures her. It's been a long winter, he says, and he always picks up something as it begins to draw to a close, starts, hopefully, to shift towards spring. He coughs again then clears his throat.

"I think you should leave off any thoughts of persuasion

where Grace is concerned," he says. "Just leave the subject of Archie alone. You've been the messenger and delivered the news and that part of your mission is over."

"You know what normally happens to the messenger," Hester says dourly. She doodles a shape on the notepad by the phone, remembers that at one time she had planned on going to art classes, sketching or watercolours for preference. Then she swiftly discards the pencil, exasperated by the butterfly darting of her mind.

"Archie is convinced that Grace is better off without him, I'm sure," Fergus says, "that she would be appalled by the idea of a… a reunion. That the thought of a reconciliation, the possibility of sorting things out, is simply not on the cards. And perhaps he's right."

"Really, Fergus, don't let me get started on… sorry, no… go on."

"It's time to step back, Hess. Let them both do a bit of thinking about what they want. We've played our parts."

"That sounds appallingly sensible and restrained, Fergus. Not my style at all. But… I suppose you're right." She taps the toe of her shoe against the chair leg. She is aware of trying to prolong the call in spite of her concerns about its expense, delay the moment when Fergus replaces the receiver and returns to his day. "Watch that cold of yours, Fergus, hot toddies and aspirin by the hour, all that sort of thing."

"When you're back, Hess," he goes on, "we'll talk again. Perhaps it would be helpful if you saw him."

"Me?" Hester is surprised. Fergus has so far seemed anxious to keep her away from Archie as if she would prove not so much an asset as a liability.

"I feel I have done all I can. And, quite frankly, I'm not sure I'm all that good at this sort of thing. I've given him space, a bit of time and shelter, but… I don't know what to do with him now. What to say. It's all so… so difficult. Words are not my strong point." He sounds weary, defeated. He coughs again.

"You've been splendid, Fergus," Hester says. "No one could have done more. In fact, most would have done far less with someone like Archie simply turning up on their doorstep."

"He's not a criminal, Hess. As far as I know he's not done anything illegal. He's just been… very foolish and made a lot of mistakes. The best of us are capable of that."

"You're a forgiving man, Fergus. I'm not sure I can be as tolerant of his misdemeanours. When I think of how he simply left Grace and…"

"The phone bill, Hess. I think we've talked long enough. We'll just go around in circles if we carry on. But when you're back here…"

"Of course I'll meet him, Fergus. If you can keep hold of him long enough."

"I'll do my best. And then if you could bring yourself to… no, it doesn't matter. Tell Grace that I… that I am very happy for her. About the baby, I mean. In fact—"

"The phone bill, Fergus," Hester interrupts.

"Yes, of course," he says hastily and puts down the receiver so quickly that Hester does not have a chance to say goodbye. She sits staring at the phone for a minute or two as if expecting him to ring back, hopeful, even, of Fergus remembering something more he intended to say. But the hall stays silent; only remote sounds from the lane outside, from Clea cooking in the kitchen, intrude. She resolves to follow his advice, to avoid any conversation with Grace concerning Archie and finds the prospect a relief. She can settle down to wallowing in the joy of this new life, her grandchild, adjust to the new status she feels this affords her. It is, after all, all too easy to be contaminated by Grace's contentment and believe with her that only the moment, this particular blissful moment, matters. Hester can entirely understand her reluctance to compromise it. Yet at the same time she remembers Grace's instinctive, unchecked response, the expression on her face, when she had first told her that Archie had been found. "He's all right?" she had said, two or three times, as if Hester might have been misleading her. "He's... not ill or hurt?" And she had brushed her hand across her face as if to still unguarded tears. Hester had held her, hugged her, then Grace had consciously moved away, shifted the subject onto the baby, the prospect of the day as if to distance herself from the thought of Archie, the complications of such news in order to retreat to safer, surer ground. Hester smells coffee. She realigns the pencils on the desk and goes to the kitchen in search of a cup.

Fergus moves to the window, sees Archie repairing the lock on one of the sheds. He's been meaning to see to it himself for months, but it is one of the many jobs that is easy to overlook since the need for security on a shed that contains so little of value is scant. He looks back at the phone, wishes he had said more, thinks even of ringing Hester back. He is exasperated with himself for his restraint, for his inability to say outright to her that he is desperate for her help, for the strength and assertion she embodies with ease and that constantly eludes him. He is gratified that she thinks of him as forgiving and tolerant, but suspects that he is, in fact, merely conciliatory, resorting to complacency rather than protest. How much easier it is to accept the given rather than to take offence from it. He shrugs on his working jacket and goes out to join Archie by the shed.

"Job well done," he says. "Thanks."

"Only took a moment. I should have seen to it before. The roof could do with a bit of attention, I'd say. But it's not urgent."

"You're not afraid of hard work, Archie, I'll give you that.

This place… you've been a great help these past weeks. If I'm honest, I'd begun to find it all a bit much. Age catching up on me, I suppose."

Archie looks away across the vegetable plots as if he finds the compliment awkward.

"I… I've enjoyed it. I surprise myself, actually, always thought of this sort of thing – working on the land, in the open – well, as not the kind of work I'd be any good at."

"Nonsense," Fergus says. A couple of crows land in the field close to them. A strong wind picks up and the first drops of rain blow into the two men's faces. Fergus starts to cough, fumbles for a handkerchief. "Dratted cold. I'm going to the outhouse for an hour or so, see to some bits and pieces." He turns to go then, without stopping, calls back to Archie over his shoulder, raising his voice against the increasing wind. "And if you want to give Grace a call any time, the number's by the phone. Her number at the place in Kronos. It would be a good idea, you know."

Archie stares after him, watches him disappear through the door of the outhouse. He lets Fergus' words run through his head, lodge there with stubborn insistence. *Give Grace a call any time, the number's by the phone.* Over the past nine or ten months, the difficulties of any communication with Grace appeared to grow, each day further eroding such possibility so that something he had always held in his mind as his intention for the next week, the following month, had begun to seem illusory. As if he had slunk back into his execrable old habit of pretence and self-deception in his belief that he would one day directly contact her.

And now this.

The idea of such an uncomplicated gesture, simply walking inside, picking up the phone and speaking to Grace, is astounding to him. He cannot imagine the consolation of hearing her voice. He has begun to believe that he will only hear it now in his head, forever hitched to a memory of it rather than the sound itself. Fergus is still in the outhouse; he sees his figure bend and stoop to pick something off the floor, reach up to a shelf and take down a box or container of some kind. Swiftly, he moves towards the front door, stands in the porch and starts to remove his boots then abruptly stops himself. He has no words that he can offer Grace. There is nothing adequate to summon. He is incapable of expressing the depth of his regret and he knows that such sentences as he can construe will sound trite, risible. And then there is the child. How can he possibly convey what he wants to say about this birth, transmit the emotions that he himself cannot even begin to define? He pushes his feet firmly back into his boots, scans the sky. Another hour or so before it rains, perhaps. Just time enough to see to some reconstruction of that bit of crumbling back wall.

***

Hester had intended staying for two weeks and had extended her visit to almost four, feeling no particular desire to go home. Grace constantly reassured her that her company was welcome and Clea encouraged her to stay. Although there was a lull before the season started at Easter there was still a lot of work to be done around the house and Hester was happy to help Clea and allow Grace more time to devote herself to the baby.

"Think of me as your maternity cover," she said to her one morning after she had dealt with a phone enquiry while Grace was resting following a night interrupted by hourly feeds. "You know how I like to busy myself. And really, that gentleman ringing from Aberdeen was absolutely charming. Evidently, he and his wife were here last year and can't wait to come back."

Grace remembered the young couple. They had been staying during her first week at Adonis House the previous June and she had been moved by their ease with each other, their obvious devotion; Archie's absence had felt like an open wound on her flesh. Hester went down to Anixi Bay and found Dimitri and Anna's *kafenion*, one of the few places open out of season. She was greeted warmly, a bottle of honey-and-cinnamon-flavoured strong spirit soon produced for endless toasts to both Hester and her new grandchild.

"They made me feel like a member of their extended family," Hester said to Clea on her return, "not merely a random visitor who happened to help them out a few months back."

"That's what it's like here on the island," Clea said. "You returned to see them. Loyalty is valued."

Grace drove them into Kronos Town and Hester abandoned her resistance to the idea of the pink stone house and insisted on buying numerous small items for it: cushions, a woven rug for the main room, another for the alcove bedroom, some simple pottery, candlesticks.

"You're spoiling me," Grace protested. "It's really not necessary. You've already spent money on baby clothes and now…"

"I want to," Hester said firmly, watching an assistant wrap a bright blue beaker, two small bowls. "Indulge an old lady."

Grace smiled. "It will be decades before anyone will be able to call you old. And even then…"

"I shall become eccentric instead. I think I'd do eccentricity rather well."

"Like my father?"

"Fergus? Oh, no, there's nothing eccentric about Fergus," Hester said, more firmly than she had intended.

"But you used to say…"

"I'm sure I said all sorts of things about your father over the years that I… that I regret saying now. Or at least that I probably got wrong. No doubt it was some sort of defence mechanism for responding to something I simply couldn't accept or even begin to understand."

They walked towards a small square where a café was responding to the warmth of the day by setting out tables, retracting protective awnings. The baby slept on in the old pram that Clea had given her, handed down, repaired and cleaned to remove signs of previous occupants.

"I find it hard to believe what he's done," Grace said after a few moments. "For Archie, I mean. My father… Fergus… he's been extraordinary. Quite extraordinary."

A young boy hovered. Grace ordered for both of them. The boy disappeared inside the café, returned with a tray of coffee and a dish of small, sweet biscuits.

"Not just for Archie," Hester said quietly, "I am sure he was thinking of doing the best thing for you. In fact, I know he was." She poured hot milk into the cup of strong coffee. "And for himself as well, of course. Parenting is all about selfless actions and Fergus has a lot of ground to make up in that area. This business with Archie… well, it has given Fergus a chance to behave as a father towards you. To show his love, you could say. Or something like that."

Grace said nothing. She nibbled a small biscuit tasting of cinnamon. The tables around them were filling up with people anxious to expose wintered limbs to the warmth of the sun. Signs of a discernible shift in season had taken place over the past couple of days and pavement tables, parasols, street vendors and even a hopeful musician or two were suddenly in evidence even though it was too early in the year to expect settled weather.

"I hardly know him," Grace said eventually. "Fergus, that

is. How could I? We've spoken so little to each other, after all. And yet now… do you think we know people more by their gestures towards us, their actions, rather than in what they say to us? Is that how we judge them? How we love them, even?"

"Judgement changes," Hester said, "or the way we view things changes. Time gives perspective. It has to. Otherwise, human beings would be a race entirely composed of embittered and resentful individuals. Of course, there is some behaviour that's so despicable and abhorrent that it has to remain forever condemned."

"The deeds of mass murderers and despotic leaders?"

"They're the ones. But most of us are fortunate enough not to encounter such types so forgiveness of their evils is never going to be our calling. Most of the time we're dealing with… what? Foolishness, vanity, pointless deceit, an excessive dose of self-importance – the sort of thing all of us are guilty of at some time or another. Venial sins, really. However hurtful the fallout for us might feel at the time. As for love…"

"Yes?"

Hester stroked the soft cheek of the baby sleeping starfish-like with the enviable abandonment of the new-born.

"That's… complex. Impossible to rationalise on the whole."

"That's very evasive," Grace said.

"Nothing is static, after all. And certainly not love. The way we love someone, what we love in them… romance and passion might start the whole thing off, but inevitably something more profound, more enduring takes hold. Or not, of course. In which case – there's only an empty husk. But it can be hard to know. That's the difficult part. Being able to tell whether love has entirely fled or just lain dormant for a while. Undergone a metamorphosis into something that's… hard to recognise." Hester drained her cup, coughed, blew her nose. "With one's children, naturally, it's entirely different."

"Unconditional love."

"Entirely. No choice in the matter whatsoever. Far more simple, really."

"So my father..." Grace stopped herself, uncertain what she wanted to ask. She found some coins in her pocket, placed them on the table. "Shall we move on? The market will be closing in half an hour and I promised Tara I'd buy some fish."

They gathered the bags of shopping acquired through the morning, stowing them under the pram, and negotiated the cobbled streets of the old town that led down towards the large indoor *agora*. Grace stopped at the entrance, leaning over the baby to tuck in the blanket that had been kicked aside.

"You mustn't ever think it's because of Archie's failure," she said abruptly, her face concentrated on the pram, "I would never... reject him because of that. As if all that can satisfy me is an entirely successful man and I can't love anyone who is less than that. In fact, in many ways it's quite the opposite."

"The opposite?"

"I've always thought how hard it must be to love someone entirely invincible. It would feel as if one was merely an adjunct in that life instead of... well, indispensable, I suppose. Vulnerability has always seemed to me to be an attractive feature to find. Essential, in fact, in order to love deeply."

"So..."

Grace said, "He hid so much for so long. He pushed me away when... as if he thought I would be too inadequate to help or... oh, never mind. It's too complicated. Fish. Let's think fish."

***

Melanie Babbington had sent an elaborately embroidered and beribboned baby jacket that Grace admired, but feared to use considering the constant washing required for the baby's clothes. She had also enclosed a present for Grace. '*No one thinks of the mother's needs at such a time*,' she wrote, '*but you are also worthy of attention as the bearer of this precious new life*.' Grace put on the simple silver bracelet and wrote back immediately. '*Thank you. The focus has certainly shifted. Before the birth, the interest was on me, the burgeoning, blossoming Madonna-figure. Now, quite rightly, I am playing second fiddle and attention is entirely on the new arrival!*'

Melanie continued to sound positive about her departure from Fletwell and, inevitably, Giles Meredith. '*Should have had the guts to do it ages ago*,' she wrote, '*but I needed a catalyst. And Peter has proved to be just that. I am renting a small flat over a travel agent's in Archway, only a stone's throw away from his place in Finsbury Park, and temping to pay the rent, the old secretarial skills from the arts centre serving me well. I'm playing the waiting game and respecting his terribly honourable ways, but it's clear he needs me as much as I need him. He's talking of a return visit to Kronos, seems very keen on the buzzards and such like so who knows? The two of us could be booking a room at Adonis House before the year is out, a double rather than the celibate single I occupied last visit, of course. I presume you and your chickababy are intending to stay put on the magic island. You'd be mad to do anything other*.'

Grace had written to Leo when the baby had arrived; she had been unsurprised to receive no answer. It seemed inappropriate to deliver the news about Archie by letter and within a day or so of absorbing what Hester had to tell her she had rung the phone number he had left with her the previous summer. Leo was away, according to the woman she had spoken to, but was due to be back by the end of the month. Grace had felt tentative about imparting too much detail to this woman who gave no indication of her relationship with Leo, so she had been brief. "Just tell him," Grace had said, "that there is good news about his brother. About Archie." Of course, she told herself, she had no idea whether Archie had already made contact with Leo, but she doubted it. Leo's constant absences hardly encouraged communication and it seemed as if they had never been particularly close.

Her small room at Adonis House was beginning to seem absurdly confined and she worried about encroaching too much on the hallway, the living room, the kitchen, with the absurd amount of equipment apparently essential to a small baby. Hester was due to return to Oxford in little more than a week and she knew she was anxious to see her settled before she left.

"We need to move on," she said to Clea one afternoon in the kitchen of Adonis House, folding a pile of clean laundry composed of cot sheets and miniscule vests and sleep suits. "You'll have guests arriving in a couple of weeks and a washing line of baby clothes is an entirely inappropriate sight to greet them."

"You're probably right," Clea conceded, "although I enjoy having a baby around the place. You mustn't feel pressurised to go, Grace."

"I don't. I just want to. I know it's earlier than I intended, but I feel ready. And the pink stone house is hardly far away so once I'm back to working full hours, you'll be seeing plenty of us."

"Of course we will. We're part of both your lives now, remember that, Grace. But I can see that it's important for you to establish some independence away from us as you're staying here on Kronos."

"I wouldn't even think of leaving now," Grace said, moving towards the sink to fill the kettle. In the corner of the room, the baby stirred in the pram as if about to wake, small limbs briefly fisting and kicking, then settling back as if deciding to slip back into sleep instead.

Clea said, "Of course, I thought there was a slight chance you might change your mind and want to go back when you heard the news that Hester brought."

Grace picked up mugs from the shelf, studied the pattern of pale blue flowers painted on the pottery. Tara's voice, rapid and excited, reached them from the hall followed by another voice as she and a friend speedily climbed the wooden staircase to her room. She had given Clea little detail about Archie's situation beyond relaying the news that her husband was well and staying, temporarily, with her father. Working with him on his Welsh smallholding, contributing tirelessly, in fact, according to Fergus, to the day-to-day running of the place. (Fergus had been insistent that Grace should know of his hard work.)

Clea, typically, had not probed.

"I find it hard to think of him as part of my life now," Grace said eventually, watching the kettle boil yet failing to fill the waiting mugs. For even as she spoke the words she knew they were not strictly true; not at all true, in fact, yet what she did feel was so hard to summon up and arrange into coherent phrases. She tried again, coming back to the table and sitting down next to Clea. "Everything that's happened over the past months, while he hasn't been here with me... well, they seem to be events unconnected with him. I mean I know that may sound ridiculous since he's the baby's father, but... he hasn't been here to share any of it. The anticipation, the... the joy of it. So much has changed since we were last together and I am not sure how all the pieces would fit together anymore."

"And what are Archie's feelings? How did he react to the news about the baby?" Clea asked.

"I've no idea," Grace said baldly. "I mean I really don't know. My mother – Hester – well, she and my father seem to have decided to relay merely the facts to me rather than the details. To Archie too, evidently. As if this will push the two of us together out of pure curiosity, make us talk to each other simply to find out. At least I imagine that's their motive."

"So he doesn't even know if he has a son or a daughter?"

Grace nodded. "I'm amazed at their restraint, actually. Especially my mother's. She seems to think it's my prerogative to tell Archie."

"It's generous of them, leaving the two of you space like that."

"Do you think so?" Grace said. "It's also quite frightening. Not even knowing what he is feeling."

"Well, one of you needs to take the first step, make the initial move towards the other, I suppose."

Grace remembered the empty mugs, the kettle, got up to pour boiling water into a pot. Steam rose into her face. She splashed milk, filled mugs with tea.

"I suppose you're right. If you put it like that."

Clea changed the subject and they spent the next half hour checking on the spring and early summer bookings that Hester had been monitoring for the past weeks, recording confirmations and deposits received in her clear, bold handwriting. The front door banged and the noise of the younger children returning from school, bags and coats spilling over the floor of the hallway, interrupted them. Clea hastily gathered together paperwork and filed it away into the deep recesses of the kitchen dresser, a haphazard-looking arrangement that worked with surprising efficiency.

"I have to see to some stuff with the kids now," she said, picking up car keys and slipping her bare feet into shoes she found discarded under the table. "Take Alara in one direction,

Venus in another and Mercury can come along for the ride. But I'll catch up with you later, Grace. So shall we fix on early April for your move into the stone house? Is that what you want? Hester can stay on until then to see you settled, surely."

Grace agreed. Early April would suit well.

She carried the baby, now protesting vehemently for attention, up to her room and heard the house grow quiet again as car doors banged in the lane outside. Hester had gone for a walk to Anixi Bay, Tara was studying in her room with her friend. Usually, a feed and a change into warm, dry clothes sent the baby straight back to sleep whilst still nestling against her, but today there was an agitation about the small form as if resisting such oblivion, sensing instead a need to be awake and alert. Grace resisted the idea of the cot and instead went downstairs and outside to the courtyard where the afternoon was mild, weak sunshine replacing the showers of the morning. She sat down on the bench for a few moments. Then, as if picking up on the baby's restlessness, walked down to the bottom of the garden, now a riot of wild flowers and overgrown greenery that were heralding spring although the mountains were still densely snow-clad. She felt uncomfortable about the inadequacy of her conversation with Clea about Archie, as if she was seeking to be evasive rather than open with her. But the truth was that even her own attempts to confront fully her feelings about him proved elusive. At one moment she was desperate to see him yet this was immediately followed by an anxiety that the man who had left Kronos many months previously was very different to the person she would now meet. And she, too, of course, must have changed. Would they even recognise each other, feel the same compulsive attraction that had hooked the two of them affirmatively together four years before? Grace was wracked by doubt. She had loved Archie with a commitment that had felt inevitable. Now she felt almost nostalgic for the simplicity of such love, for the single-minded devotion that she would no longer be capable of delivering. She stroked the soft, downy head of the baby, at the same time gently rocking with a rhythm that appeared to comfort for soon there was a relaxation, as if the child was choosing to jettison disquiet and abandon itself confidently into Grace's care. She went on standing there for some moments until certain of sleep, then gently shifted the baby onto her other shoulder and felt the warmth of soft breath on her neck, small nose and mouth flattened against her skin as if drawing life from it. Slowly, she walked the two of them back up the garden to the courtyard, regained the bench and leant against the whitewashed wall to support herself while the baby slept.

*If Archie is contrite,* she thinks now, *overwhelmingly concerned about this unexpected child and seriously considering the possibilities for the three of us, why isn't he here seeking some sort of resolution? It's weeks now since he's known and there appears to have been no overwhelming desire or irrepressible force driving him to our door. Not that I want him to act purely out of guilt or a sense of obligation. That's not what I want for us at all. I can manage alone. Or rather, I can manage because I'm no longer alone, but have a life tethered and defined by another – by our child. Archie only belongs with us if he understands the gift of such sublime ordinariness and has found the words to tell me so. And even then…*

Grace broke off in her thoughts, finding it too hard always to be sure of what she felt, conflicted in her judgement of him and too uncertain of how she imagined the future. She tried to step outside herself, tried to look with some detachment so that she could evaluate, know what she really wanted. But a long view was too abstract a notion to form; in the here and now, she felt content. It was enough, on this mild, late spring day, to watch her baby sleep, to contend only with the next few hours when Hester would return from her visit to Anixi Bay, Clea and the children would be home and a meal would be cooked and eaten in the kitchen of Adonis House. *As I see it now,* Grace thinks, shifting her position a little to ease her back, *things are as good as they can get. Given how things are. This is, possibly, the best that I can hope for. And it will do very well, really, quite extraordinarily well.*

Considering. Weighing it all up, past and present.

And it's not so much a case of settling for too little as for finding what offers the least uncertainty, the greatest chance of a calm, measured, mostly contented, way of living. *Which is what, after all, I have always wanted.*

Yet as she sits there, watching the faint flicker of the baby's eyelids in deep sleep, noting the peel of blue paint on a window shutter across the lane, she is pulled back to a remark of Hester's the day before that she chose to ignore. "A photograph," Hester had said, "when I go back to England, you must give me a photo of the baby to take with me. For when I see Archie – if I see Archie – I think he should have a photo." It had been easy to pretend she hadn't heard, occupied as she had been with filling the fridge and the larder with shopping from their trip into Kronos Town. And then Tara had come into the kitchen and taken the baby from Hester's lap and they'd talked about her idea of training to be a nurse and the conversation had expanded when Clea had arrived so that no more mention of a photograph had been made. But later, much later, around midnight, awake in her room, tired yet curiously resistant to sleep, Grace had taken out the envelope of pictures, a collection of more than a dozen taken mostly by Tara, a few by Alara, charting the first couple of weeks of this very new life. Already, she had sent one to Melanie and placed another in a frame ready to hang on the wall of the pink stone house. She had imagined that Hester would want one to take home to display in the flat in Oxford or to keep covertly in her wallet, ready to produce proudly to unsuspecting acquaintances. Perhaps she would even pick one out for Fergus.

But the thought of a photograph for Archie had confounded her.

She has found the idea of selecting a celluloid image to send to him, to her child's father, as some sort of adequate substitute for experiencing flesh on flesh, absurd. Preposterous. And now she considers it again, in bland daylight, expectant of a more rational response, an irritation with her mood of the night, and finds herself unchanged, stubbornly incapable of doing what Hester has requested. The thought, in fact, of Archie closely scanning the selected photograph, of studying features, the set of the eyes, the shape of the small mouth and nose, the colour of the tuft of hair on the soft head and trying to hook them, see them as some sort of palimpsest, disturbs her profoundly. Suddenly, she wants him with her, next to her, needs to touch his hand, lay her head onto his shoulder, with an intensity she has not felt since the first few weeks of his disappearance.

A car pulled up in the lane. Grace heard Hester's voice talking to Dimitri, to Anna, saying something about hoping to see them again before long, promising to stay again in the summer, then car doors closing and the sound of her footsteps crossing the courtyard.

"Grace? I didn't see you sitting there. Is the little one soundly asleep? I'll make us a drink, shall I? Tea, coffee? It's probably warm enough to sit outside for another hour."

Grace nodded.

"Thanks," she said. "Please. Tea. Or coffee. Yes, that would be good."

# 22

Hester stares at her reflection in the bathroom mirror. She rubs off eyeshadow, reapplies it, drops a wand of mascara on the floor and smudges her fingers retrieving it. She adjusts the pale primrose hand towel on the rail, sits the soap more comfortably in its dish and goes back to her bedroom. The purple dress she is wearing, she decides, looks too fussy, too formal for the day. Swiftly, she pulls it over her head, trampling it under foot as she yanks open the wardrobe door and ferrets between the hangers for something simpler, something suggesting a more casual, spontaneous choice. But the weather confuses. It is that time of year that constantly tips between seasons as if uncertain what is most fitting and appropriate. Hester looks out through her bedroom window and curses the vagaries of the day that had started with such promise. Now the sky is darkening alarmingly, the light breeze picking up energy and heavy showers look like a distinct possibility. She's had hopes of mild sunshine. She's even considered the three of them taking a gentle stroll through Christ Church Meadow or the university parks, noting the blossom, some late magnolias, possibly, a clutch or two of bluebells. But she has been fanciful, she knows, if she has been expecting English weather to deliver the goods to satisfy her plans. Clearly, it is going to be a wet, overcast day with a leaden sky louring heavily like a puritanical preacher determined to curb pleasure. It is not, she thinks, an encouraging sign if she allows herself to believe in such fallacies. Which, of course, she unfailingly does.

She pulls on a thin, pale grey sweater, a skirt she has rarely worn and fiddles with the clasp of a string of beads that Grace persuaded her to buy in Kronos Town.

They are due at midday.

Around midday, anyway, give or take the punctuality of the coach, the traffic on the A40, the accuracy of her directions from Gloucester Green bus station. She had woken too early. There had been no need for her to be up at such an hour, fussing over the simple lunch she had prepared the day before. Of course she has dreaded the phone ringing all morning. Dreaded hearing Fergus' voice, hesitant, apologetic in the disappointment he has rung to deliver. But the flat has stayed silent. There has been no call and surely now they will be well on their way, any last-minute retraction no longer a possibility and Hester can breathe easily, relax, in fact, in anticipating their arrival. In an hour or a little less, she tells herself, they will be here.

Of course, Fergus has been to the flat before, she remembers now. Some fifteen or so years ago when her mother had died, he had arrived without warning for the funeral. He had been well intentioned, no doubt, the gesture touching, but the service had taken place not in Oxford, but in Lincoln where her mother had been living. Hester forgets the details, but vaguely recalls returning late after a draining day to find him cooped up vagrant-like on her doorstep. She knows she was brusque with him, irritated by his error, and only later regretted the cold and detached way she had dealt with his enforced overnight stay on the living room floor, dispatching him to the early morning bus without breakfast. *Forgive our foolish ways*, Hester thinks now, *if you exist, dear Lord and Father of mankind, forgive our constant, so very, very foolish ways.*

There is a knock on the front door. Hester jumps. It is too early, surely it's too early for them to be here unless Fergus sensibly abandoned the idea of the coach and took to British Rail. But even so. Even so, she knows their route would then have been via Reading or Didcot or both and hardly a minute quicker, possibly considerably slower and certainly more expensive. She has already been forced to concede both points to Fergus in one of the several phone calls that have taken place between them over the past fortnight to set up the plans for the day. (Hester is still confounded that Fergus agreed to her suggestion of accompanying Archie to Oxford, ensuring his safe passage, as she put it, for the first stage of his journey.) So if not them, who else can be calling at such an inopportune moment, the day already fraught with tension? She is unused to impromptu callers in north Oxford unless on behalf of Christian Aid or Oxfam or the local rotary society. She wrenches open the door, ready to confront appeals to fill jingling tins, fold notes into discreet envelopes. And finds instead a man, a particularly tall man, with a face unduly tanned for the time of year, a frame that is extraordinarily lean yet notably broad and substantial. For a fleeting moment, she wonders whether her son-in-law has undergone a strange metamorphosis during his months in the wilderness, acquired a few inches in height, a anaquiline nose and distinct, notable cheekbones. But no. This is not Archie Copeland. Nor is it a flag-selling, funds-seeking individual. In fact, it's a rather remarkable looking man, the sort to attract attention, cause heads to turn in the high street. *At least*, Hester thinks, *he would cause my head to turn. Or would do if he weren't clearly three decades or so younger*. He stares back at her as if expectant of some greeting.

"Can I help you?" Hester says, wondering why she feels wrong-footed at her own door. He is carrying a small rucksack on his back and shifts it now as if ready to unload. Perhaps he has something to sell, she thinks suddenly, the dusty figure of the door-to-door salesman trailing his suitcase full of useless household gadgets coming to mind. But there is a self-possession about this man crowding her doorway, a complacency that seems at odds with the faint desperation of such characters. His foot, large and heavily booted, seems inclined to step forward into her hall, onto her pale mushroom carpet, and she finds herself retreating marginally behind the front door. A bus goes by in the road, pulling his attention for a moment and when he turns back it is as if he is starting again, amending his manner to suit the moment.

"Sorry to surprise you like this," he says, smiling broadly, holding out his hand to take hers. "I didn't mean to arrive before Archie. In fact, he's not even expecting to see me today. I'm Leo, Archie's younger brother. Leo Copeland."

***

Her move into the pink stone house was warmly acknowledged by the villagers of Aghia Kallida. Most days during the first couple of weeks, Grace would be surprised to find small gifts left at her door – a basket of eggs, oranges, jars of honey, olive oil, pots of preserves, homemade cheese, a bunch of fresh herbs. Although the house felt cool for the first few days, uninhabited as it had been for so long, the thick walls soon absorbed the warmth from the log fires she lit each evening and from the simple stove. And each day the weather grew warmer. After a brief wet and dull spell early on in the month, the sun began to appear more reliably and each day it was possible to leave open the windows and doors of the house for a few hours, to allow warmth to flood in. The patch of unkempt garden at the back of the house was a riot of wild flowers. She was grateful for the excuse to leave the thought of cultivating it, imposing some order on its wilderness, and enjoyed instead gathering armfuls of flowers every few days and filling a vase to sit on the small square wooden table. She expected, during her first week at the house, to feel alone, wondered whether she would wake in the night and question the wisdom of leaving Clea and the children so soon. But instead, she found herself relishing the space, confined as it was, the sense of her own four walls, the air empty of sounds other than the baby's cries, her own response.

She still spent most of her days at Adonis House. After Hester had gone home, back to Oxford, with promises both to Grace and to Dimitri and Anna to return in the summer, she had begun work again and had found it feasible on the whole to cope with a small baby at her side who obligingly slept for a couple of hours each morning and afternoon. She could not imagine practicalities once that same obliging baby turned into a toddler, but refused to look beyond the immediate and was gratified by the relative ease with which it seemed possible to manage in the present. Young children, she had noticed, were a familiar presence at work on the island, alongside their parents in shops, behind counters, at cafés and restaurants, their inclusion natural rather than an aberration.

Easter had seen Adonis House fully occupied and Clea was enthusiastic about the bookings for the rest of the season.

"It's almost getting too easy," she said to Grace one Friday morning after a phone call that reserved the last of the rooms available for August. "Of course it's never safe to rest on one's laurels, but even so… there's a chance I could get bored with this, you know."

Grace stared back.

"But surely, it's what you've been working towards –

Adonis House as a successful, established, small-scale holiday business."

Clea shrugged, entering the information about the new summer booking into the reservations file.

"It's exactly that, really. That word 'established.' I've never been very good at living on a plateau. Restlessness is my natural state, I suppose. Or, as my dear mother used to say, I never know when I'm well off. Except that I do. And…"

"You're not thinking of leaving?" Grace was alarmed. She had allowed herself to think of working at Adonis House, close to Clea and the children, as her security, a given that consoled her at moments of doubt about her situation. The prospect of the family suddenly leaving appalled her. "I thought you were happy here. Settled on the island."

"I am happy, of course I am. This is a good place as I've told you before. But there are other good places to discover. And 'settled'… well, I don't really do 'settled' for very long or find the idea of that particularly attractive," Clea said. "I believe that we have several lives within one life, Grace, offering entirely different experiences. Why limit yourself? Look at you, already carving out something rather different for yourself than you'd anticipated back in England, I'm sure."

"But that's been… necessary. Circumstantial, you could say."

"Nonsense," Clea said, "you've made a choice. Shrugged off one life for another. But as far as I'm concerned, don't worry, Grace, I have no immediate plans to uproot us all from Kronos. It's just that I won't be here forever. Tara will stay, I'm sure. She needs roots. She craves stability and seems to find it in what she knows. Whereas I… I'd like to try somewhere like… well, I don't know Africa, for a start. Or South America. The world's a big place, after all. So possibly in a year or two… well, we'll see."

She turned to the typewriter and rapidly typed out several letters of confirmation then sealed them in airmail envelopes and put them to one side to be posted when she went into Kronos Town later that day. Grace walked down to the village to collect the bread, trying not to be disturbed by the conversation with Clea, wondering whether she should confront her more plainly about her future plans. On her return, however, it was Clea who was direct and unequivocal. Calling her out into the courtyard, subsumed by the warmth of the late April sun, she took the baby from Grace's arms, fussed over the growing fuzz of fair hair over the soft head and asked whether she had spoken to Archie.

"Not yet," Grace said and wondered why she felt inadequate at the admission. Like a schoolgirl caught out and proffering a paper-thin excuse. "There's been so much happening with the move and settling into the house. And, of course, we've been quite busy here." She screwed her eyes up against the sun, thought of distracting Clea with a strand of news from the village then sat down next to her on the bench and drew breath. Clea, jigging the baby first on one shoulder then the other, waited as if she knew Grace would stumble towards a better explanation. "I'm frightened, I think. Of what he'll say. And… how odd it will be simply to hear his voice again. I have no idea how I will feel."

"You want him to come back to you?"

"I don't know. I mean, yes, of course I do. At least sometimes I do. Some days I'd do anything to be with him again. But then I change my mind and it's the last… you see, I'm not sure if I even know who Archie is any more. The person he's become."

"And no doubt he's thinking the same thing about you, Grace."

"No, surely not. I mean, it was Archie who left me, hid so

much from me and then ran away from everything and didn't even give me a second's thought and…"

"You don't know that. You have no idea what he was thinking."

Grace took the baby from Clea's arms, buried her face for a moment in the comfort of the soft, sweet skin.

"No. You're right," she said. "And that's part of the problem, really. Perhaps I'm simply too scared to find out. If he has fallen out of love with me, feels entirely indifferent, in fact, about the two of us… well, it would be hard to hear. And I would, wouldn't I? I'd hear it in his voice as soon as we spoke."

"And you? Will he hear anger and bitterness the way he must expect?"

"No, of course not!" Grace said, louder than she had intended so that she felt the baby flinch at the sound. "How could I be angry after everything Archie's been through?"

Clea smiled at her, shrugged her shoulders expansively as if gratified to have proved a point.

"Grace, don't let such capacity for forgiveness go wanting. Don't stifle it. It is so rare to find, believe me. And after all, unqualified forgiveness is simply another name for love. What a waste it would be if this errant husband of yours proves equally hesitant in picking up the phone." She stood up, gathered papers and a pen from the bench and headed towards the house. "We've two couples arriving early on Sunday. Tara's already prepared their rooms, but perhaps you could just do the final check."

"Of course," Grace said automatically, only half listening. "Yes, of course I will."

***

She anticipates Fergus answering the phone. She has prepared a few words, sensing he'll want to talk about his grandchild.

She has planned to say how swiftly the first few weeks go so that already this new-born has a personality, a specific set of habits and ways that are distinguishing and particular. She'll say that, yes, she's exhausted by the broken nights yet also so expectant of this phase that she would almost feel cheated if not subjected to it. And that, anyway, the constant fatigue is so overshadowed, entirely diminished by the joy of cradling her child, she hardly notices it.

But Archie answers the phone.

It is Archie's voice, unmistakably, and Grace is both alarmed and inexpressibly overjoyed to hear it. How is it possible, she thinks, to feel simultaneously an embarrassment, a temptation to put down the phone and end the conversation instantly yet at the same time a desire to talk endlessly, to extend it without limit? It takes her a moment or two to think of anything at all to say. Even her name seems to elude her. But it appears that she has stumbled it out for Archie says something in reply, a sentence or two about how good it is to hear from her and then something inconsequential and unnecessary about Fergus being out for the morning. A vacuum of sound hovers over the line; she has the need to say so much, but the thoughts refuse to form themselves into words that will carry her meaning adequately. She has to do better, she tells herself, sits down on the hard wooden chair in the hall of Adonis House and tries.

"How are you, Archie? I mean…"

"Better. Much better now. Fergus has… your father has been… so kind. Extraordinary, in fact."

"Yes. Yes, I know."

"I don't know what I would have done without him these past few months. I don't deserve it."

"But you've been working, helping him on the smallholding? That's what I've heard."

"Yes. And I've been glad to, of course. It's been... it's rewarding. The work, I mean. I've been surprised to find that."

"And now...?"

Grace starts the question unintentionally. She has no idea what she expects in answer. Archie seems equally perplexed for again a silence hangs between them. She bites her lip and thinks how entirely inadequate this phone call is proving to be. For there is, simply, too much to say. And a language sufficient to meet the needs of such a conversation has yet to be invented. Perhaps this phone call is a mistake, Grace suddenly thinks, too confrontational to elicit any useful response, to establish a clear idea of where the two of them are heading. Grace winds the phone cable around her finger, pulls it tight so that there are indents, pink whorls in her skin. She tries again and finds an overlap of voices, both of them reacting at the same moment to the awkwardness of the quiet line.

"Sorry? What was that?"

"No, you were saying? You first."

"No, it doesn't matter, it's just that..."

"What?"

Grace knows she is crying. She has not expected this, has thought herself to be too cautious and equivocal to give in to such emotion. This is, after all, the man who has deceived her, misled her in ways that would cancel any ordinary, platonic friendship. But tears splash down her face, misting her eyes, blotting onto the white cotton collar of her shirt so that she is amazed, in fact, to find any voice to speak at all. But she does.

"How soon can you be here, Archie?"

"Here? You mean Kronos? The island? Soon. Yes, of course, I'm sure I can manage it. If... if it's really what you want, Grace."

"Good," she says. "Yes, that's… at least… Then that's what we'll do. We'll talk when you arrive. When you're here… it will be… it's the best thing. We can talk properly then."

"Yes, that would be… I just wasn't sure if you would even want to see me again. I mean it would be completely understandable if…"

"I know," Grace says, "I wasn't sure either. But now… well, at least…" Neither of them seems able to finish a sentence; they are like two gauche prospective lovers, tense with the fear of blazoning too much too soon.

"And the baby?" Archie suddenly says. "I didn't know, of course. For so long, I didn't know. If I'd had any idea… I would never have gone… and even then… I can't begin to imagine what it was like for you when you realised…"

Grace silences him.

"Come to Kronos, Archie. We can't talk like this. This is not how it should be. It will be easier once you're here. To talk, I mean. We need… we need to see each other."

As soon as she puts down the phone she wants to ring again, not to say anything of any significance, but simply to reassure herself of the reality of him. Of Archie. As if until now the hearsay evidence from her mother, from Fergus, of his survival has been insufficient proof that she has only partly believed. She has expected this first call to Archie to be testing, a transaction of sorts between the two of them, sentiment necessarily subdued by reason and explanation. Instead, she has found herself simply overwhelmed by consolation, comforted by the sound of his voice in a way she has not anticipated or even knew she craved. She has, perhaps, been judiciously burying her need of him as an unconscious act of self-preservation. Now it is as if a kind of grief has lifted, a protracted mourning has shifted to allow her to look ahead, to hope, even, for something more.

***

Leo sits upright in Hester's neat, upholstered armchair yet the effect is of a sprawl, his limbs a little too loose and untidy. He swallows a first cup of coffee swiftly, accepts a second. Hester contains her confusion. Leo offers little in way of explanation except to repeat that Archie is not expecting to see him.

"But we have spoken, you see. Since he's been with this… staying with Grace's father."

"With my husband, Fergus," Hester amends curtly.

"Of course. Yes, of course. With Fergus. Anyway, we spoke just a few days ago. Tuesday, I think. Or it might have been…"

"And he said he was…"

"Coming here. To you. Here in Oxford today. To confirm his plans."

"I believe he is going to Kronos," Hester says and wonders why this conversation with Leo feels combative, a certain skirmish for pre-eminence.

"I wanted to see him," Leo says simply, placing his empty mug down on Hester's very pale cream carpet. "Before he goes. And before I go, too. I've a flight heading out tomorrow, you see."

"To…?"

"Addis Ababa. The first leg, anyway, then on to… I forget. But it's all here." Leo pats the left-hand pocket of his jacket as if containing his entire store of life's essentials.

"I see. So you and Archie…?"

Leo says nothing. He glances around her living room as if assessing it for some purpose. Like an estate agent or a prospective tenant, Hester thinks, and curbs her urge to fill the silence with banalities. His manner, detached, incurious, irritates, yet she cannot help but be drawn to his striking face and stares back at him. A flawed Greek god, she finds herself thinking, remote, impossible, yet infuriatingly charismatic. And no doubt, like most impossibly attractive men, he knows it. Eventually, she gives in to the awkwardness of the quiet room.

"You went to Kronos when Archie… you saw Grace, I believe? It was very kind of you. I know she appreciated it."

Leo smiles and for a moment Hester thinks he is flattered by her praise, but then she realises that he has glanced out of the window and seen two men approach the house. He is up and in the hall, proprietorially opening the front door in a moment.

***

They left the brothers together for an hour or so and walked down the Banbury Road towards the city. Hester suggested Fergus might be more comfortable walking in Port Meadow, but he seemed content simply to follow her lead as she took him on an impromptu tour, past several colleges, the Ashmolean, the Bodleian library, the Playhouse. The sun strove hard to make a discernible appearance and Hester regretted the grey sweater.

"More?" she asked him as they stood outside Trinity. "We could walk up towards the university parks or down to Christ Church Meadows if the rain holds off. Or do you think they'll have had sufficient soul-searching by now?"

Fergus put his hand on Hester's arm.

"Let's give them a little longer. I could do with something to eat. And a drink. Breakfast was before six."

"Of course," Hester said and thought of her quiche lorraine in its white fluted flan dish, the simple green salad sitting prepared in her fridge; already the day was taking directions she had failed to anticipate. She led the way towards a pub on St

Giles where they found the only vacant small table wedged in a bay window. She watched Fergus go to the bar, order a pie and a pint of beer for himself, a bitter lemon for her, and wondered why this situation that should be so awkward and alien for the two of them, felt so strangely normal, unexceptional. As if a casual visit to a pub for an impromptu drink was a habit too ingrained to incur comment from either of them. He pushed a packet of nuts in her direction.

"Do you think they'll be happy?" Fergus said after some moments.

"What, Archie and Leo?" Hester, in an attempt to open the obstinate packet, spilt peanuts across the beer-stained oak table. Her mind was still tethered to the two brothers sitting in her living room, wondering whether they'd discover the quiche.

"No, not them," Fergus said. "They're hardly my concern, one way or the other. I mean Grace, of course, Grace and Archie."

"Happy? That's... well, rather a tall order, I would have thought. A high expectation."

"Happiness? I thought that was rather the point. Of all this reunion business, I mean. This attempt of ours to get them together again. I thought it was what you wanted to... well, what you wanted for Grace." The pie arrived and Fergus gave his attention to eating. "Rather good, this. You're sure you don't want a piece?"

Hester shook her head. She looked across the pub's crowded lounge bar, at its cross section of students and lunch-hour office workers and foreign tourists. She disliked the fug and smell of smoke that would no doubt cling to her clothes for the rest of the day yet perversely found something comforting and cosy in the place. She turned back to Fergus.

"I don't like to think of her alone, I suppose," she said

eventually. "Grace, that is. Of course she can manage. She's making a life for herself on the island now. And what with this little one… well, I wouldn't say she's unhappy. But they need to find out, the two of them, whether there's the chance of more. Of some sort of future together. Before the damage done by such a separation is beyond repair. Long separations can be… well, irreparable, wouldn't you say, Fergus?"

He nodded, put down his fork and started to speak then hesitated, picked up his glass and downed the remaining beer instead. For a moment, Hester thought his other hand rested lightly on hers, held onto it even, as if inviting a response. But the thought was fleeting, imagined, she told herself, and she returned to her task of prising remaining peanuts from their packet. Fergus picked up his fork, returned to the pie.

"I would like to see Grace. And this grandchild," Fergus said after a while. "No doubt you think… well, I know I have no right to expect such a… I haven't earned my daughter's respect. I am all too aware of that. Let alone her love."

"No, Fergus," Hester said, more aggressively than she intended. "You've spent most of Grace's life doing the best job you could in distancing yourself from her. I'll give you that, you know. You really play the absent father to the manner born. Whereas I… I've…" She stopped abruptly, picked up her empty glass of bitter lemon and attempted to drain it. "Sorry, Fergus, that was unnecessary and inappropriate."

"You have every right, Hess," Fergus said quietly. "You are entirely right to be absolutely merciless with me."

"But that time is all gone now, isn't it?" Hester said. "I should have torn strips off you, castigated your outrageous behaviour, talked it all out and brought you to your knees decades ago. There's little point in chastising you now for past misdemeanours."

Fergus placed his hands, palms down, on the table as if

studying each span for inspiration. Hester remembered the gesture, hitched it instantly to a habit of his she had no idea she still remembered. *So often it's the little things*, she thinks, *that bind us together, hold us close, however much time and deeds try to sever us*.

"I have no idea now," Fergus said simply, looking up into Hester's face, "how I did what I did back then. Leaving you. Leaving Grace. For some foolhardy, hot-headed scheme. Not even that, in fact. It wasn't even some idealistic fantasy that I was burning to…"

He faltered, shook his head. She rapped the back of his hand as if rebuking some mild transgression.

"So come on, Fergus, what was it then? I am curious, you know, never really understood or believed your trite excuses. There had to have been some underlying dream or demon driving you away from domestic suburban bliss to a cold hillside. Was it me? Was I too demanding? Or maybe it was dear darling three-year-old Grace with that limpid, sweet and open smile of hers. Or Pinner, perhaps. Shall we blame Pinner? Suburban, I'll give you that, but not without a certain urban, small-town charm with the old High Street and the memorial park and that discernible post-war air of growing prosperity. Surely it wasn't such an appalling place to live? But something, Fergus, something compelling must have driven you so resolutely from hearth and home."

"At the time," Fergus started slowly as if grappling for a thought, a concrete idea that had long slipped from his grasp and he now hoped to find lurking in his memory, "at the time, it seemed to make sense. I suppose I thought I could be… master of my own fate. Seize the reins. Do things differently."

"Sounds all very Faustian, a touch of selling out to the devil, I would say."

"You're generous, Hester. Most people would judge me crass, utterly selfish. Ingenuous and naïve."

"Oh, all those things as well," Hester said. "I'm not relieving you of that judgement. Sentimentality hasn't yet taken up residence in these old bones of mine."

"Now it all seems so... pointless," Fergus went on as if she had not spoken. "Extraordinarily vain and unnecessary, at any rate. Here we are, sitting together and it's as if the past couple of decades have been – well, not for nothing, but lacking in significance. In importance. As if it was all a lot of fuss about nothing. Whereas what really seems to matter is..."

"Three decades, not two, actually."

"What? Surely not. Is it really that long?"

"Haven't you been keeping count, Fergus?"

"Not really," he said, "but I suppose you would know, Hess. I don't think, actually, that I ever meant it to be for... for so long. I don't think that was ever part of the plan."

Hester leaned her elbows on the table, cupped her hands under her chin. The cuffs of Fergus' shirt were fraying and the buttons clumsily sewn on with unmatching thread, she noticed, and wondered why she found such details endearing.

"You have certainly been away some time, Fergus. I'll give you that. For a man without a long-term plan, that is."

Fergus shifted in his seat then turned to look out of the window as if suddenly restless to go.

"We should be getting back to them," he said abruptly. "Archie has to catch a coach to London this afternoon if he's to make this overnight flight. It was the cheapest one to book for him although it'll mean a bit of a wait the other end before he can catch the ferry out to the island."

"You don't think he'll disappear again?" Hester said, shrugging into her jacket, "I mean, left to his own devices and all that. The man's track record is hardly reassuring, after all."

"He won't do that," Fergus said firmly, leading the way out of the pub and onto the narrow pavement. The day had lost its brief respite of sunshine and the sky was opaque with dark clouds.

"How can you be so sure?" Hester persisted, walking swiftly at his side as they crossed St Giles. "Is he really sufficiently repentant about his past actions?"

"Oh, I think so," Fergus said after a pause. "And he has a bit of money now. Not a lot, but enough to… well, it's a start. He's a good worker, you know, Hess. I don't know what I would have done without him these past few months. It's eased things considerably for me having him through the worst of the winter. I've been able to pay him a bit, just casual farm labourer wages, of course, a few hours here and there and nowhere near what he could have earned elsewhere for the work. He was very resistant to accept anything at first, said his board and keep was sufficient. But I think it's helped him to feel better about himself. And what he's capable and willing to do."

"Perhaps you should go to the airport with him," Hester said, "just to be sure. Wave him off and all that to put our minds at rest. We just don't want to find things back to square one at this stage, after all."

Fergus put his arm through hers as he steered her past a bevy of bicycles and northwards up the Banbury Road.

"No, Hess. It's not necessary. Besides, I need to get back myself. There's a bus going to Cardiff at five o'clock that will get me on my way."

"Tonight?" Hester said. She was, she realised, disappointed. As if she had been lulled into some anticipation of Fergus staying for a shared meal, a bottle of wine, conversation, even a night spent in the spare bedroom. Swiftly, she attempted to recover herself. "Of course you must get back, yes, of course.

Although… won't it be very late? Quite dark by the time you get home?"

"Probably," Fergus said, retrieving his arm from Hester's, glancing at his watch and quickening their pace. "In fact, without doubt. Especially if this rain front sweeps in. And in my part of the country, in my bit of Wales, it reliably will."

***

Archie stares from the window of the coach as it noses its way out of the city towards the M40, heading for London. Coach journeys have been a familiar part of the past year for him and he has grown used to a mood of lethargy and lassitude, both physical and mental, settling over him as he has sat back and slumbered his way through hours of travelling to a vaguely intended destination.

But this time it is different.

This time he is buoyed by an intention and the goodwill of others. The kindness of strangers, you could say. And although he is going to Kronos with little expectation, arming himself against hope, he senses an inevitability in this journey, like turning the page to confront the final chapter, the dénouement that awaits.

Yet how pretentious of him to see it in such light, he thinks suddenly, shifting in his seat, self-conscious at the thought. How typical of a man who has hopelessly devoted too much of his life to long-dead poets to consider that this act of his is so portentous. He is, after all, merely a very ordinary, flawed individual who has been given the opportunity of a second chance. He's hardly a man with the credentials of a tragic hero. He glances across the aisle at other passengers. At the plump woman in late middle age working away at a crossword puzzle in a magazine. At her neighbour, a young man slumped against the window, his face livid with acne, closing his eyes then opening them again as if sleep constantly eludes him. The woman in the seat next to him knits, loosening scarlet wool every now and again from a skein in a plastic bag on her lap. No one talks. Even when the ball of wool slips onto the floor and Archie rummages at his feet and returns it she merely smiles briefly, nods her head in place of conversation. He's noticed before how coach journeys seem to isolate rather than unite as if there is something faintly embarrassing about the close proximity of passengers that is best dealt with by pretending each other is not there.

It is the first time in months that he has been entirely alone. Apart from brief visits down to the village, half days or so when Fergus went further afield for a doctor's appointment, he has constantly had company. He has had few decisions to make. He has found himself curiously content to follow instructions, reassured even, by the acquisition of new skills and knowledge on the smallholding. He has been agreeably surprised by the satisfaction he has experienced in seeing tangible results from even the most rudimentary of tasks. And he has been cushioned quite unexpectedly, undeservedly in fact, from the storm of hostility and anger he had feared. Fergus and Hester Barnes, Leo, and, of course, Grace (most of all, most importantly, Grace), have all apparently accommodated his gross errors and failings, his profound foolishness. Or so it would seem.

He has no idea, of course, whether they forgive him.

But then it is not so much forgiveness that he seeks, but something far more essential and pragmatic than that; it is a willingness to accept him, embrace him and fold him back into their lives in some measure. Sitting in Hester's living room in north Oxford, Archie had tried to talk at length to Leo, expiating some guilt for his covert actions, but his younger brother had constantly interrupted his flow as if the wrongdoings were too out of date to concern the present moment. Archie had found Leo's tolerance unsettling for it offered him, he realised, no chance of atonement.

The coach shunts into Victoria. Archie glances at his watch. There's over three hours to go before the flight leaves so plenty of time to reach the airport. It's merely a matter of sorting out a transfer to Heathrow. He has little luggage and scant possessions. He has thought of buying some cheap T-shirts, a pair of shorts, once he reaches London. He has planned, too, to spend a few pounds on a present for Grace. And a gift, of course, for the baby. His child. But now, negotiating his way along the crowded streets of Victoria, staring blankly into shop windows, he is overwhelmed by such tasks as if he has forgotten how to handle the simplest of transactions. Besides, he has no idea what is acceptable to buy. There is, after all, nothing that will compensate for his behaviour and any material gesture seems blundering, crass. He sees his reflection in the plate glass window of a department store, and his hesitancy, his weary expression of unease, stares back at him and he panics.

He cannot do this.

He lacks the courage to go back to Grace, to confront what is only too likely to be rejection, a confirmation that all hope of a reunion is futile. *Sometimes*, he thinks, turning away from the shop window and mindlessly crossing the busy street, dodging between taxis and queuing cars, *sometimes it is better to leave things unresolved*. That way, desolation is sidestepped, kept expediently on hold, as it were. After all, even the pretence of hope is better than absolutely none at all.

***

Hester pulls up weeds with a vigour that the few recalcitrant plants lodged in her pocket-sized flowerbed do not deserve. The day has gone reasonably well if not entirely according to plan. Her plan in particular. For a start, there had been Leo to contend with, an unexpected complication although Archie had appeared to handle it well and without due concern. And Leo had not hung around, leaving within moments of their return with the air of one who had seen to tedious, necessary business and now wished to be on his way. Then there had been that curious parting at Gloucester Green, Archie dispatched to the London bus while she had stood with Fergus for another twenty minutes or so, before his Welsh-bound coach had pulled into view. She had wanted to say that he didn't have to go back straight away. She had wanted to suggest that they should walk back to the flat and mull over the events of the day, exchange some rueful remarks, even dare to reminisce a bit. But she hadn't. Partly because she felt foolish at harbouring such a fantasy of companionship between them, but mostly because she had no idea if she even wanted it to happen.

There are no more weeds to dispatch. Her garden is, after all, very small.

She goes inside and opens the fridge door, sees the bottle of Muscadet that has been chilling all day. Just in case. And the quiche. The white fluted flan dish has not been disturbed, she sees, but she pushes it to one side in favour of the bone-dry wine. Archie should be at Heathrow Airport by now, Fergus will be wending his way through undulating Welsh countryside on a slow bus from Cardiff – or possibly Swansea – watching the early summer sun sinking behind a hillside or two. Each has their purpose and direction for the evening. Whereas she…

She carries her wine glass and the bottle into the living room, settles back against the soft sofa cushions. The phone rings. She anticipates Archie or possibly Fergus, a delayed plane, a broken-down coach, or even sudden uncertainty from Grace. But no. And Hester admits to disappointment, a sense of anti-climax when the call is from a neighbour canvassing opinion on urban foxes and rubbish bins. She is brief, even curt in her response. She turns to the television to watch whatever flits across the screen for a couple of hours, feeling, Hester realises, redundant for the first time in months. Fergus had been firm in his advice. "We've done all we can, Hess," he'd said as they'd watched Archie's coach pull out, waited for the arrival of his at Gloucester Green. "They're adults with their own lives to lead. Leave them well alone now to get on with them. As you must with yours." How readily she'd appeared to agree with him! How resolutely she'd left the coach station before he'd even found his seat so that he could not see any sense of loss, any faint hint of loneliness on her late middle-aged face! "No," Hester says aloud now to her pale apricot room and forces herself to think positively. *I can't possibly see this as any sort of ending. In fact, it has to be viewed as simply the start. Now all this Archie and Grace and the baby business has been... well, possibly not resolved, but at least dispatched into their own hands and out of my head, there's the chance of a fresh venture. Something... something new. A job, perhaps, even at my advanced age. A new language or skill to learn. A holiday or possibly some sort of expedition to plan.* Of course she knows that she is currently construing her new ambitions from the comfort of her sofa, buoyed by the best part of a bottle of Muscadet, so that practicalities are entirely absent. Still, Hester tells herself, the habit helps stave off deeper, darker thoughts that can plague evenings a little too solitary for comfort.

*Like this one,* she thinks. *Like this one.*

She is in bed before midnight, the tension of the day eventually telling as she falls swiftly asleep, to be awoken sharply by the phone a couple of hours or so later. She grapples for it, knocking over the bedside light in confusion.

"Hess? Sorry. You're not asleep, are you?"

"Fergus. Well, yes, actually, but it doesn't…"

"Sorry," he says again. "I… what time is it?"

Hester shifts back against the pillow, peers at the alarm clock.

"It's nearly half past two in the morning, Fergus. When most good souls are safely asleep."

Yet she is warmed by his call, by hearing his voice.

"The trouble is I fell asleep on the coach. Then on the bus as well, both buses, in fact, so by the time I got back here I wasn't the least sleepy."

"Right. So you thought you'd take a chance on me, disturb my slumber and engage in a post-mortem of the day."

"I… I had no idea it was so late, to tell the truth. You know what I'm like with time. And when I got back… well, I suppose I've got used to having him here. Archie, that is. Or somebody. Isn't it strange? All these years up here on my own, well, mostly on my own and then… sorry, Hess, you don't want to be hearing all this right now."

Hester stares at the duck-blue curtains hanging at the bedroom's picture window, notices one hook dislodged from the runner. She must place a chair under there in the morning, climb up and re-attach it.

"You should have stayed," she says. "You should have stayed and gone back tomorrow. In the daylight. I have a spare room, after all. Grace's old room."

"Yes, that would have been sensible," Fergus says. "I did think of suggesting it, but didn't want to… well, assume. Be presumptuous. After all this time. I didn't want to… give you the wrong idea. Whatever that is."

Hester finds herself smiling as if Fergus is in the room

with her instead of hundreds of miles away on his remote hillside.

"Do you think, Fergus, at our ages, there is still the possibility of a wrong idea? Who's sitting in moral judgement of us, after all?"

Fergus laughs. Hester has forgotten how Fergus sounds when he laughs. For the past few months their conversations have inevitably lacked reason for laughter. Neither of them speaks for a moment or two. Then Hester, never entirely happy with poignant pauses, plunges.

"It's late now. Or early, more like. Too early. Let's talk in a day or two, Fergus. Perhaps we'll have heard what's going on in Kronos by then. Grace might let us know. And then maybe..."

"Yes. I'd like that. Ring me, Hess. If you hear anything. In fact, just ring me if you feel like... we could just talk."

"I will," Hester says. "I will. I'm glad you're safely home, Fergus."

"Goodnight, Hess. And... thank you. For... for today. You've hardly changed in all these years, do you know that?"

"Liar," Hester says, "but thank you. Goodnight, Fergus. We'll talk soon."

# 23

Grace finished the last page and tossed the book down on the bed beside her. She had lost interest, grown muddled by the convoluted plot and lacked the concentration to pursue it. It had been left by a recent guest at Adonis House, a withdrawn man of indeterminate age and an accent that was hard to place, who had arrived one afternoon without a reservation and taken the only spare room. He had looked astonished when he had noticed the baby sleeping at Grace's side as she had dealt with his enquiry at the hall desk and increasingly bothered when Alara had rushed in a moment later with Venus in tow. He had, however, liked the room and had appeared relieved when Grace explained that she and the baby no longer lived on the premises. He was a classical scholar, he had told Tara, although had recently been ill and taken leave from his university post. His initial alarm at the evidence of family life at Adonis House had relaxed after a day or two and on the last day of his stay he had spent an hour or more talking to Clea and Grace, complimenting them on the house, praising the island and reserving a fortnight's visit in the autumn.

"I suppose we are rather a daunting prospect at first," Grace had said after he had left. "A little too domestic, perhaps, for some people's tastes."

"Nonsense," Clea had answered swiftly, "Adonis House is a village guest house, not a plush, soulless hotel boasting meaningless stars. We are what we are. And we've yet to find any dissenters for what we offer."

And it was true. Even Grace was beginning to notice the repeat bookings, the return visits from guests she had met the year before. Only that morning, she had spoken on the phone to an American woman who had stayed the previous September, an impromptu visit caused by a broken-down car and consequent missed ferry connection. Now the woman was intending to return, bringing her partner and stepson for a planned visit. Grace had made the booking, sent off the letter of confirmation, thinking of the random nature of events. Sitting in the cool hallway of Adonis House, the voices of Clea and a Dutch visitor reaching her from the courtyard, the baby in Tara's care for the morning, the unlikelihood of her present situation just a year ago was astounding. Even in the first few weeks at Adonis House, she had imagined her situation to be transitory, a temporary arrangement to tide her over while the future sorted itself out, presented her with some discernible, vaguely tolerable option. Now it was hard to imagine any other reality than this house, the village, the island. And the child, of course. Most of all it had become impossible to think of a time when the child had not been a part of her life.

And now Archie again.

Another chance at making a life with Archie. Possibly. Or possibly not.

It was nearly nine o'clock. The baby seemed, at last, soundly asleep in the crib beside her bed and she went to prepare some supper, took a salad, some bread and cheese out to the garden. The sun had already set behind the mountain, but the sky still retained some light, the moon only two or three days away from being full. She had watched the position of the setting sun most evenings for the past year and could now pinpoint its shifting place from season to season. She tried to eat slowly, knowing that the next eight or nine hours would be hard to fill, the prospect of any sleep unlikely. She had resisted ringing her mother, had half anticipated a call from Hester and its absence felt both reassuring and at the same time, a concern. She knew Archie and Fergus were due to spend a couple of hours in Oxford. She had even written down the arrangements that had been explained to her over the phone, as if seeing precise details about coach times and flight times would lend this whole business some truth and reality instead of the substance of fiction. Now, sitting in her small garden, she tried to untether herself from her enormous anxiety about Archie's resolution. After all, either he would arrive at the ferry port in Kronos Town the following morning or he would casually abandon the carefully choreographed plan. Grace was helpless to influence either outcome and she tried to see that fact as some sort of faint comfort. It was the only way she would be capable of driving to the early morning ferry, stand waiting for disembarking passengers, if hope was subsumed by negative expectation.

Clea had suggested she should take a couple of days off.

"But you can't spare me at the moment," she had said automatically. "The house is fully booked and there's a complete changeover on Friday. It's kind, but really, it's not necessary."

Routine had sustained her over the best part of the last year. It had seemed sensible to retain it now. Tara had offered to drive to the port for her. "In case you have a bad night with the baby," she had said, "and don't want to be up so early." Grace was grateful for their efforts to protect her. Clearly, neither Clea nor Tara quite believed in the thought that her husband would return to the island and wanted to prevent a profound and very public disappointment at the ferry terminal. They knew so little of him, after all. To them, Archie was a man who had run away from his wife, abandoned her, after some years of living a life of only partial truths. They could hardly be expected to trust in the idea of his return or even consider it necessarily desirable for Grace and the child. Yet Clea had encouraged her to try, sensing, no doubt, that Grace had to confront once and for all the viability of her marriage. And of her adopted life, of course, here on the island, one that had appeared as unconsciously planned as possible yet was beginning to acquire a sense of inevitability, so naturally and easily had Grace slipped into its grasp.

She heard a sound in the lane outside the stone house and went through the side gate to find her close neighbour, Anika, standing with a bowl of fresh apricots held out in her hands. Anika had lived on the island only a few months, in the village an even shorter time, and her recent arrival had drawn them easily together. A woman in late middle age, Grace was uncertain of her past and what had brought her to Kronos, knowing only that she was originally from Finland, but had spent many years working in various posts in numerous countries as a chemist. She appeared to be unmarried with no particular ties and, thanks to her fluent English that she spoke with clarity and care as if the choice of her words was important, they were able to communicate easily. Grace liked her, felt drawn towards her calm and composed manner and her apparent independence. Their fledgling friendship was cautious, practical, as if each of them respected a certain mutual need for privacy. She was renting the white house with blue shutters just up the hill from Grace, an imposing detached village house; its large garden was profuse with citrus trees, an ancient vine and a splendid apricot tree that was just beginning to produce its annual crop.

"For you," Anika said, proffering the overflowing bowl. "I have too many. Please help me to enjoy them." She looked beyond Grace through the open front door. "The little one? I hope I don't disturb..."

"No," Grace assured her. "Fast asleep. At least for the time being. Although sleep patterns seem to have become more erratic of late, just as I thought we'd got into more of a routine. Please stay and... and perhaps a glass of wine or some tea?"

The prospect of her company for an hour or so was suddenly welcome. She had said nothing to Anika about Archie so their conversation would be a respite from her thoughts. Grace led her round to the back garden and brought out a jug of light white wine, a bowl of olives and they settled down in the softness of the summer evening air. Anika talked of the language class she had joined, determined to reach a level of near fluency within months. She shrugged when Grace admired her efforts.

"It's easy for me," she said, "I have the time. I don't need to work anymore. And I've always found it... not a trial. Studying to speak another language. Who speaks Finnish, after all? It has always been important for me to be able to communicate in the place where I am living."

"I'm trying," Grace said. "I understand more than I can speak, but even so..."

The light from the houses in the village below them and the near-perfect circle of the moon illuminated the garden and they sat outside for over an hour, falling into a companionable silence punctuated every now and again by evening village noises: dogs barking, the cry of a child, the suggestion of music from across the valley.

"Will you stay?" Anika said suddenly. "This is where you have decided to make your home and bring up your child?" She did not wait for Grace's reply. "It is a good choice. It is a place, I think, where you can be... yourself. I am not sure if I make sense, but I have lived too much in places and in roles that people seem to think I fit. And I have tried. But now… it is time to stop trying, time to allow myself not to… oblige these people. These ideas of theirs."

"So you won't go back to your home? To Finland?"

Anika waved her hand as if batting away Grace's words onto the warm night air. She picked up her glass of wine and swiftly swallowed the remains.

"Never that. It is too cold. Too far north. Anyway, it is not my home, just a place where I was born and lived until I had choice. So… yes, Kronos is my choice now. Like you, Grace, you are making it your home."

They were interrupted by a cry through the open door. Grace waited to see if the sound would subside, but it took on a persistence that she could not resist.

"Sorry, I don't think that will stop until…"

"Of course," Anika said, "but maybe your baby is sociable and wants to join us? It's too fine an evening to be inside. Falling asleep under the stars might be more acceptable, perhaps."

It took little to still the cries. Grace returned to the garden with the baby clamped against her shoulder, burrowing against her bare skin. Two dark eyes stared widely at Anika as Grace sat down next to her.

"I think you were right. My night owl was offended by being left out of the conversation."

"Routine," Anika said dismissively, pushing her clipped short hair away from her face. "You talked of getting this one into a routine. Babies know of no such ideas. They simply know what they need."

"I suppose so," Grace said, "and of course, it's such a different life here. If I were back home, in London or in Jacob's… well, where I was living before, I would feel obliged to…"

"Worry about the neighbours. Worry about expectations. Exactly, Grace. But you're not. You've chosen instead to be here, in Aghia Kallida, where things are different. You can live as you wish. This is why I am here. I can paint. I can write. I can spend time on things that I think are important. And I don't need so much money. I can manage well."

The baby seemed fascinated by the long strand of wooden beads hanging around Anika's neck, holding out a small hand as if to grasp them as they shifted with each slight movement of her head. She smiled. "And for this one, everything in the world is new. A marvel. Such excitement in each discovery. I shall feel fortunate, Grace, to watch. Privileged, in fact, to be an onlooker."

"You make it sound easy, having a life here, as if this place were some sort of guarantee of happiness."

Anika shook her head vehemently, causing the beads to jingle to the delight of the baby.

"Oh no, never that. There are always dark shadows, after all, Grace. Human beings live in a state of constant doubt; it is all too… fleeting, isn't it? The happiness and joy as well as… well, the dark times, the inevitable sadness. But this seems to me to be a better place than any other to ward off those… worries. Inevitable demons of being alive, you could say. And find something close to contentment. There is simply more time to recognise it." She stood up, placed a light kiss on the baby's forehead and headed for the side gate that led out into the lane. "And the climate, of course! Who could not find well-being living in such light, under these skies?"

***

In the end, she does fall asleep, relaxed, no doubt, by her conversation with Anika. And the baby sleeps soundly too, so that it's the sneak of light darting across the wall through the shutters that wakes her in the early dawn. It is later than she has planned to leave and she swiftly splashes water over her face, pulls on her long blue cotton dress, shoves her feet into sandals and gathers up the baby who initially protests, but slips back into sleep as soon as they are in the car, Clea's car, on loan to them for the morning. Grace loves this time of day. She loves watching the impact of the sunrise on the mountains, turning them luminously pink, the clarity of the early air, the empty village streets. She is surprised to feel so calm, driving the familiar road down to Anixi Bay, picking up the coast road, as if this is the most ordinary and insignificant of drives, collecting guests for Adonis House, perhaps, or driving into Kronos Town for the market. *And maybe it is,* Grace thinks. *Probably it will prove to be a trip with no consequence, a sort of wild goose chase made in vain to meet a man who has been absent from my life for twelve months, give or take one solitary, single phone call, some edifying comments from Fergus.*

*And it doesn't matter particularly. It really doesn't.*

*After all, Archie's failure to arrive will simply confirm my expectation and I will turn around from the ferry port and drive the two of us back to Aghia Kallida and to Adonis House and get on with the day.*

Or so she tells herself.

As she turns the corner for the descent down into the port, the wide sweep of the bay becomes visible and she sees the overnight ferry already edging its way into the harbour to dock. By now the baby is fully awake and protesting hotly at the lack of breakfast. Grace parks discreetly beyond the sight of the coaches, the usual gaggle of taxis and cars and hopeful hoteliers waiting for chance custom. She sits feeding the baby, watching the sky lighten, the pale opalescence of dawn dissolving into a perfectly clear blue morning. She knows she cannot leave this. She has grown used to the certainty of a climate that constantly delivers with obedient seasons that unfailingly perform. There is consolation to be found in these sympathetic skies, this strong bold light. She has seen the year through, watched the mountains disappear into dense cloud to reveal themselves days later, snow-heavy, iced splendidly like some extravagant wedding cake. She's grown used to driving down roads heavily scented by orange groves, tyres squelching inevitably through the windfalls. She finds a natural fit, an easy accommodation with the reliable shift of the year as if this place, the island, is somewhere that has always been intended for her and has simply, patiently been awaiting her discovery. The baby feeds steadily then stops abruptly, breaks away from Grace and stares around as if sensing something of more interest. Restless now, back arching away, it is clear that sleep is not going to follow. Even from their position at the edge of the port, Grace can see more movement, a steady trickle of cars beginning to leave, foot passengers edging past them. She feels tired suddenly, the brief night inadequate and she has an overwhelming desire to sidestep whatever the next half hour or so will hold, close her eyes and succumb to the warmth and comfort of Clea's cluttered, pleasantly untidy car. The baby, however, clearly has other intentions. So she pushes her bare feet into her flat sandals, loosens her hair from a careless ponytail, wipes a slither of milk from the baby's mouth and gets out of the car.

He sees them first.

For a moment, Archie is unsure whether his sleepless night in a stuffy cabin is to blame for an illusion. But the woman standing at the far end of the meeting area, long cotton dress, hair loose over her shoulders, looks too like the figure held in his mind's eye for him to ignore. She, however, seems distracted, occupied anyway, with something too important to bother watching disembarking passengers. He walks hesitantly towards the woman, wanting to dispel his foolish thought with discretion to avoid an ignominy of sorts. He pushes his hair back with his hand, tries to think whether he has even remembered to comb it. Suddenly, it seems most important to remember whether he has combed his hair. A taxi crosses his path, then a couple of cars and by the time the small stream of traffic has cleared, the woman in the long dress – pale blue, he notices now – with the loose long hair, has seen him.

Grace has seen him.

She smiles, walks swiftly towards him. As if it is the most ordinary and commonplace of meetings, he thinks. He puts down his small suitcase so that he can take from her arms what she appears to be holding out to him, at the same time keeping her hands firmly in place as something, a wriggling bundle in white, is carefully shifted into his care. Thus, their hands rest on each other's for a moment. Neither of them speaks. Then Archie kisses the top of the baby's head, leans forward and kisses Grace's cheek.

"What is her name?" he says, so softly that he is uncertain whether she has heard and repeats the question.

"It was hard," Grace says tentatively, "naming her without… choosing without you. I put it off for ages and then…"

"Grace?"

"I wanted something that sounded right in both languages. And something not too… So… Lucy. She's Lucy Rose. But if you don't like that, we can…"

"Lucy," Archie says, "Lucy is… I like it very much. And anyway, it's for you to…" Then he looks at Grace fully for the first time, searching her eyes for resentment, anger, inevitable reproach. Instead, he sees only an offering of unqualified love, of understanding that he knows is utterly undeserved. He wants to pull her close, but he needs to keep a firm hold on the little girl so that she is secure in his arms.

"Grace, I don't even know where to begin to say everything that has to be said, to try and…"

Grace stops him, places a hand across his lips.

"Not now," she says firmly, "please, not yet. Later, in a few days, we can start to talk. Of course we need to talk. I need to understand why – but soon. Over time."

He feels uncertain, but now she gently takes their daughter from his arms and leads him back towards the parked car. He watches as she buckles Lucy safely into her seat and lets her take his suitcase, stow it in the boot. She opens the passenger door, walks round to the driver's side. Hesitantly, he takes the seat next to her.

"Where are we going?" he says. Grace looks at him as if surprised by the question. She smiles, reaches over and briefly holds his hand. Then she switches on the engine, urges the car into gear.

"Home, of course," she says, "to Aghia Kallida. I'm taking the three of us home."

***

Hester looks across the table at Fergus, watches him pile his plate with more food. She refills his glass, pushes back her chair and glances at the clock.

"It's an early start for us," she says, not for the first time that evening. "I'll set an alarm."

Fergus nods, eats more chicken then puts down his fork. "There's cheese," she says, "if you're still hungry." He shakes his head.

"That was a very good dinner, Hess. You shouldn't have made such a fuss for me. I wasn't expecting it."

"Just chicken," Hester says, "cooked in some leftover wine with a few vegetables thrown in. Hardly a fuss." Nevertheless, she is touched by the compliment. She cannot remember the last time she cooked a meal for Fergus, has grappled in her mind for any knowledge of his tastes and found only a memory of him once refusing a stuffed heart; 1958 or thereabouts, she thinks, at a squalid restaurant in Harrow. A hundred and fifty decades or so ago or as good as. She watches Fergus look around her kitchen, spy the prepared dish of cheese.

"Well, perhaps..." he says, "just a small piece."

Outside, the September evening is blustery, leaves from a tree in her neighbour's garden falling over Hester's patch of grass. Grace has said that temperatures on Kronos are still high, summer still strongly in evidence.

"You won't find it too hot?" Hester asks. "After a Welsh hillside, you know, it's going to seem..."

"A welcome relief," Fergus says. "In fact, I'm not sure how I've endured the cold so long. I used not to notice, but now..."

"Age," Hester says swiftly.

"Possibly. Very probably. I can't tell you how much I... well, thank you for organising it all for us, Hess, this trip. Getting them to agree to my visit."

"No persuasion was needed," Hester says honestly. "They are both delighted."

"How did they seem? When you were there last month?"

Fergus has already asked. They have already had several phone calls following Hester's return from Kronos, but Hester is touched rather than irritated that he wants to hear again.

"Grace and Archie? Together," Hester says. "They seemed together. Of course I didn't probe and I'm sure they are still – what is it called these days – working through things, talking about a lot of stuff, but, essentially, they are a couple with a young child. Busy, tired, but remarkably ordinary. Normal. Calm. Apparently content. What else can I tell you? I didn't stay with them, of course. I was quite happy with my room at Anna and Dimitri's at Anixi Bay, doing a few shifts for them in the bar. And naturally I turned my hand to a bit of babysitting so the two of them could have the odd night out on their own."

"And they are definitely staying? Going to try and make a go of things out there? You said something about some land."

Hester nodded. "You taught him well, Fergus. Archie's months with you were clearly not wasted. He's already taken Clea's bit of garden in hand and planted all sorts of things. And they're taking on more land soon, of course, when they rent this bigger village house they've found themselves. He seems to have got the bug for self-sufficiency, determined to grow their own fruit and vegetables, all that sort of thing. I wouldn't be surprised if they didn't get themselves a couple of goats and a brood of hens before long."

"It must be a darn sight more congenial having a smallholding of sorts in that climate," Fergus says ruefully. "Not so much in the way of frozen clods of soil to shift, I should imagine."

"No," Hester says. "No frost-nipped Brussels sprouts, that's for sure."

"So all the teaching's gone by the wayside?"

"Not quite," Hester says. She considers refilling her wine glass, compromises with half. "There's a language school in Kronos Town and evidently Archie picked up a couple of courses when a tutor was sick. There's likely to be some more work there for him according to Grace. Then there's Adonis House. Clea was actually able to get herself and her brood of oddly named children away for a week leaving Grace and Archie in charge."

Fergus nods, replenishes his glass to the rim.

"I imagine the soil's good," he says, "an effective irrigation system needed in that climate, of course, but provided you've got that – well, everything grows well in sunshine."

"No doubt," Hester says. "I don't suppose you get a lot of that in deepest Wales. Coffee? Tea? Decaffeinated or otherwise?"

Fergus shakes his head. He stands up, stretches, yawns. He picks up a postcard propped on Hester's dresser, stares at the image, replaces it.

"I'm not going back, you know."

Hester is confused. She begins to pile plates, carries them to the sink.

"No, obviously not, Fergus. Tomorrow morning at some ungodly hour you and I are off to the airport to catch…"

"I mean I'm not ever going back to the smallholding. To that life. I don't want to do it anymore. I can't do it anymore."

She turns to face him, her hands wet with water from the tap, waits for him to go on. But he says nothing, leads the way instead down her long hall to the sitting room, folds himself onto her apricot sofa as if relieved of some burden. Hester joins him.

"So?" she says after some minutes. "So what are you going to do instead? Where are you going to go?"

He smiles as if at some private joke, touches the back of her hand for a fleeting moment then laughs aloud.

"I have absolutely no idea. I haven't really got that far in my planning. It's all a bit of a… spontaneous decision, you could say. I've known, deep down, for some time, but I've only just allowed myself to say it out loud."

"You'll change your mind," Hester says more sharply than she intends.

"No," he says firmly, tapping the arm of the sofa as if

in emphasis. "No, I won't. It's… it's time. It's clearly time. Before it's all too late, you know. Before it's all over."

Outside, a dog barks, a car door bangs. Some laughter, someone shouting, loud knocking at a neighbour's front door. The sound of warm greetings, a door closing. Hester looks around the room as if she is carefully inspecting and assessing her pale walls, the small stain on the cream carpet, the cracked tile on the Edwardian fireplace.

"I might not be staying here myself," she says. "In Oxford, in this flat. There's so little to keep me here, you see. Now Grace and Archie have a life over there with Lucy… it's just something they said when I was there. And I would like… it's an opportunity. For something different. Something better."

"You'd move to Kronos?"

"Perhaps. It's just an idea. But I think it's a possibility."

"I see," Fergus says. He leans back against the sofa cushions, closes his eyes, looking suddenly very tired. Hester notices that his hair is shorter, neater, his blue shirt pressed and tidy. For some reason she finds such details unbearably touching. Even the sight of him, at ease and relaxed in her home, comforted by her warm food, moves her. Briskly, she stands up, plumps a cushion, straightens a small table.

"We need to get to bed, Fergus. I've put you in Grace's old room so you should sleep well and I'll set an alarm for five or something around there. We can always catch up on some sleep on the plane."

Fergus does not move. But he opens his eyes, watches Hester fuss with window latches, curtains. She is saying something about the bathroom and the stubborn tap and the clean blue towel she has left for him when he stands up, catches her arm.

"Is there any hope for us, Hess? Any hope at all after all this time? Or am I just a foolish, fond old man?"

She cannot look at him. She knows that if she lets him slip an arm around her shoulder, if she allows herself to think of the comfort and consolation she finds in his company, considers a future in which he is neither absent nor estranged from her life any more, she is lost. Entirely and utterly lost. And she needs to hold her course for just a little longer. To be sure. She breaks away from his hold, moves to the door.

"I need to finish packing," she says as firmly as she can summon. "Tea in the morning?"

"Yes. But I'll make it," he says.

"Thank you, Fergus, that would be kind. No milk for me."

"I'll remember. The blue towel, did you say?"

"I've left it on your bed."

He kisses her on the cheek.

"Thank you. Goodnight, Hess."

"Goodnight, dear Fergus. Until the morning."